To Lizzie

You were always meant to be ours

Cer

STARTING LINE
FOR PUCK'S SAKE
BOOK II

CREA REITAN

dragon fire fantasy

Starting Line

For Puck's Sake | Book 2

Copyright © 2023 by Amber Reitan writing as Crea Reitan

www.facebook.com/LadyCreaAuthor

Cover Copyright © 2023 Rebeca Covers

Editing by Lindsay Hamilton

Proofreading by Chaotic Creatives

Alpha Readers: Lindsay H, Cassandra F, Carrie F

Beta Readers: Sarah Jane, Amanda B, Margarida T, Kirsty E

Patreon pretties: Jennifer Colleen, Rosa, Taylour, Tamara, Rachel, Suzanne, Anthia, Carrie, Cindy, Fawn, Gina, Jen B, Lauren, Megan, Heather F, Miriam, Sarah Jane, Tara, Terriann, Zuria, Ay Bee

All Rights Reserved. No part of this publication may be reproduced, distributed, or transmitted in any form or by any means, including photocopying, recording, or other electronic or mechanical methods, without the prior written permission of the publisher, except in the case of brief quotations for review purposes.

This is a work of fiction - all characters and events portrayed in this book are fictitious. Any resemblance to actual persons, living or dead, places, or events is purely coincidental and not intended by the author.

Dragon Fire Fantasy, Inc.

dragonfirefantasy@gmail.com

ISBN:

ASIN:

Version 2023.10.31 - P.NA

❦ Created with Vellum

Welcome to my world of MM hockey romance. If you're familiar with my writing, you know that I write polyamorous romance (whychoose) with a lot of different relationships all within the family group. Especially over the last year, I've had to pre-empt my books with 'this story is heavy MM' because my main characters were not *always* female.

This book is about love and the different forms it might take. Although the world is becoming more accepting of what's considered non-traditional lifestyles, it has a very long way to go. Not only do our characters have the challenge of being gay athletes and all the extra pressure that puts on them, they now have the added judgment and bigotry for being polyamorous *on top* of being gay.

This story is very much about navigating a new relationship with different dynamics between three people while being put under the microscope by everyone else in the world who thinks they're entitled to an opinion on their lives. Not only do our characters have the challenge of building something together to which there are no guides, but are also challenged with outside pressures. While I'm by no means a celebrity, no one is immune to seeing how the world watches them as if they have a right to their private lives.

Simply put, this story is about falling in love and fighting for the acceptance of that love.

In this book, you'll find a secret marriage, a polyamorous lifestyle, an open marriage. There's an alpha character who thrives on being the caregiver, spoiling and nurturing his love interest/s, but also demands obedience in the bedroom on occasion. There's a threesome scene, a cuckold scene, exhibitionism, and sensation play.

You'll also find that the characters, because of their situation, are thrown into the storm of their triad relationship (on top of their sexuality) being suddenly made public. This causes them to react to certain characters' backgrounds and beliefs in the same way that they're being targeted though not in the same limelight or with the same intent. There is a single mention about an illegal immigrant. It's brought up for prosperity purposes more than anything. There is also the musing of how religion has played a role in the movement *against* LGBTQ+ people. I acknowledge that this sentiment does not reflect all religions and those practicing, nor is the part within my story meant to reflect that.

I'd like to remind you that this is a work of fiction and while it takes place within a contemporary setting based in real life situations, these thoughts, opinions, and beliefs do not reflect that of the author. However, that doesn't mean I haven't seen such things in the world. Like it or not, this ugliness happens. It's real. Every day, someone lives through these scenarios.

If you choose to take offense, that's on you. You have been warned.

I am still very much a new hockey fan so please forgive any mistakes or liberties I may have taken with the hockey elements of this book. I've had one kind reader correct the amount of games in a hockey season for me and I really do appreciate that feedback. While I take my time and look up a lot of unnecessary research, sometimes I find conflicting information and just go with the one I think might be right. If you're so inclined and feel like you need to correct me on something, you can reach out to me or one of my PAs via email or socials (links in back of this ebook) or on my website.

If anything you just read bothers you, makes you uneasy, or isn't what you're looking for, please do not read this book. Otherwise, enjoy this story about falling in love and battling being in the public eye while doing so.

ONE
ETHAN "WILDMAN" WILDER

"Faster."

I groan, my back arching slightly as I stroke my dick. My body is already covered in a sheen of sweat. It passed 'light sheen' and now I feel like I just got out of the shower after hours on the ice. Sweaty. Shaky. Breathless.

"That's it. Look at you. So needy for me."

When he's horny, his Czech accent gets thicker. Over the last eight years, it's thinned out and become only slightly accented. Enough so that you would immediately know that English isn't his first language, but not quite enough to figure out his natural tongue. Not unless you're familiar with the Czech accent. Since hockey is big in the Czech Republic, many hockey fans can pick it out easily.

My cock is throbbing. My balls ache. He's been torturing me for what feels like a goddamn day! Since I only got back to my apartment around six, I know it hasn't been that long.

"Come on, kocourek. I want to see tears in your eyes."

"Sadist," I mutter, my hand moving faster over my hard dick. My hips come off the mattress as I groan. His answering chuckle makes everything inside me flutter. "Fuck, Jakub."

"Soon, zlato. I will fuck you soon."

His words make my ass clench. Jesus, it's been far too long.

"Slow down, lásko. You will come when I do." His voice gets sharp when he says, "I didn't say you could touch your balls."

I pull my other hand away and push it under my head. Every muscle in my body is tight. Needing release. It's his favorite way to torture me. I mean... please me. Especially when we're almost 3,000 miles apart, like we are most of the year.

"No, lásko. Keep touching yourself. Begin at your neck; wrap your hand around it."

A pathetic whimper escapes my throat as I do what he demands. My fingers wrap around my throat and I whine like a bitch. "That's it," he says. "Squeeze. Apply pressure, kocourek."

His terms of endearment simultaneously make my chest warm and turn me the fuck on. You'd think with as angry and needy as my cock is right now that I couldn't get any more turned on. That would be incorrect. The combination of his words in that sexy fucking accent of his, him calling me a little male kitten (yeah, I don't get it, but it's apparently a really sweet thing to call your male lover), and the restriction of my airway, my cock is leaking like a sieve. Thankfully, it just adds more lubricant to my hand, so I'm not rubbing myself raw.

"Yes, good. Do not slow your stroking, lásko. So sexy."

"Please," I mutter. My eyes squeeze shut.

He ignores me, of course. "Down your chest. Rub over your sexy pecs." I do, touching my chest and running my hands over my nipples. My hips leave the bed again. Fuck, I'm acting like I'm touch starved. "So hot, Ethan. Pinch your nipple." He makes a sexy sound when I do, which only gets me hotter.

"Your stomach, lásko. Like that."

Fuck, I'm going to burst. Words leave my mouth, but I'm not really here anymore. I can hear Jakub telling me what to do and I immediately obey. Running my hand over my sweaty torso while my other abuses my dick. My ass clenches over and over as my hips leave the bed, desperate for sex. For my husband.

"Please," I whine.

"Touch your balls, now."

I do, squeezing them hard to try to stave off my impending orgasm until Jakub says I can. He likes to come together. It's more important to him when we're apart than when we're together. Hell, when we're together, it's like I'm a horny teenager all over again. I orgasm so fucking easily. Often. It's disgusting and hilarious.

"Slip your fingers down, kocourek. Slip into your hole."

"It's over if I do that."

"It is not over until I say it is, Ethan."

Gooseflesh rises all over my skin as I bend my body slightly to do as he commands. The feel of my finger against my hole is almost enough to push me over. It's barely been a month. I shouldn't feel so desperate. Christmas is right around the corner too.

But it feels like years since he's touched me. Years!

"So needy."

"Talk Czech to me," I say, my voice breathless.

One of the things I love about this man—and there are many things—is that his version of dirty talk in his native tongue is all sweet. He keeps the dirty words in English so I understand every word.

"Moc mi chybíš, lásko," he says. His voice is almost a purr. I groan, pressing my finger against my aching hole. My pre-cum has dripped all over the place, as has the excessive amount of lube I used because I was too anxious to keep myself neat. The tip of my finger slides inside just as he says, "Nemůžu se dočkat, až tě zase uvidím."

I moan as I work my finger into my tight hole. My breathing stops as I try to deprive myself of oxygen in an attempt to keep my orgasm at bay.

"Look at me, miláček. Now."

Shifting my head, I force my eyes open to look at his gorgeous face on my tablet screen. He's completely exposed to me. I can see his large hand moving frantically over his even larger dick as he watches me. His light blue eyes are almost silver, and I swear, I can feel them like a caress over my body.

I'm so close.

"Miluji tě."

His breathy voice, his words, his hot as hell accent have me coming with force as if I hadn't just jerked off this morning. I spray all over my chest, continuing to work myself over with his words ringing in my ears. Our eyes are locked as we come together. I can barely make out through the blurry image the way he drips long threads onto his thigh as his open mouth pants near the screen.

He's so close that the camera is having trouble figuring out what to focus on.

I drop limply to my bed and stare blearily into the screen. "That's it," he says, breathless. Voice deep and gravelly. "Run your fingers through your juice, lásko. Look at me when you clean your fingers."

My hand moves slowly, as if it's a limp noodle. I drag my fingers through the river of cum on my sweaty skin and bring my fingers to my lips. Making sure my eyes are locked with his, I dip my two fingers into my mouth, closing my lips around them and suck them clean of my release.

Jakub groans. "So pretty."

I snort quietly. Then we stare at each other for a long time until he finally says, "Get cleaned up, kocourek. Then come back."

It takes a lot of energy to force myself to get up. I'm shimmying a bit as I try to move my way across the bed, staying somewhat vertical to avoid making a mess with the dripping semen on my body. There's nothing more annoying than leaving behind a trail that you need to clean up before you can drop boneless once more to enjoy the effects of a good release.

Jakub's already clean and waiting for me when I return. I drop onto the bed, on my side, and stare into the screen at his handsome face. Light hair kept short. Scruff along his jaw and hinting around his upper lip. He has a lean face, though it's not hard.

Then there are his eyes. They're like something out of a children's tale. Magical. Such a color shouldn't exist in real life. Blue turning silver with a shine and sparkle all their own.

If anyone is gorgeous, it's this man. And he's mine.

As if he knows what I'm thinking about, an amused smile curves his lips. "Stop lusting over me."

"I'm allowed to. You married me."

This time, he grins. We met eight years ago playing for the farm league in Detroit, where we spent a year together. We got married. Enjoyed three months of married life. Then Jakub was traded to Anaheim. I'd have followed. I'd have given up my career to be with him. Except three weeks after he left, and I was ready to go crazy, I was offered a contract by Colorado. We've been traded a handful of times since then.

We talked extensively about whether I wanted to continue with my career or be his trophy husband. Often, I'm not sure why we agreed to do this long-distance thing. It's difficult. Sometimes more than others.

Like right now when I'm feeling needy, lonely, and slightly vulnerable. I know that's why he called me tonight. I know that's why he made sure I had some extra torture to break down my resistance, so I'd talk about it without trying to shove it away. After a good orgasm, my inability to curb my thoughts and feelings is higher.

It's been a long seven years apart. Anyone who tells you marriage is easy is lying through their teeth. It takes a lot of communication and compromise. It's made all the more challenging by the distance between us. The infrequency of our time together.

And the fact our marriage is practically a secret to the world. Why? How do we keep it that way?

Many reasons. For starters, being an openly gay man in any high-profile sport puts an extra layer of pressure on you that you're not always prepared for. My life was always going to be seen through tabloid headlines, but now it's under a microscope.

Add to that the fact that we have an open marriage? The world hates both those things—homosexuality and non-monogamy. Imagine having those two things together!

Nope. It's easier on both of us if we keep our personal lives a secret. Which isn't hard since we rarely see each other. No one is looking for this scandal since I'm openly gay and Jakub is perceived as straight. He's not. He hasn't been with a woman since before he met me. But what the world believes will keep them happy.

"Ready to talk?" he asks.

"Sure. How's the team?"

He smirks. "Luca is a pain in my ass. If he wasn't the only other player on the first line worth a shit, I'd kick his sorry ass."

I laugh.

"Yours?"

I sigh. "Same as usual. Gilpatrick is never where he needs to be."

It's been a struggle since Credence Ayrton was drafted fresh from college. He and I just... gel. We're fucking amazing together.

There's some magical connection that has our moves, our thoughts, our plays completely synced.

We've been accused of shutting out the third on the line, but for fuck's sake. We've been through three right wingmen in the last few years as management tries to find us one that gels with Creed and me. I think the rest of the league is hoping that doesn't happen. We're a force just the two of us. If we had a third who harmonized as well as the two of us together…?

Then again, there are those who say that the reason Creed and I are just a powerhouse together is because of our chemistry. While I might give that hypothesis thought under other circumstances, the only thing on my mind when we're on the ice is hockey.

Not how the pants spread over his ass and display the outline of his jockstrap. That's locker room observation and bathroom fodder. *Not* what I think about during a game!

"Is there talk of a trade?" Jakub asks.

There's that little voice that says I shouldn't share what I know about my team with the competition. But Jakub and I always agreed that our marriage is our first priority. It might not look that way since we've chosen careers that take us to near opposite ends of the continent. But our conversations, our relationship in general, are a safe place. We can talk, vent, whine, cry, whatever about whatever we want. And it stays between us.

"Not that I know of. I think they still have hope for him." I shrug. "He's forced to take extra practice that Creed and I attend twice a week as we try to sync up."

"Not happening."

I shake my head. "Not yet. Once in a blue moon there's a glimpse of perfect harmony. It's always during practice, of course. But the plays, the passes, his position—it's just right. Like he finally found our wavelength. But fuck if he can keep it. I think it's enough of a promise that the coaches are really pushing him. He's better than Vinny, Kain, or Romanov were."

Yes, the three wingmen that came before Gilpatrick. Owen Vincent, Vinny, was here when Creed was drafted. He and I had worked well together for the previous season. It was good enough, but once Creed's skates hit the ice, he and I were just… perfection. Vinny was traded for Noah Kain within the year.

Kain lasted six months. Honestly, it's like our playing styles were complete opposites. I liked him. Especially since we were already friends. As one of a handful of queer hockey players, we get thrown together often as the poster boys for 'even the gays can play' campaign. No, it's not as crude as that, but it's the message that the world sees.

Kain was traded for Kozlov Romanov, an amazing and aggressive wingman whose Russian is so thick, I was rarely sure what he was saying. He lasted through the end of the season and was traded over the summer for Ryan Gilpatrick.

Here we are.

"Now we talk about Creed," Jakub says.

Ah, the segway into my growing crush on my best friend and teammate. I grin and drop my face into the pillow.

Our marriage works like this: our communication is almost embarrassingly frequent as we talk about *everything*. Like even when one of us finds something new we like in bed (or don't like, as it's happened once or twice). Especially when it's more than a hookup, someone we want to see repeatedly, we talk about it incessantly. To the point where it could get annoying and uncomfortable.

As it happens, more often than not, a lover being the frequent topic of conversation has killed the attraction.

But when I found I could talk about Creed and never get tired of it; when just the mention of his name in conversation makes me smile and fills my body with tingles and cliché streaks of warmth; when I realized that my attraction to him was far more than physical... that's when I decided that I *couldn't* be with him.

I was going to fall for Credence if I allowed myself even a peek of what it might look like beyond the friend zone.

"Jakub," I say quietly. "I can't do that."

"Talk about him?"

Laughing, I shake my head and pull my face up to look at him. "You already know how I feel about him. If I let it, it's going to go too far." Biting my lip, I study his face for a minute. "I'm afraid of what will come of that. How this is going to work. Hookups are simple and careless transactions. Meaningless. A means to an orgasm." I shake my head again. "Creed is none of those things."

"You already love him, lásko." My chest tightens at his words because I fear they're true. "I trust you. Same rules apply."

I swallow the lump in my throat.

"Nothing will break us, Ethan. Our marriage, our relationship, is strong and healthy. Our love is solid, flexible, enduring. Eight years, kocourek. In eight years, I have grown to love you more. Fallen in love with you all over again. Many times. No matter what other relationships we explore, ours will always flourish."

In these conversations, when I hint that I might want something more, Jakub is always quick to tell me these same things. But he left one thing out this time. That our marriage is a priority over any other relationship.

As if he knows I can't go into a relationship with one partner taking priority over another, he has already modified our standing.

"We talk every day," Jakub says. "That will continue. We will video when we can. We will make time together when we're close or can sneak away, as we always do. And this summer, the three of us will spend time together. Look at me, Ethan. Look into my eyes."

I hadn't realized my gaze had fallen until he said so. Meeting his eyes again, I see nothing but his love for me. Even through a screen. Even 2,700 miles away, I can feel it. It makes my heart beat erratically. My breath stutters.

"I have known since you first spoke of Creed that he has a piece of your heart, lásko. It is time to see where that goes."

"It could break the team," I say. "What if we... don't work?"

The thought alone makes my chest tight. Losing Creed would be devastating. Not just because he's a teammate, but because he's my best friend.

"I have confidence in the two of you," my husband tells me with a soft smile. "It's time to make that man yours, Ethan Wilder."

"Miluji tě," I whisper.

He chuckles. "Your pronunciation is shit, miláček. But I love you, too."

TWO
CREDENCE "CREED" AYRTON

THE BALL WHIZZES BY. I CRINGE AS I HEAR IT SLAM INTO THE little goal with a *slap*. "Fucksauce," I mutter, making Caulder laugh as I reach for the ball. "Seriously, I have good reflexes. I don't appreciate you making it look like I suck balls."

"You do, though," he says, smirking.

I glare at him and drop the ball into the middle of the table. Foosball is fun with anyone else, but Caulder kicks all our asses. I'd hate him if I didn't like him so much.

The ball bounces lazily toward his line and I'm already groaning before he can twist the handle. The ball snaps forward and by some miracle, I have my little stick figure kebabed guy in the right place to stop him.

"Ha!" I say in a moment of triumph. Sure, it's dumb luck, but I'll take it. Luck is all I have playing this stupid game with his stupid self. However, I might have stopped the ball, but it bounces off my guy's fused legs and sails right back to his waiting line. Then he flicks his wrist and the ball sinks into my goal again.

Caulder grins.

"You have to actually major in something that's not a table game in college," I say.

He chuckles. "You know that show about the six besties who live in NYC? The two bromance dudes have a foosball table for a table and cover it with plexiglass?"

I nod. "Yep."

"That was our dorm for the last two years of college in the hockey dorms. There were like three of them between our rooms and once Egon moved in with his husband, he gave us the key to his dorm room. We added two more in there, standing his bed up against the wall so we had the full use of the floor space," he says.

I frown at him. Only half of that makes sense. "I'm not sure which question to ask first," I say as I drop the ball between the guys again, thinking that maybe if I keep him talking it'll be a distraction and he'll suddenly suck.

He doesn't. He sinks three more goals while he tells me about how the school rule is that if you're on a sports team, you have to live on campus. His teammate got married before his last year and though the school refused to let him move, he refused to live on campus. So he gave the key to his dorm to Caulder, who passed it on to another teammate when he was drafted.

"Huh," I say. "That's a lame rule."

Caulder shrugs. "It's not like they truly tried to enforce it with Egon. He was up front about refusing to live on campus and insisting that he live with his husband. But he was there on a hockey scholarship, so he didn't argue too loudly. I still talk to him. He's still married. He works for Los Angeles."

"Ah. That's where you disappear every time we're on the West Coast," I say and somehow sneak one past his little goaltenders. Do I jump and cheer like I just won the Cup? Yes, I do. Even though the score is probably 13581 to 3.

"Yep. Or visiting Coach Adak with Anaheim."

"Your old coach, right?"

He grins. "Yes."

See? I pay attention.

"You have any plans this weekend?" he asks as he continues to effortlessly kick my ass.

I glance up and spot Ethan at the bar laughing with Lucien Medcalf, our second line D-man. My stomach flutters as I quickly look back at the game. "Nope. Not yet." I don't say I'm hoping to hang out with Ethan.

It's not like the entire team doesn't know I'm crushing on the man. Hell, I was basically a drooling mess when I was drafted to

Buffalo three years ago. He's been one of my hockey idols, even though he'd only been playing for the NHL for four years prior. Before that he was in the AHL for a year. I even followed his college hockey career for his last two years!

I'm not pathetic. He wasn't the only player I followed. But he was certainly one of my idols. So meeting him in person was like meeting an A-list celebrity for me. He's a phenomenon, breaking records and shit all the time. It's like watching a legend in the making.

But then I found out that he's really thoughtful, sweet, and humble. He's also fucking gorgeous. It makes my gay heart just swell to know that he's my teammate. A friend. My bestie.

Talk about living a dream, though. The way we just came together on the ice that first time and worked together as if we were of one mind was the kind of thing every hockey kid dreams of. Finding your person. The other half to make you both exceptional hockey players. To bring your team wins and elevate you all to something of myth.

At first, I thought the chemistry I felt between us was just me. I was starstruck. Not even I could deny that. But it wasn't long before I knew it was more than awe at meeting the man that I'd watched since he was in college. I was crushing on Ethan Wilder.

Hard.

Imagine my surprise when he started flirting with me. The chemistry between us isn't one way. We both feel the attraction. That irresistible pull between us.

What's more, he trusts me with his secrets. I know the one he keeps closest to his heart. He's married to another hockey player. They have an open marriage. This is something the world doesn't know. Only me.

It makes me swell with pride to know that he trusts me with those things. It also makes me question why—if he feels the same things I do—hasn't he made a move? I've definitely given the invitation more than once. Hell, I can even see it on his face how much he wants to.

But he hesitates and ultimately doesn't take the offer.

I'd feel horrified or rejected if I didn't think that there was an actual reason for it that he fought against. At first, I thought it was his husband; maybe *he* doesn't like me. Or I've unwittingly done something to offend him. Maybe it's something more serious that I don't know.

I've met Jakub Bozik several times now. Hell, I even had dinner with the two of them after a game last year in Vancouver. I didn't feel any kind of unease or resentment from him. He was friendly, open. And I liked the way he spoke.

The worst part of my crush by far, is seeing him hook up with others. Early on, before I had made it known that I had a thing for him, I had to see him with someone else for seven months. It was crushing. Painful. I'm a little ashamed to admit I nearly celebrated when they broke up.

"You?" I ask, pulling my thoughts from musing on Ethan any longer. I could fall down that rabbit hole for a long fucking time.

"Photo shoot," he says.

I ping my gaze to his face for a minute, brow raised. "Really?"

Caulder gives me a wide, laughing smile. "Yep. I swear, Rigo is already setting me up for retirement." He shakes his head. "I've always got something going on."

Tilting my head, I lean across the game table with the ball in my hand. "What's working with him like?" I ask.

He grins again. "He's amazing. I worried about my public perception since the company is called Pride Sports and Rigo is known for taking all kinds of queer athletes under his command. But it hasn't been bad. And even though his company has been growing leaps and bounds since I've been with him, he's always the one to call me. He remembers shit that I forgot I told him. Rigo constantly has things lined up for me to keep my profile growing. To keep my face and reputation current and positive." Caulder leans closer, as if he's going to tell me a secret. "Better yet, he makes sure that everything he lines up is something I support and that I like. The photoshoot is for underwear with players across all sports. But fuck, it's underwear I've been wearing for years. I didn't tell him that!"

I laugh at the look of perplexity on his face.

"Man," I say. "My agent is a deadbeat. He only calls when he needs to talk about my contract. Which is agent speak for wanting another payday."

"Lame," he says as he takes the ball from my hand and drops it. "Trade up."

I snort. As if it were that simple.

The sound of giggles makes me shift my attention from the table and I watch as three of the most well-known puck bunnies in Buffalo begin meandering their way to our table. I can tell by the way they're walking that they're tipsy. I can also tell by the way one is batting her lashes at me that I'm going to have to remind them *again* that I'm gay.

Caulder sighs, likely having seen the same thing I did. He's relatively shy. Only when we're on our own or in smaller team groups does he talk much. Add a stranger or two to the mix and he's a chameleon. He basically turns invisible.

I'm not proven wrong when the girls step up to the foosball table. One of them, I think her name is Anabeth, stumbles closer, her hand falling to my forearm. I cringe and pull away.

"Take a step back," I say. "Respect my personal space."

She pouts. Literally pouts. I hate the rhetoric in the world where it's always men disrespecting personal space. Like masculinity is the only thing that is capable of being pushy and ill-mannered. As if women don't also take liberties to get close and touch because they think they can and that men are always open to it, welcoming it.

I, for one, do not.

"Seriously," I tell her, frowning. "Back up by ten steps."

The woman sighs and I get a whiff of alcohol on her breath. Thankfully, the teams in Buffalo are well acquainted with these three. She's never touched with a ten-foot pole. After another minute, she does as I tell her and backs up to her friends. They wrap her in their arms and give her drunken, hiccupping coos.

"Awe, sweetheart," one of the others says, looking at me with a flirty smile.

"I'm gay," I deadpan. I leave off 'and desperation doesn't look good on anyone' because professional athletes have their reputation to protect. Instead, I add, "Very, very gay."

As with nearly every single time we have this encounter, the surprise on their faces makes me roll my eyes. However, I barely have time to acknowledge it when the vultures turn their sights on Caulder. The color literally drains from his face at their attention.

Before I can say anything, Bianca steps into Caulder's side and wraps her arm around his waist. He visibly relaxes as she pats his cheek. Then turns her shrewd eyes on the girls. "These boys are mine. Go away."

"You're only married to one of them," the drunken lady in a short skirt says. She looks between me and Caulder as if to study us before she can confidently say, "And neither of them are your husbands."

"Sweetheart, all these boys are mine. I'm mama bear. And you can't read a fucking room. Go. Away. Or I'll get security over here for harassing my boys."

I smirk, bowing my face to hide the expression. The three hem and haw before they turn and stumble away. "I'm so in love with you, Bee."

She laughs and kisses Caulder's cheek. "Just holler if you need rescuin', babes."

We watch as she returns to Lucien's side. He looks down at her as she snuggles in close and he drapes his big arm around her shoulders, kissing the top of her head tenderly. His gaze flickers up to mine and he grins.

Lucien is the old man on our team at thirty-one. If he wasn't such a driving force, he'd probably have retired. He's been dropped to the second line, but there's no doubt in my mind that he's someone management would like to keep until he's ready to go.

Then again, I've been wrong before. What do I know?!

My heart stops when hands on my hips and lips at my ear make my entire body light up. I don't need to look to know that this is Ethan. My body knows. Everything in me knows.

Caulder's attention has already moved on to talk to Asael and Astor, our teammates who just walked in the door. With his attention off me, I don't quite manage to stifle the groan when Ethan's hips sway into mine.

Images of us naked, touching and kissing flash before my eyes and my dick is not happy that I wore these specific underwear to try to contain myself. Every time we come to Sceptre, I wear something restricting or I end up with a very noticeable bulge in my fucking pants.

Ethan Wilder just does it for me.

"Dance with me."

Though his request isn't a question, I nod and he pulls me away. There aren't many people on the dance floor. It's relatively early in the evening on a Tuesday, so the party crowd isn't here and loud yet.

When he turns me around, we come face to face. We're pretty much the same height, but somehow, I feel like he's leaning over me. Pressing into my space like the puck bunny was. But this time it's welcome. Wanted.

It's always the same when we dance. He doesn't touch me. Even with as close as we are, his hands are never on my body. His mouth hovers dangerously close, but never meets mine. My dick is so fucking hard right now that if he gets even a little bit closer, it's going to brush against him like a waving flag. A viper ready to strike.

"Your name wasn't on the list for the charity event in two weeks," he says.

His words almost sound foreign. I hear them. They're English. But my brain is sluggish to make the sentence make sense. Eventually it does and I smile a little. Words fail me, so I don't speak.

His lips quirk into a sexy fucking smirk, making my entire body shiver. "Come with me?" he asks, his voice low, barely heard over the beat of the music.

I nod. I'm pretty sure I'd follow him over the side of a bridge right now. He takes a step closer and our clothing brushes together. The friction across my hot body is delicious and painful at the same time.

"Come over this weekend? We'll watch a movie?"

I nod again. I'd watch paint dry with this man. "Yes," I breathe. He grins, swaying toward me. I swear, I *almost* feel the brush of his lips against mine, but he moves away and I nearly sob in frustration.

THREE
CREDENCE

I DIG IN MY BLADES AND PUSH OFF, GAINING SPEED SO I CAN catch up to Ethan. I already see the play in my head and contemplate moving to the left of him because, once again, Ryan isn't where he needs to be.

Instead, I bear down and shoot forward, coming up behind him. Ethan looks for Ryan, and I see his scowl when Ryan's a dozen feet too far away for the play. Instead, Ethan passes the puck through his legs behind him and skates forward, around the goal.

As he's passing back in front, the one defensive player moves to block Ryan. Halfheartedly, I might add. Everyone seems to know that Ryan just can't cut it right now. He's off his game tonight. The other defenseman moves to block my pass back to Ethan.

Which is fine. Even as Ethan moves between me and the goal, his stick ready to accept my shot, I slide further right, make to pass, and slap the puck. It sails straight through Ethan's legs, and the goalie is distracted as he waits for the shot from Ethan.

Instead, it hits the net after bouncing off the goalie's pads. Okay, it barely hit the net, but it did, and that's what counts. Especially as the light flashes the goal.

"Fuck, yeah," Ethan says, skating into me and grabbing the top of my pads in front of my neck. His smile is radiant as he grins. "Way to score," he says, winking at me.

No, my cheeks don't flush at all.

"Gilpatrick!" Coach Melvin Mickerson barks.

Ethan and I wince as we skate to the bench. Our second line is climbing out as we move in through the little door. An intern hands both of us water bottles and we all try not to listen to the coach admonish Ryan for not being where he needed to be.

It's not really his fault. Sometimes you make it with someone, or you don't. It's all about chemistry. Ryan just doesn't have it with us.

Me and Ethan aren't good at communicating plays on the ice since we've never had to before. It's like we can read the situation and just *know* what will work. We fall into line as if it's second nature. Ryan just isn't on whatever page we are. I'm not even sure he's in the same playbook, to be honest.

We ended up beating the Arizona Sand Riders 3-1. Ethan made a goal and then one of our defensemen, Brighten Shepey III, made a goal. I assisted on both goals that I didn't make, which feels like an even bigger win than my own goal.

By the time we're back at the hotel, stoked and ready to party, I'm flying high. Not just because we get to hang out with some of our friends from other teams who are in the area, but because when we have away games, I always share a room with Ethan.

I don't think it's my imagination that things are shifting between us. Last weekend, we spent most of it at his apartment, curled up together on the couch. Sharing a single blanket and huddled close. Always with skin touching. At one point, we were holding hands.

All weekend, I waited with bated breath for *something*. Even if it was just a conversation. It didn't come. But I didn't think it was because he didn't want it to happen. Ethan is rarely nervous, so when he is, it's really fucking obvious.

Now we're on a series of away games and that means endless days with Ethan nonstop. I'm so here for it.

But after dropping our bags in our room, we head back down to the hotel bar and restaurant.

Ethan claps Shepey on the back. "Nice fucking shot, Three," he says, giving him a half hug from behind. "You trying to move up to wingman?"

Shepey laughs, nudging his shoulder into Ryan's, who's standing next to him. Ryan sighs, rolling his eyes. Luckily, he's a good sport. He's also not blind or dumb. He knows that if he can't somehow get on our wavelength, then his days with Buffalo are numbered. All our ribbing is good natured. Besides, I really like him. And it's not like we don't try to work with him.

The thing is, what Ethan and I do works for the team. We're winning shit more times than not. We had a ten game winning streak earlier this season to prove it. The coaches have made it apparent that we need to keep doing what we're doing. That means they need to find us a third member for our starting line that works *with* us.

"Nah, man. That's far too much pressure," Shepey says, shaking his head. "I feel bad for anyone who's in that position."

"Thanks," Ryan deadpans.

Shepey grins broadly, winking at him. "Want to head to a club instead? Getting sucked always puts me in a better mood."

"That all you think about, Three?" one of the Arizona players asks, knocking him forward.

Shepey turns and grins, hugging him like they're old friends. I think they are.

Ethan drags me away, and I wave. Shepey nods me off and grins at his friend. If I'm not mistaken, it's that guy who gave him the nickname Three. Not because that's his number or ever was. But because he's some posh rich boy with Roman numerals as part of his name. Brighten Shepey the Third.

Thus, he's Three. Something that makes him roll his eyes, but he doesn't mind telling the story when someone asks why they call him that when there's another guy on our team that has the number.

In the back, we find the guys we're meeting. Azure Dayne is the goalie for the Las Vegas Crowns and Larson Faulkner VIII (also with Roman numerals in his name to which those giving nicknames were completely original and dubbed him as Ocho) is the center for the DC Hermits. Both gay players.

Sometimes it feels like the league pushes us gay players together and then, on a bigger scale, gay athletes. I don't usually mind. There's a bit of solidarity to it. Support we can offer to each other.

It's actually really nice to know that we're not alone in our experiences and the pressure we feel.

That's how I met both these men. Azure and Larson were at a charity event and the gay athletes were rounded up like cattle to take a photo. While it might have felt like they were herding us like cattle, what really happened was they were trying to get a bunch of puppies to sit still and look at the camera. Those photos were some of my favorites of my career.

"Hey, man," Larson greets as he gets to his feet and offers his hand. Azure follows, though he stays silent.

There's something about that man that has always made me slightly uncomfortable. Like there's a threat just beneath the surface. I'm not sure if it's in the way he watches, almost silently, like he's studying us. Or how he sometimes reacts a beat too late, as if he's determining what's an appropriate response.

Also, there's something in his eyes that always gives me the impression that he's not really human. I mean, he is. Obviously. But... it's almost absent. Or... I don't know. Just inhuman. That's really the only way to describe it.

As if he's read my mind, his gaze flickers to mine and the smile he gives me feels chilling. I swear, he was a murderer in a past life.

"Where's Dylan tonight?" Ethan says as he pulls out my chair.

With everything in me, I try not to get all giddy and warm at the gesture. He's always thoughtful. Doing kind gestures like this. But damn, does it feel good.

I must not hide my pleasure at this, because Larson notices. He smirks and turns his attention back to Ethan as he takes his seat at my side. He even scoots his chair closer and his fucking hand rests on my lower back.

Fuck, he's going to make me swoon!

Larson sighs. "He's home because apparently he causes a debacle in the box when he comes to a game."

"Nooo," Ethan says, mock disbelief thick in his voice.

Larson's husband is a pint-sized diva queen. He's not spoiled in that he demands velvet cushions or anything. Though I'm almost surprised at that, given the few times I've met him. But man, does he get offended and go off the rails when Larson is slammed against the board.

It's funny and cute seeing them together. The way Dylan dotes on Larson is so... counterintuitive to what you would stereotypically expect. It's adorable as fuck, really.

I think Larson secretly loves every minute of it, though he pretends to be put out and just tolerates the attention. Honestly, those two are goals to the max. If it were up to Dylan, he'd be at every game cheering his husband on.

Larson chuckles, shrugging. "It's fine. He watches the game on Sports Spot Live and already called me by the time I got back into the locker room."

I can only imagine how those voicemails go. A smile curls my lips. Honestly, it's just too sweet.

Attention turns to Azure since he's been quiet as he listens to the conversation. "What about you?" Ethan asks. "Who have you tied up lately?"

Azure's brow raises and a smile flickers across his face. "Lately? No one."

"Ohhh. Kink discovered," Larson says, leaning his elbow dramatically on the table and placing his chin in his palm. "Spill the tea, Dayne."

His gaze moves to mine, and it feels like someone has walked over my grave. Ethan's arm moves more fully around my back and I'm not sure if it's in response to the way I shivered or something else. Maybe he sees the crazy in Azure's eyes, too.

"What's to tell? Don't you think it's... maddeningly arousing to have someone helpless beneath you?" His dark gaze moves to me. "At your complete mercy."

"Bondage is not my kink," I say.

He chuckles. It's low and... dark. It's the thing of nightmares. I'm building this man up to be a serial killer in my head, but he makes it all too easy!

"To each their own," Azure answers.

"I don't know," Larson says, sitting up again. "I let Dylan tie me up."

"Do you?" Ethan asks, tilting his head. He looks Larson over. "I took you for a power top."

Larson laughs and shakes his head. "You really want to know?"

Ethan nods. "Now I do. Blow my mind."

He snorts. "Quite the opposite. Totally a power bottom."

"With Dylan?" I ask.

Larson laughs again. "Honey, don't let him hear that surprise. And yes. My queen is definitely a Dom top, hands down."

"Well fuck. I don't know shit," Ethan says, looking at me with a wide grin. I don't know why, but that smile makes everything inside me turn hot.

"You guys had a killer game tonight," Larson says, shaking his head. "But you know your line is supposed to be three men, right? Not three defensemen?"

Azure snorts, his eyes traveling the room and I have no doubt that he's seeking out Ryan.

"Give him a break," I say. "We've got a unique game."

"Yeah. You need to let someone else in on your game to complete your lineup, boys," Larson jokes. Though there's truth in his words. Kind of.

It's not a conscious choice. Not really. It just happens.

"We'll get there, eventually. And then be unstoppable," Ethan says, tossing a chip across the table. It bounces off Larson's cheek, making him chuckle.

"Where to next? Winnipeg?"

"Nah. Tampa, then Winnipeg. Ending in Minnesota, then we're home for a couple weeks," I say.

"All over the place in temperature."

"Hot. Hell. Cold, cold, cold," Ethan agrees. "About sums up the life of a hockey player."

We talk for a while longer and I try to ignore Azure. I don't think he's a bad guy. Or an actual serial killer. He's just unnerving. Then again, I could compare his tendency to sit back and listen as opposed to talking to Caulder. He's much the same. I don't even think Caulder is downstairs.

I tease him about having a secret girlfriend because he doesn't like to be rowdy with us. But I think it's probably social anxiety more than anything. He doesn't care for big crowds or a lot of people he doesn't know surrounding him. I get it.

If it wasn't for my craving to be close to Ethan all the time, I'd probably check out too. We don't get enough sleep during the season as it is. There's nothing wrong with catching up on that.

Ethan leaves us for a few minutes when his husband calls. I watch as he walks away, trying to find a quiet place so he can hear the phone. When I look back at Azure and Larson watching me knowingly, I flush because I'm caught lusting after a married man.

Then I have to remind myself that they don't know he's married. So... I'm just lusting after my teammate. Right?

I'm not sure that's better.

"You two are cute," Larson says.

I huff. "Thanks. Probably."

He chuckles. "What's taking you two so long? Is it the whole teammates thing?"

Shrugging, I try to brush it off because *I don't know!* And I don't want to think about it in case I don't like the answer. "Yes," I say.

"Liar," Azure says, then coughs.

Larson laughs and pats him hard on the back. "Dude, you have to say it *while* faking a cough."

Azure doesn't look like he did it wrong unintentionally. When he looks at me, a hint of a smirk on his lips, and I know I was fully intended to hear that.

"Fine. It's just not the right time."

"Uh huh," Larson says. "Hockey doesn't last forever, Creed. You're already getting old."

In hockey, maybe. I'm twenty-four. Already half way through the average length of a five-year NHL career. But I'm good. I know I'm good. And as long as I keep being good, I can keep playing.

I look up when I catch sight of Ethan walking back in. Making his way through the crowd, stopping periodically to talk to someone for a second. He's past the average five years at eight. But then, he's in the top 25% of all-star hockey players.

As long as we're together, we're an unstoppable team. As long as we're together, I think I'll be able to keep my career going.

It's not just the prospect of my career ending that looms ahead but when it's over, that means I won't be spending at least part of every day for more than half the year with this man who I've been crushing on since before I've known him.

Larson's right. This isn't forever. There's potential to go separate ways in the near future. The thought of it makes me sick to my stomach.

Maybe one more invitation for more? And this time, make it clear I'm definitely interested!

Sure. Easy as a hat trick.

FOUR
ETHAN

I CAN FEEL HIS EYES ON ME. IT MAKES ME INCREDIBLY AWARE OF every inch of my body. As if I'm on display. Being stared at. I'm self-conscious about how much I'm smiling. How long the friendly casual touches between me and someone else are. The hairs on the back of my neck stand up.

As I'm making my way back toward the table with Creed, Azure, and Larson, an image flashes behind my eyes of Creed looking at me while I'm completely naked before him.

Not that I haven't been before. We share a locker room. For the past two years, we've shared hotel rooms for our away games. We've definitely seen each other naked. Too many times to count.

But the scenario that keeps flashing before my eyes is very different.

"I support you."

Jakub's words are still ringing in my ears as I finally break away from the rest of the crowd and meet Creed's dark eyes as I make my way to him. Azure and Larson are also watching me; I can see their expressions out of the corner of my eye. But I can't take my gaze from Creed.

It's always been Creed. Since the day we met, I've barely seen anyone other than him and my husband.

I smile as I retake my seat, replacing my hand on Creed's back. There's always been this need to touch him. Something that I can't always seem to stop myself from doing. Especially when we're in crowded areas and there are people around.

It feels like I need to claim him. *This man is mine.* He's not. But it's never been because we don't want it to happen that way.

"Good call?" Larson asks and I study him for a minute.

Does he know?

I am well aware of what looks suspicious. The rhythm of your breathing. The inability to keep eye contact. Eye twitching. There are other smaller ticks, too.

However, while Jakub and I keep our marriage a secret, it's not because of the reasons everyone would accuse us of. We have an open marriage because that's what we talked about from the very beginning. When we started fooling around, it was never exclusive. Our love, our commitment, has always been solely for each other. But sex? That's not what's important in a healthy relationship. It's a bonus. It can definitely be a point of contention. But for us, it's not an end-all. Like conversation and laughter, it's not something that needs to be kept strictly for our spouse.

This isn't something the world understands or approves of. Pick your battles. Being a gay hockey player has enough challenges. I don't fancy being the headlines for the constant accusations of cheating on my husband. That's more pressure and attention than he needs too.

So, I don't lie. My smile remains easy as I nod. "Yep. Been expecting the call."

Azure's cool gaze remains locked on me. There's something about him that always makes the hair on the back of my neck stand on end when his attention is reserved for me alone for a long period. Uninterrupted. As it is now. While he watches me like a science experiment.

An image that's nowhere near as sexy flashes before my eyes. I'm still naked. But now I'm splayed out as Azure dissects me. Looking for the answers he seeks that he can't see with his naked eye.

Chills race down my body, leaving my flesh prickly with awareness.

Larson's stare isn't nearly as unsettling. The playful smile on his face counteracts the unease I feel from Azure. Don't get me wrong;

Azure is good people. An amazing player. But fuck. Some people just give you a vibe.

"What kind of call?" Larson asks.

Creed glances at me and it's his flushed expression that's hinting at something scandalous more than my behavior or answers. I flash him a smile, wrap my arm more fully around his back until I can hook my hand at his hip, and pull him against me.

"Don't be nosy, Ocho," I reprimand. "A man can have private conversations."

He rolls his eyes. "Every time Dylan calls when we're together, you demand to hear the conversation."

"Because he's a fucking riot," I say. "Keeps you in your place. I can't stop seeing the juxtaposition of you two next to each other and the way he just naturally dominates."

"I'd like to see you try to get your way," he says, pouting slightly.

I raise my hand. "Definitely not. No thanks."

Creed laughs, shaking his head. His laughter is cut by a yawn. It's quickly followed by Larson and me yawning too.

"On that note," I say, pushing my chair back and getting to my feet. "I think I'm heading up. These long stretches of away games should be reserved for the young guys."

The three of them snort. None of us can be considered old. Not by any means. Two hundred years ago when people were only living into their thirties, sure. But not today. And not one of us is in our thirties yet.

The others get to their feet as well. There are bro hugs and all the expected exchanges that those watching are waiting for. The masculine form of affection between athletes. We even give the flashing phone cameras brief, but fake rivalry banter for our next games.

This time it's my turn to yawn first. Once the dam is open, the yawns don't stop until I'm passed out. I'll probably yawn a dozen more times before we even make it to our room.

Creed and I walk closely, our shoulders brushing. My body becomes incredibly aware of him once again. The backs of our hands graze together. I'm even more aware of him once we're alone in the elevator as we make our way to the eleventh floor.

Jesus, when's the last time I was this nervous? It feels like I'm taking my prom date back to the hotel room for our first fuck. And with that thought, I'm pretty sure my cheeks heat, so I turn away to stare at my reflection. And Creed's.

His gaze is straight ahead.

"Why is this so awkward?" I mutter through anxious laughter.

He grins as I turn to meet his eyes. The hair on top of his head is getting long. Falling in his eyes. Before I can think better of it, I reach for him. Brushing it away. My heart is racing in my chest.

The ping of the elevator announcing we're on our floor makes us both jump away and stare as the doors open.

Creed laughs, shaking his head. "Honestly," he huffs.

We're once again awkwardly quiet as we move down the hall. I use my phone and the digital key to let us in, then throw the lock and the extra bar to secure us inside.

Now, we're alone. Great.

Creed moves right for the bathroom, and I breathe a sigh of relief for the moment alone. I need to pull myself together. I'm being weird. This is ridiculous. He's Creed. At this point, we've been alone together probably more times than I have with my husband this year.

As soon as he comes out, I trade places with him and brush my teeth. Wash my face. My hands. I contemplate taking another shower, just to extend the time in the bathroom and maybe work my dick into submission since it thinks now is a good time to wave.

I don't because I'm pretty sure that would look like I'm avoiding him.

Even though I am. For stupid reasons.

"I support you."

Jakub's words fluttering through my head make me smile. I know how lucky I am.

With a breath and a silent pep talk as I stare into the mirror at my reflection, I resolutely move to the door. When I walk back into the room, I stop and stare for a minute before I laugh. Creed is in bed with the blankets tucked all the way up under his chin. Like he's hiding.

My laughter makes his gaze snap open and lock with mine. Though my laughter dies, my smile doesn't. Of course, once Creed's eyes dip to my waving dick in my boxer briefs, my smile falls in favor of trying to catch my breath and settle my hormones.

He visibly swallows.

There's a part of me that wants to climb into his bed. Get close and comfortable. Rub against him until we cover each other in cum. Kiss him until we fall asleep.

My body sways forward slightly and I don't miss the way his blankets tent a little more as the seconds tick by.

I can't just crawl into his bed. We need a conversation first. That has to happen. The last thing I want is to ruin our friendship. While that's the most important thing to me, I'm also aware of how it could fuck with our chemistry on the ice.

There's too much to lose to fuck this up. Discussion *needs* to happen first.

I'm not sure where the strength comes from, but I force myself to move to my own bed. From my peripheral vision, I catch Creed wince. And now he feels bad. Rejected? That's definitely *not* how I want him to feel. And I'm not fucking rejecting him.

Sighing, I drop onto the edge of my bed and stare at him. My cock has not taken notice of the somewhat fragile moment, though. It fucking throbs.

With a somewhat high school idea, I sit up. "Get up," I say. "Sit on your bed. Face me."

Creed stares at me for a minute before doing as I suggest. Slowly. As if he's trying to figure out what I'm doing and whether I'm leading him into a trap.

When he's facing me, I unabashedly stare at the way his dick strains in his underwear, too. They're white, designer with the word LUSH centered on the waistband. My stare becomes transfixed at the wet spot where his pre-cum is being soaked into the fabric.

I bite my lip, hand moving to cup my cock in my underwear. A groan nearly escapes at the pressure.

Meeting his eyes again, I can feel the way his desire fills the room. His pretty lips are parted as he tries to breathe. I can't keep my groan in this time. He's too perfect.

"Jerk with me," I whisper.

The whimper that meets my ears has me nearly falling off the bed to get to him. Somehow, though I shift, I remain where I'm seated. I stare. Waiting for his answer.

He doesn't say anything as he holds my gaze. Doesn't move. For a long time, we remain frozen except our breathing and my hand squeezing my frustrated dick.

Finally, he shifts on the bed to push his underwear out of the way and I can't stop myself from looking. Seeing that perfect specimen come out, hard and needy. He's thick, though not long. His head is red, glistening, and angry. Needing attention.

"Fuck," I murmur and hurry to shove my underwear down, too. His moan is quiet and while I really, truly try to look up and into his face, my attention is locked when his hand wraps around his cock. Squeezing the base. Moving up the length. Covering his crown for a minute. When he pulls his hand back down, his thumb traces over the slit and rubs in another drop of pre-cum.

"Ethan," he whispers.

It's his voice that draws my attention to his face. I meet his eyes just as his settle back on mine. The want there is so bright, so unabashed. My free hand grips the bed tightly to keep me there. Somehow, I can still recall that I can't fuck this up with him.

We're not touching. Just staring at each other. Enjoying this moment where we both need release. *After* we'll talk. After we take the edge off, I'll be lust drunk enough that my inhibitions will have lessened, and I'll find the courage to tell him how much I want him.

"Match my rhythm," I say, breathless.

His hand hesitates for just a moment before I can practically feel him under my touch as I move my hand, his syncing with mine. Even as I run my fingers over my cockhead, he does the same. As with on the ice, it's as if we're reading the same playbook. He's doing just what I need him to. His motions, his touch, are so in tune with mine that it's like I'm touching him and not myself. Combined with his hard breathing and the beating of my own heart, this no longer feels separate.

My balls are tight, and I know that this is going to be an embarrassingly short session. Words try to come out to excuse how quickly I'm going to come, but they get lost on my tongue as he moans, his hips rocking on the bed.

"Yes, Ethan," Creed murmurs, moaning my name. It's enough to make me dizzy.

"Come for me," I say.

He does. His hips buck up as he suddenly drips long cords of cum onto the floor, nearly reaching my feet. I follow. Or maybe I echo his orgasm. My moans feel like they're a beat later than his. My release crossing his seconds after it hits the ground.

"Oh god," he says through another moan.

My head is heavy. I really want to drop it back and feel the pulse of my climax as it travels through my cock, but I can't take my eyes off him. He's so perfect.

Another image flashes in my head, and I imagine Jakub sitting behind me. Telling me exactly what he wants me to do. How he wants me to touch myself. He commands Creed too. I groan. Fuck, do I want that!

It takes me a few minutes to catch my breath. The room comes back into focus, and I blink a few times to take in Creed. His mouth is open wider now as he stares at our mixed cum on the hotel floor. Thankfully, this room doesn't have carpet. Best idea ever was when hotels started removing carpet. Far more sanitary.

"I'll be right back," I say and slowly get to my feet. They're slightly wobbly. As if I just got off the ice and have to retrain my muscles how to move on solid, rough ground.

I grab a washcloth and wet it. Quickly cleaning myself up, I rinse it and return to the room with a second towel in hand too. I drop the second on the floor, covering our mess. Creed is laying back, his arm covering his eyes. His cock is softening, leaning against his thigh.

Carefully, I kneel next to him and set the warm cloth on his leg, wiping up where he dripped and sprayed himself. He twitches and drops the arm over his head to look at me. His expression is guarded, and I know I put that there.

Gently, trying to be somewhat professional, I clean him and then drop the cloth onto the towel before laying next to him. Close enough that I can feel his body heat.

There's so much to say. But I don't know where to begin.

"I've always known that every guy I mess around with is temporary," I say, watching as he swallows. "They're a means to an end. A body to cut through the loneliness that surrounds me during the season when my husband is across the country."

Creed nods and I'm sure I glimpse hurt in his eyes.

I touch his chest, laying a hand across his beating heart. "The reason I've always kept some distance between us despite the mutual attraction we feel for each other isn't because I'm not interested, Creed. It's not because of hockey or because we're friends. Or even because of Jakub. It's because—sometimes when you meet someone, you just know that they're a permanent part of you. Life is a little complicated for everyone who'd be involved in this, even by extension. I'm afraid of us somehow fucking up and… everything falling apart."

He releases a breath and I feel his body sag. There's no mistaking the relief he feels. Before he can say anything, I add, "I didn't mean to make you feel unwanted."

Creed smiles a little and rolls onto his side to face me. We're inches apart. "I feel sheepish saying that I kept thinking I was imagining this because I wanted it."

I laugh and shake my head. "No. You're not. You never have. I kept waiting for my attraction to fade because it usually does. Mixing work and personal life isn't the best idea even when you work in an office, but in the public eye? It really has the potential to be a nightmare. It's added pressure on us and I'm not sure if you've noticed, but I'm shit at hiding my attraction and affection for someone."

"That's why you and Jakub never remain somewhere you're recognized during the offseason," Creed says, nodding in understanding.

"Yep. Our marriage was an accidental secret, but it's a happy accident. Celebrities who live the open lifestyle are constantly under fire and they're generally straight. Gay athletes are a new phenomenon and the pressure on us is unfairly more intense than everyone else. When it became apparent that no one knew we were married, we talked about it and kind of went with the flow. I was already openly out but Jakub is a private person, so his sexuality was always just assumed straight since no one ever sees him with another person."

"I wondered," Creed says.

I nod. "So yeah. That's where I'm at." Sliding my hand up his chest, I touch his cheek. "I'm finding it's harder to keep the distance between us that I've always tried to create. I don't want to anymore."

His smile makes my stomach flutter. Creed leans in and I feel his breath against my lips. "About fucking time, Wildman."

Grinning, I press my lips to his and kiss him for the first time.

FIVE
CREDENCE

"This is wild," Max says as we step onto campus.

The next big event in professional sports is a program where we talk to young athletes about being queer in the big league. There's a dozen of us from hockey, including some straight athletes, and there are a couple dozen from other sports, too. I wasn't sure if it was put on by one of the professional leagues or an agency like Pride Sports. They're constantly putting on these events to try to make the world a little more inclusive.

Of the dozen hockey players, four are from Buffalo. Ethan, of course, since he was the one signed up for this event. I'm here because he asked me to go with him. Asael Rhavn is our second goalie and Isak Lokken is our first line defenseman and one of Ethan's best friends. I have to admit; Isak is Norwegian and listening to him talk is like a wet dream.

Walking with our Buffalo group is Felton Badcock, the goalie from the Winnipeg Wendigos; Noah Kain, a wingman from the Florida Manatees; Max Latham, a wingman from the Philadelphia Hatters; and his coach, Tavis Davenport.

The campus we walk onto is certainly wild. There are pride flags everywhere. There is rainbow colored everything. I'd think it's set up for the event except that we just walked by the football stadium and the bleachers are definitely permanently painted the colors of the rainbow in a very familiar pride pattern.

There are students everywhere, and I stare a little at their clothing. For no reason except that it's loud and there are a lot of people dressed this way. It's like walking into a gay club but... a campus that's entirely gay!

"This is blowing my mind," Noah says, watching as a guy stares at him with a flirty smile and wearing just a salmon colored speedo.

"Welcome to Rainbow Dorset University."

As a group, we turn to the man addressing us. Fit and distinguished in a suit with salt and pepper hair, heavier on the silver than the dark lines. He's got slight crinkles around his eyes as he smiles widely at us.

He offers his hand to the first person to reach him, which happens to be Coach Tavis. "We're so glad you could make it."

"Thank you for hosting the event," Tavis says. "I'm Tavis." He steps aside to introduce the rest of us. He does really fucking well, not just with the hockey players but with the soccer, football, and baseball players, too.

"I'm Provost Kendrick Keller," the silver fox says and steps aside as Tavis did. "These are some of my faculty from the athletic department. Our football coach, Lemon Frost. Don't let his size fool you; I've seen his tackle."

The man in question is small, almost dainty, with the loudest clothes of all, including a neon pink tutu. He smirks as he takes us all in, waving his fingers with matching pink painted nails.

"Our soccer coach, Alka Lennon. One of our athletic trainers, Declan Whitaker. Both of our lacrosse coaches, Danika and Davyn Elmyra." He continues down the line as Tavis had and introduces his people.

There is some general talking where we intermingle before the 'adults in charge' split us into groups to head off for different events. Ethan is pulled to a second group, but he shoves the baseball player, Ian Roe that way instead, giving him a kissy face as Ian scowls but doesn't argue.

Ethan stops next to me and looks around our group. Asael has been split away from us, but Isak is still there. We also have Noah, Max, and the soccer pro, Gabe Zanderman.

We are paired with Alka Lennon and Declan Whitaker. For a moment, as the other groups move away, the group of us take a few minutes to check each other out. Until Isak says, "Okay, stop that. You can compare junk later. What's first on the agenda?"

Max shoves him playfully before turning back to our hosts. I recognize that smirk. He's ready to make an ass of himself. "You know how to work a stick, Whitaker?" he asks, and I raise my hand to cover my mouth, hiding my smile when the athletic trainer raises a brow at him.

Another man appears seemingly from nowhere, moves in front of Declan Whitaker and crosses his arms over his chest, giving the beast that is Max Latham a look that should be lethal. "You will keep your hands and your comments to yourself, fuckboy."

"Hey," Declan says through laughter and pulls him back. "Rude, Ehsan." He continues to chuckle as Alka Lennon shakes his head, doing his best not to smile and remain completely neutral.

Declan looks at us somewhat apologetically. "This is Zarek, my boyfriend. Although he gets the sports confused, he'll be with us, too."

"They're barbaric," Zarek says, his eyes narrowing on us. I have to say, I'm intrigued. He's shorter than Declan by a few inches and definitely on the softer side. But fuck, does he look like he's ready to tear down right now. "Especially hockey. I don't think it's necessary to compare dick size by throwing your opponents into the window."

"They're called boards," Max says, "and we don't do it to compare dick size. We do it to cop a feel." He raises his brows suggestively a couple times.

Zarek scowls. "Keep your hands to yourself, savage."

I chuckle, unable to hold it in any longer. That is, until Zarek looks at me and I immediately stop laughing. Hell, it feels like I was caught passing a note in class.

"Anyway," Alka says, eyeing Zarek while trying to keep his smile small. "We're going to be heading to the soccer field and playing with the kids there. Most of the students attend Rainbow Dorset, but we have some local high school kids in attendance as well." He gives Max a once over. "The high school kids are in school shirts announcing which school they belong to. So... keep that in mind, please."

"In other words, don't hit on the minors," Noah loudly whispers to Max.

Max rolls his eyes. "As if they could keep up."

"Ew, stop," Isak says, shoving at him and turning towards the fields. "Don't be a creep."

Max rolls his eyes again. "I'm not into anyone who isn't old enough to get drunk." He pauses before adding, "In the U.S. That's an important distinction to make."

"Indeed," Isak mutters.

Declan links his hand with Zarek and motions for us to follow them. When they've moved a few steps ahead, Ethan asks Alka who has fallen into line with us, "Why does it feel like he's going to give me a detention?"

Alka snorts but covers his mouth when Zarek looks back with narrowed eyes. Once he's facing forward again, he answers, "He will. He's like a terrier, but his bite is that of a wolf. I've been on the receiving end and not in a fun way."

"You have a hockey team here, don't you?" Isak asks.

Alka nods. "Yep. They're pretty good. Didn't make it to the Frozen Four this year since we had a bunch of injuries toward the second half of the season."

"Barbaric," Zarek singsongs ahead of us.

Alka grins. "As much as I loathe to admit it, our football team is really our pride. Though we don't win at the championship level often enough, we have more drafts to the NFL than any other college in our region. The spitfire coach they have is... well, he's not to be messed with on the field."

"I'm as surprised by that as I love it," Ethan says.

"It's definitely a love/hate feeling concerning him," Declan says with a cute smile that he throws over his shoulder at us.

"If he keeps looking at us like that, I'm going to challenge his boyfriend," Max hisses.

"You'll lose," Alka says, "but I think the school would love to see that throw down. Let our prize mathematician make a giant pro hockey player cry."

Max is about to take the challenge when we all fall silent, catching Zarek looking back at us shrewdly. "I'll do it," he says. "Try me."

I'm surprised when Max remains silent, though he's definitely contemplating it. The man is a PR nightmare that Philly keeps on the roster because he's their top scorer. Though there are rumors saying he's on a tight leash right now. Most of his antics seem pretty harmless as far as I'm concerned, but no team wants negative attention.

Unless you ask our PR rep. Even negative attention is attention. He's pointed out to us a few times that every time Max makes headlines, their games—both away and home—are nearly sold out. Not that she encourages us to be hellions. Far from it. But... she's not wrong.

"Okay," Alka says, clapping his hands. "Gather 'round, kiddos."

"You're barely older than us," one of them says.

It's pretty easy to distinguish the difference between the college kids and the high school students for the most part. I have to wonder if there's magic that happens once they step foot on campus. Like they suddenly look... older. Not mature, but older.

"I'm older," Zarek says, stuffing his hands into the pockets of his tight pants. Now that I'm looking, I can't stop. Does he have a fucking soda bottle stuffed in there?? Am I gawking at it? "Fall into line."

"Maybe I should be hitting on him," Max whispers. "I bet he's fun in bed."

"He is," Declan says, smirking. "But keep your hands to yourself."

Max huffs. "This school is no fun."

"We have a porn star sponsor that we proudly display on our home page," one of the college athletes states with a grin. "I think that's pretty fun."

"No shit," Isak says.

"I'll give you my husband's number," Alka says. "He'd love to do a collab with you." He winks and Max just stares. Ethan, Isak, and Noah laugh.

"Fuck's sake. This entire experience is surreal," Max mutters, crossing his arms over his big chest.

"Anyway," Zarek says, making a pointed look at Alka. "On with it, coach."

Alka shakes his head and turns to look at us with amusement

before addressing the students. "We're going to match you up for some practice. Besides Zanderman, I think you can all show these hockey players how to… handle a ball. Have fun and feel free to ask them questions about their sport, the spotlight, pressure, and—respectfully—how their sexuality has been a factor in their lives, personally and professionally."

We're each given a few students. I end up with two high school girls and a college boy. Nora, Stephanie, and Brandon. I can tell by the way the girls kick the ball back and forth as they lead us down the field that they're soccer players.

"I'm gay," Brandon says when we find a corner to ourselves. He looks at the girls. "You?"

Nora points at her chest. "Pan." Points to Stephanie. "Ace."

"But straight," Stephanie says.

"Are you familiar with hockey?" I ask.

The girls shrug. "The game, not so much. So, just in the way that you are when you're told someone is like you and thrust into the spotlight," Nora says. "I know that there's an openly pan player for New York and I admit that I follow him on social media. Women's sports aren't as big as men's but it still feels like a win for me that there's a pan professional player, you know?"

I nod. I do know. The moment that Ethan Wilder came onto the scene as an openly gay athlete was the day my obsession with him began. Because I loved hockey, and I'd just come out a month or so before he came onto the college scene. There'd been issues on my team with a couple of assholes and there were moments where clinging to the fact that there was a gay man making his way through all this noise despite the assholes standing in his way was what got me through a lot of rough patches in school.

"I do," I say, managing to catch the ball with the side of my foot when she sends it my way. "I'm going to pre-empt this conversation by stating that I've never touched a soccer ball in my life. Be easy on me." The girls grin as I send the ball toward Stephanie. "What about you? Familiar with hockey?"

"I have three older brothers. One is a professional hockey player," she says, giving me a bemused look. "I'm familiar."

"Who?" Brandon asks.

"Colby Minden, he plays for Anaheim."

"Fuck yeah, he does," Brandon says, grinning. "Man, the way he moves on the ice—"

Stephanie covers her ears and says, lalalala, until we're laughing. When she drops her hands, she gives Brandon a deadpan look. "Not only does the whole concept of sex kind of gross me out, but I sure as fuck don't want to hear anything sexual in relation to my brother."

Brandon laughs. "I was commenting on his speed. I swear."

Stephanie kicks the ball to him hard, but Brandon stops it with a smile. He looks at me. "I *am* familiar with hockey. Though, like Nora, I think my interest lies in the number of out players in the league. There seems to be more per capita than other professional sports. Why do you think that is?"

I shrug. "Honestly? Our teams are small. We spend weeks on the road together in tight quarters."

"If you're going to say that being close like that all the time makes you realize you're gay…" Nora begins.

Laughing, I shake my head. "No. I was going to comment on our camaraderie. The closeness of our teams. The frequency in trades. You'd think that knowing we could be shifted to another country at the drop of a hat means that we don't have time to build connections and lay down roots, but it's actually the opposite. It facilitates learning to trust those around you quickly. Hockey is a team sport, even as you're battling for your individual career when it averages five to twelve years at the most. But that team camaraderie is important."

"The trust is what allows you to feel comfortable coming out?" Brandon asks.

Nodding, I agree. "I think so. I was out in high school when kids are still dickwads. So it wasn't a pleasant experience for me. I can appreciate those who have gone pro already being out. But I think that more who are already pro coming out is a result of the close ties we have with each other."

"Have you had any issues because of your sexuality?" Nora asks.

"Not professionally. At least, none who have openly expressed their distaste to me. Again, I think that has to do with how close we become as teammates. A person can find their bravado to show their disgust toward one hockey player. But when you're facing twenty hockey players? Not so much. I've only played with Buffalo, though, so I can't speak for every team. What I can tell you is that there's a trend of professional leagues throwing their queer players together often to make sure the world knows that we have a place in professional sports."

"By singling you out," Stephanie mutters.

"It's a double-edged sword," I agree. "But because of that, we find friends across the country who experience the same shit we do. It's a comforting feeling knowing we're not alone."

"You're friends with the guys who came here today?" Brandon asks.

I nod. "Obviously my teammates, yeah. But Noah and Max are friends too. Gabe I've only met a couple times, but he seems cool."

Our conversation is broken up when Alka calls us back for a scrimmage. The professional players are divided up between the students. There's more laughing and mishaps happening on the field than any actual playing.

However, by far my favorite moment is when Zarek kicks the soccer ball and it hits Max in the nuts. From the way Alka and Declan stared at him with shock and the way the Rainbow Dorset students stared at him in awe, I have to think that it surprised everyone. I hadn't taken him to knowing shit about sports.

But he smirks at Max before retaking his position on the field and waiting for Max to stop groaning.

"Well fuck," Isak mutters. "You gays don't mess around."

Ethan shoves him, but he's still staring at Zarek like the rest of us are. I think we all just unlocked a new level of attraction. Possessive math nerds for the win!

SIX

JAKUB BOZIK

HE'S BOUNCING OFF MY BOOTY CHEEKS; I LOVE THE WAY HE RIDES...
The country song breaks through my sleep, and I squint into the dim light of my room. My phone screen is the only source of light as I groggily roll over and reach for it. The combination of the words of the song and the voice I know will greet me when I answer makes me smile. Despite the ungodly hour.

"Miláček," I murmur.

There's a smile in his voice when he responds. Butchering the Czech word, of course. "Manžel."

I chuckle and close my eyes.

"What're you doing?" Ethan asks.

"Not sleeping anymore."

I can almost feel him wince. "Sorry, love. I forget the time difference when I want to hear your voice."

"Mm," I answer.

There's a pause before he asks, "How was your hookup last night?"

"Not you," I say. The same thing I always say, which makes him hum in appreciation this time. It's the truth, anyway. Random hookups are what keep me from being a grumpy man, but no one measures up to my husband. Not even those who keep me entertained for more than a night.

"What's wrong, kocourek?" I ask.

"Nothing," he answers, then sighs. I hear his car start and there's a moment that the sound shifts before his phone switches to Bluetooth. "Jakub, I really need you to tell me that you're okay with me and Creed."

"I already told you I am," I say as I roll over to look at the picture of us on my nightstand. Because of the darkness, I can barely make it out, but that's fine. I don't need to see it in order to *see* it. Our wedding wasn't anything special. It was just us on a beach with a couple random witnesses and a justice of the peace. But I'll not only forever see the image of the memory captured within the photo, but also the way he looked at me when he told me he loved me that day. It'll be burned into my mind for the rest of my life.

"I know," he says quietly. "But I know I'm going to fall for him. That's never happened before. I just—"

"Ethan," I hum, hearing him sigh again. "I've watched you fall in love with him over the last three years and, zlato, it's been beautiful to see."

He huffs.

"I know what you're worried about. You're afraid that loving him is going to mean you love me less."

My husband sighs. "Yeah," he whispers.

"But it hasn't. Has it?"

"No. Not at all. I still love you with everything in me. You've always been the future I see for me. As much as I love hockey, I'm so fucking excited to retire and just *be* with you."

"But," I prompt, knowing it's there.

"What if I want him too?" he asks quietly. "What if I love him as much? Or if I see him in my future with us?"

"Let me ask you something. Do you think if I thought for a minute that you were in love with him and I *wouldn't* be okay with him in our future together, that I'd encourage you to pursue something with him?" I ask.

"No," he answers with a sigh.

"I know you love me, Ethan. I know no one could ever take your love for me away. No matter how much you love another person. That love is separate."

"Miluji tě," he says, and I hear his car shift into park.

"I love you too. More than hockey."

He chuckles.

"We need to get back to working on your Czech," I say. "And I know this goes without saying, but the same rules apply with Creed as they do with any other relationship. Your ass is mine and mine alone. He doesn't get to touch it."

Ethan laughs and then groans. "I know. I miss your dick."

I grunt in response. Sure, I might have just gotten my dick squeezed last night, but I meant what I said. He wasn't my husband. Sex has never been just sex for me. When I love my partner, it's all the better, regardless of what we do.

"Have a good practice," I tell him.

"Sorry I woke you up."

"You feel better?"

His car door closes. "Yeah. I think I needed to hear it again. And I wanted to hear your voice. I miss you."

"Miss you too."

"I'll see you next week for Christmas," I tell him. It's a very short break, but it's something. "Then less than a month later when our teams play. Yeah?"

"Yeah," he answers.

"We'll get together for dinner or something. With Creed. Okay?"

He hums and I can hear the smile in his voice. "That sounds good. Thanks, Jakub."

I hear his name called in the distance and the phone makes a rustling sound. "Call you later, love," he says.

I say goodbye and we end the call. Glancing at the time, I groan, knowing I'm not going to be getting any more sleep this morning. Instead, I drop my phone back on its charger and reach for the remote.

As per usual, my television is set to Sports Spot. Since it's so early, I'm a little groggy when the bright colors flash across my screen with dozens—hundreds?—of people dressed in rainbow colors. It's not June, though. Why the pride parade?

Turning up the volume, I pause when my husband's face flashes across the screen as he moves behind Creed, wrapping his arms around him and grinning. He's completely unaware of the camera and the move is so natural, so affectionate that it makes me smile at the way they look at each other.

As I watch the highlights of the event that took place a couple days ago, that one shot keeps getting recycled to play over and over again. I wonder if he's aware they're using it as a cute draw in. Then I burst out laughing when Max dropped on the soccer field from a ball to the crotch. He probably deserved it.

I spend the next couple hours watching the highlights and catching up on the rest of the sporting world.

By mid-morning, I've watched enough sporting news that I can hear the broadcaster's voice when I close my eyes, so I head down to the gym in my apartment complex. I spend a couple hours messing with different muscle groups and wondering how Ethan's practice is going. While he isn't outwardly upset at the lack of chemistry between him and the second wingman, I know it's a point of frustration for him.

For the entire team.

I get it. I really do. Buffalo would be the team to beat if they could get their starting line in order. Sadly, that doesn't seem to be the case right now.

When noon comes around, I'm bored in the gym, so I head back upstairs and shower. These are the days that I hate being away from Ethan. I'd love to just sit in the stands and watch him skate around the ice. There's no one I've ever loved watching more than him. Not just because he's sexy as fuck, but because he's just so natural. So confident. His moves are fluid. It looks like he's on a machine that skates him around with perfect balance, smooth transitions, and talent coming out of his ears.

Instead, I piss away the afternoon until I feel like I've spent enough time at home that I could reasonably go to the arena and skate around on the ice for a while without someone asking if something is wrong. Nothing's wrong. I'm just bored.

Unlike Ethan, I don't make friends easily. I'm friendly enough, but I don't find I have the interest to create bonds and shit with my teammates. Even though I've been in Vancouver for two years, I've had very little interest in making friends.

Part of me thinks it's because if I let someone in, they're going to find my secret. Home is my sanctuary, and I don't let anyone come over. There are pictures of Ethan and me everywhere. There'd be no way to explain why that is without someone getting suspicious.

Especially right now when he's already struggling with his feelings for Creed, I don't want him to have something that could potentially get in his way. A new relationship, especially one that's been boiling just under the surface for so long, is a fragile thing. Our marriage leaking could cause an early death to it, and I don't want to see either of them hurt like that.

Besides, I think our relationship could be a very beautiful thing adding Credence to it. Not that I'm inserting myself into their romance. I'm certainly not. I'm not even sure how I feel about him personally on a romantic or sexual level. But that doesn't mean that I don't think that the three of us could be great together. With Ethan as our fulcrum, we're going to be a very happy household.

Eventually.

I step inside the arena and head for the locker room.

"Bozik."

Pausing, I turn at the sound of my coach's voice and meander back down the hall until I reach his door. There I stand until he looks up at me. I'm not even sure how he saw me walk by.

"Come in."

Dropping my bag, I sit in the chair facing him with his desk between us. I can see my file open and for a minute, I'm concerned.

"Your records state that one of your interests is animals, yeah?" he asks.

My shoulders relax. "Yes, coach."

"There's a charity event for the local shelter that I'd like you to attend on Christmas Eve. It's only a few hours, but the shelters are bursting at the seams, so they need some animals adopted as soon as possible."

My stomach drops. Fuck. I was definitely heading into Buffalo for Christmas. My dismay must show on my face because my coach raises a brow.

"Did you plan to head back to Czech for the holiday?"

Hockey is like any other employer. You give them your personal information on the prescribed government and local forms. This includes marital status. I'm almost *positive* that my management team knows I'm married. As I'm pretty sure Ethan's knows. I think that they don't say anything because they legally can't. It's protected information that management can't share.

So… is he backing me into a tough spot intentionally so I'll come clean? What would he gain by doing this? Coach has never appeared to target me for any reason in the past. I'm a good player. I don't make any drama on or off the ice.

"No, coach," I tell him. "It's fine. It's just a few hours, right?"

"Exactly."

I nod. "Done. You'll email me the details?"

"Already have. You going to enjoy the peace of the ice for a bit before it gets loud?"

Nodding again, I get to my feet. "Yeah."

"All right. See you before the game."

I head out of his office, slinging my bag over my shoulder on the way. The arena is silent this early before a game. Everyone is doing their thing whether that's spending time with family, unwinding with friends, getting laid, catching up on sleep—whatever their normal routine is before a game.

It's just me here. I drop my bag again on the bench and sink into my cubby. Leaning back, I pull out my phone and catch the time. Four. Ethan should be home by now. Probably.

Dialing his number, I close my eyes and wait for him to answer.

"Hey, sexy Czech man," he greets. He sounds like he's in a much better place than he was this morning. His easy confidence and happy demeanor are back.

"Hey, zlato. Busy?"

"Nah. Shouldn't you be getting ready?"

I open my eyes and look around, confirming once more that there's no one here. "I'm already at the arena. Got bored at home. Listen. We're going to have to change plans for Christmas."

"Why?" I grin at the whine in his voice.

"Coach just dropped a Christmas Eve event in my lap. It's only a few hours that day, but it means it no longer makes sense for me to come out there. Can you come here?"

"Yeah, that's fine. Are you going to be able to cancel your tickets, though?" he asks.

No idea. Probably for airline credit, which sucks, but it's not like I won't use the credits. "It'll be fine. You can bring Creed if you want to."

He hums and I can just see the smile on his face. "I think he's already got plans to go home for Christmas, but I'll ask him."

"Good." A beat passes. "You okay?"

"Just miss you, but yeah, I'm good. You?"

"Same. We have a few days together next week, then in less than a month we have a game."

"Then three months with nothing," he says with a sigh.

I smile. "Miluji tě," I murmur. "Summer is soon."

"Go enjoy the ice in peace. Call me later. Win. Love you."

Grinning again, I tell him I love him again and we hang up. I don't move from where I'm leaning inside my cubby, my gear uncomfortably digging into my back. The locker room smells like a locker room but covered in bleach to try to get rid of the rancid jock odor. It's not awful and I can tell it was recently hosed down. For a few peaceful minutes, I don't move.

When I open my eyes, I'm startled to find Luca Billsworth standing just inside the locker room door, watching me. He's our center on the starting line with me. We're not the best of friends, but I think we tolerate each other pretty well. However, the way he's looking at me says that he's likely been there for a bit.

"Have a girlfriend you're not telling us about, Bozik?" he asks, smirking as he comes further into the room.

Pressing my lips together, I get to my feet and start pulling off my clothes. "Something like that."

We don't speak again and after a few minutes, I tune him out completely as I gear up. With a handful of pucks, I waddle my way down the chute until I hit the ice. As soon as my blades make contact, I take a deep breath and close my eyes again, letting my momentum move me forward a few inches.

There are days when I consider retiring so I can be with my man. Today is one of those days.

The time apart never felt so... cold and long. But lately, it's becoming more and more unbearable. Lonelier. Every time I come to the conclusion that I'm ready for retirement, I walk into the arena. As soon as I get on the ice, my determination shifts and I think *well, just a little while longer*.

Dropping the pucks, I skate around for a few minutes, letting the cold air brush against my skin. Yeah, just a while longer. But there's no doubt in my mind that I'm definitely getting closer to throwing in the skates. I love hockey. But I love Ethan more.

SEVEN
ETHAN

I LOOK AT MY HAND: 10♦, 9♣, 3♦, 4♦, 7♣, A♦, 3♥. FROWNING, I decide that we didn't shuffle the deck very well. After rearranging my cards, I frown further. "What are we playing again?"

Isak chuckles. "Gin."

"I'm not even sure I know how to play gin," I say, once more rearranging my cards so that they're still in numeric order but now by suit as well. I pick up another card. 4♥. Yep, I don't know how to play gin.

Glancing up, my gaze catches over Isak's shoulder to where Creed is sitting with Caulder on the couch as they play video games. They're laughing and for a minute, I can't stop myself from staring. He's definitely one of the most gorgeous men I've ever known. His laughter. That smile. Everything about him just makes me... warm.

"Ugh. It's sick the way your eyes morph into hearts when you look at him," Isak says.

I toss my cards on the table. "I demand a better shuffle."

He laughs and gathers the cards, giving into my petty tantrum and shuffling. I watch as he does. Not because I think he cheats, but because the action is so rhythmic and mesmerizing. There's a steady *shhhh* when he shuffles them together. Then, instead of aligning them all again, he flips them the other way and makes a bridge that sounds like *ffllppp*. Watching it is like magic.

Then he's dealing again. I pick them up as he tosses one to me. 8♣. 2♦. 10♦. 9♣. 4♥. 8♦. 5♠. "This is shit," I tell him.

"You watched me shuffle," he says.

I harrumph and glance at Creed again. This time, his eyes flicker to mine too, and he grins broadly before looking back at the screen. Does my stomach flutter? Not at all.

"Seriously, what's taking you two so long to hook up?" Isak asks. "I swear, we've been watching you two give each other fuck me eyes for years."

Glaring at him, I toss down my 4♥ and choose another card. I really have no idea how to play this game. 2♣. "It has nothing to do with hooking up," I say, frowning at him.

"I know, man. But seriously, what's the holdup?"

Obviously, I don't tell him the reasons. Not only would it take too long to fully explain, but... I haven't told anyone but Creed about Jakub. Not everyone would agree with our reasons. In my experience, most people have an opinion that they feel they need to tell you as if we asked for it. I don't have the patience for that. I can't take a chance on that stress affecting my career and neither can he.

We have our reasons—whether anyone agrees with them or not—and I really don't care what others think.

Except that I truly like Isak, and I *do* care what he thinks. While I think he'd be fine with it and at least verbally supportive, even if he doesn't agree with our lifestyle, I don't want to take the chance that he won't be.

"We're not talking about this," I say. "Tell me about your college girl. You still fucking her?"

He snorts. While at Rainbow Dorset, Isak somehow picked up a girl that wasn't even part of the athletic shit we were doing. He probably went to the bathroom and found her on the way. Or maybe while we stopped in their queer café or whatever it was called. The memory makes me smile. We had a lot of fun with the names of drinks—blue ball ballerina, bear sauce, hairy fairy. That campus was probably the most fun I've had in a long time.

"She looks like she's thirteen," I say.

Isak bristles immediately. "She's twenty."

"IDs can be faked, man."

I'm not joking when I say that he growls at me. It makes me grin. "I have a friend at Van Doren Technologies. He checked her out before I stuck my dick in her."

Laughter bubbles out of me as I shake my head and stare at our cards. Am I looking for pairs? A full house? What's going on right now?

"I wouldn't risk my career for sex," he grumbles. "I can get sex anywhere."

"So you still seeing her?" I ask.

"She's four states away," he says, frowning. "We talk, yeah. But I don't know, man. Long distance kind of sucks, you know?"

Do I ever? I nod vaguely.

"Just a fling, then?"

"Meh. We still chat sometimes. She sends me nudies and I don't send any in return because I really don't need that scandal on me." Our gazes meet for a minute and we chuckle. Wouldn't be the first time a celebrity or pro athlete had their junk all over the internet. "We're talking about getting together for a while this summer, but that's five months away, so who knows what could happen between now and then."

"You could fall in love with a puck bunny," I say.

"Or you could," he says, raising a challenging brow at me.

"I'm not sure if you're aware, but I'm really not interested in bunnies. Show me an otter or wolf or even a cub and we can talk."

His eyebrows scrunch together, making it clear he's not at all familiar with LGBTQ+ terms and it makes me chuckle. I laugh and throw down another card. Isak might be playing gin, but I'm closer to playing Go Fish at this point.

Our game is interrupted when his phone rings with the previously mentioned college girl calling him. He avoids my eyes, and I don't miss the slight tinge of pink on his cheeks as he excuses himself to take the call. Smirking, I get up and stretch.

We're at Isak's house, which is where we usually end up hanging out because he has a basement full of entertainment. We're not bothered by drunken puck bunnies who don't seem to remember that we reject them every time (or that I'm gay, for fuck's sake) and there aren't more than a dozen kids running around like Lucien and Bianca have in their mansion.

Though, to be fair, they have a bowling alley in their basement. And a team of nannies. So the team sucks it up to hang out at their place from time to time.

Since Creed is still laughing with Caulder on the couch, I head for the daylight basement door and step into the freezing December air that encases Buffalo this time of year. There's no snow right now, thankfully, but I know from experience that's something that can change overnight. Being so close to Lake Erie means we get some nasty lake effect shit that you only dream about.

Then there's Lake Ontario thirty-five miles north and yeah... winter can be devastating.

However, right now, the only thing we're dealing with is the cold weather. It's below freezing, but that doesn't stop me from stepping outside to stare into the clear night sky. For a minute, I stare at the stars and contemplate being a kid again and making a wish. But do I need to wait for a falling star?

Honestly, that would be really cool to see. Knowing that somewhere deep in space, a star is meeting its death and 'falling' through the universe as it goes out. Obviously, that's not what happens. I'm sure there's a whole bunch of scientific explanations as to why it looks that way, but I'd really love to see one someday.

I muse for a few minutes longer about how my husband is under the same sky nearly 3,000 miles away and technically in a different country. His side of the sky isn't quite as dark as mine is right now since it's probably just reaching sunset in Vancouver.

The door behind me slides open, and then there's a blanket being wrapped around me. I grin and turn my head to look at Creed. He shivers as he watches me, his eyes so dark in the night air that they look black right now. I pull him in front of me, wrapping the blanket around us both.

"Why are you out here without a jacket? Coach will kill you if you drop dead from pneumonia," he says.

I snort. "I wasn't planning on being out here long. Just getting some fresh air. Musing about falling stars."

"Uh, huh."

Pulling him close, I curl the blanket tightly around us. His hands move to my back and wrap around me, so I bury my face in his neck. He shivers, wincing from my cold nose on his skin. We stay like that for a while. Not speaking. Just enjoying each other's body heat and feeling his heart beat against mine.

"Tell me something," he says after a while, his voice quiet.

"Like what?"

He thinks for a second. "My college roommate has a ReachMe account, and he's now making bank. I used to walk into our dorm so many times while he was in the middle of filming a solo session."

I burst out laughing. "Jesus," I mutter.

Creed chuckles. "Yeah. We still keep in touch. He's a good guy using his... assets to make him money and get him the things he wants in life."

The sex content scene has blown up in the last handful of years when the new adult subscription platform ReachMe launched. It basically gave any Joe Moe the ability to create porn and get paid for it. No longer do they have to go through studios or whatever the procedure was for professional porn stars.

But it's not just ReachMe that they've inundated. While they stay off Spectrum because their 'community guidelines' basically advertise that they're prudes and terrified of seeing skin (when in reality they haven't been able to enforce a way to keep adult content separate from underage users), they've flooded ShareIt and Viraly with their thirst traps, glimpses into their lives with fun skits, solo and with other creators, plus teasers of what they're posting on ReachMe.

Then there's ClickDrip, which has a far more lenient set of guidelines, and you can see the full goods that they post. We're talking naked pics and short clips. Of course, this is just to get you drooling so you'll subscribe to their ReachMe channel.

"Anyone I've seen?" I ask.

"ASStrid," he says. "That's his social media name."

I laugh. "You're kidding. He's everywhere. Adorable little twink."

He chuckles. "Yep. That was two years of my life. I'm pretty sure that he intentionally recorded some of those videos when he knew I'd be coming back. The thrill of getting caught, I guess."

"Or hoping you'd be tempted into joining him..."

"Yeah, that too. But I'd already made it perfectly clear that I wasn't about to let *that* be the reason I wasn't able to go pro. What team was going to want me when I have sex videos out in the world?!"

Laughing quietly, I shake my head and bury my face some more. He smells so good.

"What about you?" he asks.

"I don't know that I have anything that can live up to that," I say. "The only thing I really got is that Noah Kain, the wingman for Florida? We attended the same high school and fucking hated each other. We were awful rivals. Like, completely nasty to each other. I'm pretty sure it was our goal to get the other kicked off the team, as if the NHL only had room enough for one of us and we needed to take out the competition."

"That's ridiculous," he says, laughing. "You appear to get along now."

I shrug. "We've grown up, I guess. He's not a bad guy."

Creed shakes his head, and for a content minute, we remain quiet. "What about family?" he asks. "Are you close?"

"I have a younger sister who just passed her barr exam. She's a full-fledged lawyer now and I'm slightly terrified for the world. I have an older brother who has his fifth kid in the oven with his wife and two from previous relationships, but his only ambition in life is to be a barista."

"Not that I'm judging, but how does he support his family?" he asks. The horror in his voice makes me laugh.

"Thankfully, his wife makes some decent coin, but I don't know, honestly. Our parents and her parents help out a lot with the kids. And I receive a text now and then from my mom that tends to be code for 'they need some help financially' and then I transfer a few thousand, depending on the tone of her text. I doubt my brother is aware of that; which leads me to believe that he doesn't do anything with the finances. But I mean, at least he's healthy and happy, right?"

Creed shakes his head in disbelief. "That's like Lucien and his wife. They just announced their eighth kid, right? Or are we at seventh?"

"No, you're right. Eighth. But at least they can afford it. My brother? Not so much."

He huffs.

"What about you? Siblings?"

"No. I'm an only child. I think when I began showing an interest in hockey, my parents made the decision to support that instead of giving me a sibling. I have a huge extended family, though. My mom has four brothers and a sister. My father comes from a very, very large family. They all have two or three kids. So I grew up surrounded by aunts, uncles, and cousins. Until I announced that I'm gay and suddenly, they all disappeared."

I wince and hug him tighter. "Sorry."

"Eh. My parents and I are still very close. They've separated from the rest of our family, though. My father's side is blindingly religious. I don't know what the issue is with my mom's side. After it became clear that they thought I was a pariah, I deleted them all from my life and blocked them. Being an out athlete was the only thing I had the energy to focus on. Not dealing with whether my family could love me the way I am."

"It never ceases to amaze me when I hear things like that," I say. "I know that I'm fortunate. My family doesn't give a shit about what gender I love. My sister spent a great deal of time in law school focusing on LGBTQ+ rights and laws and whatever. I know that it's because of me, though she claims that it's just sickeningly underrepresented. The shop my brother works in has little hints of rainbows everywhere, making sure that it subtly advertises that it's a safe space without throwing it in everyone's face. But my parents?!" I shake my head. "You'd think that they were the gay ones. There's no less than half a dozen flags outside our house in various spots. There's a rainbow garden and little gay gnomes in the yard. The mailbox is a fucking cloud with a rainbow coming out of it!"

Creed laughs. "I love that."

I nod and sigh. "Yeah." I glance at the sky. "I'm really looking forward to telling them about you and Jakub. They're going to eat you up."

"They don't know you're married?" he asks, surprised.

"No," I say. "Neither does his family. Between the two of us, there's a handful of people that know. Our agents, you, and my sister."

"I understand why you don't share it, but that seems like a heavy burden to carry," he says.

"It never was before and it's not really a burden now either. But I'm beginning to hate the secret. Sneaking around was fun for a while but... it's lost its appeal. I think we're both ready to be a family, but right now, this still just makes the most sense for us. The media is nasty. I already deal with the gay haters who demand that gays can't play sports. This is just a nightmare in the making if it comes out, given our current situation."

"Meaning me," he says quietly.

I hold him tightly to me. "No. Well, yes. But also, I've never been quiet about hooking up. Imagine the field day the haters are going to have. Even those who support me are going to turn nasty for my supposed infidelity. But yeah, you, too. Even though I don't spend a lot of time on social media, I can see the way our fanbase ships us. They're not blind to our chemistry and our budding romance. I sure as fuck don't want to put you through all that nastiness, either."

He sighs, and we stay quiet for a while longer. Until we go in because I can't feel my toes.

EIGHT
CREDENCE

We've got two more games before the short Christmas break, tomorrow and the day after. That means today is practice. I skate to the box and reach for a water bottle as I catch my breath. I can hear Coach yelling at Ryan to get his head out of his ass and pay attention to me and Ethan.

Ethan stops next to me, watching the scene with a pinched expression. "I hate that," he mutters.

I nod, sighing. "Yet, if we change up what we're doing, we get yelled at. I really hate getting yelled at."

He chuckles, knocking his shoulder into mine. I grin and hand him the water bottle. We wait a few more minutes until Coach is done reprimanding Ryan for the dozenth time in the last hour. Eventually, he skates toward us with a wary expression.

"Please tell me what play you're planning next," Ryan says tiredly.

Ethan and I exchange looks. "That's not how we play, man. You know that," Ethan says, clapping his shoulder. "We just respond to what the other team is doing."

"And magically communicate that," he says with an exasperated sigh. "Honestly, I fucking love that you can do that. But fuck, what am I supposed to do to get in sync with you guys when you don't actually *speak* to each other?"

I tap my stick against his and give him a sympathetic sigh as

Coach blows his whistle for us to return to the ice. "Just watch us," I say. "I know that's not exactly helpful, but... try to predict what we're doing. Alright?"

Ryan frowns as he follows us to the ice. We're in the middle of skirmishes, where our first line plays against our second line. This gives us all time to work together as a team and allows both of our goalies time on the ice. We trade in the remaining team players on occasion, too, but I know we spend so long on these skirmishes because the coaching team is trying to force our starting line to fully click together.

At this point, I don't think that's going to happen. He's been with the team all season now. Then again, maybe we just need that one moment for it all to fall into place. We get into position. I grin at Lucas Dueck across from me, our left wingman for the second line. He grins back.

It's during that friendly moment that the puck is dropped and Ethan steals it away, sending it toward me as he breaks away around Mattias Jönsson, our second line center. Ethan is always in my peripheral, even as most of my attention is on keeping the puck as I skirt around our second line defensemen, Astor Tyson and Lucien Medcalf.

"Come on, Meddy," their center calls in frustration as I shoot the puck between his legs. Honestly, it was a lucky move. I'm laughing as I send it back to Ethan, who just came around the back of the goal.

While I'm pretty much blocked, I know I could shove through to get to the puck, but since we're trying to get Ryan to gel with us, Ethan flings it his way.

It's just not Ryan's day, though. Where he predicts Ethan to go right, Ethan gives every indication that he's going left. The puck sails by Ryan and into the wall, where Astor recovers it and sends it sailing down the other end.

Thankfully, Phalyn Rioux, our goalie, is on point and stops the goal attempt made by Lucas, catching it in his oversized mitt.

Coach is yelling again but we don't stop the play as Phalyn drops the puck, making eye contact with Ethan, but sends it to me. Once again, I try to give Ryan the benefit of the doubt and send the puck to him right away.

Thankfully, he catches it and I release a breath as he brings it down to the other end. But I'm not sure what he's trying for as he flings the puck away and it sails straight into Astor's stick.

I groan as I adjust directions and follow, hunkering down and gaining speed. Coach is yelling again and I feel like Ryan is on thin ice. While Ethan and I continue trying to feed Ryan attempts to get into our plays, it's clear that it's just not going to happen.

There's a pause when I make a goal on our second goalie Asael, and Ethan crowds me, hugging me as if this is a game. We pause like that for a minute. While I'd like to say it's because we can hear Coach tearing Ryan apart for losing every chance we gave him, it's really because we seem to be stuck in each other's gaze.

I love his dark eyes. They're such a pretty brown. He's just pretty. I love everything about this man.

"Come over tonight," he says, voice breathless.

That can be explained away by the exertion we were just expelling on the ice, but I know he feels the same thing I do. I nod. "Yeah."

Ethan flashes me a smile when Coach blows the whistle and we push off each other, returning to our positions. I'm no longer facing Lucas since he's now replaced Ryan. Instead, our third line right wing Sacha Ivanov is across from me. I inwardly cringe and wonder how many more chances Ryan is going to have.

Honestly, it's not fair that he has all the pressure put on him. We should be trying to find a way that the three of us can work seamlessly together. That would be the right thing to do. But the coaching staff doesn't seem interested in that right now. Hell, they've never been interested in that.

As soon as it became apparent that Ethan and I clicked the way we did on the ice, it became about finding a third lineman that could match that. It's not fair. I feel like they're just setting the new guy up for failure every time.

But as much as hockey is a team sport, I know I'm replaceable. And I want to play. So I take my luck and run with it. Besides, this keeps me on the ice with Ethan. There's nearly no other place I'd rather be.

Practice continues and while we're not keeping score, the first line wins against the second but only by a single shot. I think that has more to do with Asael keeping a lockdown on his net more than anything else. Both of our goalies are fucking amazing. While technically, Phalyn is starting goalie, Coach Melvin switches them out sometimes just because.

Unless there's a reason we just don't know about. So many of our positions remain pretty fluid, with players coming and going. Not our goaltenders. I think Phalyn has a no trade contract because he's just that good.

We head into the locker room and strip down, but we aren't heading home yet. It's time for a couple hours of conditioning. Low impact since we just had two hours on the ice. I actually really enjoy cooling down in the gym as I sit on a bike and cycle for a bit.

When I get in there, Ryan is already on a bike, looking defeated. I'm not sure he wants me around right now. I'm not sure I'd want me around if I were him. But I head for the bike next to him and offer a smile. "Sorry, man. We tried."

"I know," he says, shaking his head. The resignation in his voice rings in my ears. "Honestly, I'm not sure why they're not looking to trade me yet. We're before the deadline for the season. Yet, not even my agent has heard anything."

"We'll figure it out, Ryan."

He gives me a sideways smile. "No, we won't. I have no idea what kind of god needs to be your third lineman, but it's not me. Or those who came before me. I overheard Coach saying he's thinking about bringing Lucas to starting line tomorrow."

"I sure as fuck hope not," Lucas says as he settles on the bike in front of us. "I don't want that kind of pressure."

Ethan walking in catches my attention and for a minute, I forget that I'm having a conversation as I watch him step into the room with Isak and Asael. Speaking of a god. I'm pretty sure I'm looking at one. Especially when his face splits into a smile. His eyes crinkle to almost closed as laugh lines frame his mouth and the corners of his eyes.

"Something has to change," Ryan says, and I blink, turning back to the guys with me. "It's gonna be me."

"Don't quote a boy band," Lucas says, snorting.

Ryan chuckles, shaking his head. "I don't know how to do what's expected of me. I can't just suddenly become a clone of Creed, which I think is what they want from me at this point. Two Creeds; one for each side of Ethan."

I smirk and bow my head as I pick up my water bottle and take a long drink.

"What do *you* want?" Lucas asks.

With a heavy sigh, Ryan shakes his head. "I'm at six years. I could just retire and be done with it. But I hate the idea of doing so and having such a shitty season personally. I'd at least like to score a handful of goals and at least as many assists in my last season. But fuck, it's definitely not going to happen here. This is my worst fucking season to date."

I glance at him and frown. Not that I keep track of many players' stats, but I hadn't realized that about him. It's not that I thought he was having a fantastic season or anything, but damn.

"I'm really sorry," I say.

He reaches over and claps my back. "Seriously, don't sweat it. I get it. And it's not like you or Wildman are selfish with the puck. You give me every opportunity. You give everyone equal opportunity while still managing to remain our fucking stars. At the risk of sounding sappy, you both are really great teammates."

"Thanks, but I think we have a great team all the way around. I know that this is the only pro team I've been on, but compared to high school and college, it's a world of difference between the guys I played with at both stages of my career and here."

"Ugh," Lucas groans. "You're not fucking wrong at all. High school was cutthroat. Those guys were a bunch of dicks."

"Not that I disagree that this team isn't great, but my high school team was fucking awesome. I still keep in touch with a lot of them. They're some of my best friends," Ryan says. "Shit, I sometimes wish I could go back to playing with them."

"I'm glad someone had a good high school experience on their hockey team," I said. "Although I think my problem was homophobia. It's rampant as a teenager."

"You make it sound like it disappears when you become an adult," Lucas says, glancing over his shoulder at me with a half-smile.

"Oh, no," I say, laughing. "Not at all. I think I'm just better equipped to deal with it now. College wasn't awful, but..." I shrug. "I guess I didn't fit in much with them. I was there for the position and played my ass off for the chance to be drafted. Though nothing was ever said to me or in my presence, I think there was probably homophobia surrounding me there, too. It became pretty clear early on that we weren't friends."

"That sucks," Ryan says, frowning.

"I'm used to it," I say, shrugging.

"You shouldn't have to be used to it, though," he says. "It's disgusting."

I shrug again. "Technology has made the world think that they have the right to broadcast their opinions and beliefs on everyone else. I've learned to ignore it."

We continue talking about my gay experiences with hockey for a while and a sense of comfort settles over me. I'm not an overly sentimental person but at this moment, I really love how my team rallies around me. Supporting me. Sympathizing with my situation. I've never had this from anyone outside of my parents growing up. It's almost surreal.

I love everything about it.

Ethan catches my eye from across the room as he heads for the door. I give him a few minutes before I excuse myself and follow. We're not alone in the shower and while the team has never shown us any hostility or bigotry concerning our sexuality, we've both been pretty careful not to be overt about it.

So we don't speak. We don't even shower near each other. That's just a recipe for a boner and I'm almost positive *that* would garner a reaction. Again, I wait a solid couple minutes after he leaves the shower before following with my towel as I hurriedly dry off and think of anything not sexy to keep my body in check until I at least have my pants on. I can hide a growing chubby in my pants. Not possible when I'm fucking naked.

Once dressed, I head for the exit and stop short when I nearly run into Ethan. He laughs as he catches me from stumbling. His smile makes my stomach flip as I flush. "Sorry."

He's still grinning as he brushes my wet hair from my eyes. "You're going to catch pneumonia if you don't at least dry your hair." He pulls my hood up. "Come on. Ride with me?"

I nod as I follow him to his car. Thankfully, it's already running, so a blast of warm air meets us when he opens his trunk, and we drop our bags in. I'm thankful that we have home games for the next two days before the short break; otherwise, whatever time we have together would be cut short while we pack and make sure we're prepared for our away games. That's not the case.

Then he opens my door for me, and I try to hide the way I love that as I climb in. He waits for me to settle before closing my door. Fuck, I can understand why girls like this. I feel... special.

Ethan climbs in next to me and flashes me a smile. "Hungry?"

Though I'd like to say no, my stomach clenches at the mention of food. With a slight grumble, I nod. "Yeah. Want to grab something on the way?"

He nods thoughtfully for a minute. "I think I already have something thawing in the fridge. That okay?" he asks, glancing at me again.

"Yep. Perfectly fine. As long as you're not going to poison me with undercooked meat."

Ethan laughs. "I'm a great cook."

"Right," I say, drawing out the word.

He shoves me playfully when we pull up to a stoplight, but then drops his hand and grasps mine. Everything in me flutters with nerves and excitement. I've been in his car with him too many times to count. I've been over at his house more times than I can even remember.

Fuck, I've spent the night so many times, I feel like I'm a teenager and having sleepovers.

But this feels distinctly different. I'm as eager for this change as I am slightly terrified of it. I've been wanting this man for so long, building up these moments in my head as a teenager fantasizing about his idol and crush... What if it doesn't measure up?

Worse yet, what if we get into it and he realizes I'm just not fucking good enough for him?

NINE
ETHAN

I DON'T HAVE ANY ACTUAL PLANS FOR TONIGHT. THE ONLY THING going through my mind when we were on the ice and I had him pressed against me was that there were far too many layers between us. The minutes we spent wrapped in each other's arms under the stars and wrapped in a blanket a couple nights ago have been replaying in my mind ever since.

It wasn't long enough. It wasn't enough. It's never enough. I need more.

The words came tumbling out before I could stop them. Not that I regret it. I'd likely have suggested he come over, anyway. But that hadn't exactly been the appropriate time to ask, right?

Who am I kidding? Any time to ask him over is appropriate!

He follows me inside and I drop my bag in the laundry room. We shuck off our winter gear before heading into the kitchen. Creed leans against the counter to watch me prepare dinner for us. There's chicken in the fridge which I'd cubed when I bought it and froze it in a marinade. When I unseal the bag, I'm met with a wonderful parmesan garlic aroma that has my stomach groaning with hunger.

"Chicken okay?" I ask.

"I'm not picky."

He's really not. I could probably put a whale liver in front of him and he'd eat it. Ew. That's enough to make my stomach turn sour. Back to the skinned chunks of chicken it is.

We talk about Ryan for a while and try to determine how we can change our play so that it remains effective, while also getting him on board. If we actually communicated in some way about any plan at all, it would be different. But we don't. I'm not sure that there's ever a plan. Honestly, I think we just react to each other and the situation.

While I'm aware of his every move, I don't think that has to do with hockey at all and everything to do with what's been sizzling between us since we met. I feel him in every atom of my body. I'm aware when he takes a breath, when he blinks, when his heart races.

There's a moment when I pause, wondering if we answer that chemistry in a physical way, if it'll break our game. Maybe it's the constant physical tension between us that keeps us as smooth and synced as we are.

With plates piled with vegetables, carbs, and protein, we head into the den to watch Sports Spot while we eat. It's just highlights of the games played today across all professional sports, which is fine. There are three live broadcasts on the right side of the screen showing the current Tennessee versus Jacksonville football game, Montreal versus Detroit hockey game, and Kansas City versus Los Angeles football game. I don't follow much football until this time of year, and I only watch now to see who makes it to the Super Bowl. It's out of curiosity more than interest usually.

When we're done eating and I've cleaned up the kitchen, loaded the dishwasher and made sure that all that I need to do tomorrow is reheat the leftovers, I turn and face Creed who is now standing in the door watching me with his deep blue eyes.

Everything inside me heats as I watch him. As soon as our gazes lock, there's an electric current that sizzles between us. I swallow around the lump in my throat and wonder if it's too soon. Have we talked enough about what we want? Have we talked at all? I'm so lightheaded with the way I ache for him, I can barely think of anything else other than he's here right now. In my apartment. And we're alone.

Creed takes a step towards me and that's it. I'm crossing the room and pull him against me, covering his mouth with my own. I groan into him, pressing our bodies flush. His hands, strong and sure, land on my hips and wrap around me. His fingers dig into my hips, my lower back, and then down to my ass.

He squeezes, forcing me harder against him until our growing hard-ons press together. My heels leave the floor with the way he pulls me tightly.

"Bedroom," I say against his lips.

We stumble our way through the apartment until we fall onto my bed. There's a moment of wrestling awkwardly with our clothing until we're naked. And then I'm hovering over him, looking down at his hard, sculpted body and the way his chest heaves.

"Fuck," I murmur, washing a hand down his smooth chest. "You have no idea how long I've wanted to touch you."

"Not as long as I have," he says, his hands moving along my sides, gliding his fingers up over my ribs. "Is it too soon to do this?"

"Oh, fuck yes. But I'm not sure I want to stop." Especially not when he rolls his hips and his dick rubs against mine, making my eyes roll.

"In everything we've talked about, sex has never been a topic," he says as he spreads his legs wider, letting my body settle between them. His fingers dance across my skin, leaving goosebumps in their wake, until they're digging into my ass cheeks again.

My breath catches, making me groan.

"I have one rule," I say, panting now. "I can't bottom with you. Is that okay?"

Creed grins. "Yep, though I never took you for a strict top."

I shake my head. "I'm not. It's just... that's mine and Jakub's one rule. Besides the complete honesty and constant communication thing, which I actually really love. Otherwise, he's the only one who gets to touch my ass."

"So I shouldn't touch your ass," he says, pulling his hands away.

I smile, leaning down to kiss him. While I mean for it to be quick, we get lost in dirty, wet, sloppy kisses for a while until we're both panting and aching for something more.

"No," I say, shaking my head to clear the fog. "You can touch, you know, here." I shift my weight and reach down to cup his ass cheek. "Just not here." I shift again so I can stroke between his crack and press my finger against his hole.

His breath catches and lips part. "Fuck me," he breathes, pressing his body down so his ass is firmly against my finger.

I'm sure there are so many reasons not to right now. But I can't find them. I don't remember them.

I scramble off him and fumble blindly in my nightstand for the lube and a condom. When I can't seem to grab just one, I take a handful and bring them to the bed. He laughs quietly before I cover his mouth with mine and make a mess with the lube as I soak my fingers and the bed as I can prep him.

Creed groans when I slide a finger inside him. Already his body rocks on it and I don't spend much time with a single finger before I'm pressing a second inside with the first. "Yes," he moans, his body continuously moving against mine. "Ethan, yes."

I'm so fucking dizzy right now and become even more disoriented when he pushes me off him but demands I keep fingering him. I do, adding a third finger unceremoniously and making him grunt. He moves with steady hands as he covers my leaking dick with a condom and then slathers lube on me before pulling me harshly to him.

I lose balance and crash into him, making us both 'oof' and then laugh. But he's already pulling my hand away and wrapping his legs around my waist, urging me to get to the good stuff.

Under different circumstances, I'd show him how good this part can be. But I think we're both far too needy for that right now. We've been toeing the line of more than friends for far too long. There's no time for the lead up during this moment. No time for anything but finally coming together.

He takes both my hands, lube and all, and links our fingers before drawing them above our heads. His heels dig into my ass cheeks as he urges me inside him.

I laugh in frustration. "This is easier if you let me—"

"I know," he says, locking our hands together tightly. Keeping me completely stretched out on top of him with no leverage for anything. Fuck, it feels so goddamn good that my hips are moving on their own. "You got this, Ethan. Put your dick inside me."

His words make me grunt and somehow, my cockhead catches on his hole, and I shimmy until I'm pressing inside him. His lips part as I breach his tight ring of muscles, his hands are tight in mine. It feels like he's taking away my volition. Like I'm at his command.

Have I ever told him how much I like that? That I crave the release of having someone else take the reins and commanding me to do what they want? Just like Jakub does. Only this time, there's something very different about it, because I'm not the one being fucked right now.

"Deeper," he hisses, and I realize I've frozen. "Ethan, I need to feel you."

His mouth covers mine as I moan and press inside him a little more with every rock of my hips. So good. So tight. Motherfuck, I've dreamed of being inside him for ages. A lifetime. He feels so good.

I move inside him slowly, taking my time to feel every single inch of him that I can reach. He doesn't ever give my arms any slack as he keeps me drawn out over him with his legs wrapped securely around me, guiding my thrusts with his body.

It's heady. It's so fucking good.

"Your dick is just… fuck, Ethan," he murmurs as I bury my face in his neck. He tastes like sweat and I find myself licking him. His moans are addictive. Intoxicating.

I move faster, burying myself over and over inside him as deep as I can get. I need to hear his moans and the way he chants my name. How his body opens for me and how he keeps me exactly where he wants me. How he wants me.

"Keep doing that," he says. "Keep sucking me."

It's only then I realize that I'm no longer licking him, but I've latched onto his neck like I'm sucking a dick. His body shakes beneath me, and I can tell he's close. There's desperation in his voice. In each syllable of my name.

I come hard, needy whiny sounds leaving my mouth as I practically bite his neck as if I'm a fucking vampire. A hint of blood even meets my tongue.

"Keep fucking me," Creed says. "Almost there. Don't stop, Ethan. I want to come on your dick."

If I'd known he had such a dirty mouth, I don't think I'd have had the willpower to stay away for as long as I did.

"Just like that. Yes. Don't stop fucking me. Suck my neck. God, Ethan. You're better than I've ever dreamed."

I shiver in appreciation as I continue to shove my cock inside him.

His heels slide down and lock around my thighs. He shifts my hands, somehow managing to secure them both and then reaches between us to jerk his dick.

I get lost in the words falling from his mouth as he demands that I keep fucking him. Faster. Faster. Hell, I'm going to come again if he keeps saying these things to me.

Then his hot seed sprays between us and he lets out a deep, throaty sound that settles in my balls. I may come again. My body tingles in the most delicious way as pleasure just travels through me in a continuous circuit.

We still for a heartbeat before we simultaneously go limp.

The only sound in the room is our heavy breathing. And maybe my heartbeat since it seems to be hammering in my ears. So loudly. It's all I hear.

Creed releases my hands, but I don't move until he brings his hand from between us and wiggles until he can get his messy fingers to my lips. I open without further prompting and suck him clean.

"I never thought you could be more perfect," he whispers.

I hum as I move down our bodies, seeking more of his cooling seed and licking it off his smooth skin. The moments that follow are filled with slimy filth as he runs his hands over my sweaty body, still covered in his release. It's like he's rubbing it in, and I can't stop myself from wanting to wear him like another skin.

When we finally catch our breath and realize how disgusting we are, we laugh quietly before struggling out of bed and to my bathroom while trying not to leave a disgusting trail behind us. I turn on the shower after I drop the condom into the trash, and we step under the stream of water and wash each other.

We're still damp when we return to my bed, and curl up under my blankets wrapped around each other.

"Is this okay?" he asks quietly.

"I want this," I say. "So fucking bad. I can't pretend not to anymore, Creed."

"Mmm," he says, but I can feel the hesitation in that sound. "What about Jakub?"

"I wouldn't be in bed with you if he didn't support this, you know. He's good. He's happy. We're good."

Creed sighs, his arms flexing tighter for a minute. "For the record, I'm fine not topping. Though I'm a switch, I tend to lean towards bottoming, anyway. That's never been a concern for me."

"What concerns you?"

"I've never been involved with a married man," he says, amused.

I laugh and cuddle into him a little more, pressing a soft kiss to his collarbone. "If it helps, this married man has the full support of his husband. Jakub is always aware of what goes on between us. I know that might feel a little... invasive and like we don't have privacy, but it's not like that. My marriage is always going to be a priority, so keeping it strong and healthy is important." I shift so I can look at him. "You're just as important, though. He knows that. I'm not trying to just fuck, Creed. Sex is easy to come by. I need something deeper from you if you can accept this untraditional relationship."

He bites his lip, and I hold my breath waiting for him to respond. I'm pretty sure it's going to break me if he tells me he can't. I've never hidden my marriage from him. It's like I knew as soon as I met him that I was going to fall in love with this man. That's why I made him aware of my situation and gave him almost three years to get used to it.

Now, here we are.

"Ethan, I—" He pauses and then sighs, closing his eyes. I brush a kiss to his jaw. The words that come out of his mouth aren't what I'm expecting. "I've loved you since I was sixteen," he whispers. "I don't think you having five husbands could convince me that I don't want to do this."

My heart is beating so rapidly that I can't take another breath as I stare at him. Did he just say...?

"I love you, too," I whisper, almost inaudibly.

His mouth seals over mine in a long, sweet kiss filled with everything we've been longing to say to each other, but never had the fucking balls to do so.

"Does he know?" he asks after a minute. "That you love me?"

I laugh as I rub my face against his like I'm a cat. "Yeah, he knows. I've refused to call this more than a crush for the entire time I've known you. Fucking husband called me out just the other day, telling me he's loved watching me fall in love with you."

Creed looks at me incredulously. "I always suspected he's a really great guy, but fuck's sake. He might be a saint."

I grin. "He's perfect, Creed. I can't wait until you can spend some time with him this summer. He's the sweetest fucking man. He's the only other person I've ever fallen for as soon as I met him."

He smiles. "I'm going to brush past that because it's too sweet and I think I'm going to cry if I concentrate on it, but are you trying to push us together? You want a threesome, don't you?"

Laughing, I kiss him over and over. "Nah. I mean, I'm certainly not opposed; but whether you two get involved or not, I don't care. I think it would be great, but again, whatever happens between you two does. There's zero pressure or expectations from me. All I want is for you two to get along and become friends. And I think that's going to happen easily."

Creed sighs, relaxing in my arms completely. Although, I think I might be in his arms. "Me, too," he whispers.

TEN
ETHAN

It's nearing two in the morning when the driver pulls up outside Jakub's building. He inches beside the curb as he leans forward, looking out the window.

"I hear there's a hockey player that lives in this building," he says before sitting back. Glancing at me in the rearview, he adds, "Maybe if you're lucky, you'll get to meet him."

I grin and nod. "Yeah. Maybe."

I'm not sure he's an actual hockey fan. Granted, I've let my facial hair grow out over the last couple days when I tend to remain clean shaven, which I usually do when I travel. It can make a world of difference as to whether I'm recognized or not. Especially by someone who is only marginally familiar with the sport. With my beanie low on my head and the lower part of my face tucked behind a scarf, it'd be hard to name me.

"Thanks," I tell him, grabbing my bag and slipping out of the car. He waves as I move toward the entrance to the tall building.

The driver is kind enough to wait until I get to the door and let myself in before he drives off. For that, he deserves a big tip. As I wait for the elevator, I open the app and modify the tip to $50. It's more than the rideshare cost, but it's an ungodly hour of the morning two days before Christmas. He's earned it.

The elevator pings and I step inside, staring at my slightly distorted reflection in the stainless-steel doors as I make my way to the eleventh floor. We both rent our apartments, mostly fully furnished, since our lives can be impermanent depending on whether the teams want to keep or trade us. Neither of us has a no-trade clause and I'm not even sad about it. I love Buffalo, but I wouldn't mind warmer weather or being traded closer to my husband.

I let myself in and lock up behind me as I drop my bag and kick off my shoes. Peeking into the apartment, I notice a flickering light and pause to watch it. A fire? It takes me a minute to remember if he has a fireplace or not. Probably. It gets stupidly cold in Vancouver. When was the last time I was at his apartment?

Sighing at how sad it makes me that I can't remember, I hang up my outside clothing and step around the corner where I freeze and stare. It's definitely fire that I saw flickering, but it's not from the fireplace. It's from dozens of candles covering every surface. All lit. There's a soft, romantic glow to it and for a while, I just stare.

How tired am I?

Moving slowly through the space, I find a trail of them through the apartment leading to the stairs. Their flames flicker in reflection off the tile floors and the glass banister as I make my way up, careful not to touch any of the candles. I'm too tired to put myself out if my pants caught fire.

Jakub may live in an apartment, but these are high end condos, basically. He's got three floors all to himself. His bedroom is the only room on the third floor of his space. Since the second floor is dark with no candles lining the hall, I follow their trail to the third.

The space opens into a beautiful room with a solid glass wall that overlooks the city and the Strait of Georgia. I pause for just a second as the backdrop of the city lights against the dark night sky grabs my attention.

That's only until I look around at the dozens more candles covering the surfaces here, too. And there are red rose petals scattered all over the large bed, standing out starkly on the white comforter, and a single red rose lays in the middle.

Everything in me feels warm and sappy as I take it in. Jakub has always been a very sweet and thoughtful man. His gestures of love and affection know no bounds. But this?! I've never seen anything like it.

I turn and find him standing in the doorway, probably having followed me up. Words are on the tip of my tongue, but I can't do anything but just stare at him for a minute. He's taller than me, which has always been something I fucking love about him. There's something that makes me feel delicate about having to look up into my husband's face.

His lips are pulled into a soft smile. The fire dancing across his features makes the light dusting of hair on his jaw look longer in the shadows. His light eyes almost glow in the dim room, bathed in candlelight.

I'm glad I didn't bring my bag upstairs with me. I probably would have dropped it into the candles as I moved toward him and wrapped my arms around him. He picks me up and my legs lock around his waist as our mouths come together.

In reality, I know it hasn't been all that long since we were together. A month and a half. We've gone and will go much longer. But it feels like it's been a year. Two years. Feeling his hands under my thighs, holding me to him, there's a moment where I think I have to memorize this moment because our time together is so limited and there's a chance I'll forget what his hands feel like on me.

"You didn't have to do this," I whisper.

Jakub smiles. "No. But I wanted to. The look in your eyes when you saw it was worth it."

"I love you," I say.

He brushes his nose against mine. "Love you. Let's go take a bath and wash the travel off you."

I nod and he carries me into the bathroom. There's more than travel on me. We played Anaheim less than twelve hours ago. I barely ran through the shower before Creed drove me to the airport. There's no doubt in my mind that I need a thorough washing.

The bathroom looks like the rest of the apartment I'd made my way through. Tile floors and surfaces covered in dancing shadows caused by the plethora of candles. There's a large soaking tub that's lightly bubbling, and has a scattering of rose petals too.

Jakub sets me on my feet and undresses me. He's slow as he removes each article of clothing, running his fingers over my skin as if he's reminding himself what I feel like. Maybe he is. I plan to do the same later. His lips brush over me and I bury my fingers into his short hair. It's not even long enough to grab a fistful of but I love the feeling of it over my palms and between my fingers.

When I'm fully bare before him, he wastes no time stripping off his shorts and shirt before picking me back up. I grin because he makes me feel like I weigh a hundred pounds less than I do. Like I'm so dainty he can move me around with little to no effort at all.

We sink into the hot water just as we are; with me wrapped around him. For a long time, that's how we remain. No talking. Hands still. Just breathing each other in. Enjoying the feeling of our bodies pressed together. Our heartbeats thumping against each other.

"Is it just me, or do the times apart feel harder now?" I ask.

He huffs quietly. "Definitely not you, kocourek. I was just thinking that maybe it's time I retire."

I sit up and frown as I look at him. "No. We agreed that we would retire when we're ready. Not for each other. We don't want any resentment to build."

Jakub takes my chin between his fingers and brings my lips to his. The kiss is soft; just a press of our lips together to keep the connection. "I'm growing to resent much about hockey because being away from you is just... awful."

His words make my heart patter unevenly.

"I haven't made a decision. We will talk about it this summer, but I'm seriously considering it, Ethan. The idea of three more months has never felt so long before. This year I've dreaded the time we spent apart."

I kiss him again and nod because I know what he means. But unlike Jakub, I have Creed to keep me company. I have my team. Jakub doesn't make friends often. Not because he's an unapproachable man. He's not. And he's kind. But he's not very social.

"This summer, the three of us will spend time together and talk about a future," he says and everything inside me leaps. That he's already including Creed into our lives nearly brings tears to my eyes.

Jakub pulls me against him again and, for a while longer, we remain quiet. The only sounds are the gentle bubbles around us and the quiet whir of the motor that creates them.

"You won your game last night," he says.

I chuckle. "I'm not going to discount the hard work our offense played, but man, our defense was on fire. That's Phalyn's second shutout of the season."

"I'm sorry you didn't have time to celebrate with them."

"Nah. At least half the team was leaving right away or very early in the morning for the holiday, so we'll just celebrate when we get back."

"You didn't bring Credence," he says.

I grin. "I'm glad you noticed." He pinches my ass, and I laugh. "He had plans with his parents, as I thought he did. No big deal."

Jakub nods. His hands move over my wet skin. All the pleasant, peaceful sounds have me nearly lulled into sleep before I blink several times to wake myself up. I'm exhausted, yes. But I only have a few days with my husband.

"What are our plans?" I ask.

He hums quietly, his fingers slowly tracing the ridges of my spine down to the apex of my ass crack. He doesn't go any lower, though. His fingers move back up my back.

"Today, we're going to sleep and just enjoy each other. We'll order delivery for whatever meal we want. Tomorrow, I have that event for a few hours. Unfortunately, I anticipate being gone for longer than Coach suggested, but it's early in the morning, so I shouldn't be gone much past midafternoon. I'm not above walking out if it carries on much longer than that. I figured we'd go all out when I get home and cook until I have no food left to cook. We'll eat and save the leftovers for Christmas day. We'll spend the day together and the next until you have to get back to the airport."

"Sounds perfect," I say. "I'm a little bummed you have that thing, though."

"I know. I'd drag you with me but there'd be questions about why you're here when your team is on the East Coast, as is your family."

I shrug. "It's alright. We go months without being together. I can probably survive a few hours."

He hums again. "Sit up, miláček. Let me wash you. Then we can get into bed."

Jakub's already maneuvered me how he wants me before the words have finished coming out of his mouth. Our hips are pressed tightly together as he has me leaning backwards, his hand under my neck and head to support me as I lean back in the water.

"Relax, lásko. Let me take care of you."

I close my eyes and let my muscles do just that—relax. It's almost like I'm floating as he moves his fingers softly through my hair. I'm reminded of how someone might hold a baby over the tub to wash their hair. His fingers are soft as he touches me.

"You are the best thing that's ever happened to me," he murmurs, making my heart flutter. I open my eyes slightly to look at his gorgeous face. His gaze is focused on how he's taking care of me, not me watching him. "I was in love with you the moment our eyes locked and you smiled at me. I used to think that there was nothing better in life than being on the ice. Scoring. Living the life of a professional athlete. But none of that holds a candle to you, Ethan Wilder. I cannot tell you how much I'm looking forward to the next chapter of our lives together."

I try not to get emotional, but there's no mistaking the sting of tears in the corners of my eyes. My lips part to respond, but his finger is suddenly there, preventing me. His blue eyes meet mine and he shakes his head with a gentle smile. "Just listen, zlato. Okay?"

Nodding, I kiss the pad of his fingers and close my mouth.

"I love that you trust me so completely," he murmurs. "With every piece of you. Your secrets, your body, your heart. I love your smile, how it creates laugh lines all over your face because every bit of you smiles when your lips do. I love your eyes, how deep brown they are. So pretty and shining with mirth and joy. The pretty color of your skin, like creamy coffee."

His finger traces down my neck, making my skin prickle with awareness.

"I love how soft your hair is. How perfectly dark it is. I love to see you on the ice, moving with such fluid moves and speed that you appear to be a part of it. I love to witness your greatness, your kindness, your talent, your loyalty. And I love to have watched you fall in love with your best friend."

My heart races for a minute as his eyes flicker down to mine. His smile widens. Then his fingers are moving against my scalp and my eyes flutter as I groan. He's quiet as he massages me, only speaking again when he begins rinsing my hair.

"I love how much you love me," he murmurs. "How your face lights up every time I video call you. I love how happy you are to be with me. To be against me. I love how you let me take care of you completely. How you just let me smother you in my affection and care. You don't even look put out by it."

"I'm not," I say. "I love receiving it as much as you love giving it."

"Mmm," he answers. He's got my head cradled in a single hand again while his other moves to my chest, rubbing the soapy suds over my skin. Then his hand dips beneath the water and feathers against my hard cock. I'd barely noticed I was turned on, but now that he's touching me, there's no way to *not* know.

His hand moves around my cock, circling it with a strong grip, as he slowly, almost reverently, strokes me.

"I love how completely obedient you are when I want you to be. How still and pliant you remain, no matter what I do to you." His hand drops to cup my balls, rubbing them until I let out a harsh breath. Then he's back to stroking me. "I love how well you listen. How you keep your ass for me alone. I love that I'm the only one who gets to see you that way. Who gets to be inside your body."

I shiver. My hands clench. Jakub smiles a little more.

"I love how you tremble when you're so turned on that you can't stand it, and are struggling to do as I say. I love how your entire body tenses with the need to come, but you won't until I'm ready for you to. Oh, how I love your cock; so perfect and hard for me. Dripping. I love your tight ass; how it squeezes my dick so hard that I swear that hold is around my neck, and I can't breathe."

"Jakub," I whisper.

"You want to come for me?"

I nod. "Please."

He leans forward, pressing his mouth to mine. Our tongues meet in a licking, wet, deep kiss. He doesn't stop jerking me. "I love how your dick twitches," he murmurs into my mouth, making me whine. "Come for me, zlato."

A shudder wracks my body as my orgasm crashes through me. My body jerks, making the water slosh at the sides and the candles on the edge hiss. Most of that barely registers as little rivulets of pleasure shoot through my cock while I shoot my seed into the water.

When I finally blink back into focus, my body feels limp. His finger traces up the underside of my dick, concentrating at the base of my cock for a minute as he rubs little circles. I whine slightly, shivering at the feeling on my oversensitive dick. Then his hand moves up to wipe over my slit.

"I love how your cock throbs when you come," he says, grinning.

I laugh breathlessly.

"Ready for bed?"

"Yes. However, I'm concerned about the candles. I don't want to die in a house fire."

Jakub chuckles as he pulls us to our feet. I'm out of the tub and standing on the mat as he wraps a large, warm towel over me before flicking the plug on the tub and turning off the bubbles. "Dry off, lásko. Then get in bed. I'll take care of the candles and meet you there."

He kisses my forehead as he wraps a towel around his waist and leaves the bathroom. I dry off and carefully set my towel down as far from the flames as I can. Taking a few minutes, I blow some of the candles out. Just to be safe.

I don't move the flower petals but slide in under the covers to wait for Jakub. A yawn overtakes me and my eyes close. I had every intent of waiting for him. Of being with him tonight. But the long day and all the travel catches up and I'm asleep within minutes.

ELEVEN
CREDENCE

I LOVE HOW HE FITS PERFECTLY IN MY ARMS. WE'RE LAYING ON the couch, his bare back to my chest. His hip is digging into my thigh where he's laying between my legs, but I don't fucking care. With one of his hands on mine where they cross over his chest and the other on my thigh, I could stay like this for years. I might lose a leg due to lack of circulation, but I have no fucks to give.

If I could go back and tell sixteen-year-old me that all the hell he's going through in high school and with his family abandoning him is going to end up with my teenage celebrity crush falling in love with me, I'd do it. I'd give myself that bit of sunshine to look forward to. There were a lot of really dark moments in those years. Sometimes, I'm still not sure what got me through them.

I press my lips to the back of his shoulder, just because I can. It's still surreal to me. It's been less than two weeks, but everything about this has felt easy and natural. Like we were always supposed to make it to this point.

After having a crush on him since I was sixteen to pining for him when I was drafted to the same team, I was beginning to think that we were just destined to keep missing each other. There was a roadblock there that I didn't understand and didn't know how to get around.

I kiss the back of his neck and take a deep breath, breathing in his shampoo. His natural scent coming off his skin. His fingers flex on my thigh.

It's been fuckin bliss since coming back from Christmas. We spend so much time together, both at my place and his. I don't think we've driven separate cars once since I picked him up from the airport.

I love everything about it.

Which means something is surely going to fuck it all up. That's what happens, right? When something's too good to be true, it's not going to last.

When I kiss his shoulder again, Ethan turns his head to look at me. He's smiling. I fucking love his smile. He twists a little so our lips can meet.

Just when our kiss is starting to get heavy, his phone rings. It's not a typical ring, though. It's that very distinct sound that indicates a video call.

I expect him to get up and take it to the other room. But he doesn't. Ethan reaches for his phone and answers it, propping the phone against a couple full bottles of water and grinning broadly into the screen where his husband smiles out.

"Hey, love," Ethan answers, making my stomach do all sorts of acrobatics.

"Miláček," Jakub answers. I swear his voice is a purr. "I love your smile."

Ethan laughs. "How was the game?"

Jakub rolls his eyes. "Would have been better if Luca hadn't had to sit out because of an injury he tried to hide. Such a dick."

"Does that mean you lost?" Ethan teases.

Jakub smirks. "No. It means we would have won by a bigger margin if the fucker took care of himself better." His eyes flicker to me. "Hello, Credence."

I shift slightly so I can look over Ethan's shoulder better. Offering him a smile, I pretend this isn't awkward at all. "Hi." Nope; my boyfriend isn't married and his husband is not currently looking at us half naked wrapped around each other on the couch.

Not awkward at all.

"You didn't have a game today," Jakub says.

"No, but we lost against fucking Boston again yesterday. Fuckers," Ethan says with a scowl.

"The score was only 2-1," I say. "It's not like they creamed us."

Ethan grunts in acknowledgment but doesn't retract his comment. I hide my smile behind his shoulder, pressing my lips to his skin again as I watch Jakub on the screen. His indulgent smile for Ethan has me smiling.

I've seen them together less than a handful of times. Only twice, I think. Once, during my first season, Ethan brought me to dinner with them after the game we played against Jakub's team. The first thing I remember thinking was how incredibly obvious it is that they're so in love. There's honestly no mistaking it. Even when they're sitting across the table from each other.

It became clear then why they don't go out in public during the offseason. There's no way that would be missed.

I also remember how heartbroken I felt because, while Ethan had shared that he was married, he also emphasized that they had an open relationship. To me, that meant that their love couldn't be that strong, right? How can you love someone and still be with someone else? It just felt wrong to me. It gave me hope that maybe there was room for me in Ethan's life.

Seeing them together changed my opinion. Joining them for dinner also leveled up the trust between Ethan and I and he began sharing more about his marriage and Jakub and why they live the way they do.

It was probably when I began seeing the truth about them that I actually began to fall for Ethan. Seems kind of counterintuitive—witnessing the man you've been pining over for years express how much he loves another man. But instead, I longed to be a part of it. To have just a fraction of the love he's capable of.

And thus... My life is surreal right now.

I listen to them talk about nothing as I muse over how strange this feels. But it's not strange in that I'm uncomfortable. It's because this situation is new and not something I ever imagined for myself.

When you grow up, the concept of family is a man and a woman. The image and expectation is forced down your throat until you're convinced that absolutely anything outside of that is wrong, unhealthy, disgusting, and unnatural.

But I don't hate this at all. Considering I'm pretty sure it was Ethan's love for his husband that truly pushed my childhood crush into legit, full-blown adult feelings, I'd say I'm very okay with this unusual relationship.

That doesn't mean it's not slightly awkward at times because all the outside pressures and expectations say that this is wrong. So I *feel* like maybe I'm doing something wrong. Even though I'm not.

I know it's these exact reasons that keep Ethan and Jakub from going public with their marriage. They're going against the grain. They're doing what's right and works for them. Their marriage and lifestyle make them happy. Loving more than one person isn't only accepted but supported.

"You have an off week right after our next game, yeah?" Jakub asks and I tune back into the conversation.

"Yep. Would be better if that was your complete off week too," Ethan says.

"I know. But I think we can use that to our advantage. Do you have home or away games from January 24 through February 1?"

I pull out my phone since we're using Ethan's for the video call. It doesn't take me long to pull up my calendar and flip to next month. "Toronto on the 25th and Philly on the 26th. Both away. Otherwise, we have one home game."

"And I have two home games on your off week. So, how about you both stay out here for the first part of your week off, we can choose something to do together for the five days we share off, and I'll come out there for the rest of mine when your season continues," Jakub suggests. My breath catches at the idea as my mind races.

Ethan grins and twists in my arms to look at me. His smile is breathtaking, and I forget to breathe for a single beat. "What do you think?"

Honestly, I'm not sure that Ethan could ask me for something I'd say no to.

"It's okay if you're uncomfortable with the idea," Jakub says.

"No," I say quickly, hugging Ethan tightly, though I try not to make it obvious. It's not really a possessive hold. I just don't want to lose any more time with him. Those few days at Christmas when we were still so new last week were hard. Though I know the worry was unwarranted, the unbidden idea that he was going to spend the holiday with his husband and come back to tell me that he changed his mind. "It's a good idea," I say and give them both a smile.

"It's really okay if you don't want to," Ethan says. He touches my face and his soft smile just fucking melts me. "I'm selfish, and I want to be with both of you together. But it's completely fine if you need to take that a little slower. I know this is new for you."

"It's new for all of us," Jakub says.

"I'm talking about the poly thing," Ethan says, "but yeah, it is. And I'm not going to be upset if you'd rather take our time together before this summer, when the three of us get together."

Honestly, I'm a little conflicted because I still feel so conditioned to the concept of love triangles and that the fulcrum has to choose someone. There isn't a happy ending for all three people. Someone loses.

I don't want to be that someone, but if it came down to me or his husband, Ethan will choose his husband. Right?

"I want to be with both of you together."

It's like my mind reminding me that the world isn't black and white like that. Not everything is a choice. Sometimes you can keep both options.

"Yes. Let's do it," I say.

Ethan smiles, pulling my face down to his and our lips meet. I'm never unaware that Jakub is there. Watching. My face heats knowing that.

He pulls away and turns back to the screen of his phone. The smile doesn't leave Ethan's face for the rest of the call. Neither does mine, because seeing him so happy just fills me with warmth. I am the cause for some of that happiness.

I recognize the smile on Jakub's face is partially there for the same reason. Our gazes meet for a minute, and I know we share a smile because we have this same understanding about each other. It's reassuring.

When the call ends, I hug him a little tighter, dropping my top arm to circle his stomach. He sighs in contentment.

"You're really okay with that?" he asks.

I nod. "Yes. I might be a little awkward at first, though. Fair warning."

Ethan laughs. "Creed, I'm not trying to rush this," he says, his body wiggling as if he can possibly cuddle back any closer. "I just don't want to lose a minute with either of you. I know that could make for some uncomfortable situations in the beginning, but... I'm selfish."

"That's not selfish. I had the same thought. I don't want to be without you, either. So we'll just have to work through the awkward moments."

He hums in contentment. Again, we lay quietly for a while, my fingers moving absently over his stomach. There's a hint of hair there, as there is all over his torso. Whether he shaves or waxes or whatever, he's between sessions and I kind of love it.

"Jakub's thinking about retiring," he says quietly.

"Really? But his game is great," I say.

Ethan nods. "This last year, maybe more, being so far away has really sucked for both of us. I think it's worse for Jakub because he doesn't get along with his team like I do ours. I think we're just growing up and ready to be a real family, you know?"

"You don't sound happy about something in that," I note.

He laughs quietly. "Believe me. I'd love nothing more than to come home to that man every single day for the rest of my life. I'm looking forward to it, Creed. Long distance is hard, but seven years?" He shakes his head. "I just worry that he's going to become resentful that he gave up his career for me. He says he won't but..."

Many marriages end because one party sacrifices for their relationship and later becomes resentful of the fact. I can understand why he feels that way.

"You're going to talk about it before he makes that decision, right?" I ask.

"Yeah. We'll talk this summer. I'm conflicted about it because I'm growing to hate being away from him for so long, but I don't want him to give up hockey for me. You know?"

I nod. "I get it."

Ethan shifts so he's laying on his back and looking up at me. He's so beautiful. I just want to crawl into his chest and live there forever.

"I know it's really soon to truly have this conversation, but I don't want you to think that when I talk about my future with Jakub, that I'm not including you in that. Even if I don't say so."

There really aren't words to describe what that does to me. The way I catch my breath and tears sting my eyes. How my chest gets tight and my stomach flutters almost violently.

Because he wants me.

I can't find my tongue right now, so I just nod again.

His fingers touch my jaw, and he smiles. "I know that, officially, we've been doing this for what, a week?"

I laugh and nod. "Yeah."

"But in reality, this has been coming for years. I know it's my fault that it took us so long to get together because I *knew* you weren't a fly-by-night hookup. Just as I knew when I met Jakub, he was my endgame. I knew it about you, too. But those aren't waters I'd navigated before since I'm married and we've only ever done casual outside of each other. Talk about unlocking a whole new set of anxieties."

Leaning down, I press my lips to the corner of his. "I don't ever want to be a cause for anxiety, Ethan."

He grins, tangling his fingers in my hair and pulling my mouth to his. "Not what I meant," he says against my lips. "You're not. You're always my Stanley Cup."

I grin as he kisses me and, for a minute, we do nothing but kiss. It's sweet and drawn out. The kind of kiss that you can feel in your soul. In your bones. In every ethereal part of you, and you *just know* that this person will forever change your life.

Ethan shifts slightly and groans. That one sound, quiet as it was, sends a jolt of heat through me, making me shake as if I were suddenly plunged into a vat of Arctic ice water. My hand slides down his stomach and slips beneath the waistband of his pants.

Unsurprisingly, I find him hard and weeping for me. Grinning into our kiss, I grip his cock tightly and stroke my hand down his length. He gasps into my mouth and I take full advantage to plunder his as I bring my tight grip up his shaft.

His hips follow me off the couch and I chuckle. "How many times can you come in one night?" I ask.

A shudder races through his body, his moan indecent. "I don't know."

"I think we're going to find out, Wildman."

"Fuck," he whines, shoving his hips up again, pushing his dick further into my grip.

TWELVE
CREDENCE

"My house, yeah?" Mattias Jönsson says as we part ways at the elevator. We stop in the parking lot outside the players' entrance.

We just won by a fucking landslide. 5-1 against the New Jersey Captains. Two of those goals were by Mattias. His Swedish ass was on fire tonight. However, we weren't in the mood to go out to celebrate. Ethan and I were going to head back to his apartment when Caulder caught me and asked if we'd hang out for a while.

I might have made an excuse not to, but Ethan grinned and said we would. Mattias overheard and decided that the three of us were coming over to his house and we were going to play video games to celebrate our win.

"Since I scored two, I choose," he declared.

We clearly couldn't argue with that logic and thus, we nod and tell him we'll follow behind. Ethan opens my door for me as he usually does and there's no way I can keep the grin from my face. He leans forward when I'm inside and kisses me.

If it wasn't so fucking cold, I'd have held him there for a longer kiss. It's in the forties, but it's rainy. Not a comfortable way to be.

Mattias lives close in a small townhouse. Seriously, I think we're in the low-rent district. There's nothing wrong with that, except that I'm at least marginally aware of what he makes. Though the inside is modern and filled with all sorts of technology, it's... tiny.

"Do the Swedes live in shoeboxes?" Ethan asks as he lets us in.

Mattias looks around before facing us. He blinks a few times before shrugging. "I don't need space. Just me here."

"I guess it's an American thing to flaunt your salary with the biggest place you can afford," Caulder says as we four big guys squeeze into the tiny entry.

"Yes. Guess so," Mattias says as he turns away. "This way. Want beer?"

"I'm good," Ethan says as he follows. "But I'd definitely like some water. I'm still dehydrated."

"Same," Caulder says.

"Water is fine," Mattias says. "TV that way." He points down the hall and we obediently go where we're told to.

The space is decent sized. Two entire walls are taken up by a large sectional. A third wall has a television that practically covers the entirety of it.

"I think he's compensating for something," Ethan mutters with a smirk.

"Yes," Mattias says as Ethan pushes me toward the corner of the couch. "I search specifically for a room like this. All comfort. Make up for small interior."

Ethan smirks at him as he climbs into my lap and settles. So I don't look like a fool and smile ridiculously, I turn my face into his hair. His hands fall to my legs and he shimmies until he's slouched just enough to be comfortable.

Caulder shakes his head as he passes us drinks. "It's sickeningly sweet watching you two," he says.

"Yes. Sometimes I want to vomit," Mattias says matter-of-factly as he starts turning on the electronics. "Sweet love is nauseating."

"What you're really saying is you're lonely, tired of your hand, and jealous," Ethan says. "I hear ya."

Mattias snorts.

"I kind of want to watch the highlights of the game," Caulder says. "We spanked them good."

"We just played," Mattias says. "Fresh in mind."

I chuckle. Listening to Mattias talk has always been one of my favorite pastimes since he's been on the team. He's only been in the US for two years. We're his first and only team. While he speaks

English clearly enough and is decently fluent, the arrangement of sentences needs some work. Combined with his thick Swedish accent, I could listen to him for hours.

I'm handed a controller as the game starts up.

"How did your photo shoot go?" I ask Caulder.

This, of course, turns Ethan and Mattias' attention to him with interest. Caulder glares at me, but I'm seriously curious.

"It was fine," he says.

"Just fine?" Ethan asks. "What were you modeling?"

Sighing, Caulder says, "Underwear."

"Ooh," Mattias says. "I want to model underwear. The only acceptable way to have public pictures of me in skivvies."

We laugh, but Ethan knocks Caulder. "Seriously. Spill."

After giving me another glare, Caulder says, "There's not much to tell. It was me and six other guys from other professional sports. We had a dozen different styles and colors each. And we posed in various settings and shit."

"Will we see you on billboards?" I ask.

He groans. "I really hope not."

"Oh, yes. Dick size of my whole body." Mattias nods in appreciation. "Where we find these images?"

"I'm going to regret offering this information, but I was sent a few proofs for my professional portfolio." He pulls out his phone and clicks a few times until he hands the phone to Mattias.

Mattias whistles. "That is hot. I like girls, but I can see it's hot."

Caulder rolls his eyes, though I don't miss his cheeks flushing. When Mattias hands his phone back, Caulder tries to put it away.

"Oh, no," Ethan says, plucking it from his hand. "Share it with the gay boys."

"Fuck's sake," Caulder says and turns away. "Just scroll right."

The first one is of him standing against a solid gray background. His weight is leaning toward one side and his face is turned that way too. His hands are in front of him, one looks like he's massaging the wrist of his opposite. He's wearing boxer briefs but they're long.

The second has him looking in the same direction as the last, though he's leaning on the opposite leg. His lips slightly parted and eyes dark. His solid color and shorter boxer briefs are somehow more form fitting and hinting at what's beneath. He's wearing a tank, one hand holding the side of it up and showing off a hint of his stomach.

"This one is hot," Ethan says. "I'm sure you're giving some girl fuck me eyes."

Caulder sighs in exasperation.

The third is of him in a bright orange jock. He's turned slightly to the side so we get a full on view of his package and his ass cheeks. His upper body is turned so that we also see his ripped torso.

"Well, fuck, Caulder. Is that what you're hiding under there?" Ethan asks, whistling under his breath.

"Give me my phone," Caulder says, his face bright red.

Ethan moves it out of reach as he flips to the next shot.

Ultrathin underwear pants in a baby blue with a matching shirt. And they show his junk almost better than the jock. The color offsets his eyes and you can see them stand out.

"Fuck," Ethan says and scrolls to the next.

This one is a group shot and they're all in different versions and styles of bikinis. Some with ties. One is unmistakably a thong. I'm pretty sure that one guy's balls are hanging out.

"When you retire from hockey, this is what you need to be doing with your life," Ethan says, handing back his phone when he can't scroll any longer.

"You are good for ego," Mattias says. "I will model my underwear before you leave, and I want your compliments."

"I don't give them out for free," Ethan says. "You best have something impressive to show."

"I think they should put the jock one on a billboard. You're going to put the entire city to shame," Ethan says.

Caulder sighs and stares resolutely at the TV as Mattias moves through the menus. With my face on the other side of Ethan's, they can't see my grin, but this right here, this silly camaraderie and teasing, is what friendship is supposed to be about. While I know Caulder is embarrassed, I can feel the way he's sitting a little taller. I can see the hint of a smile on his lips at Ethan's constant compliments.

Friends should always build each other up.

Not that I knew anything about that until I went pro. The 'friends' I had in college were fleeting and definitely not people I'd share these moments with. They were the 'friends of convenience' kind of friends. You're here now, so we can hang. There was no investment. No trust.

They were just there.

I've never felt more accepted and at peace until I joined Buffalo. I'm not sure how the world truly perceives teammates and how they get along, but I love the atmosphere and easy friendships that I've been given over the last three years.

I also know that's not how all teams are. This might not be a completely unique environment, but it's not the rule, either. One of the Florida teams is rumored to be downright hostile.

After a while we order delivery and eat Chinese as we watch the highlights on Sports Spot. There's talk of trades and rumors of old rivalries getting together. Most of that I tune out as I eat. However, when they're showing the highlight reels from the game between us and New Jersey, I definitely watch that.

The play where Mattias is basically laying flat and sends the puck through the goalie's legs is just fucking epic. It gets played over and over. Slow motion so we can watch the puck (with the assistance of a large red arrow so no one can miss it) and at normal speed are both just awesome.

"Damn, Mattias," I say. "That's the best thing I've seen all season."

He grins. "It is beautiful, yeah?"

The three of us agree as we nod at the replay.

It's a good day that ends with a great evening with our teammates and friends. When we finally head back to Ethan's apartment, I'm looking forward to sleeping in and lounging around over the next couple days.

And riding Ethan's cock. Wonder if I could get him to model underwear for me.

THIRTEEN

ETHAN

THERE ARE MOMENTS IN YOUR LIFE THAT JUST FEEL LIKE THEY slow down and part of you is watching it happen. Over the span of twenty-four hours, that's exactly what happened to me. Everything felt so surreal.

Creed and I were sitting on the couch watching Sports Spot and reliving yesterday's game. Hockey is a low-scoring game as it is, and usually the points are within three of each other. To win by four points felt really good.

I know that thinking about it too much is going to bite me in the ass later. Our team is good. But we're probably middle of the pack as far as the league is concerned. We win enough and show enough promise that the franchise keeps us around. But we don't win championships.

That's okay with me. I can break records without winning a Stanley Cup. Having said that, I *really* want to win a Stanley Cup.

"I've been thinking about looking into changing agents," Creed says, and I shift to look at him. It's a commercial break, though there are highlights rotating around the NFL right now since the Super Bowl is set for February 3. I'm betting on New England but man, that would be six championships in a row for the same freaking quarterback! I want to see it just to see it.

"Why?" I ask.

"After talking to Caulder and knowing all his agent sets up for him and knowing that yours does the same thing, I feel like mine is only concerned about my hockey career. Nothing in conjunction or after."

"That's stupid. A good agent will know that you can still make money after you retire from hockey, too," I say.

He links his fingers with mine and a silly smile breaks out across my face. "I know. I'm not sure how to even get out of my contract."

"That's what contract lawyers are for. But have you been talking to another agent?"

"No, though I think I'm going to look into Pride Sports." He shifts to look at me. "What do you think? Do you like your agent?"

I shrug. "Yeah, he's cool. I have no complaints. Though, I'll be honest; in hindsight, I'd totally go to Pride. My agency is good enough and they serve my purposes, but in reality, Pride has set themselves up to handle everything having to do with an LGBTQ+ athlete. They do something new every year and... yeah, I really love that."

"But you're not considering leaving?"

"Nah. My agent is good. I chose him because he's gay and I'm sure he'll have my back and best interest at heart. He does what I need him to, as well as sets me up with other avenues for the future." I shrug again. "But if yours isn't, there's nothing wrong about changing."

"I know. But I haven't even told them I want something more." He laughs. "It kind of feels like I'm making excuses."

"I guess that depends on your contract. What does it say about other endorsements and whatever?"

Creed nods absently. "No idea," he mutters and laughs.

Our conversation pauses when the anchor returns, breaking through the NFL talk with a hockey announcement. Since we're less than a month away from the Super Bowl, I know it must be big.

"Vancouver Phoenix's head coach has just announced an upcoming trade." Avianna Zayn turns to look at Reese Davie. "They've had a slow year this far with an eight-game losing streak. While they managed to break it, they just came off two more losses. What could a trade mean this far into the season for the Phoenixes?"

"They've got a solid starting line with Luca Billsworth, Jakub

Bozik, and Antonio Polleska. So I don't think it's their offense that they have an issue with. I think their defense needs some work. I could see the team increasing their success if they traded Tom Eli and got someone who was more concerned about defending the goal instead of throwing down on the ice," Reese says.

"He spent a total of twelve minutes in the bin last game which, in my opinion, is part of the reason that they lost in Toronto," Molly Zubin says.

I text Jakub while we're listening to them discuss the team to see if he knows something about it. He doesn't answer me right away, but as the way things go, sometimes the team is last to hear about a trade. He might not know anything, anyway.

"Listen, we all know that a single person doesn't make a team," Reese says, "but it certainly has the potential to break it."

"They really need to be rotating their second line through. Eli isn't doing anything for them at this point," Avianna says.

"It's weird that the daughter of an A list actor and a rockstar chose to go into sports reporting and analytics," I say. Avianna is the daughter of actress Zyaire Legend and rockstar Royalty Zayn. I have always admired Zyaire. She refuses to use gender-specifying titles in her life except as mother, where her kids call her mom. Otherwise, she's a parent, a performer, a spouse. She's a huge advocate of the movement to remove such gender separation in the world, claiming that the reason there's such a gender divide is because everything we do separates one gender from another.

I really admire her.

"I think I donate to like eight of her charities," Creed says, laughing.

We half-heartedly listen to the anchors picking apart Vancouver as we talk quietly about the charity gala that Zyaire recently held and how much money they raised for one of the charities that are constantly fighting for LGBTQ+ people to be given the same rights and liberties as everyone else in the world. They raised well into the six figures, impressive for a first-time event.

The commercial break ends, and the team of four commentators come back.

"Here it is, in a twist that I'm not sure we saw coming," Reese says. "It's just been announced that Vancouver wingman Jakub

Bozik has been traded to the Buffalo Skidmosses for wingman Ryan Gilpatrick and center Mattias Jönsson."

The air whooshes out of me and for a minute, I feel like I'm floating over my body as I stare at the screen. I can hear their words from a distance, saying that if they look at this trade from Buffalo's vantage, it makes sense. They're constantly looking for someone to mesh with their star starting linemen and while Gilpatrick had been the most promising to date, he definitely doesn't make the cut.

My heart beats loudly in my chest so that there's an echoing *thud, thud, thud* in my ears, drowning out the newscasters. My team traded to get Jakub here...

Everything in me is warring. Excitement. Dread. Eagerness. Fear. Elation. Horror.

The ring of my phone makes me jump and I answer it without looking. I know who it is.

"What just happened?" I ask in greeting.

He snorts. "Looks like retirement can be put off for a while," he jokes and while I try to laugh, it sounds slightly unhinged. "Take a breath, miláček," he says quietly. "I know this is... going to be interesting, but..." he trails off.

"Jakub, this could be horrible. What this could do to our team!" I say, slightly hysterical.

He sighs because we both know I'm right. It's one thing having a gay couple on the team. One of which they've seen get closer and witnessed their relationship evolve for three years. Now, my *husband* is being traded to the same team where me and my boyfriend play. When that gets out...!

There's no if anymore. It's a when. It's going to happen.

"Does your management know?" he asks.

"I mean, I didn't announce it or anything, but yeah, you're on all my legal shit. Jesus fuck, I've never felt like I've been living as part of a hidden marriage so much as I do right now."

"It's only going to get worse," he says quietly.

A moment of silence passes between us and I ask, "When will you be here?"

"Twelfth," he says.

"Three days. They really gave you time to pack your shit, huh?"

Jakub chuckles. "Ethan." I take a heavy breath. "It's going to be okay. We'll figure this out. Alright?"

"Yeah. I know. It's just... I can't help but see this team imploding. *I didn't tell them I'm married, Jakub.* That's not the kind of thing you keep from your friends," I say.

"You didn't," he says. "You told Creed."

At his name, I realize I'm gripping his hand so hard that I'm going to leave bruises. I look at him and there's concern written all over his face as he stares at me. Taking a breath, I lean against his shoulder, wanting nothing more than to curl into his side.

"We'll figure it out, lásko. It's going to be fine."

JAKUB'S WORDS ARE STILL RUNNING THROUGH MY HEAD THE NEXT day. It's just practice, which is fortunate because I'm fucking all over the place. Not even Creed can predict what I'm doing at this point. There's no chance for Lucas, who has stepped into Ryan's position since he's not at practice and won't be again. I managed to have enough presence of mind to call Mattias and wish him luck, telling him to keep in touch. I haven't gotten around to Ryan yet.

By the end of practice, I'm a riotous mess. I can feel the concerned looks as my teammates watch me move around. All I can see is them freaking out and our chemistry imploding. It makes it so looking them in the eyes is too much of a chore, so I keep my face down.

When I dress, I head for Coach Melvin's office. I'm pretty sure he's expecting me since he's already looking into the hall when I stand before his door.

"Come in, Wilder," he says.

Shutting the door behind me, I take my seat and stare at him. I really need for him to tell me this entire thing is a mistake. An early April Fool's joke. But the grim look he's giving me says that it's not at all funny.

"What happened on the ice today?" he asks.

I'm pretty sure my expression turns incredulous. For a minute, I can't find my voice. Is there a chance he *doesn't know* that Jakub is my husband? Staring into his eyes, I try desperately to read him. To figure out if he knows or not.

Deciding that he must, I say, "You just traded for my husband to be on this team," I say, keeping my voice quiet.

There's no response. No shift in his expression. Minutes tick by and we're frozen. Once more, I feel like I'm floating outside my body, staring down at this scene.

Finally, he sits back. "Since Credence was drafted and you two clicked like you're made of the same fabric, we've been searching for a third for the two of you. Our methods of finding a fantastic player weren't enough. We tried Gilpatrick because his play style is the same. When it became clear he wasn't working out, we decided to dig into your past and came across your AHL games with Jakub Bozik. He's the only other player who you've had chemistry with." He gives me an amused smirk. "I'm beginning to think your personal chemistry and your game chemistry are directly tied."

For another few seconds, I just open and close my mouth like I'm a mindless fish. "You're bringing him here intentionally?!"

"Ethan," Coach Melvin says as he leans forward and places his folded hands on his desk, "your personal life is your own."

"Oh, come on, Coach. You know this is going to be a fucking chaotic explosion when the press finds out. We've intentionally kept our marriage a secret and I know you can imagine how much fun PR is going to have when they bring up all my hookups," I say. "I'm not even going to say what this is going to do with the team dynamics."

"PR is already on standby. However, you're going to have to have a statement prepared for when it does come to light as to why…"

"I haven't been faithful?" I deadpan.

He doesn't answer.

With a frustrated sigh, I say, "We have an open marriage. Even before we were traded to separate teams, we had an open marriage. Being gay *and* poly is going to be fucking fun in this environment, yeah?"

Coach Melvin laughs.

"He knows about Creed," I say, hearing the defense in my voice.

"Listen. I didn't make the trade. I warned against it, not just because of the concerns you just listed, but also because we were going to lose Jönsson in this trade. He's a fucking good player and definitely a loss. But management does what it wants. I suggest you figure out how you want to handle it," he says.

"You're not going to demand we make a statement or something?" I ask.

Coach shakes his head. "This is your business. As far as I know, Bozik isn't out publicly and I sure as hell won't be the one to demand he announce it if he's not ready."

My shoulders relax. We have some time. Probably.

"I do suggest you tell your team, though. Sooner rather than later."

I sigh. The feeling of relief was short-lived as my shoulders tense again. He's right. I know he's right. "Thanks, Coach. I'm sorry about practice."

He waves me off. "As long as you have your shit together for tomorrow's game, I'll excuse today."

Leaving his office, I head for the empty hallways that are rarely used and call Jakub. "They knew and decided the risk all around was worth the potential payout," I say when he answers.

"I figured as much," he says. "Take a breath, zlato."

I do. Several. It does little to calm me. This is going to be hellish. I can feel it. I've never wanted to retire before, but if there's something that's going to set me over the edge, it's this pressure. Right now, I kind of want to jump off the ledge and freefall into an anonymous existence. I can't deal with this kind of stress.

In words that I'm not sure make much sense, I repeat to him what Coach told me. Then he tells me to go let Creed comfort me for a while. But when I go to find him, he's not here. Isak says he left twenty minutes ago and my stomach falls.

I've been a bit of a dick, I think. Getting in my car, I drive to his home. Sure enough, his car is parked outside, and I know that I need to apologize until he takes pity on me and wraps me in his arms.

This doesn't just affect me and Jakub. It affects Creed too. In some ways, a lot more. He's the one having an affair with a married man, after all.

FOURTEEN
CREDENCE

The words of the news anchors felt like a punch in the gut.

My boyfriend's husband was moving home...

Watching his face turn white and then excited and then horrified all within a matter of sixty seconds, said how well he was taking it. His hand became a vice around mine, but I was clinging to him just as much.

I wasn't sure what to think or how to feel. Through the rest of the night, we stared at the television absently, waiting for something to happen. But the anchors went between the upcoming Super Bowl and the breaking hockey trade as Buffalo continues to search for the needle in the haystack for the player to jibe with Credence Ayrton and Ethan Wilder.

Did I flinch every time they said 'threesome' concerning the starting line? Oh, fuck yes, I did.

The next morning, I felt sick to my stomach. Ethan moved around like a shadow, barely seeing anything at all. I didn't dare talk to him because I wasn't sure he knew I was there, anyway. Practice wasn't any different and when he disappeared after his shower, I went home, almost gasping for breath.

This isn't fair. My love life isn't supposed to fall apart before it even truly gets started. Shouldn't I be allowed to have at least a little while with him before it all turns to hell?

Until this point, I could have maybe convinced myself that I wasn't in love with him. Sure, I was falling for him, but I wasn't there yet. But by the way my chest felt like both goalies were sitting on it and my ribs were about to crack from the pressure... Yeah, I think I'm already there.

Of course, I am. I said as much to him not long ago.

"Fuck," I mutter, as I literally kick my shoes across the foyer and listen to them hit the wall with a resounding *thud* before thunking to the ground. A wet patch on the wall makes me scowl. This isn't supposed to happen like this.

Then there's the other voice in my head saying, what did you think was going to happen when you got involved with a married man? You *knew* he was married!

I strip from my clothes and get into sweats, needing the comfort of the soft material against my skin. Heading into the kitchen, I load up my pot with milk and dump a stupid amount of chocolate in. For a few minutes, I stare at the milk as it gets hot, melting the chocolate and turning the milk brown and delicious.

Stirring it until it's all dissolved, I try not to think of anything at all. For just a minute, I can pretend this isn't happening. I can enjoy my thick, soft sweats and this super sweet and doubly chocolatey milk and pretend that I'm not trying to drown or smother my feelings.

Just as I pour it into a large, insulated travel mug, there's a knock at my door. I contemplate ignoring it. I'm definitely not in the mood to talk to anyone. They're going to have questions and I don't want to pretend to know what to say or that I'm fine.

I'm not fine.

Somehow, I find myself at the door anyway and am surprised to find Ethan there. His brows are knit together as he looks at me. "Why did you leave without me?" he asks.

My stomach drops at the tone of his voice.

You abandoned me.

Immediately, I reach for him and pull him to my chest, still bundled in his winter layers. "I'm sorry. I just thought..."

He sighs and hugs me tightly. "I'm sorry. I didn't mean to push you aside. You're stupidly important to me."

"Yeah, but..." I take a breath and while my doorway might not be the ideal place for this conversation, I say it anyway, "he's moving home, no? To your place? We can't keep—"

"Yes, we can," he says, picking his face up from my shoulder and looking at me. He searches my eyes for a minute. "I'm keeping you. We're just going to have some very strange growing pains for a while."

While I try not to let hope take hold, my stomach flutters at his words. I pull him inside and strip his clothes from his body, letting them fall where they do. Then I'm yanking him farther inside, where we tumble onto the couch as if I forgot the placement of my own furniture.

We're tangled together with our asses and legs over our heads, but we kind of turn limbless and just lay there wrapped around each other. Silence passes through the room for several minutes.

"You really think we can keep seeing each other?" I ask.

Ethan sighs, hugging me tightly to him. "Of course we can. This —between you and me—was never contingent on where Jakub is located. I told you; it was never going to be temporary with you. That means there was always going to be a time in the future when the three of us existed together. In the same place. But, you know, ideally not a couple weeks after we finally get together."

"You really think he's going to be okay with this?"

He kisses my forehead. "He already is, Creed. My concern with him coming here isn't you. It has nothing to do with you except for how it's going to affect you in the greater scheme of things. You're going to be the other man in the world's opinion. That's more stress and negativity than you need or deserve. But everything that has me stressed isn't because you and Jakub will be in the same place. I'm really excited about that part. It's everything outside of us that I'm worried about."

While that doesn't take away all my concerns, I feel much lighter now. I take a breath, inhaling his scent. "What are we going to do?"

"I don't know," he says. "Our reasons for living as we were are our own and the reasons we kept it to ourselves are legitimate concerns. Which will be evident when the truth finally comes out and will only prove that we'd made the right decision. What I'm afraid of is the hurt and resentment it's going to cause with our team because I've been here for four years, am close with several guys, and they don't know."

"It would be easy for someone to let it slip accidentally," I tell him. "I get it."

"I told you because I knew how I felt about you and you needed to know my situation. Otherwise, I wouldn't have even told you," he says. He pauses. "Does that bother you? Would you have been hurt if you found out three years later now that he's moving here?"

"It's easy to say that I wouldn't because I know the situation… but yeah, I imagine I'd be upset," I admit.

He sighs. I shimmy on the couch until we both end up nearly rolling off. The laughter is a nice break between the heavy moments, but eventually, we curl up together in a position where I can stroke the soft skin of his face. He's so fucking beautiful, this man. Inside and out.

It would be easy to brush this off if his concerns were selfish, but he hasn't mentioned once how this is going to affect him except that he's glad his husband will be moving home. Otherwise, it's been about the team. About me.

There's really no wonder why I fell in love with him. It would be difficult not to at this point. He's so fucking sweet.

Ethan spends the next few minutes telling me he went to talk to Coach Melvin and repeated what he was told. I can't help but think that it was ridiculously selfish on management's part to do this trade without considering how it would affect him.

I get it. Their goal is to win. To build the best team with a chance to get the Stanley Cup. And it sounds like they had considered some things because they apparently have PR statements in place.

But they didn't consider the important things, like the team and those personally involved. Like it or not, Ethan Wilder is the face of the Buffalo Skidmosses. He's been on more tabloid and legit news covers than the rest of our team combined. He's a force in hockey. A true role model for so many reasons.

This means his affairs are all public. As is our relationship already.

His marriage isn't going to just damage him and his figure, it's going to fuck with the entire team. I know our PR rep isn't concerned about negative publicity, but there are those who will go on a rampage about a team supporting a known married man having an affair. Even if that's not the case at all.

For just a minute, I let anger sour my mood. I'd love nothing more than to tell management off for this fuckery. And then scream at the world for being the reason we now have this kind of stress. If people would mind their own fucking business and keep their unsolicited opinions to themselves, then this wouldn't be such a huge deal.

But every athlete knows going into a professional career that your private life is no longer private. It's impossible to keep it that way. Every celebrity or royalty or whatever *knows* this. That doesn't make it right or fair, but it is what it is. That's why people say we signed up for it.

"When will he be here?" I ask.

"Two days. His flight doesn't come in until the evening, but yeah. Two days."

I nod and try not to think of that as a deadline. An end point. It's not. I know it's not. But I can't stop myself from feeling like it is.

"We're going to be fine," he says, his fingers tangling in my hair. "I promise. If you still want to do this. I guess I never asked, and I should have asked how you felt."

Shifting so I can look into his face, seeing his concern just breaks my heart. "You're the only one for me, Ethan," I say quietly. "I knew it as a teenager. I'm literally living every kids' dream where I get to be with my idol."

Ethan rolls his eyes, laughing. "I'm not an idol."

"You've been mine for as long as I can remember. It was about your talent at first. For being openly out and proud. For how you just dominate and break records. Then when I met you in person, for the man you are. I saw the surface of you as a kid; everything that the world sees and what you stand for. But learning who you are as a person? That's been the best thing to ever happen to me."

His lips part as he stares into my eyes. "You can't really be real," he whispers. "There's no way two perfect people have come into my life to love me."

I laugh and wiggle closer, pressing my face to his. "I'm not perfect, but I am real. Yes, I want to be with you. I'm not going to lie and pretend that I'm not worried about how this is going to work when Jakub gets here. But I'm committed to you."

"That's a lot of pressure, you know."

"What is?" I kiss his lips lightly, making him hum.

"Being your idol. I'm going to fall from that pedestal, eventually. All idols fall at some point."

"You'd have already done so if that was going to happen. I'm pretty sure you just become more divine in my mind every time I learn something new about you," I say.

He laughs, wrapping his arms around me. "I really do love you, Credence," Ethan whispers, sending my heart racing. "So much."

"I believe you," I say quietly. "And I love you too. I've never had my heart broken, but I think that's unusual, isn't it? Everyone has their heart broken at least once. I think that's why I'm afraid that somehow, something is going to come between us and force us apart."

His arms tighten. "As much as outside forces can suck and put a lot of stress on us, they don't have any relevance in our decisions and how we live our lives. If we don't work out, it'll be because we gave it our all, and that wasn't enough. But that's not going to happen."

"You sound so sure," I whisper.

"I am sure. When you meet your person, you just know. I knew you were mine the moment we met, Creed. That's why I *didn't* jump in your bed right away."

I laugh and bury my face in his neck. I can feel his smile against my head as he holds me to him, his fingers still running through my hair.

This is where we spend the rest of the night. Mostly in silence, but sometimes talking. Voicing concerns and reassuring the other. My hot chocolate is forgotten until morning when I find it sitting on my kitchen counter. It's a testament to how high-quality my travel mug is that it was still warm.

FIFTEEN
ETHAN

WE LOST THE AWAY GAME AGAINST THE CAROLINA BLUE HAWKS on the eleventh and then lose again at the home game against the Tampa Bay Pirates on the twelfth. In all honesty, I'm not surprised we lost against Tampa Bay. They're a bunch of dick players. I don't think they play the game to win; they play to be assholes.

Jakub will be arriving sometime after midnight and while I plan to be home to meet him, I'm currently laying naked on Creed's bed with him sprawled across my chest.

I've tried to remain completely present with him over the last forty-eight hours, which has been difficult since my mind keeps performing a deep dive into what's going to happen when Jakub gets here and our secret is spilled. Coach is right; we need to tell our team first. I'm not sure when is the best time to do that, though. During the season seems like a shit move since it has the potential to create a lot of ill feelings toward me, and that's not the kind of shift we need in our game.

But Creed is here now, and he needs me to remind him he's not a second priority. He's just as important as my husband is.

"What are you thinking?" he asks.

My fingers continue to trail up and down his body, feeling his smooth skin stretched over his sexy muscles.

"You know the only part of Jakub moving here that I'm worried about on a personal level?" I ask. Creed immediately stiffens and I kiss the top of his head. "Nothing to do with you, Creed."

He sighs.

"We met and immediately hit it off. But even then, I was openly out, and Jakub wasn't. We kept our relationship a secret, but I think back then, it was more because we didn't want to call attention to something that might be interpreted as a con on our personal profiles for recruiting teams. It's one thing to be a gay player. It's another thing to have that flaunted out there in the world by creating a spotlight on yourself for marrying a player the world didn't know is gay."

"I hate that our sexuality plays such a big part in anything we do," he says.

"Yeah, I know. But it is what it is. We could talk for hours about how society is moving backwards instead of progressing. The ancient cultures all show homosexuality in their paintings—especially of their gods. Hell, more times than not, their gods were bisexual. And here we are, a few hundred years later, and suddenly it's a fucking sin," I say.

He snorts. "You're not at all bitter about it."

"Yeah, well."

Creed turns his head and kisses my chest. "Back to what you were saying."

"Anyway, yeah. Even when we got married, that was a complete and total secret. We made sure the person we hired to marry us wasn't a hockey fan. Either way, we made everyone in attendance sign an NDA. We were just starting out and didn't want anything to reflect negatively on our chances. But during that time, we kept our separate apartments. I know we were almost always together, but we had our own places; somewhere all our own where we could escape to. We've lived apart more than we have in the same city."

"You think this is going to be a bad thing? Don't you spend summers together?" he asks.

"Yes, but that's different. We go out and travel. Somewhere anonymous. Somewhere we're left alone. In hindsight, it's actually pretty remarkable that we've managed to remain out of headlines this long, but we're careful. I guess the part I'm worried about is living with my husband." Laughter bubbles out of me as I hear how silly that sounds. "We've never lived together. In our entire relationship, we've *never lived together,* Creed. I've never shared a space with my husband."

His arms tuck under me so he can hug me. "You think it's going to cause problems? Is he going to move in with you?"

"For now, he is. There are apartments open in my building, so it's an easy enough reason that he's here and why we might carpool. My building always has apartments open. But yeah, I don't know. Is it going to be weird that this has been my space alone for four years and now he's moved in? How do we make it ours? And I don't want you to feel like you're intruding. I know you feel that way already, and he's not even here yet. I get it. Fuck, I can only imagine how awkward it's going to feel for you, and I don't want that."

He kisses my chest again, over and over, spreading soft, feather-light kisses across my skin. "I admit that I think it's going to feel like I'm interfering. But I think maybe it might feel more so for him since I've been here for three years and I've been to your place a lot."

My breath catches because I hadn't thought about that. "Well, fuck's sake."

Creed chuckles. "You said it best. We're going to be experiencing some weird growing pains for a while and as much as you'd like to nullify them all, it's not going to happen. I think you need to stop worrying about it and we will just have to see how it goes."

"I kind of hate that," I admit.

He grins against my chest before pushing himself up. "You should get back soon," he says.

I pout, gripping his hips to keep him from moving. It's only ten. I have a couple more hours until Jakub's plane even lands. Really, I'm a little concerned with being alone and how all of my growing list of worries is going to affect me when I'm surrounded by nothing but silence and my own thoughts. I might have a panic attack.

Creed smiles softly and scoots down my body. He grips my wrists and pins them to my side as his mouth descends over my dick, circling it until I'm groaning, my entire body rolling with the feel of him.

We've been lying long enough since our mad dash in here to fuck when we got back that my body feels it's up to the challenge of becoming hard again. Actually, there's no challenge at all. My dick is already throbbing as he sucks on me.

"Creed," I murmur, his name ending on a groan as he brings me to the back of his throat.

He moves off me with a pop of his lips. The way he licks them after is indecent and I drip my appreciation. Moving back up my body, he keeps my hands trapped when he straddles my hips again, locking my hands against my thighs.

Creed continues to stroke my cock as he grabs another condom, ripping the package with his teeth, and then rolls it down my length. I try to pull my hands out, but he keeps them still. Not going to lie; him restraining me is stupid hot. Especially when his eyes don't leave mine the entire time he touches me. Lubes me up, reapplies to his tight hole, and then shifts so he's hovering over my cock, holding it in place for him to slide down on.

My mouth remains open as I stare at him, breathless.

"God," I murmur as I break through his tight ring and he's suddenly strangling the tip of my dick. "You feel so good."

"Mmm," he answers as he slowly works his way down me. His body swallows me whole, sucking me in. Strangling me until I can barely take a breath.

"Creed," I groan as his ass finally rests on my pelvis. My entire body shivers as he tenses around me over and over. I whine, the sound coming out in almost a sob.

"I really love how you come apart for me," he says, his voice low and sexy. "I've barely got you inside me and you're already shaking."

I almost laugh because Jakub has said the same thing before. "Only with those I let myself go with," I manage to get out.

His body suddenly releases mine, and I suck in a breath. He's hovering over me, his clenched cheeks keeping the very tip of my cock at this entrance, just barely pushing me inside. "What do you mean?" he asks as he slowly moves down my shaft again.

My groan lasts as long as it takes for him to sit again. He can't really expect a conversation right now, can he? When he stills, I assume it's because he's waiting for an answer. Words are floating around as if they're in soup right now, so I'm not sure what kind of order they're going to come out in.

"You're not transactional," I say, panting. "I love you. I give you all of me."

I watch as his lips part and his expression softens. Creed leans down and kisses me slowly. I kiss him desperately in return, trying to keep his mouth on mine. "I love you too," he whispers. "You have no idea how surreal it is to hear you say you love me and know that you mean it."

My head leaves the bed, trying to capture his mouth again. But he's already sitting. He starts to ride me with his hands planted firmly on my chest. Sometimes tweaking my nipples, but usually just to keep his balance.

Everything inside me swirls with pleasure, but it doesn't compare to how good I feel when he arches his body, his hands leaving my chest to touch himself. Over his chest, his stomach, around his throat, and his dick. His head thrown back as he bounces on my cock over and over.

There are tears in my eyes as he brings my orgasm closer and closer. My moans fill the room as we take pleasure in each other. When I come, I try to force my eyes to remain open so I can see the vision that is Credence Ayrton on top of me, lost in his pleasure that he's taking from my body.

I gasp when his spurts of hot, stringy cum land on my chest and stomach. He says my name like a prayer, and I try to wrench my hands free, again to no avail. I desperately need to kiss him, though. Like, yesterday. I need his mouth on mine yesterday!

As I knew I would, I pace around my apartment as I wait for Jakub. Again, as per usual, I don't pick him up from the airport. We've gotten the technique of hiding our acquaintance down pretty well. We know that being seen together in public at all when we weren't on the same team would only raise questions. It would make people look at us.

It'll be easier to be in the same place now. Our presence together will be easily explained. But if we don't want someone else to figure out our situation before we have a chance to announce it on our own terms, we still need to be careful.

Anything to draw someone's attention to him or me wouldn't be a good thing.

I try not to think about it. Or about how having him move in is going to work. I don't live with a lot of furniture in the same way I know Jakub doesn't. But my apartment isn't huge. Where will we put all his things?

Stopping in my room, I stare into my closet. It's not massive, but it's big enough that I'm pretty sure my minimalist clothing husband can squeeze in there. He'll fit into my bathroom fine. What if he wants to keep his bed, though? Did he even bring his bed? Does he have art he'll want to hang?

I'm biting my lip as I contemplate this and so deep within my worries that I don't hear the door open, nor his footsteps as they come down the hall. I don't feel him standing behind me as I stare at my bed and then look at my bathroom again. It's not until his hands land on my waist and I nearly scream that I finally feel his presence.

"Shh, zlato," he murmurs, amusement in his tone. "You're going to wake the neighbors. I'm not sure they're going to believe you're suddenly into kinky sex."

I laugh, though my heart is racing as I turn in his arms and hug him fiercely. For a minute, all my worries, all my fear, my trepidation, my anxiety—it all melts away and I sink into the embrace of the first man I have ever fully loved.

He's here. My husband is here. Where he'll be every single day. When I wake up. When I go to sleep. After not seeing him for months at a time, we will suddenly be spending every single minute of every day together.

And I can't be more thrilled about it.

"I know it's only been a couple weeks, but it feels like it's been months," I say, pressing my face to the soft skin of his neck.

His arms tighten. "I've made a decision," he says quietly, kissing my ear. "When Buffalo decides it's time to trade one of us, I'll be announcing my retirement."

I laugh, even though I know he's serious. "Jakub—"

"No, lásko. I'm done living away from you. I can't do it anymore. Even though we have some mountains to climb for a while, I don't even care. They're ant hills. The only thing that matters is spending every day for the rest of my life with the man I love more than hockey."

While I know that there are reasons we said these decisions needed to be a discussion and agreed upon together, I can't stop the silly, sappy smile that spreads across my face because more than anything, I want that too. I want him here. Every day. I want him and Creed every day.

I finally have that.

"I won't argue right now because I'm too fucking happy to see you," I say.

"Where's Creed?" he asks.

"Home. He thought it was important that it's just me and you tonight."

"That's not necessary. I know that he's important to you. I don't expect—"

Raising my face, I kiss him to cut his words off. He smirks against my mouth, his hand coming up to rest at the back of my neck.

"Tonight, I'll agree with him," I say quietly. "Just tonight. I'm very conscious of making him feel left out or… not as important. And right now, I can't let you go. I don't want him to feel out of place."

Jakub brushes his lips across mine. "Okay. Just tonight. Although since you smell like sex, I'm guessing you didn't leave him that long ago."

I laugh, feeling my cheeks blush. "I could have taken a shower, but this idea was so much hotter."

His grin is wolfish. "It really is, kocourek. It's time to break in your ass again."

For the third time tonight, my cock rises to the occasion. Only this time, he's not the one getting the action. And fuck, I was looking forward to this change in position.

SIXTEEN
JAKUB

I'VE ONLY HAD A HANDFUL OF HOURS OF SLEEP AND WHILE MY internal clock says I'm still in Vancouver, I'm wide awake at seven in the morning. We have practice late morning but it's not for a while. Turning my head, a smile takes over. It's been so long since I've woken up to my husband and not had a date looming ahead in which we'd be going our separate ways again.

I'm here for good. I live here now.

At least, until next season, when the option to trade me is fresh again. But regardless of the conversation we've yet to truly have, I'm not going anywhere. There comes a time when you have to listen to what your heart wants over everything else.

Hockey still makes me happy, but waking up next to Ethan makes me happier.

He's laying on his stomach, all that smooth coffee-colored skin on display for me as he sleeps soundly. Rolling onto my side, I trail my fingers softly along the curvature of his back, slipping it beneath the covers to trace his round ass.

While I'd really love nothing more than to wake him up and bury myself inside him again, I let him sleep and creep out of bed, careful not to disturb him.

I've only been to Ethan's house a handful of times. Usually when I was in town, we'd get a separate hotel room in a different hotel than where my team was staying. We didn't want to risk coming to his apartment often for no other reason than explaining it away from someone who randomly got a picture of us would be too difficult.

We didn't necessarily go to extremes to keep our secret. Thankfully, like most professional athletes, we kept much of our private life private. No one gave it much thought, and there was no reason to try to link us.

Honestly, it was fucking luck.

I make my way through the bathroom and then stop in the closet to pick through his clothing. My dozen boxes won't arrive until later this week, so I only brought a suitcase, focusing on what I'd need for hockey over casual clothing.

We don't wear the same size. Ethan is a couple inches shorter and has more of a compact body shape. It means that most of his clothing is a size smaller than mine. But for lounging around the house, I could wear a pair of gym shorts and a tee.

For a while, I wander through the rest of the apartment. There is another bedroom that looks like it has never been used. It probably hasn't. Another bathroom, which I'm pretty sure is used more frequently than his en suite. A large living space that you walked through to the kitchen/eating combination. Then there's the foyer with the laundry off it.

It's a nice size for a single person. I'm fairly certain it will be comfortable enough for two people. But I wondered about three. Would Ethan object to upgrading his apartment to something slightly bigger?

Or am I jumping the gun?

Deciding that the discussion isn't necessary immediately, I make my way to the kitchen and pull the air fryer and the blender forward. In just a few minutes, I'm sipping on a smoothie and have the makings of a couple breakfast sandwiches cooking up.

It isn't long before I feel arms wrap around me from behind and my husband presses his face into the back of my shoulder.

"Morning," I say, laying my hand over his.

"I like this," he says, sleepily. "You being here."

"So do I."

I turn and pull him into my chest, kissing his forehead while I hug him close. For a minute, we remain like that, just enjoying the feel of each other. The moment is interrupted by the air fryer.

Giving him another kiss, I release him and turn back to my task. It isn't long before I've assembled the pieces and hand him one. Ethan gives me a sleepy grin.

"Why did you get up?" I ask as I watch him head for a stool. He's only in a pair of underwear, which I love seeing.

He shrugs as he takes a bite. When he's done chewing, he says, "The bed was cold, and I thought I imagined you here."

I sit next to him, bumping my shoulder to his. "Going to take some getting used to, huh?"

He nods, but gives me a smile. "In a good way, but yeah."

We eat in silence for a few minutes before he steals my smoothie and drinks a few mouthfuls before giving me a sour look. "I don't know what you have against honey, but this thing is bitter as fuck."

"You know what I like."

Ethan laughs. The sound makes me smile. He leans into my side, and I wrap an arm around him, sighing happily.

"You think we're going to be okay living in the same space?" he asks quietly.

"You don't?"

He hesitates before shrugging. "We've literally never lived in the same place. Besides the outside concerns, it's the one thing I haven't stopped thinking about. Is there a chance we work as well as we do because we've always had our own places?"

"No," I tell him, shifting in my seat so I can grasp his face and make him look at me. "We work well because we love each other and everything else comes second. Though it's always looked like we put our careers first, we've only done that so we could put this first in the future. That doesn't mean we haven't always made our marriage a top priority. It really doesn't matter where we live, Ethan; my home is where you are."

"You say such sweet things," he teases, but I can feel the way he relaxes against me again.

I kiss his nose and get up. "It's the truth."

I take care of our few dishes and push the small appliances back into their places. We spend the next couple hours lounging around, laying in each other's arms, just because we can. When we decide to shower and get changed for practice, it's still a couple hours away.

"You going to come to the rink with me?" I ask.

Ethan shakes his head. "If it's okay with you, I'm going to Creed's. I don't want him to feel like a second thought even though it was his insistence that he not be here last night. I know what he's afraid of."

I kiss him and nod. "I'll see you later, then."

"Want me to drop you off?"

Shaking my head, I kiss him once more, just because I can. "Nope. I'll take a rideshare and think about a car later. I think I might lease."

Ethan grins and we head downstairs together. "Something fast and sexy, I hope."

"Sure, but you're not driving it if it's fast."

He laughs. We part ways as I order a ride and wait. I like this part of the city. Still close enough to walk to things, but not surrounded by so many towering buildings that they're the only thing you see when you look out the window.

It's freezing. Well below freezing. But the sun is out, giving the impression that it might get warm. I doubt it, but we'll see.

My ride comes and I'm dropped off out back of the arena. Thankfully, the door is open, so I meander my way down the dim corridors as I make my way to the locker room. The floor is a heathered blue gym floor. That rubber feeling that's easy to clean but not hard on your feet. There's a yellow line that boxes in the cubbies that outline the round room. Running in front of the cubbies is a wooden bench that opens for storage.

In the center of the floor is the Skidmoss logo, which is reflected in the large light above. The ceiling is a large stainless steel light panel with starlight holes throughout. The room is also lit by a continuous light that follows the perimeter.

There's a television set into a wall of drawers where I'm sure we'll find things we might need, such as tape and whatever. The set of double doors that opens to the chute has sticks lined up against the wall in their holders.

I take a few minutes to get acquainted with the rest of the area, finding the bathrooms, lounge, and conditioning room.

It doesn't take me long to find my cubby in the round room. My jersey and pads are hanging on the hooks, my helmet and gloves on the top shelf, a skate on its hook on either side. More pads on the second shelf. In the cubby within the cubby, standing up, are more pads. My thermal pants are sitting on top of the bench. And my name with my number is already affixed to the bar: Bozik | 37.

I look around and spot Creed's three down on my right, number twenty. Ethan's is across the room, almost directly opposite mine, number eighteen.

When I turn back around, Coach Melvin Mickerson is standing just inside the door. He's smiling at me and I give him a grin in return.

"I take it you found your way here alright?" he asks as he approaches.

I take his hand and nod. "Yep. Nothing exciting to report. Thought I'd come and check out the ice before practice. See if it's as cold as Vancouver."

He chuckles. "Is it?"

"It's pretty fucking cold," I say. "I think it might be colder here."

"There's something to be said about the lakes," Coach agrees. "Buffalo isn't for the faint of heart."

Chuckling, I shake my head and drop my bag. Coach watches me for a minute. He glances around before saying, "Everything okay?"

I know what he's asking. "Yeah. He's… nervous, but not because of us. He's worried about what the team is going to think about him keeping it from them."

Coach nods. "I don't want to push or force your hand, but now that you're here, it's only a matter of time before some nosey tabloid reporter digs it up. This team will support you. But you need to be honest with them. Sooner rather than later. Again, I don't want to push. Everyone is entitled to come out on their own terms. I just don't want the public to be the reason that happens."

"I agree. It's not something we've had a chance to talk about, but we will."

He looks at Creed's locker as if seeing him there. "I really hope this isn't going to get messy."

The laugh that tries to escape is only marginally stopped. "I mean no disrespect, but management had to have known the risks it was taking when bringing me here, Coach. Whatever fallout happens, it's not on any of our hands but theirs."

He claps me on the shoulder. "I don't disagree. Enjoy the ice. The rest of the team will begin trickling in within the hour."

I watch Coach walk away and debate whether that was a supportive and understanding exchange or if he's expecting shit to hit the fan. I'm pretty sure it's going to hit the fan, but not because of any drama caused by the three of us.

It doesn't take me long to change, and I'm hobbling my way down the chute with my stick and a few pucks in my hands. It really is wild how different the temperature is between here and Vancouver. Vancouver was further north, but it was right on the ocean, which tends to keep the temperature moderate. Not warm by any means, but not freezing like this.

Lake effect is nasty. Ethan's told me about the storms they get out here. I've seen pictures. I've seen the news. It's wild.

Even their rink feels colder. Like it doesn't need to be cooled because the outside air has that under control. I'm thankful for all my layers.

Dropping the pucks on the ice, I take a few laps and just let the cold air prickle my skin. Then I'm shooting pucks and going through some maneuvers as I contemplate practice. There's a lot of pressure on me to measure up to some standard no one has reached before.

It's a misconception that there's communication between Ethan and Creed on the ice. There isn't. They simply read each other and the situation. They can usually predict what's happening in front of them as if they can see three steps ahead and they react.

The challenge with other players is that they don't play like that. Management looks for those with the same playing style, hoping that will be enough to make magic happen. But what they needed to find all along was someone who could adapt.

They weren't wrong to take a chance on me. Ethan and I were young when we played together, but I know that if given the time, we'd have found a similar routine to what he has with Credence. Some people just click. For Ethan, that click needs to happen on and off the ice. He needs to be able to feel his teammates and know them in a way that he can predict what they're going to do.

Coming around the net a while later, I come face to face with Brighten Shepey and nearly careen into him. I spin and stumble before righting myself, making him laugh hysterically. I chuckle, shaking my head as I slide to a stop beside him.

"Welcome," he says, grinning. "I'm Brighten. They call me Shepey, The Third, or Three, usually. Take your pick."

I nod. "Why not Brighten?"

"Because it's a stupid name and I hate it. Only management is allowed to call me by my name, and I'll respond. Otherwise, I don't hear them at all. Weird how that happens," he says.

I laugh again, shaking my head.

"You liking Buffalo?"

"I've been here for less than twelve hours, but yeah, so far, it's fine." It's perfect. My husband is here. What more could I possibly ask for?

We skate around for a while and, one by one, the rest of the team streams onto the ice. Ethan flashes me a huge grin when he steps on, following Creed whose smile is a lot shyer. After we've skated around for a bit, Coach calls us all together.

"I think you've all informally met Jakub Bozik, either in games or just now. Let's give him a warm welcome." He looks at me and gives me a smile. "I can imagine you're aware of the weight that's been placed on your shoulders, Bozik."

His gaze glances over my shoulders. I, like many of my teammates, glance that way. I'm not at all surprised to see that management is here. Not the owner, but definitely some bigwigs in suits under their parkas.

I glance at Ethan and he smirks my way before turning his attention back to Coach.

"We're going to give them what they want, which is to see how you mesh on the starting line. You warmed up?" Coach asks.

"As well as I'm going to be," I say.

"I take it you've met Ethan and Creed?" he asks, raising a brow.

I laugh, nodding. "We're acquainted."

Creed's cheeks are red, but Ethan just laughs.

"First and second lines—get ready," Coach says.

The team splits, and Ethan comes towards me. "Bozik, is it?" he teases.

I smirk, licking my lips. "Show me your moves, Wildman."

His laughter floods my system, and I grin as I follow him.

It's been a while since I've skated with him. Against him, sure. But never on the same side of the ice in the last seven years. It's going to take a few rounds to get reacquainted. That is, if I manage to. There's a chance our styles won't work well together after all these years.

The puck drops and Ethan shoves it my way before taking off down the ice. I dodge the defenseman and fling it back, further than I should have, which means he barely catches it. It barely touches his stick before he's sent it to Creed as he rounds the goal.

Creed glances at me but sends it towards the goal. It bounces off the goalie's pads and one of the defenders takes it, shooting it to the other end.

When the puck gets back in Creed's hands, Ethan is blocked, so he sends it my way, but I'm not quite where he needed me to be. I dive, sending it flying at a weird angle and end up starfished on the ground. Laughter follows as I grin, getting back to my feet.

It's the fourth play before I'm where they both need me to be. It's one of those perfect situations where the stars align and the angels sing, or some shit, but the passes are perfect, the synchronization and harmonious movement are gold. The goal that Ethan sinks is magic.

When we repeat the same cohesion for the next few rounds, I chance a glance at the bigwigs and find them grinning. This was what they were looking for. Hopefully, we can keep it up during an actual game.

SEVENTEEN
CREDENCE

WE GET SPANKED ON OUR FIRST GAME WITH JAKUB. EDMONTON kills us 2-7. We're wincing by the time we get back into the locker room, though Ethan, Jakub, and I get pulled for a press conference right after we're cleaned and dressed again. Our team was on fire tonight, though the score doesn't reflect that. Edmonton simply kicked ass a little more than we did.

"A lot more," I mutter to myself.

We're lined up behind microphones just as we would be on the ice. Ethan between us, with me on his left and Jakub on his right.

Flashes blind me for several minutes while we stand there, waiting for it to get on with so I can get out of here.

"You played remarkably well tonight," a reporter says, causing the room to fall marginally quiet. "It looks like you were their missing piece, Mr. Bozik, despite the heavy loss."

Jakub gives them a charming smile. "Sometimes you just gel. I'm proud of our performance tonight. Edmonton was just a bit stronger than us. We'll get there."

"You and Wilder played together in the AHL, correct?" another reporter says.

I try not to stiffen. Since everyone's focus is on Jakub, I'm hoping it was missed. Both Jakub and Ethan nod at the question.

"How has the reunion been? Do you find your past has lent a hand in how well you worked together tonight?"

Ethan's smirk says that his answer is going to be something that has a double meaning. I'm not disappointed. "Our reunion has been great. Falling back into old routines while creating new ones." He looks at Jakub but somehow just keeps the amused grin on his face and the hearts out of his eyes.

His gaze moves to mine, and he winks, his smile broadening.

"How are you feeling about this new relationship, Mr. Ayrton?"

Fucking Christ. Talk about a loaded question. "It's new, but as with everything, we'll have some growing pains, but I'm sure in no time, it'll be like he's always been a part of our team."

Ethan's beaming grin says he heard other things that may or may not have been there. I smile and duck my head, trying to hide it from the press.

"I'm going to ask the question we're all dying to know the answer to. Mr. Bozik, how do you feel being on the same line with hockey's sweethearts? They're so in sync that it's been almost painful to watch someone else try to match their level. You did remarkably well tonight, but we all want to know how you're feeling being inserted into their love affair."

Ethan's head snaps back to the press as he glares at them.

Jakub's hand lands on Ethan's forearm, as if to hold him back and quiet his remark. It's his quiet, cool voice that answers. "I appreciate that you're trying to make this hockey related when that's not really what you're asking. So I'm going to keep my response hockey related because that's what this press conference is about. When players work well together, it's because they find a common language. For three years, Ethan and Creed have spoken the same language while everyone else Buffalo tried on their line couldn't interpret it." He pauses, staring at the camera. "I know their language and I can speak it fluently. Their personal lives are personal and have no bearing on the ice at all."

I'm furious and scowling as our PR rep pulls us from the room after that, despite the dozens of questions yelled after us.

Arms circle me and I stiffen, aware that Jakub is close. "Relax," Ethan says. "We played amazingly tonight. We knew these questions were coming; they do with every new teammate. And after this string of away games, we get a week off."

STARTING LINE

"Fuck yeah," Isak says. He tosses his glove at me. "You can go fuck on a tropical island for a while."

I roll my eyes, my gaze flickering to Jakub. Though I love Ethan wrapped around me, I gently brush him off and offer him a smile. It's weird having his husband here. It just is. I feel like I'm doing something wrong.

Ethan kisses my cheek before retreating across the room to grab his bag.

"So, you have a problem with gays?"

I spin around at the casual question that's edged with blades. Isak is standing in front of Jakub, where he's sitting on the bench in front of his cubby. Jakub looks at him in confusion.

"What?" Jakub asks.

"Are you homophobic?" Isak says, the entire room falling silent and still.

Jakub tilts his head, no doubt trying to figure out what he's on about. "No. Why?"

"Then there's no reason my boy Ethan can't kiss his boyfriend in front of you then, right?"

I nearly choke on my tongue, my face heating like a fucking beet as everyone's gazes moves between the three of us.

"Ohhh kay," Ethan says, hobbling back across the room with one shoe on and the other off, though I'm not sure why he's missing a shoe right now. He wraps an arm around Isak. "Calm down, man."

"I'm just saying. You two have been weird and eyeing him since he got here. If he made you uncomfortable—"

"Jesus," I mutter.

"No," Ethan laughs. "We're just conscious that not everyone likes public displays of affection, regardless of the sexes involved."

"We are not opposed to sex involved," Sacha says, Russian accent thick, raising his brows playfully.

"Mmm," Isak says, giving Jakub a sideways glare.

Ethan laughs. "Seriously. It's a courtesy. Not because we're uncomfortable. We appreciate you having our backs, though." He kisses Isak's cheek, the loud *smack* filling the locker room.

Isak glares at him next and pulls away. "Fine."

Ethan meets my eyes, grinning. But I just turn away and continue digging my stuff out my cubby and shoving it into my bag.

I hadn't realized I'd been acting so strangely. I'm feeling very self-conscious as I head to the bus and take a seat. Ethan falls into his next to me shortly after.

His fingers lace with mine and he smiles. We don't talk for the bus ride, but I make it a point to kiss him in front of the team, just so they can see that it has nothing to do with Jakub. Except that it does, and I hate the way my stomach churns.

"Let's order pizza," Ethan says. "Bozik, want to join us?"

My breath catches as I turn to find Jakub walking toward us. With the little row in the locker room, I assume this is going to look like a means to soften any hard feelings.

"I'd love to," Jakub says with exaggeration.

Ethan winks at Isak and we head for the elevators. He keeps me in his grasp until we're upstairs and in our shared room.

As soon as the door is shut, I turn to Jakub. "I'm so sorry for that. Putting you in that position—"

He chuckles, raising his hands. "Not your fault and it's fine. I really appreciate that they support you enough to not only notice but do something about it. That's never been my experience."

"We're close," Ethan says, kissing Jakub on the way to the bathroom. "Told you this was nothing like Vancouver." The door shuts and I'm left in the room with Jakub.

Alone.

He looks at me and I feel like I'm frozen as a freight train barrels at me. I'm pretty sure my eyes get wide.

Jakub chuckles. "You want me to leave?"

"No," I say quickly. "Sorry I'm being weird. I don't really know how to act right now."

He shakes his head. Dropping his bag by the wall, he sits on the edge of the closest bed. "It doesn't have to be weird, Creed. I'm not discounting how you feel, but just so you can hear it from my mouth, I'm completely supportive of you and Ethan."

My breath rushes out of me, and I relax a little. "Thanks. I know that. I trust it, even. But I've lived my entire life believing that being with a married man is wrong."

He chuckles. "Because usually when you hear it being talked about, someone is having an affair. That's not the case here."

I scrub a hand over my face and sigh. "Thanks. Again."

Ethan comes out of the bathroom, and I slip in before anyone else can say something. For a minute, I lean against the door. There aren't any voices in the other room. None that I can hear, anyway. I wash my face, brush my teeth, and then stare at myself in the mirror. It might be time for a haircut. It's hanging in my eyes now. The sides are still short but the top needs some attention.

I'm making this weird. Me. I'm the reason for Isak's confrontation this evening. That means I need to get my shit together. Everyone is on the same page. Just because I don't know how to be in this situation doesn't mean it's wrong. The world makes me feel like it's wrong, but then again, I'm used to feeling that way.

Gay is wrong, after all. My entire family will attest to that.

Scowling at the mirror, I turn and leave the room. Jakub is now in a chair with his phone out while Ethan is sprawled across the opposite bed that Jakub was sitting on. While I think I'd usually crawl on top of Ethan, I'm still far too aware that Jakub is here.

Would I feel this way if someone else were in the room? Our teammates don't mind seeing us together. We're not overly clandestine in front of them. We're affectionate and we sit close. Hold hands. Kiss sometimes. But we're not vulgar or anything.

So, no, I probably wouldn't crawl on top of him. But I would sit with him. Maybe it will feel more natural if I begin by approaching this situation as if Jakub is a friend and not my boyfriend's husband.

"Sausage okay?" Jakub asks, and I pause on my way across the room.

"Sausage?" I ask.

Ethan snorts. "He likes sausage just fine."

I smack his knee, and he grins. "You do. In both ways I'm implying."

Rolling my eyes, I sit next to him before scooching back, so my back is against the headboard. He follows, lounging between my legs. Just as we always would. A minute later, he reaches for the remote and flicks on the television.

"All right. Two pizzas on their way. Sausage on one, cheese on the other. In case either of you need a break from sausage," Jakub says.

Ethan snorts. "Hardly."

I'm not surprised that when Ethan settles on Sports Spot, we're faced with coverage of the recent games. Vancouver won against the Florida Manatees 5-1 yesterday, though Gilpatrick didn't see much ice time. The channel is enjoying showing that game compared to ours today. Apparently, our game play is top-notch, but that's still not enough to pull off a win.

I roll my eyes, resting my chin on Ethan's head. "I'd like to see their asses on the ice," I mutter.

He chuckles. "Don't let it get to you."

"I'm not. I'm just saying. It's so easy to judge someone when you're sitting pretty on the sidelines."

"They're not even on the sidelines," Jakub says as he moves to the bed and sits at the end to face the television. "They're hundreds if not thousands of miles away watching it through a screen."

Ethan nudges him with his foot, making Jakub turn around. He holds his hands out like a child asking to be picked up. Jakub grins but turns his attention to me, as if asking me permission to touch his husband.

I nearly blurt those words, but I just smile and nod.

"You sure you don't mind?" Jakub asks.

"I don't," I say.

Jakub moves up the bed and lays between Ethan's legs, his head on Ethan's stomach. Ethan sighs, one of his hands tangling in Jakub's short hair and the other gripping my wrist. It's so clear to see how incredibly happy he is to have us both here right now. Seeing his happiness helps me relax further. I kiss the side of his head and catch his smile widening.

"You happy?" I ask.

"So fucking happy," he says. A minute later, he shifts to look up at me. "Are you?"

I brush my finger across his cheek. "Yeah."

"It's not too much for you?"

I shrug. "No." Tracing his lip, I add, "I love to see this smile on your face."

He gently bites my finger. "Good, but I'm asking how you're feeling. We all know that this is what's going to make me happiest, but only if we're all happy, too."

"You know how I am in new situations," I say, leaning down to kiss his forehead. I let my lips linger for a minute, though I'm never *not* aware that Jakub is there. "This is brand new territory for me, so it's just going to take me some time to get comfortable."

"I get that, but you know, it's new for all three of us. Neither of us have, essentially, brought home our boyfriends before," he says. "You know that, right?"

I nod.

"We're always completely open and honest about who we're seeing or sleeping with. We know their names and the situation. But this is very different. You're different. Everything about how I feel about you is different."

The way he makes my heart race will never get old. The knock at the door has Jakub getting up from the bed and Ethan twists in my arms. He cups my face, staring into my eyes. "I love you," he whispers. "You're every beat of my heart. I've known that from the beginning. Even if I wasn't willing to admit it to myself at the time, we all know that's why I introduced you to Jakub early on. I was letting you two get used to each other. Because my endgame doesn't just have my husband by my side; it has you, too."

"You're a fucking romantic, aren't you?" I mutter, pressing soft kisses to his face. He grins as I continue to press my lips to his skin, over and over again. "I love you too. And I'm glad you gave me three years to get used to this idea. I'm pretty sure I'd have freaked out if you suddenly threw in my lap that you were married."

"And that's why I'm concerned about telling the team," he says, sighing as he sinks into me. "They're going to be furious."

"They're going to understand," Jakub says as he comes back into the room with two boxes of pizza. "Especially when we explain why we kept it private for all this time. And even if they're upset about it, they have your backs. Nothing you throw at them will change that."

EIGHTEEN

JAKUB

Two days later, we win the game against Calgary. I'm fucking relieved because as much as the world is seeing that Buffalo's starting line is on point now, it means nothing if we're not winning games.

I take a sip of my drink and lean back against the bar as I watch Ethan and Creed play pool. We're at a bar in Calgary, celebrating our win and they're playing pool against Caulder and Asael. Creed steps up behind Ethan, running his hand down Ethan's spine, making Ethan grin like it's his birthday.

A smile tugs at my lips, and I pull my phone out to sneak a picture of them. It's cute, so I text it to Ethan before sticking my phone back in my pocket. Shepey sits down beside me, glancing at my phone as I shove it away.

"You texting a secret wife, mate?" he asks, smirking as he waves down the bartender.

"Something like that," I say, looking back at the pool table. Sacha and Astor sit on my other side and Sacha elbows me.

"Look. Pretty lady wants to take you home," he grins, winking at me as I follow his gaze.

Pretty enough, sure, but I definitely don't swing that way anymore. So I give Sacha a wave, telling him that he can totally go for it if he's interested.

My gaze finds my husband as Creed wraps his arms around him.

Ethan's grinning as they rock slightly. Creed meets my eyes briefly and flashes me a smile. I take another sip.

"They've been pining over each other for three years," Shepey says. I glance at him to find that he's watching Ethan and Creed too. "If you're into dick, I suggest looking elsewhere."

Before I can say something, my attention is snagged by Isak, Phalyn, Lucien, and Lucas moving toward a small group of scowling men who are watching the pool table. It doesn't take me long as I witness the confrontation to know what I'm seeing.

"Do you run into that a lot?" I ask, nodding in their direction.

Shepey glances at them and shrugs. "More than you might think. But we don't let them know that. There's no reason they should feel the hate because of who they love."

"You protect them," I say, surprised, as our four teammates escort the two assholes out.

"We do," Astor says. "It's the only time PR doesn't hate it when we get shoved into the spotlight for being rowdy. There's no room in hockey for bigots."

"I'm not sure the entire league feels the same way," I say, glancing back at Ethan and Creed again. Creed is taking a shot so they're not touching, but Ethan is leaning on his pool stick as he talks to Asael and watches.

"Enough do, but I'm not sure they handle it like we do," Shepey says. "We don't keep it from them to keep them in the dark and pretend they live in a rosy world. They have enough pressure on them."

"We all do," Sacha says.

"We do, but being gay in the spotlight of a decidedly masculine *straight* industry is enough of a hurdle for them to navigate without the added judgment from assholes," Shepey says. "So, yeah. I don't think they're aware that we remove the hostility before it makes it to them as often as possible."

I can honestly say they do not. At least, Ethan doesn't. I smile knowing this. Knowing that someone is here protecting him when I haven't been. He's a strong man. He's proud of who he is. But being hit with little stones over and over eventually hurts.

"Look," Sacha says, nodding toward the dance floor. It takes me a few minutes to figure out what he's looking at. With his phone out, he has an account up, and sure enough, there's a man on the dance floor who is also dancing on his phone. "This is Shooting Star. From Viraly."

"Shooting Star," I say, leaning over to look at his screen. Because I know that name. I laugh when I see that he's following a gay twink. I grin at him.

"What? I support the creators," he says. "I am sure that those are the twins. Uh… blond official or something."

"How many gay accounts do you follow?" Shepey asks, leaning forward to look at him from around me.

Sacha shrugs. "I am safe place. I support all creators. I follow many thousand accounts."

Astor laughs. "They're with a couple more. Do you recognize them too?"

It takes Sacha a couple minutes, but he finds their accounts. One he's following, who he tells us is a twink called Psyche.01 who has recently come onto the scene. He has a sweet, cute face, but he needs a bit of a haircut. The last, it takes him a while to find, but eventually he does, naming him Noble Bold. He followed him once he found him.

"It's cute that you think you're not a touch into cock," Astor says, eyeing Sacha.

"I am comfortable with my sexuality to follow gay men. I follow Ethan and Creed and other queer hockey men," he says, shrugging. "Look," he says, pointing to the dance floor and I find myself grinning when three of the five of the online creators are dancing with Ethan and Creed. Sacha grins hugely. "See! It is cute."

We watch them for a while, and I find that I'm smiling. It's not hard to do when I see that smile on Ethan's face. He's talking to the creators, and I don't miss when they pose for pictures and candids are taken too. How many videos are they going to end up in by morning?

I chuckle as I take another sip. While they're happily occupied, I study the rest of my teammates. Caulder is still at the pool table with Asael, now joined by a couple of giggling women. Caulder inches away from one standing too close, but Asael is all about getting a little personal. Isak and Lucien are sitting at the table where the assholes had been. I'm not sure where Phalyn and Lucas disappeared to.

"This really is nothing like Vancouver," I murmur to myself.

Shepey looks at me. "We're really not far from Vancouver. It's not that different. Colder. More snow, but still Canadian."

I laugh, shaking my head. "Not what I meant."

"They are not friends?" Sacha asks, having caught my meaning.

Shrugging, I say, "It's probably partially my fault, but no, not really. I wonder if they'd have the same courtesy to protect a queer player that you do. This feels rather judgmental of me, but I can't see them doing the same."

"They are not good teammates, then," Sacha says.

"It's called being a decent human being," Astor says. "You don't have to agree with the way someone lives, but you do have to respect them. If you can't, just leave them the fuck alone."

I nod. "But we're public figures," I say, quoting the articles that used to bother me and Ethan way back in the day. "We're supposed to be setting an example for the young. Give them someone to look up to and be a role model. Instead, we're flaunting gayness."

Silence follows my words and I realize that maybe I might have just hinted about my sexuality when the three of them look at me. Or they're trying to determine whether to take me seriously or not.

"Gaga said it best; we were born this way," Astor says, shrugging. "I was born liking vajayjays. They were born terrified of them."

Sacha bursts out laughing. "No, but are they afraid of lady bits?"

"It's not something I've asked, but we totally can if you want to," Astor says. "I'm just saying. It's not like deciding what to wear today. They just are who they are. It baffles me that someone would think that it's a choice they make to be ridiculed and harassed. Told they're going to hell. That they're not normal. Like, who would fucking choose that shit?"

I smile at him, deciding that I really like Astor. How offended he gets on someone else's behalf is just... peaceful.

"They're good people. Most of the gays I've met are better people than so many of the straight people. That really says something," Shepey says.

I nod absently as I watch my man dance with his boyfriend. They're cuddled together now, dancing slowly among the rapidly moving bodies around them. I see Ethan's mouth moving, so I think they're talking. It's just a sweet moment that I try to commit to memory. It would be too weird to take their picture now, right? Now that I have everyone watching me?

WE'RE NOT LEAVING UNTIL MIDDAY TOMORROW, SINCE OUR NEXT game is not until the following day in Vancouver. So I booked a hotel room down the street from where the team is staying. My roommate will think I've snuck off with a hookup and will think that Ethan is in his room with Creed. But I slipped Ethan the room key earlier.

I've barely changed out of my suit when the door opens. I turn to find my husband beaming at me. He shuts the door before walking into my chest, wrapping his arms around my waist.

"Good game today," he says.

"We did have a good game. And you're going to be all over the internet as a thirst trap with a whole bunch of ReachMe creators."

He laughs. "Yep. Remember, all attention is good attention."

"I'm thinking that the PR guy will take that back when he sees you're tagged with a bunch of self-made porn stars."

He laughs again and steps back. "Creed will be horrified."

"He okay alone tonight?" I ask.

"Yeah. I tried to convince him to come too, but he's going to hang with Caulder for a while."

"In that case." I push his jacket off and toss it on the back of the chair where mine is. Slowly unbuttoning his shirt buttons, I let my fingers skim his smooth flesh.

The serene yet aroused look on his face is so beautiful. I can't help watching his expression as much as I am the rest of his perfect body. When he's completely naked, I shove off the rest of my clothes and pull him against me once more.

"Love you," I tell him quietly.

"No Czech tonight, huh?" he asks.

Covering his mouth with mine, I kiss him until he's breathless. "Later." Picking him up, I lay him on the bed and crawl over him.

Already I have condoms and lube out, but for now, I just lay my naked body over his, content to feel his heated skin against mine.

Ethan sighs, his fingers tracing over my back as I lavish kisses along his neck and collarbone. "Your teammates really look out for you," I tell him.

"Mmm," he answers. "They're your teammates now too."

"Yes. And I apparently watch you an exaggerated amount. I've been told if I'm interested in dick, I should look elsewhere since you're happily committed."

He laughs. "Oh, fuck."

While I have every intention of ravishing my husband tonight, we lay quietly together for quite some time. His fingers continue to move over my shoulders as I listen to his heart under my ear. It's been so long since we've just laid like this.

Would it be too corny to tell him how much he completes me? How much I'm looking forward to these lazy moments where we don't have to be anywhere but can just enjoy each other's company.

"I hope Creed will be comfortable with us eventually," he says quietly. "It feels like I'm in some kind of limbo right now because he feels awkward when you're around. As much as I love that you're here, I think he would have benefited from us having time just the two of us to get his bearings before you were here full time. Not that I want to change this. I was so fucking excited that you were traded." He pauses. "And a little horrified."

I chuckle, turning my face to his chest again. "I know. The fucking emotions that went through me when I got the call, man. I thought I was going to have a heart attack the way my heart was racing. These last couple of months have been hard, and all I've wanted is to begin my life with you. I've never experienced that longing before, and it was difficult to get through each day when you were so far away. So I was beyond thrilled. But I was also aware of... everything else."

"I know. Then there's the guilt for thinking of all the weird and heavy shit that comes with you moving here. Because I should just be happy and let the rest of it happen as it will."

"It's more complicated than that," I say. "You don't have to feel guilty, Ethan. Believe me, I'm very aware of all the storm clouds hanging over our heads, waiting to bust a leak before drowning us."

"That's dooming," he mutters.

"Maybe. But storms pass. It's going to be rocky when we finally tell everyone, and when the world knows, but there are beautiful skies that follow."

He chuckles. "You're so corny. I love it. Before I pass out, and it's fucking coming, I need you to fuck me," he says, as if this is just the next checkpoint on the agenda that our conversation was moving through.

Laughing, I pull off him and look at him spread under me. "You're feeling needy."

"No one touches my ass," he says, eyelids drooping. "So yeah, I'm feeling needy. I need to be fucked."

"Then turn over. Get on your hands and knees. Let me see your neglected hole."

Ethan scrambles to his hands and knees, moving quickly until his ass is presented to me. I reach for the supplies, bringing them closer as I rub his cheek. "Whose ass is this?" I murmur.

"Yours," he says, shifting his hands forward. "Always yours. Only yours."

"You want to feel my dick?"

He groans. "Hit my throat through my ass, manžel."

I grin because his pronunciation is atrocious. But I fucking love when he talks in his heavily American accented Czech. Because I know he does it for me.

After slicking up my fingers, I massage his hole slowly, listening to him whine. Only when his whine turns into a growl of frustration, do I push my finger inside and slowly fuck him with it. Just one finger. Again, I wait until he gets annoyed with me before I add a second, but I reward him by pressing against his prostate until he jumps forward, hitting his head against the headboard with a loud *thud*.

He laughs, his face falling into the pillow.

"Give me your hands," I tell him.

Ethan shifts his legs wider apart to keep his ass up before he reaches his arms behind himself for me. I gather them both at his back while I use my other hand and my teeth to open the condom and slide it on. Once I'm properly lubed up, I grip his wrists tightly and line my cock up, holding it at the base.

"Ready?"

"I've been ready," he says.

The moment my cockhead pushes through that first ring of muscle, I groan and lean forward. With one of his hands in each of mine, I pin them to the bed beside him as I ease inside.

"You feel like a goddamn furnace," I say.

"You feel like a fucking butternut squash," he grunts in return.

I laugh as I continue to press into him. Slowly. Inch by inch. Until I'm completely sheathed within his hot body. His muscles contract around me, making me nearly roll my eyes in pleasure. Fuck, he feels good.

Bearing my weight down until he collapses under me, I press kisses to the back of his shoulders and neck. Linking our hands together as I work my way out before sliding back inside. His heavy breathing fills my head. The quiet grunts and gasps shiver through me. How his fingers tighten around mine.

"Whose ass is this?" I ask again.

Ethan groans. "Yours, Jakub."

"One day, we'll have Creed underneath you. Your cock buried in him while I fuck you like this." The whimper that fills the room along with his shivers makes me grin. "You like that? You want that?"

"So much," he whines.

"Someday, lásko. For now, you just get me."

"That's okay," he says, breathlessly. "I love you. Make love to me until I fall asleep."

I kiss his neck, sucking on the shell of his ear until he moans, and I do just as he requested.

NINETEEN
JAKUB

THE WHIR OF THE HAND MIXER MAKES ME LOOK UP FROM WHERE I'm seated at the kitchen nook. Creed is on the counter, watching Ethan mix the frosting for the cookies that are cooling as another batch bakes in the oven. I forgot how much he enjoys baking. It's one of the things we used to do together in the AHL when we first met. Hell, I'm surprised we weren't both filled with sugar and sluggish more often than not.

I glance back down at my phone as I scroll through the ShareIt app at all the images, getting sidetracked occasionally with a reel or two. My scrolling pauses when a video catches my attention and I smirk at the faces dancing.

Noble Bold: @Ethan.Wilder18; @The_real.Credence; @blondtwins_official; @ShootingStar; @Psyche.01 *Dancing like a rockstar with these super hot hockey players from @BuffaloSkidmoss. Who's a new hockey fan?*

There's over 100,000 likes and 153 comments. I scroll through them and smirk at all the fire emojis, the kisses, the comments of 'I'm definitely a hockey fan now.' I don't pay much attention to social media, but I click on Ethan's name to take a look at his page, wondering how many followers he had before the trip to the club in Calgary. He's up to 800k now.

The mixer turns off and I glance up as Ethan dips his finger in and moves to Creed, offering a taste. I witness a cute, sweet moment pass silently between them before Creed groans. "Damn, that's fucking good."

Ethan grins. "It's my great grandmother's recipe. I've made it so many times, I think I could make it in my sleep."

He moves away when the timer for the oven goes off. With an oven mitt that looks like one of those big foam fingers, he pulls out the tray of cookies and replaces it with another, setting the hot one on top of the stove to cool. After closing the oven door, he resets the timer and tosses the oven mitt onto the counter.

"Did she teach you to bake?" Creed asks as Ethan moves his bowl of frosting to the already cooled cookies and begins frosting them with very generous dollops.

"Nah," he says. "She was already deep into dementia when I was born. But I grew up hearing stories about her so often, it was like she was there. I think I was slightly obsessed with her life, so I was always asking to bake her recipes." He looks at Creed over his shoulder. "She was one of the first women to own a brick-and-mortar business in Virginia. Unsurprisingly, it was a bakery."

Creed grins. When Ethan's done with the first cooled batch of cookies, he brings one to Creed and places it in his mouth. I swear, Creed has a mini orgasm judging by the sound that escapes and the way his eyes roll as he chews.

Ethan grins and swipes another cookie, coming over to me. Like he did with Creed, he places it in my mouth. Before he can pull his hand away, I catch his wrist and bring his finger back to my mouth, encasing it and licking off the excess frosting.

He bends down to kiss me, whispering, "Love you."

I smile back, watching him return to the kitchen. Creed snaps a few pictures and turns his attention to his phone. "I talked to my mom the other day."

"Yeah?" Ethan says. "She okay?"

Creed nods. I look back down at my phone as I continue to scroll, though I listen to what they're talking about. While I could certainly give them their moment alone to bond, I really want to facilitate comfort in my presence with Creed. Especially since Ethan convinced him to spend the night tonight. It'll be the first time since I was traded.

"Yep. Apparently, one of my cousins has been kicked out of his home. They found out he has a ReachMe account."

Ethan pauses, taking the cookies off the cooling tray, and looks at him. "So?"

Creed glances at him, raising a brow. "Given the little that I've told you about my family, you think that was going to be considered an appropriate career?"

Ethan rolls his eyes, turning back to the cookies. Creed looks at me and says, "Outside of my parents, my entire family disowned me at sixteen when I came out. Having a ReachMe account is obviously sending my cousin to Hell alongside me."

"This is going to sound a little awkward, but what's his account? I'll follow him and boost his income," I say.

Creed nods, shrugging. "I don't know. I haven't talked to him since I was sixteen. He was ten."

"See if you can get it," Ethan says. "I'm sure we can get the entire team to support him."

Creed smiles and turns to his phone. "That would be awesome." He pauses for a minute as he types. "You know, this is going to sound arrogant... But concerning this, I don't care: I fucking love that I have made it big. One year of my salary is more money than every single person in my family will bring in during the same year—combined. After all the nasty things they said to me, how they made me feel, it's really one of the best feelings. When they look up my name, I'm going to be remembered. Not a single one of them will be."

Ethan stops what he's doing and looks at Creed. "That's not arrogant. That's finding closure to the hurt they've caused in your own way. You're entitled to feel that way. I think to some extent, when a person reaches a certain level of accomplishment, they can't help but look back, feeling smug toward all those people who were shit to them growing up."

Creed smiles at him, nodding. His shoulders relax slightly, and I realize that he thought he was going to be made to feel bad over that. Personally, I think Ethan's right. It might be the wrong reason to do something but when someone tells you that you'll never make it in something you pursue, that you'll fail at what you're passionate about, or you're not good enough to *be* someone—I always say to use that as motivation to prove them wrong.

Like it or not, it's human nature to feel good about what you've accomplished. To be proud. And there's little better motivation than the promise that one day, you can shove it in their face that you didn't crumble under their bullying and cruelty.

It's made sweeter when you find that they're the ones who turned out miserable. Karma.

The only noise in the kitchen is Ethan manning his cookies for a while. Eventually, Creed announces that he's sending us both the link.

I immediately click on it and begin the process of proving my age and then signing up to follow his account. The account name is Surfing Chaos. Out of curiosity, I click the first video in the set, the most recent, making sure the sound is off. My mouth drops slightly when I see the fat dildo he shoves up his ass as soon as the camera rolls. Even though I have the sound off, I can nearly hear his shout.

After perusing a couple more, I look up at Creed. "The only thing they pushed him out for was this account?" I ask.

Creed looks at me, shrugging. "Yeah. That's what mom said. Why? Do I want to know?"

"Is he gay?"

Creed's eyes widen slightly. "I don't think so, but as I said, I haven't even seen him for the last eight years."

I nod.

"What did you find?" Ethan asks.

"Well, without oversharing for family purposes." Creed grins at me. "While this is a solo account right now, I don't think it's going to stay that way, given what your cousin is into. I'd be willing to predict that *if* he starts out with a female partner, he's going to eventually find that a man is more to his liking."

Creed stares at me before bursting out laughing. "Oh, no."

The doorbell rings and I get to my feet, checking the time. We have Chinese food being delivered, but it looks like they're ten minutes early. I head to the door, listening to Creed and Ethan continue to talk about Creed's cousin.

Without thinking anything of it, I pull the door open and come face to face with Caulder. He looks at me, eyes widening, and takes a step back. He looks at the number on the door and then around the hall as if to make sure he has the correct apartment. Then he looks at me, his eyes scanning down my body.

I look down and realize immediately how this is going to look since I'm only wearing gym shorts. Only. And it's very obvious there's nothing on under them.

"What the fuck are you doing here?" he hisses.

It's not often that I'm rendered speechless, but I just stare at him, trying to think of anything to say at all. But the only thing I can think is, *oh fuck*.

"What are you doing here?" I ask instead and wince when I see the way his face contorts into fury.

"Are you fucking kidding me right now? You know Ethan's with Creed. What the actual fuck, man?!"

As if this situation couldn't get any worse, Ethan's voice calls out, "Need help with the bags, love?"

Caulder glares beyond me, and before I can stop him, he pushes his way into the apartment and past me. I go to follow him but see the delivery guy down the hall. Fuck's sake.

It takes far too long for him to reach me, and I quickly take the bags from him before kicking the door shut and rushing after Caulder.

The kitchen has been frozen. Ethan is standing between the stove and the island, his eyes wide with barely concealed panic. Creed is now on the floor, partially blocking Ethan, as if to protect him.

It's incredibly clear that Caulder simply doesn't know what to think.

I set the bags on the table and move around the far side of the kitchen island until I can wrap my arms around Ethan. His heart is beating wildly. His entire body is tense, and he's breathing rapidly.

"It's not what it looks like," Creed says after a minute.

"I'm not even sure what it looks like right now," Caulder says, frowning.

Creed grabs a cookie and shoves it into Caulder's mouth. "Eat this and go take your boots off. You're getting the floor wet."

Caulder chews on the cookie as he turns away. For a beat, no one else moves, but then Creed heads for the pantry and grabs the wet mop to clean up the puddles. By the time he's done and standing with me and Ethan, Caulder comes back into the room.

"That cookie has drugs in it, doesn't it?" he asks, eyes narrowed.

Creed laughs. "I think so and I even watched them being made." He pauses. "Why are you here?"

"Because I wanted to play a video game and you weren't answering your damn phone."

Creed looks at his phone and scowls. "Sorry. Was... I have a porn account I need you to subscribe to. Is now a good time to distract you with that?"

Caulder's expression is almost comical as his eyes move between Creed and us. "No."

Sighing, Creed looks back at me. I nod, giving him permission to tell our truth. Looking back at Caulder, he says, "He's not having an affair. They're married."

"What the fuck? When have you even—"

"They've been married for seven years," Creed says over Caulder's incredulity. That's enough to render him speechless once more.

The timer goes off and I kiss Ethan's forehead and let him go. I pull out the last batch of cookies and set them on the stove before turning the oven off. Then I move back behind Ethan and wrap him up. He takes a breath, avoiding Caulder's gaze, but when Creed reaches for his hand, Ethan releases a heavy breath and finally looks up.

"Guess you'll be the first to know," he says quietly. "Want to eat with us? I think we bought enough for the entire team."

Caulder glances at the bags before shrugging. "All right."

It's another minute before we're gathered around the small table in the kitchen with a plethora of takeout containers spread between us. We pile our plates, but no one takes a bite as we wait.

"So, Jakub and I met in the AHL, which I think everyone's aware of." Caulder nods. "We..." He looks at Creed and gives him a small smile. "I guess it's a story much like Creed and me. We fell in love as soon as we met. Everyone knows I was drafted into the pros as an out athlete. Jakub didn't. It became increasingly obvious that life was going to be a little more challenging for me as such, so we made the decision to keep our relationship a secret for as long as possible. We married in secret. And we maintained our marriage as a secret for the past seven years."

"How?" Caulder asks, shaking his head. He laughs. "Fuck, nothing is private. How did you manage that?"

"Luck," I say. "And never giving anyone a reason to look at us together. Or me at all."

"And you're okay with Ethan and Creed together?" Caulder asks, looking incredulous again.

"We've had an open relationship since we met," I say. "Even before we got married. Sometimes we shared lovers but usually we just... did our thing solo. I knew about Creed right away. I met Creed within a couple months of him coming to Buffalo."

"Our relationship works because we're almost embarrassingly honest with each other," Ethan says. "So yeah, he knew about Creed, how I felt about Creed, and he's given us his complete support since the beginning."

There's a moment of silence as Caulder looks between me and Ethan. Then his attention turns to Creed, but it seems we've still rendered him silent. Finally, he says, "You realize that there's going to be shit going down when this comes out, right?"

Ethan sighs, dropping his face in his hands. "I didn't tell the team for legit reasons, Caulder. I trust you all." He looks up. "Really, I do. But it's so easy to let it slip. To be accidentally overheard. We couldn't afford that. It was selfish self-preservation."

"It wasn't selfish," Caulder says, frowning. "As much as I'm annoyed and shocked, I get it. The press will have a fucking field day with this."

Creed sighs and picks up a spring roll.

"The other reason I haven't said anything yet is because Creed and I had *just* gotten together when they traded for Jakub. We'd all been counting on a few months for Creed and I to... I don't know, get established? Let them get used to each other and this relationship while they weren't constantly together," Ethan says. He looks at Creed. "It's a strange situation that comes with a lot of factors and stressors. We wanted to navigate that in private as much as we could before letting the world know about this. Before we had the team up in our business."

Caulder nods. He takes a slow bite of his food before he says,

"Thanks for trusting me and I'm sorry I didn't give you a choice by showing up unannounced. I'll help you run interference wherever I can."

"Thanks," Creed says, grinning at him.

"I suggest you get away during break, though. I doubt I'll be the only one who drops in." After another bite, he snorts. "Isak is going to feel like an idiot when you tell him."

Ethan grins, but I can see that he's still feeling the stress of the conversation. So I change the subject. "Want to talk about the porn channel now?"

Caulder chokes on his noodles before looking up. He looks at Creed. "You were serious about that?"

Creed laughs. "Yep."

We spend the rest of the meal talking about Creed's cousin. After a while, Ethan relaxes. We finish frosting the cookies and head into the living room to play video games. Ethan being unusually quiet isn't missed by anyone, but we let him remain that way for now.

We knew that telling the team was going to be hard for him. I'm just not sure how to take that pressure off his shoulders.

TWENTY
CREDENCE

WE PLAY UNTIL NEAR MIDNIGHT WHEN ETHAN YAWNS. HE SHIFTS to look around me and gives Caulder a pointed look. "You're keeping me awake now, Haines."

Caulder laughs. He tosses the remote on the far end of the couch and stretches. "Fine. Fine. I'll go watch some cousin porn or something."

"Ugh," I say, glowering at him.

Caulder grins as he gets to his feet. He pauses on his way to the entry and turns back. "I'm sorry for busting in like that earlier. In my defense, I'd been texting Creed for like two hours and he wasn't answering. I was bored."

Ethan shrugs, nodding. "You're not going to say anything?"

"No. This is your business, and I won't tell you what to do, but you should tell the team. We can't have your back if we don't know what we're up against."

I nod, leaning back against Ethan's side. We wait until the door closes a few minutes later before speaking.

"He's right," I say. "I already know what's going to happen if the tabloids find this before we tell the team. They're going to defend us to the point they get themselves into trouble and then we're going to be forced to tell them the truth, flustered and frustrated, and it's going to come out a mess."

Ethan groans. "You're not wrong, but I think it's going to be worse than that. They're going to ream us new assholes, too. It's just... I've kept this hidden for so long, from some of my closest friends. I don't want to see the hurt on their faces. Like I betrayed them. Like I didn't trust them enough with something personal in my life. I don't want to be the cause of that hurt. Every one of them has had my back against some asshole who thought they had the right to spew their hate at me. And I didn't trust them with my entire truth."

Jakub kisses his head and hums quietly. "We'll talk about it tomorrow when we're fresh," he says. "Go to bed. I'm going to watch Sports Spot for a while so I can get the sound of shooting guns out of my head."

Ethan snorts. "We didn't have to play that game."

Jakub shrugs and urges him to his feet. Ethan takes my hand, pulling me up too. He looks back at Jakub with a smile and then pulls me to the bedroom, leaving the door wide open.

Wide open with the bed in clear view of where Jakub is sitting on the couch.

I give the living room my back as Jakub turns the light out so we're all plunged into the dark with the only light coming from the flickering television and the moon outside. Pulling Ethan to me, I kiss him. He tastes like frosting and sunshine.

His fingers slide under my shirt, along my skin, making my muscles dance under his touch. While it begins slowly, it doesn't take us long to hastily get rid of the clothing and then fall onto the bed. I try to roll us away from the view of the door, but Ethan keeps us on that side of the bed.

I'm not sure if he's doing it so Jakub has a clear view or because this is the side of the bed we're always on. I try not to think about it as his fingers trace over my cock.

"How do you want me tonight?" he asks against my neck. I close my eyes and decide that I'm going to completely ignore the fact that his husband is here. It's just us. Like it always has been.

Just us.

Swallowing, I gently push him off me until we've switched places and I'm moving my naked ass down the bed. It's just us, but I know that the way I'm on my knees with my legs spread wide has my ass well on display.

Nope. It's just us. No one can see my ass because no one is here.

Kissing down Ethan's body, I lick along his dick. "Lube," I say quietly.

He nods. I can feel it in his entire body. Ethan shifts, stretching to reach into the drawer. A pile of condoms and two different lube bottles land next to his hip. I chuckle and grab one of them.

Coating my fingers, I concentrate back on his cock, licking him and teasing him while I reach behind me. My cheeks flush, knowing that I might as well be making my own porn video right now as I slip my finger into my tight hole. At the perfect angle for Jakub to see.

If he were there. Watching.

Which he's not. Because we're alone.

I take Ethan into my mouth, sucking on him hard as I work myself open for his dick. Pretending that no one can see us. Imagining that I'm not getting even more turned on by the idea that *someone might be watching*.

When I can't take any more of Ethan's porn sounds and my entire body is tingling, I quickly cover his cock with a condom and then more lube than necessary—enough that we're going to be a slippery, sticky mess after—and then climb back up his body.

I waste no time sliding down his cock, gripping his hands in mine. With our fingers locked, I bear down, staring at his face. His expression twists to pleasure and his entire body contorts from the pressure I'm squeezing around his dick as I bring him into my body.

"Creed," he moans, his hips bucking up into me with no rhythm at all.

My mouth remains open as I try to clear my airway so I can catch my breath. With our hands still locked together, I use that leverage to lean back and ride him.

No one is watching. No one is here.

But I can feel his eyes on me and it makes this even hotter. God, yes. Fuck, yes. There's no cadence to how we're fucking at all. We're not keeping pace or creating a pattern. But every one of his thrusts, every downward bounce I make, my entire body heats by ten degrees of pleasure. I'm fucking dizzy by the time I let go of one of his hands to quickly jerk myself.

Ethan comes as soon as I do. Probably because I clench around his dick so hard he shouts, his body convulsing as he grips me to him. I still have one hand linked with his, but the other is rubbing my dick until I'm empty. Ethan's second hand is on my hip, keeping me in place as he fucks me until he's dry.

Or wet since I'm sure he's filled that condom.

For a minute, when we're both spent, we just stare at each other with what are probably similar expressions. Mouths open as we pant, staring into each other's eyes. The intensity of those orgasms still shivering through us.

I bend down and kiss him slowly.

"Love you," he whispers.

"I love you too," I tell him and gently pull his cock from my body. After another few breaths, I pull the condom off and slide from the bed. On legs made of gelatin, I head for the bathroom to get rid of it and grab a towel to clean us.

"That was so good," he murmurs as I wipe him down. His fingers keep splaying over my bare skin. His eyes never leave me. Goddamn, I love this man.

I drop the towel on the floor and climb back into bed. Facing each other, I'm beginning to fall asleep when the bed dips. Ethan hums but when he suddenly inhales, I open my eyes in time to see that his back is arched as he stares at me with arousal quickly covering his face again.

He groans. "I'm not twenty anymore," he grunts, his hips jerking slightly, making him gasp.

My heart races as I watch. Frozen. Unable to move. Ethan's hand shoots out, gripping mine again. He moans and writhes, his eyes rolling back. I know what Jakub is doing. He's recreating the show I gave him, but with Ethan's fine ass.

I swallow as I hear the condom wrapper. Blood rushes in my ears and I watch as the next minute feels like it happens in slow motion. Jakub pulls Ethan's leg up, so it's hooked at my hip, his hand under his knee to keep him there.

Then he's pushing inside.

The sounds that Ethan makes have my cock hardening painfully. As he said, I'm not twenty anymore. Yet my body can't help it when I see the lust and desire surge through Ethan right before my eyes. He's less than a foot away. His hands—both of them now—grip me so fucking tightly I think he's going to leave bruises.

I bear witness to something so incredible, so beautiful and filled with pleasure, that I feel like I shouldn't be here. This isn't something I should be witnessing. It's a private moment between husbands.

But I can't look away from Ethan's face. I can't stop hearing the sounds he makes or how Jakub speaks to him with such demand, but with praise so sweet, I'm fucking melting.

I've never seen someone so filled with pleasure that they're almost glowing.

It makes me feel... inadequate.

A war brews inside me while Jakub pleases Ethan. His orgasm is loud as he covers me in cum. He shakes and whines low. A sound that grips my balls until I'm spilling with him.

I'm still panting and breathless when Jakub is suddenly there, moving us apart so he can clean up the mess. My cheeks are red. Fuck, my entire body is blushing. When he's done, he pushes us back together and Ethan presses his face to my chest, sighing. He's already asleep, his body relaxing completely.

Jakub wraps around his back, and the room is silent. Still. Except for our labored breathing, there isn't a sound.

For a long time, I lay like that. Trying to silence the troubled thoughts that keep shouting at me that I'm getting between a married couple. I don't belong here. I add nothing to this relationship at all.

When my head starts pounding with a headache, I decide that I just can't stay here anymore. Slowly, so fucking slowly, I pull out from Ethan's arms and slip from the bed. I stand still for a minute, just looking at him.

I've never loved someone like I do Ethan Wilder. And I never will again.

But I just don't think I can be a part of this. As much as I want to, I can't live up to the relationship that they already share. They deserve to give each other everything; their full attention and love.

I'm just getting in the way.

As silently as I can, I find my clothing and gather them into my arms before heading for the door. It's still wide open to the living room and my cheeks flush again, knowing that Jakub was there. He might have been watching.

I step into the hall and glance back at them together. They're perfect. Beautiful. Without me as a third wheel, the world won't attack them quite as hard, right?

Turning away, I try to force air into my lungs and keep myself upright when all I want to do is keel over and cry. I was stupid to think that I could do this. That I'd be offering anything valuable to their lives when they're already gods.

"Credence."

I pause, holding my breath, clutching my pile of clothes to my chest. When I turn, Jakub is coming out of the bedroom. Butt. Ass. Naked.

Jesus motherfucking shit he is gorgeous.

He stops a couple feet away and stares at me. The only light is the moon shining in through the window across the room, so we're thrown in shadows. Hopefully, he can't see the distress in... every single inch of me!

We stand in silence for several seconds. Maybe minutes pass. It could also be years.

I'm surprised when he offers me his hand. I stare, blinking, before I meet his eyes. Not sure what I'm doing, I take a step closer and place my hand in his. Then I look at our hands together, how his long fingers close over mine. I swallow.

And jump when the fingers of his other hand gently grip my chin and guide my gaze back to his.

"Why are you leaving?" he asks quietly.

Quiet panic starts to shiver through me, and I glance beyond him to the dark bedroom where Ethan is asleep. I feel sick. Fuck, why am I leaving him right now?!

"Because I..." Words don't come to me. I can't manage to put into words what I'm feeling. How out of place I feel. Seeing them together... it just... made me feel like I didn't belong there. Like I was interfering in their lives. Stepping in where I don't belong.

"You're a part of this, Creed," he says quietly. "You're a part of our relationship. A wanted part. A vital piece." His finger brushes over my lip and I fucking tremble. What is happening right now? "If you don't want to be here, then you can go, and I won't stop you.

But if you're leaving for any other reason, I think we need to talk about that."

My eyes drop and I end up staring at his chest. Licking my lips, I close my eyes. "Maybe it's self-preservation?" I whisper. "I just keep thinking that you two have something amazing together and I'm... meddling."

His grip on me tightens as he brings my gaze to his once more. I force my eyes open and look into his gorgeous light ones. I swear, with nothing but moonlight illuminating either of us, his eyes glow in the dark.

He's ethereal. Angelic.

"I'm not sure how many more ways there are for me to say it," he says. "You were always going to be with us, Credence. Your fear and anxiety are keeping you from looking beyond this moment, but we can see it clearly. You were always meant to be ours. If hockey hadn't brought us together, something else would have. We're inevitable. If you need to slow down, we can do that. But don't let your fear make you run away from this. Especially when we all know how much you want to be here, too."

I swallow again and nod. "I want to be here," I whisper. "Everything feels so... big. Difficult. I'm exhausted and afraid that... I'm just not going to be worth it in the end."

Again, Jakub surprises me when he pulls me into his chest and hugs me. "You're already worth it," he says quietly, his fingers running through my hair. "No outside force gets to dictate our lives, Creed. Their opinions just don't matter. Yes, it's probably going to be a whole lot of fucked up for a while, but eventually, we'll be old news and the assholes behind cameras and shit-stirrers who just want hits will eventually find something else to word vomit about. The only thing we need to concentrate on and give any shred of our attention to is each other. This relationship." His fingers grip my chin again and turn my face toward his. Our mouths are so fucking close, my heart races. "That's it. Just this."

I nod, a subtle bob of my head. He mimics me.

"Come back to bed?"

I nod again. My tongue seems to have become glued to the roof of my mouth. His hand drops to mine, our fingers lacing together, and I have another fear that maybe Ethan isn't going to be happy if something happens between me and Jakub!

"Stop overthinking," Jakub whispers when we step into the bedroom. He kisses my temple and urges me toward the bed.

Dropping my clothes back on the floor, I climb in. Ethan immediately turns into me and wraps me in his arms, burying his head in my neck. Jakub pulls the blanket up, tucking it under me, before climbing in behind Ethan and wrapping around him. I can feel his arm slide under Ethan's side and between us, hugging Ethan to his chest.

But his other hand? It slides into my hair and gently massages my scalp.

Ethan sighs in his sleep and I take a breath. There really is no place I'd rather be than right here. I just need to remind myself of this every time those doubts start to take hold again.

I can do that. Right?

TWENTY-ONE
ETHAN

When I wake up the next morning, I'm feeling thoroughly fucked. I can't remember when I've had a night so damn perfect. However, I wake up alone. The bed is cold.

For a minute, I just lay there with a stupid smile on my face because I can still smell both of them. In the room. On the sheets. On my skin. There's a very large part of me that wants to keep it that way and not shower. But I'm aware of the slimy sensation left over from the lube that's still in my ass and that's just uncomfortable.

Sighing, I pull myself from my bed and note that the floor has been cleaned up of all our discarded clothes last night. I'm still grinning when I get into the shower, and that grin doesn't leave when I finally move into the rest of my apartment.

I can hear their voices as I move through the space, keeping quiet because I don't want to interrupt. Pausing in the door, I just stare at the two men I love with every piece of me. Jakub is still in just shorts, which doesn't surprise me. If he had his way, he'd wear nothing but shorts all the time. I'm not complaining; I love to see his thick dick hanging between his legs. Pressed against his thigh.

He is a thirst trap but doesn't take advantage of that.

Jakub is moving around the kitchen preparing breakfast, while Creed is back on the counter where he'd been last night. He's wearing shorts, his I think since I don't recognize them as my own, but he's wearing the hoodie I wore yesterday. My stomach flutters and my smile is stupidly big.

I feel all sappy.

That feeling only magnifies when they laugh at whatever they're talking about. Creed looks relaxed. More so than he has since Jakub was traded here. There's an easy quality in the way he leans against the side of the fridge where he sits, watching Jakub move around the kitchen.

I'm so caught up in just staring at them I barely realize that they're talking to me until I register that both men are looking my way.

"Sorry, what?" I ask.

Jakub chuckles, shaking his head. "You done drooling, kocourek?"

"Not even close," I say and move into the kitchen. I stop in front of Creed and pull him forward with a fistful of hoodie so I can kiss him. He grins against my mouth, and I admit that I'm a little more aggressive than necessary this morning.

"Morning," he murmurs as I let him go.

"Morning," I answer and look into his dark blue eyes. "I'm really glad you're here."

His smile is soft. "Me too, Ethan."

Kissing him again, I turn to face my husband and watch him. When he pauses what he's cooking to look at me, I can't stop from jumping up and wrapping my entire body around him, legs locked around his waist as I kiss him breathless.

He chuckles. "It's like you weren't fucked at all last night, lásko."

"Best night of my life," I murmur. "Definitely in the top three or four, anyway."

Jakub grins and deposits me on the counter next to Creed. "Unless you want burnt French toast, you're going to have to wait a little bit. Or Creed can take care of you before breakfast. Your choice."

I look at Creed with a grin, making him laugh. "You can wait. Jeez."

Pretending to pout, I lean my shoulder against his while we watch Jakub move around my kitchen as if he's always been here. There's a quiet comfort this morning where nothing needs to be said and we're content to just enjoy each other's company without needing to fill the silence.

After another ten minutes, we're gathered around the small table and wolfing down French toast.

"Going to need the gym later," Creed says as he hauls another piece onto his plate. "You're going to make me fat if you keep feeding me so much."

"A daily struggle," Jakub says, eyeing me.

I grin without comment. I'm definitely the eater of the three of us.

After we make a mostly hysterical effort of doing the dishes together that ends up with us sopping wet and the kitchen dripping with soapy water, we land on the couch curled up together. The three of us.

I literally have to bite my tongue to avoid spewing something too sentimental. I'm turning into a sap. At least I'm marginally good at keeping that shit to myself.

The television is on, but I don't think anyone is watching it. We're wrapped around each other, limbs tangled and hearts beating to a rhythm all our own.

"Can I ask you something?" Creed asks.

"I'm not sure why you think you need permission to ask a question, but go ahead," I say.

He huffs and I know that was mostly for Jakub.

"Of course," Jakub says, pinching my ass and making me yelp.

"It might be a little... weird. But I'm just curious," Creed says. "Did you always know you're gay?"

I'll admit, that does take me by surprise. I shift to look at him and he gives me a wry smile. "I was thinking about Kalel—my cousin who is now doing porn, I guess—and what Jakub reported on his content."

"Ah," I say and shrug. "Well, I think on some level I always knew, but not in a way that made sense. I grew up playing hockey; which, as you know, is dominated by men. I was always surrounded by boys, and it never occurred to me to look elsewhere for anything. It wasn't until I was a teenager and the other guys started talking about getting laid and girls and shit that I realized I was definitely *not* like them. The things they said used to make me fucking cringe." A shudder races through me.

Thinking back on it, I try to remember the catalyst that made me say, 'hey, I'm gay,' but nothing specifically comes to mind.

"I'm not sure what happened, but one day, I ran home hysterical and just... freaked out. I think I was inconsolable for hours. My siblings were so freaked out they called my parents, who came home early. I remember thinking that I was going to lose hockey. All my friends. That the world hates gay kids for no reason except that we don't conform to what their opinion of a healthy, *normal* man is supposed to look like.

"I don't even think I said that I'm gay in that entire afternoon. I just kept... losing my mind over the unfairness of it all. This mountain stood before me, and I was never going to be able to scale it. A fortress that I was never going to get out of. Life was just going to... suck, and I was going to have nothing."

"Jesus," Creed murmurs.

"Yeah. The next day, I told the guys on my team to stop talking about girl bits unless they wanted me to throw up on them. Silence engulfed us for a long fucking time. By the time someone spoke, I was clinging to the wall of my cubby, dizzy as all fuck. One of the guys, Derek, asked what my problem was. Was I gay? I think I just nodded, trying not to vomit all over them as I waited for their response. I was fucking shocked when he apologized and said he didn't mean to make me uncomfortable."

"That's wild," Creed says. "I literally can't imagine that."

I laugh a little. "Yeah. I had a privileged childhood. The fact that my team had my back against everything through high school was just... unreal to me. The first time they fucked someone up for trying to bully me about my sexuality, they received a single detention, but the principal didn't enforce that they had to miss a game. And the guys who were being dicks? They were suspended for three days."

"That's how a school should react," Jakub says.

"Yeah. So, I guess I knew I was gay, but didn't really know what that meant until I was a teenager." When silence follows, I nudge Creed. "You?"

"I knew when I was really young. My disinterest in girls was very apparent. As a kid, no one thinks much of it. You know, boys will be boys and all that. Rough and tumble, we're naturally drawn to each other to roughhouse with. Except I knew right away that my reaction to them was very different from theirs to me. I officially put it together when I was sixteen and told my parents. You know what happened from there."

Hugging him close, I say, "I wish you had someone to support you. I'm so sorry you had to go through it alone."

Creed brushes his face against my chest, burying himself. "I... at my lowest, when I was sure that... maybe my family was right, and I'm not supposed to exist... there you were. You had just broken some college record that I'm going to pretend I haven't memorized. A proud, gay hockey player. I obsessively followed you as a lifeline and I kept thinking, if you're this amazing hockey player *and you're gay,* then clearly there's nothing wrong with me."

"There's nothing wrong with you," Jakub says, his fingers digging into my arm.

"I know that now. As a teenager, when it feels like literally everyone hates you for something you can't change about yourself? It was difficult to accept that I wasn't the problem."

"I hate that," I say, frustrated that I couldn't gather everyone from his past onto the ice and run them over with the Zamboni. "Fuck them."

He huffs quietly. "Yep. And this is why I'm secretly smug about being where I am when *no one* from my high school has truly accomplished anything for themselves and I'm making more than $2 million a year. People know my name and *they're* always going to be nobodies. Maybe that makes me a shitty person, but they were shitty first."

"You're not a shitty person," I tell him. "You've been bullied for a long time. You've been abandoned. You deserve to feel contempt and arrogance on occasion. You're a good person, Creed. You're kind, thoughtful, and generous."

He kisses my collarbone. "Thanks, Ethan."

I nudge Jakub, and he nods against me. "I don't think I'm gay."

Creed picks his head up to look at Jakub with skepticism. I laugh.

With a grin, Jakub shrugs. "Until I came to the US, I had only been with women. Then I met Ethan and now I've only been with men." He shrugs again. "I don't know that I've ever had a preference before meeting Ethan. I have a suspicion that it was expected of me to fuck women, so I did. Now that I've been with Ethan, I just don't feel... drawn to women. I'm not really drawn to anyone outside of this room."

Creed licks his lips. "But... didn't you hook up in the years you were apart?"

"Yeah, but it was to answer a frustration inside me more than anything else. I needed release and my husband wasn't close. Maybe I'm pan. Or bi. Or... a touch demisexual. Sex is good with Ethan." He brushes Creed's cheek with his thumb, making Creed flush. As if he's trying to wordlessly communicate that this doesn't quite apply to him. "But everyone else is just meh. It's a means to an end. This is different."

Creed exhales. "Can I ask another personal question?"

Jakub chuckles. "Ask whatever you want."

"Do you always wear a condom?"

"Yes."

"*Will you* always wear a condom?"

Jakub pauses to study his face. I do too, trying to decide what he's really asking.

"You want to know if we plan to remain open," Jakub guesses.

Creed takes a deep breath. "I don't know. Kind of? But you're married, so I just kind of thought... you'd stop wearing one."

I can feel the way he's tense in my arms. I'm sure Jakub does too. Tangling my fingers with Jakub's on Creed's face, I ask, "Would you prefer that we're no longer in an open relationship?"

Creed's skin pinks up, and he nods slightly. "Yes." Then he quickly adds, "But that's not really fair of me to ask. You shouldn't have to change for me."

"We've been waiting for you," Jakub says quietly. His words making Creed inhale sharply and me smile like a fucking loon with how happy they make me. "We don't need to go elsewhere for anything, Creed."

Creed's breath rushes out, and he closes his eyes.

"I suppose at some point in the future, we can stop using condoms if you want. I like them because they make cleanup easier and, you know, it makes everything safer. But we can talk about it," Jakub says, once more making my heart race.

I've never given the condom thing much of a thought. I don't hate them, or even find them an inconvenience. It takes like thirty additional seconds to wrap up and re-lube. They provide peace of mind and I appreciate that.

I'm not even sure that I care whether we go bare at some point in the future. If it makes Creed happy and we're not open to strangers anymore, then I'd be fine with that. As long as we still get tested regularly. I need *some* reassurance.

"I think we should tell the team," Creed blurts.

My brows knit together, and I try to determine what telling them that we're discussing not using condoms someday has to do with anything and why they should know that.

"That we're together," Creed says, looking at me with an amused smirk.

"Oh," I say, laughing. "You really need to begin at the beginning of a thought if you want us to have a meaningful discussion."

He grins. "Sorry."

"Nah, it's good. I'd be open for that," I say, but the dread sits on my chest again, its claws digging in.

Jakub kisses my neck. "Let's wait a bit. Doesn't Meddy have a gathering or something later?"

"Yeah. Gender reveal for baby number eight," I say, chuckling. "I think they should use condoms."

Creed laughs.

"I'm not sure that's the appropriate venue, though. It's their day," I say.

"But most of the team will be together in a casual setting," Jakub says. "They'll have time to get used to it before practice the next day. We can pull Meddy aside and see if he's okay with it first if you want to."

Lucien is probably one of my favorite people. He's older than most of us by a decade. He's been playing for fifteen years and while he's not on the first line anymore, he definitely gets pulled up frequently enough from the second to make him a valuable player.

His wife, Bianca, is an absolute sweetheart. She minds us and protects us like a mama bear would her cubs. We joke that they're both our hockey parents. Momma B and Daddy Meddy.

"Let's think about it," I say. "But I think maybe we should consider Caulder's idea first. While I don't hate staying home when you're here with me, maybe we ought to get out of here for a while. A few days. Where we can just be together and no one is going to recognize us."

"Is there such a place?" Creed asks.

"There are a few," Jakub says. "We get away every summer with this in mind."

I smile and close my eyes. Perfect.

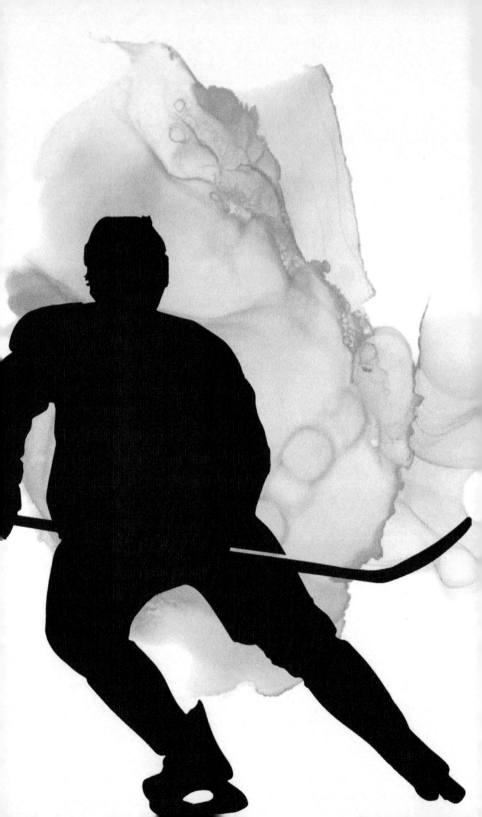

TWENTY-TWO
JAKUB

By the next day, I'm definitely feeling the tentative attraction between me and Creed. I suppose there was a part of me that kind of thought that if Ethan fell in love again, that I'd continue fucking around on occasion. Just to give them some privacy.

But since the morning two days ago when I caught Creed trying to sneak away, there's been something brewing between us. It's in the shy looks he gives me. In the way he bows his head to hide his smile from both of us. In his quiet, subtly flirty remarks that have Ethan beaming.

Since the first time I met Creed, I knew he was exactly the kind of man who would pair with Ethan perfectly. He's strong, stable, and has just enough dominance in him that Ethan will happily give up control, which has always been what he prefers, anyway.

The way they looked at each other, even in those early days, screamed that this was different from any other guy Ethan had ever told me about. There was something fundamentally locked together between them.

I wasn't lying when I told Ethan that I've loved watching him fall in love with Creed. And I knew that over the summer, when it became the three of us, that Creed and I would get along just fine.

What I hadn't anticipated was that something might spark between us. Not that I'm sure why I felt that way, but it's surprising that I feel so different now. When I told him he was definitely a part of this relationship and he was always meant to be here, I'd meant with Ethan.

But even the words leaving my mouth weren't being spoken as I initially intended them to. Because I knew subconsciously that it wasn't the entire truth?

Creed fits into our lives seamlessly. He isn't an addition to our marriage, but a missing piece. And I know that we're going to grow stronger together—the three of us.

Now we just need to work on the voices in Creed's head, telling him that he's a visitor and not an integral piece of our lives.

Ethan suddenly laughs, causing Creed and I to look at him. He shakes his head. "Sorry, but I need to go rescue Isak. He's having an existential crisis."

"Again?" Creed asks.

Ethan laughs more. "Oh yeah. This man has no self-regulation." He gets to his feet and heads into the bedroom to put on some real clothing. It's a shame since I love to see him walk around in underwear and a t-shirt.

He comes in and says he'll be back. Creed and I watch him head to the door. The rustling of his outside clothes carries down the hall and then the door opens and shuts.

A minute passes as I stare. Did he really just leave like that?

Then the door opens and he reappears, looking sheepish. He crosses the room to bend down and kiss me. It lingers and he sighs. "Sorry. It's still surreal that you're actually here."

"Mm-hmm," I answer, frowning. "You best start remembering. I expect an actual goodbye when you leave."

He chuckles and kisses me again. "Miluji tě," he murmurs.

"Love you too, kocourek."

Ethan gets up and moves to Creed, dropping into his lap, cupping his face between both hands, and kissing him sloppily until Creed pushes him away laughing. "Ew. I don't want to be covered in your spit."

"That's not what you said last night," Ethan says, making me laugh.

Creed rolls his eyes, bringing his face back for a quicker, softer kiss.

"I love you," Ethan murmurs, pressing his forehead to Creed's. What's becoming one of my favorite things is watching Creed's cheeks pink as they do now. "I love you," he repeats.

"Will you be here when I get back?" Ethan asks.

Creed nods. "Yeah."

With another quick kiss, Ethan gets to his feet again. "Good. Keep my husband entertained. I'll be back soon."

Creed nods again and we both watch him go once more. The door clicks shut, and then Creed looks at me.

"They're close," I say.

"From what I understand, Isak experienced some horrific accident right after he was traded to Buffalo. He wasn't involved, but it left him devastated. Ethan was at his side the entire time. They've become inseparable since."

"Until you were drafted."

"No," he says, laughing. "That's different. I realize it might not seem that way since you've been here, but I think usually he was equally with Isak as he was with me."

"I see. Isak doesn't have a thing for him?"

Creed grins. "I think everyone has a crush on Ethan Wilder." I share his grin. "But no. If he does, it's bromance-y. Not like, legit, he'd act on it, type crush."

I nod.

"Are you concerned?" he asks.

"No," I say, chuckling. "Still just learning these men. Trying to figure them out."

"Oh. In that case, I'll just tell you." He waves his hand. "At least about the guys we're closest with. My bestie is Caulder. He was drafted straight from college and had been coached by Adak Nemaczekk. You know, the super hot coach who's with Anaheim now? He's kind of quiet, but super loyal and protective. He's only been here a year or so.

"Meddy is our resident daddy, in case you haven't figured that out. He and his wife kind of baby us and take care of us. They're always throwing parties for our birthdays or any big achievement. Bianca rescues us from the crazy puck bunnies all the time.

"I just told you about Isak. The only other thing you need to know is that he falls in and out of love many times during a season.

We're thankful he was taught to wrap it early on or we're pretty sure he'd be filling a stadium with his offspring."

I flinch, laughing.

Creed grins. "He's a good guy. Other than them, it's the same crew that comes out with us when we go—Lucas, Phalyn, Sacha, Asael, Astor, and Three. When we get together at someone's house, it's usually with them, too. Mattias, too, when he was here."

"Ethan always told me that Buffalo wasn't like the other teams I've played for. You have real camaraderie here," I say.

"I think that's why admitting to them that he's been keeping such a big secret for so long is such a struggle for Ethan," he says. "He's always so concerned about everyone around them that he hates the very idea of being the one to let them down."

"One of the reasons I fell in love with him was because I could see how good a person he was right away," I say. "His concern was never for himself. He's incredibly, almost unbelievably, selfless. One of the first thoughts I had concerning him when I realized I really liked him was that he needed to be spoiled, since he takes care of everyone else. And I wanted to be the one to spoil him."

Creed smiles, nodding. "Yep. I've had those same thoughts."

We fall into silence for a while before Creed asks, "So... where do you think we should go?"

I shrug. "We've been to a lot of places over the years. One of our favorites is renting a yacht or something. It allows us to travel, set our own destinations, and privacy. But we can also rent entire islands and the like."

Creed nods, turning his gaze to his phone. The conversation ends and I think he's moved on until he suddenly gets up and leaves the room, returning with Ethan's tablet.

Then he moves to the couch next to me instead of retaking his spot in the chair. He sits close and I adjust to drape my arm behind him.

His cheeks pinken but he settles in closer to show me the screen. "Look what I found."

The site is to a resort called Isle of Kala. It's an island chain in the Pacific that boasts an anonymous getaway. No technology allowed of any kind. (There are emergency stations, of course.) Everyone is checked thoroughly at the one place of check-in on the island and all technology is locked away until we're back in the airport to head home. In addition, everyone who sets foot on the islands signs an NDA.

One of my favorite things that catches my eye is that the entire resort—all six islands—are largely geared towards the LGBTQ+ community.

One island—Ceto—is basically a party all the time. It's the smallest island, but the entirety of it is broken down into different kinds of parties. Gays, orgy, kink, etc.

While it's not restricted to those who identify within the LGBTQ+ community, it's made clear that this is a safe place and always attracts a lot of those who are a part of it. So if that's not your thing, then you're not welcome here.

There are other things too. Hiking in old ruins. A nude beach. Catamaran rides. Dune buggies. Sailing, snorkeling, zip-lining. There are a handful of restaurants on each island. And an array of different accommodations.

"This is sick," I say.

He grins. "What do you think? Want to give it a try?"

"Absolutely. You want to choose a suite and I'll book the flight?"

"We don't need to wait for Ethan?"

"No. He's going to love this surprise," I say.

Creed smiles and navigates to the tab with the different rooms available. I watch him scroll for a minute until he pauses. "This is overwhelming."

"See about filters. That should narrow it down."

"What am I filtering for?"

I kiss the side of his head, making him bow to hide his smile. "We're going to be happy with whatever you choose, Creed. And if we like it here and want to try a longer stay, we can take turns booking the room."

"You think they're going to have an issue with three of us in one room?" he asks as he navigates to the filters.

"If there's an issue, we'll give them a call, but usually there are accommodations for larger parties who travel together."

"What dates am I looking for?"

I pull up the calendar. "It's going to have to be a short trip. Especially since this is basically on the other side of the globe. If we leave tomorrow, that gives us two full days there and we'll be home in time for Lucien's party."

Creed nods and I turn my attention to booking flights. I choose the ones that will put us there as early as possible but also leave as early as possible, allowing us room on either end to relax after a long day of travel.

By the time I'm finished, I lean in closer to Creed and he shifts the tablet to show me the two rooms he's looking between.

"I think I'm going to forego the butler level this time, but I think that would be so cool. I'd rather make the expense worth it and I'm not sure it is for the two days we'll be there. We're already not going to have time to visit all six islands."

"Which one are you leaning towards?" I ask.

Creed changes tabs and shows one bungalow that's built over the water with a glass bottom. There's a net over the water, a slide that dumps you into the water, a pool with an infinity edge that looks out over the water... And it faces the mountainous island in the chain.

"It's almost a tease for two days, though," he says, sighing. "I almost think we're not going to want to leave the bungalow if I choose this one."

I hug him to me, chuckling. I love the way he grins and snuggles in further. "Then let's save that for a second visit. What's the other one you're looking at?"

He clicks on a different tab. This one says that we're looking at an active lava field and the volcano that is constantly drooling lava. Yes, it says drooling.

"That looks dangerous."

Creed laughs. "It says the volcano is active, but it doesn't actually erupt. They monitor it closely. I think it would be a once in a lifetime experience to stay in a hotel that's this close to an active volcano. We can even walk along the hardened lava rock! It says that the island expands by a couple feet every year due to the volcano's drool."

I can't stop laughing. "That they call it volcano drool makes me want to visit this place all the more."

"So, this one?"

"Yep, let's take a chance on dying. Management is going to shit a brick if they lose their entire starting line to fucking volcano drool."

He laughs, too.

This is where Ethan finds us when he returns home a few hours later. We're booked and looking through the long list of excursions and features the resort has to offer when he steps into the living room. As soon as he sees us, he's beaming.

"Crisis averted?" Creed asks, sitting up a little straighter, though he doesn't pull away entirely.

"Yep. Don't worry; he's not in love for real."

Creed rolls his eyes.

"Come here," I tell him. Ethan basically falls into our laps. I fucking love that Creed immediately starts petting him in the same way I do. He looks at me, grins, and then looks away. "We have a surprise for you."

"Please tell me it has to do with me between you two," he says.

Creed chokes as he laughs. "Fuck's sake, Ethan."

"Not this time, no," I say, shaking my head. "Horny fucker. But you're going to need to pack for a few days. Clothing for a warm climate. Lots of swimwear. Make sure you bring your manscaping goodies. And... don't you have a full-face snorkel mask?"

Ethan stares at me for a minute before his dark eyes move to Creed. "Really?"

"Yes," Creed says, grinning just as widely as Ethan was when he walked in. "And don't forget to pack your passport, baby."

Ethan inhales sharply and I swear, I see little hearts dance in his eyes. Then he's beaming again. We each receive enthusiastic kisses before he basically rolls off our laps onto the floor. Then he's practically running to the bedroom.

"I worry that he's going to hurt himself when the surprise really is a threesome," I murmur.

Once more, Creed nearly chokes on his tongue. His face is bright red as he covers it with his hands. "Jesus," he murmurs.

I grin and kiss the side of his head. Maybe I'll trip on my way to such an event, too. I'm suddenly looking forward to it in the worst fucking way.

TWENTY-THREE
ETHAN

FLYING OVER THE CHAIN OF ISLANDS WAS BEAUTIFUL. AS WAS THE sun glistening off the water as we flew low to the airport on the largest island, Anapos. I could see mountains and forests and gorgeous land-locked lakes. Lower still and I found the cabanas over the sea, boats moving between islands, and a huge fire that the pilot assured the passengers was a bonfire that's constantly burning. It helps with waste and gives visitors a beach bonfire any night they want it.

When the small plane lands, we are escorted off the plane on the runway and brought to a checkpoint that serves as our initial check-in. Basically, just making sure our names are on the guest list.

Then we are brought to a luxurious room filled with gay art. Some abstract and some obscene. I don't stare at the blowie for too long—I swear. But fuck, it's hot.

"Good afternoon."

I turn at the voice to find a man in uniform with a single large lockbox. He smiles, his teeth almost alarmingly white, but the three of us smile in return.

"This box is to store all your technology, including but not limited to laptops, phones, tablets, cameras, beepers, and any other recording devices, be it audio, visual, or otherwise. You read the releases?" he asks.

We nod and turn our phones off before putting them in the box.

"Then you know we will need to conduct a search of your belongings. This is for the protection of all of our guests who wish to remain anonymous. Do you have any questions before I begin?"

"What's the most alarming thing you've found in luggage?" I ask.

"I can't really say," he says, pressing his lips together. "But if I were using my imagination, I would say chain. A whole lot of chain," I glance at Creed, whose eyes have gotten wide.

"Why would someone bring chain?" I ask.

The gentleman shakes his head. "I would imagine there was no offered explanation and since it's not on our banned items list, it couldn't be confiscated." He picks up my bag and, with gloves on, begins going through the pockets. "If I ever found chain in luggage, I would report it to security, and they would keep an eye on that person."

"Please tell me he's not currently on the island," Creed says.

He laughs. "We're talking hypothetically but I feel confident that I haven't checked anyone in with chain in their luggage recently."

My shoulders relax. The man nods at the pile of books to the side. "That's our island guide. You'll find a thorough list of things to do, places to eat, locations to see, events to experience, adventures to have, and anything else you can think of. Have a look while you wait, if you like."

I eagerly pick up one of the books. It's eighty pages long, high gloss, and the pictures inside are gorgeous. Within the first ten pages, I find a dozen things to do. Moving to stand with my men, I lean against Jakub, pulling Creed in close, and we flip through the pages.

"Oh! A naked beach!!"

Jakub laughs. "Of course, that's what catches your attention."

"I've never been to a naked beach. That's too shameful for a pro athlete."

Creed snickers.

"Fuck, they have a toy store!" I say, reading the little snippet of the kinds of items we'll find there.

"Jesus," Creed says, and I spy his cheeks pinking.

We've made it through a third of the book when the man finishes. "You're welcome to take that book with you, if you'd like."

"We will," Jakub says.

"We're here for two full days. What activities do you suggest we do?" Jakub asks.

He looks us over before stating, "Is it safe to assume you aren't afraid of a little exercise?"

"He's clearly not a hockey fan," I say, grinning hugely at that. Anonymity is a wonderful thing when hundreds of thousands of people know your name.

"I'm not. I apologize." He grins at us.

"We're not afraid of exercise," Jakub says.

"Do you like adventurous activities? Relaxing activities? Partying?"

"All of the above, but I think we can pass on the partying for this trip," I say.

"For one day, I suggest taking a hike up to the ruins. There are caves and houses and battlements to explore. The glimpses into the past and the views are spectacular. In the afternoon, take a catamaran ride. You can knock off a few experiences with this—boat ride, island views, snorkeling in the clear blue waters, visiting shipwrecks, and swimming with manta rays and giant sea turtles."

"Damn," Creed says.

I'm grinning too big to comment right now. That sounds like a fucking blast.

"The second day, maybe relax a little. We can have a throuple massage set up that takes place in your room. Then maybe check out some of our pristine beaches. We've had a reviewer of our paradise state that every hundred feet around the island is a different and unique view."

"It's almost a shame that we can't take pictures of it," Creed says.

"We have a gift shop where you can purchase some of the hundreds of pictures taken. There are also resort photographers all over the place snapping pictures. Upon check out, you can check the wall to see if there are any you'd like. These are complementary and can be sent digitally. While there are some inconveniences to not allowing our guests technology, we find that even our most disgruntled guests check out with a feeling of peace they can't describe from being unplugged or bothered with the kinds of demands placed on them by always having their entire lives at their fingertips."

"Oh no. We're completely happy about not having any technology," Jakub says. "It's one of the reasons we chose this resort specifically."

"We'd like to book all the things you mentioned," I say.

The man tags our bags, bio-locks the case with our phones in it with our fingerprints, and then leads us from the room. It's through this second door that we enter the actual lobby of the primary building and it's simply stunning. I get caught staring out the floor to ceiling windows that span three floors (we're on the middle floor) that are set in the wall beyond an open, enormous staircase.

Jakub grips my hand after a while and pulls me along. I'm far too overwhelmed with everything to look at to pay attention to check in. Even as we make our way to our room, I'm distracted by the windows and the art—just as gay and vibrant as that in the holding room.

As soon as we walk in, my mouth drops. Not because of the room itself but the enormous window beyond is overlooking a motherfucking volcano! I move straight to the window, finding that it's not a window but a door that opens onto a large balcony with hanging seating and a small infinity edge pool. While that's impressive and everything, I can't stop staring at the volcano.

"There are rivers of lava," I say, pointing. I feel like a goddamn child right now. Then I point into the water where I can see another island in the distance. "Look!"

Behind me, Jakub chuckles. Moments later, his arms wrap around me.

"This is amazing," I say. It takes me several more minutes of staring at everything I can before I turn to look at him. "I can't believe you brought us here."

"Creed found this resort and chose the room," he says. "This isn't my doing."

"You helped me choose," Creed calls from inside the room.

"You spoil me," I chastise them both, narrowing my eyes.

"Every single day of my life," Jakub murmurs and I can't help but fucking melt into him.

Creed steps onto the balcony then and I pull him towards us so that he's pressed to our sides.

"I love you," I say. "So fucking much. This is the best thing ever and I'm pretty sure we're going to have to come back. I want to do everything in that book."

Jakub smiles, kissing my forehead. I don't get all giddy or anything when he kisses Creed's, too. "We can make this an annual holiday. It took us far too long to decide on a room alone."

Creed squeezes my wrist. "What do you want to do tonight? We still have several hours of daylight."

"The beauty of moving back in time," I muse. Looking out at the volcano, I contemplate walking the trails where I saw others but when the island in the distance catches my eyes, I turn to them with a grin. "Nude beach!"

Jakub grins and pulls away. "I'll check the map."

I turn to Creed with a wide smile, but I can immediately see the unease that he's trying to hide from me. "What's wrong? We don't have to do that."

"It's alright. I don't mind."

It's a lie. I narrow my eyes and bring him closer. "Tell me the truth."

His face heats again. I can feel it under my hand. He drops his gaze and in a voice I can barely hear, he says, "I'm just... not confident in myself."

I frown. "Creed, you're fucking gorgeous."

He sighs and I swear, if his skin gets any hotter, it's going to burn my hand. "No. I mean." He takes a deep, shuddering breath and then quickly says, "I have a small dick and I'm self-conscious about it."

For a minute, I just stare at him, not believing his words. My eyes drop on their own as if I can see said dick that's hidden within his jeans. "Creed—"

He shakes his head and I pull him close, hugging him tightly. "It's fine. I know what I have. I've heard it enough to understand that everyone else knows what I have too."

"What the fuck?!" I say, anger fizzling through me. "That's definitely not okay."

Creed laughs, but I can hear the self-depreciation in the sound.

"Not a big deal. I know it's small. Not micro, I guess, though I've been called micro before. I just—"

That's all I can handle. I step back and grip his face, forcing him to look at me. "You're fucking perfect," I grit out. "Every single thick inch of you, Creed. Do you hear me?"

The shine in his eyes and the way he shivers in my hold tells me more about how he feels concerning this than his words ever could.

"Thanks, but I know—"

I cover his mouth, preventing his words. "Credence," I say, getting right in his face, pressing my body against his so all of our hard lines are lined up. "I have zero complaints about your size. You're perfect and I wouldn't change a thing about you. I'm going to need every fucking name who's ever made you feel this way, baby."

He laughs and it sounds shaky, but he drops his forehead to mine. His arms wrap around me and hug me tightly. "Thank you," he whispers.

"You have no idea how furious I am right now," I tell him, gripping him like he's going to fall apart and I'm holding him together. "What the actual motherfucking fuck?!"

Creed's face tucks into my neck. "I've never loved you so thoroughly," he whispers. "Thank you for loving everything about me."

"Everything," I confirm.

I feel Jakub back in the room, but he remains against the wall as he watches. After he's given us a minute, he approaches and tucks a few strands of Creed's hair behind his ear. "How about we get in the pool here. Naked. We can satisfy Ethan's sudden curiosity for nudity right here and never wear clothes once we walk into the room."

Creed's laughter is quiet. "We can go to the beach. It's fine."

"No," I tell him firmly. "Look, it's a curiosity thing. Because we can. Because no one here knows us and will probably not recognize us. This isn't a bucket list moment."

"But I don't want to keep you from doing things you want to do," Creed says, picking his head up to look at me. "I want to do everything with you. I want to experience everything you want to do with you."

"We will, but I'm all about compromise, Creed. And I will never ask you to do something that makes you uncomfortable for any reason. You don't think I'd actually enjoy it if I knew you were uneasy, do you? Besides, I will never put you in that position," I tell him.

His soft smile says it all.

"Oh!" I say, grinning again. "Let's do Jakub's idea, but *first*, I want to go to the toy store."

Creed looks at me warily again. "What do you want in a toy store?"

I can feel the way my grin turns wicked when I glance at Jakub. "My husband has some shopping to do."

Creed looks between the two of us, but it's not the same unease that he radiated concerning the beach. Gripping his hand, I kiss him softly. "You're my Stanley Cup," I whisper. "The thing I've been striving for my entire life. I already have it, right here in this room. No matter what we do or where we go, don't forget that, Credence."

His eyes shine again, and he swallows when he nods. I give him another peck and then kiss Jakub. "Alright," I say, clapping my hands together. "Let's go spend some money, find food, come back, and get naked!"

TWENTY-FOUR
JAKUB

Watching these guys enjoy themselves has me in a state of constant and deep contentment. Ethan's youthful enthusiasm just emanates from him. His excitement and constant wide smiles are contagious. He's just so damn happy. Everything we pass or see is like Christmas morning for him. Filled with magic and enchantment.

He's always been excited to explore places and we've gone to islands plenty of times. We've even gone to a couple LGBT-only islands. However, our stay is usually short and we are never around too many people for fear of being recognized.

The freedom in not caring if we're recognized since there's going to be zero proof of that is so damn freeing that it's like he's seeing the world for the first time. I can't stop watching him.

When I'm not watching Ethan, I'm watching Creed. His enthusiasm isn't nearly as bright as Ethan's, but it's clear that he loves everything. With every hour that passes, he's relaxing a little more.

I'm not sure Ethan realizes how stressed Creed is. I have a feeling my presence puts that constant tension in his shoulders. Even though we get along fine and will continue to do so, and while I'm confident that the relationship between the two of us—and the three of us—will grow, the stress he feels weighs him down.

I think I'm proving to be less of a factor in that stress. But he's never unaware of the storm that's hanging out just over the horizon. Ready to hit land and turn our lives into a media fiasco. There's nothing I can do to take that away.

Ethan isn't ready to tell his team. Which means we're not ready to tell the world. We've talked about it a little here and there, but Ethan is usually quick for a topic change. Creed and I will exchange a look when that happens now. We both know that Ethan is in avoidance mode.

I get it. He's feeling like he's been leading a lie for so long that finally coming clean is going to hurt the people he cares about most. Never mind the fact that we haven't even told our parents. His parents are more familiar with Creed than they are with me. When we agreed not to tell a soul, we meant it.

Not that any of that matters now. I'm watching my men get massages, having already finished mine. While I enjoy a good massage, I'm not keen on having a stranger's hands all over my body so I opted for neck and shoulders primarily. I let them do my arms, wrists, and hands, too. Hockey is rough on all parts of the body, but constantly swinging our sticks can lead to shoulder strain and whatever.

When the masseur has given me the warning that they'll be finishing up in twenty minutes that I asked for, I quietly head back into the room. We spent a great deal of time in the toy store the evening that we arrived, and I may have dropped a small fortune on a few things. Honestly, I could have just brought my stash from home, but it hadn't come up.

Since Ethan and I had such infrequent time together, other things usually took priority over our sensation play. It became more about bonding and strengthening our relationship than it was exploration with sexy things as we used to do. But when Ethan's face lit up at the listing for the toy store, I knew what we were going to spend this afternoon doing and it wasn't exploring the beach.

I wasn't sure how Creed was going to feel. Hopefully, he'd watch and maybe participate if he was feeling comfortable about it. I'm sure he's going to love the way Ethan just turns to putty before falling apart completely.

After ordering room service for ice and a cart with extra

towels and starting the wax melt warmer and the electric teapot, I grab my bag of goodies and head for the bathroom to sanitize them all. I'm nearly finished when my ice arrives with the cart, and I begin arranging all the supplies. I drop one glass dildo into the ice and another into the hot water of the electric teapot and then wheel my cart onto the balcony where the masseurs are finishing up.

There's an outlet out here so I plug the wax melt warmer back in and then wait until the men leave. For a minute, I stare at my boys laying face down and boneless. They're so calm and relaxed. There's a moment where I imagine that we can all give up hockey right now and live our lives just like this. Together and pampering each other.

Or, as I prefer it, them letting me spoil the fuck out of them.

Before one of them can decide that they need to get up, I move between the two tables that I asked to be left here and rest my hands on their backs.

"Just five more minutes," Ethan murmurs.

I chuckle.

"Actually, how about we do something else that requires you to remain right where you are?"

His entire body responds with a shiver. Chills rush down his exposed skin and he nods. "Yeah. I want that."

"Roll over, kocourek."

Creed has turned his face sideways to watch and though I keep my hand on his back, he doesn't make any move to change position. Ethan looks at him with a wide smile, but Creed's gaze has dropped to Ethan's half hard cock now exposed when the sheet falls away. It won't be long before that thing can cut steel.

I brush my fingers through Creed's hair, calling his attention to me. His dark eyes meet mine and he gives me a small smile. "Are you familiar with sensation play?" He shakes his head. "It's a stimuli exercise where I take away two of your senses and heighten the others by touching you with various objects. There's no pressure to participate but you're welcome to if you want."

"I'll just watch for now," he says.

Nodding, I smooth back his hair and move to the cart to grab a blindfold. I bought two—just in case. After kissing Ethan's pretty lips, I pull the blindfold over his face. Then press his hands to the side of the table he's on. They immediately curl around the edge. "Don't move them. Understand?"

He nods eagerly. "Can I hold Creed's hand?"

Creed grins and moves to his side to reach. I move his table, closing the distance between them so that they can comfortably link their hands together.

"Ready, lásko?"

"Yes," he says. It's more of an exhale than it is actual words.

With a Bluetooth speaker connected to the television, I turn on a quiet ambiance track. Rustling of sheets. The occasional heavy breathing. A low moan. Kissing. Whispers.

Ethan's body breaks out in gooseflesh.

I begin lightly with a feather cluster and move it over his face. Tracing his jaw and down his neck. Moving it around his pecs and then his nipples. Down his body, over his stomach. Teasing the tip of his dick but never fully touching him. Just a whisper. A hint. A brush of displaced air. His lips part as I glide over his balls, move down his legs, and to his calves.

He lets his legs fall open and I grin, rubbing the feather toy over his crack.

When I follow his crack back up, I brush the pom of feathers along his shaft this time, but avoid the bit of pre-cum beading at the slit. Not something fun to get out of feathers. Glancing at Creed, I find him watching intently, eyes wide with interest and a hint of arousal.

Still moving the feather pom over Ethan's skin, I pick up the spike roller and move a cup of water to the side of the table he's on, careful not to let it touch him. I just want him to feel what I do to him.

I remove the feather toy and immediately replace it with the spikes. They're sharp, but I don't intend to press into his skin. I don't want to mark his body, rather I want him to feel the hint of the needles. I roll it over his chest, around his nipples, down his stomach and back up, this time grazing a nipple.

He groans, his hips coming off the bed slightly when I move away from his pecs again. This time, I follow the trail of the needles with drops of water from my fingers after dipping them into the cup. His breathing is heavy when I get to his cock and lightly run the sharp toy along his length.

"Oh my god," he murmurs. He trembles slightly, and I know it's in an effort to remain still. Especially when his cock twitches as I bring the roller back up the length of his hard dick.

"That feels good?" Creed whispers.

"I'm going to come in two minutes flat," Ethan groans.

Removing the wheel, I offer it to Creed while I concentrate on dropping water over Ethan's body and letting him feel the way it drips, running along his contours and pooling in his navel or dribbling off the side.

Creed touches the toy and pulls a hand back. I smile and lightly run it along his arm with the same pressure I used on Ethan. His lips form an O as he looks at me in surprise. I smile.

The indecision in his face is clear. He's curious. So damn curious. But not sure he wants to play.

"We can forgo the blindfold," I tell him, "but I suggest you try to keep your eyes shut otherwise it doesn't have the same effect. And you can tell me to stop at any time."

"I won't let go of your hand," Ethan promises, his face turned toward Creed though he's still blindfolded.

Biting his lip, Creed nods and shifts on his table again. With one hand still firmly attached to Ethan's, he glances at the sheet covering his waist down. His cheeks heat again as his eyes flicker to mine.

I'm glad Ethan is blindfolded right now. Seeing his insecurity would only fill him with anger again. Instead, I keep that anger for myself and gently direct Creed's face up so he's looking into mine. "You're perfect," I whisper, letting him see the truth in my words. "But you're not required to be completely bare. I can stay on your torso."

He swallows and nods before laying back. Once he closes his eyes, his cheeks heat to a delicious bright red and he shoves the sheet off him. His body is stiff, right down to his cock.

He's not big. Sure. And he is thick, just as Ethan has said. But he's completely perfect. Tracing my finger over his skin, close but not touching his dick, I bend down and whisper in his ear. "You're magnificent, sweetheart. I promise, you have nothing to be ashamed of."

Creed's lips part and he takes a deep breath, nodding slightly. There's no more talking after that. I set the needle roller down and sprinkle droplets of water on them, one drop at a time. I try to hit the same spot on each of them, so they feel the same thing and I can watch their reactions.

Creed's nipples are very sensitive. The first time I hit one with a drop of water, he shivered, his cock leaking. I store this information away for later. He also loves his dick touched with water. His reaction is visceral.

While I do bring the needle roller to his flesh, I don't use it for a long time, and I don't touch his dick or nipples with it. He tenses every time I get close, so I figure we'd bypass it for now.

I move onto wax. I purchased this melter at the toy store, and it's specially designed for this. So I can take out the internal ceramic ramekin with the melted wax and drip it as I had with the water via a specifically designed spout made for just this purpose.

Beginning with Ethan, I pour thin lines of it along his body, avoiding his nipples and cock this time. He moans. Glancing at Creed, I find he's watching, but his lust is as apparent in his eyes as it is his hard dick. His gaze flickers to mine before he turns his head up and closes his eyes again.

Letting the wax dry on Ethan, I move to Creed and make the same pattern on him. His moan isn't as quiet, and he mutters a few curses as he squirms. Ethan's grinning at this. So am I.

I set the wax melter back in its base and slowly begin to peel the wax from Ethan's body as he wiggles and his breathing becomes heavier. Then I move to Creed. He's biting his lip as he tries to keep his sounds in.

Following the hot wax—which doesn't get hot enough to actually burn skin—I trace the slightly pink pattern on their flesh with an ice cube. Creed gasps, his eyes squeezing shut.

"Ethan, plug your ears."

He laughs and brings both his hands up to cover his ears.

Then I get close to Creed and lower my voice to a whisper. "Part of the fun of sensation play is that the person receiving doesn't know what's coming. But this is your first time, so I'm going to tell you the finale and you can decide how much, if any, you'd like." He nods and I see the appreciation on his face. "There are two glass dicks—one hot and one cold. Neither so hot nor cold that it'll hurt you, but enough that you're definitely going to feel it. I have leather gloves. I plan to play with your hole and then use your choice of glass dick on you. When it's fully inserted, then I'm going to let you fuck up into my leather-covered hand until you come."

"Oh my god," he whispers, his hand grasping his cock tightly.

"Are you comfortable with this? Do you trust me?"

He nods and though I'm not sure which question he's answering, I take pride in that I think he's answering both. "Do you have a preference, hot or cold?"

This time he bites his lip, but when he answers, he chooses hot.

"Blindfold me?" he whispers.

I touch his cheek. "Are you sure?"

"Yes. I want to feel it like Ethan does."

I kiss his forehead and reach for the second blindfold. Gently, I secure it over his face and urge him to lie back again. When I'm sure he's settled, I pull Ethan's hands back down and secure their hands together, so they're linked once more.

"Ready?" Both respond by nodding.

To let the glass toys regulate a little so they're not such a shock, I pull them out of their baths to warm and cool, respectively. Slipping my hands into the leather gloves, I alternate between the melting icy water and the hot teapot water and massage their holes but never press inside.

Ethan is always vocal, and this moment is no different. Creed tries to keep his sexy sounds in, but I work extra hard to make sure that some escape him.

Touching each of the bases of the glass cocks to my neck to check on the temperature, I decide that we're good. Using the water to keep them slick with frequent dunks back in, I begin working them inside both men. Their reactions are almost mirrors and yet completely different. The muscles in their arms strain as they try to keep themselves still and gripping each other in vice holds.

Little by little, intentionally slow and drawn out with frequent complete removal for water baths, I work these toys into their tight bodies. Using just the toys to really prep them and stretch them. I handle them both so fucking slowly that by the time I'm halfway inside them, they're both begging me to come.

I appreciate that they both manage to keep their hands off their cocks. Ethan has had years of practice obeying my demands. Creed hasn't. So I'm so fucking proud of the fact that he is so self-restrained.

When I finally get them fully impaled, I spend the next few minutes slowly fucking into them with the toys. Same pace. Same deep, moderate thrusts. I keep this up until Ethan has tears running down his face from behind his blindfold.

Conceding that they've had enough, I push their glass cocks all the way inside and then bring my hands to cover their cocks by laying them flat along their shaft.

"Get off now," I tell them.

Both respond immediately and they rub up into my hands with fervent need. Creed comes first. His cum streaks up his chest and dribbles down his neck, much like the water droplets I'd sprinkled on him.

Ethan isn't long after and I'm sure that the guests in the surrounding rooms hear him coming.

Keeping my hands on them for a minute longer, I let them relax before slowly pulling my hands away. I remove their glass cocks and set them on the towels. Leaving their blindfolds on, I bend down to kiss Ethan. He's still moaning softly.

Then I bend over Creed, pressing my lips to his ear. "Thank you for trusting me," I whisper. Then gently press my lips to his. I feel his inhale, but he definitely returns my kiss.

I grin the entire time I clean up, letting them relax where I've worn them out.

TWENTY-FIVE
CREDENCE

THE WORDS SUGGESTING THAT WE BLOW OFF HOCKEY AND JUST stay here for the rest of our lives were on the tip of my tongue as we headed to the airport. It's early. So fucking early. I'm pretty sure we all slept through the flight across the Pacific. Our layover in LA wasn't long but I don't remember much of it. I'm pretty sure if it wasn't for Jakub, Ethan and I would have missed the flight.

When we get home, Jakub forces us to stay up until eight. Yep, he's cruel like that, but he insists if we don't want to deal with jetlag for the next week, it's necessary. We grudgingly do, and while I'm a little grumpy about it (I can't help myself!), Ethan whines a lot. I find it amusing and adorable, which might just have been the sleep deprivation talking.

But what makes me realize I can easily fall for Jakub too is that he is so fucking sweet and indulgent toward, not only Ethan, but me as he keeps us awake. By the time he lets us crawl into bed that evening, I'm pretty sure I'm swooning.

In fact, I think I even mumbled to Ethan in something not quite a whisper, "Your husband is dreamy."

Ethan giggled. He fucking giggled. Which, of course, made me giggle. It was then that I knew what happens to hockey players when they're overly tired. We turn into giggling messes where everything just begins to make us giggle uncontrollably.

Jakub remains amused and indulgent the entire time, and it's not long before I fall asleep and remain that way for a solid ten hours.

I'm not sure what wakes me up, but I'm suddenly bolting upright the next morning. There's one wild minute where I have no idea where I am. My heart races as I frantically look around.

"What's wrong?" Ethan asks groggily as he reaches for me.

Breathing a sigh of relief, I fall back into the bed and let him curl around me like a sloth. We lay quietly for a while before I ask, "Where's Jakub?"

"My dreamy husband is likely already up and making breakfast," Ethan answers, his lips quirking.

I groan. "I really said that then."

He chuckles. "You certainly did. And you're not wrong."

"I've never met someone so... sweet," I admit.

"Should I be offended?" he asks, nipping at my neck.

Rolling into his embrace, I press a kiss to his lips. "No. I just mean... He's so damn patient. We were annoying bitches last night, and he never once acted like we were putting him out."

Ethan smiles. "Jakub *is* the sweetest man you will ever meet," he says. "If you let him, he'll give you the world. All he wants is to make those he loves happy. He loves romantic stuff, thoughtful gestures, and just... to take care of us."

"You keep saying us but—"

"Silly, Credence," he whispers, licking up the side of my face and making me squirm. "I say what I mean. Us."

My stomach flutters.

Jakub comes into the room, his smile making my stomach flutter further. I don't feel like he's just looking at Ethan anymore. It's like his smile is for me too. He approaches the bed and brushes his fingers through both of our hair.

"Time to get up, láskos. Breakfast. Then we need to shower and head to Meddy's," he says.

I'm not sure what láskos means, but I've heard a variation of it before. He has a handful of nicknames that he calls Ethan. The way Ethan grins at me says that it's probably something else really sweet, too.

Jakub leaves the room again as Ethan and I make our way out of bed. Since Lucien's party begins at eleven, that only leaves us a couple of hours. While we don't rush, we also don't dally while we eat and then pass through the shower.

Ethan turns quiet when we head out. I know what he's nervous about. We've unofficially decided that today is the day, providing Lucien and Bianca don't mind. I doubt they will. That's just the kind of people they are.

We're not the last to arrive, but considering the crowd of cars in their large driveway, half the team is already here. I recognize most of them as belonging to our closest friends, though I don't see Caulder yet.

Since it's still January in Buffalo, we aren't having this gathering outside, though the past three I've been to were in the spring and summer months and were held in their large backyard. Ethan lets us in, and we move through the enormous space until we find the solarium. It's basically an outdoor space, but under glass windows that amplify the heat of the sun. Though, again, since we're in Buffalo and it gets stupidly frigid out, there are a bunch of heaters, too.

I know immediately that something isn't right. Their chatter was already quieter than usual, but when we step into the room, everyone falls silent and turns to look at us. Chills race down my back.

"What's up?" Ethan asks.

For a beat, no one moves. Eventually, Isak gets up, glaring at Jakub as he approaches, and hands Ethan his phone. Before I even look at the screen, a pit forms in my stomach. Jakub and I move to crowd around him so we can see.

ETHAN WILDER IS CHEATING ON WINGMAN BOYFRIEND CREDENCE AYRTON WITH SECRET HUSBAND, NEW VANCOUVER TRANSFER, JAKUB BOZIK.

The image auto-scrolls right, and there are two pictures smashed together. One with Ethan and I cuddled up together after a game, just the second day after we had made our relationship official. It's juxtaposed with a grainy one of Jakub kissing Ethan with me behind them, looking at them. I have no idea where that photo was taken, but fuck, they somehow captured my expression that could easily be assumed as betrayed. When to me, I just look exhausted.

"Oh no," Jakub says.

Ethan's phone rings and he absently pulls it out of his pocket. I see the name flash across his screen and his wince echoes through my body. He hands Jakub Isak's phone and turns away to answer our PR manager.

As he walks away, I take Isak's phone and expand the words. It's not an article per se. It's a social media post by some trashy reporter on ShareIt. Of course, we're tagged in the post. As is our Buffalo Skidmoss team account, which is probably why everyone has seen it already.

The 'article,' if it can be called that, is just trash talking with every single fucking word of it complete and total garbage. There isn't a word of truth in the whole of it. I shove the phone back at Isak and turn around to search for Ethan. I can feel his stress from across the space. His head is bent forward as he talks into the phone, a hand gripping a fistful of his hair.

"Bullshit," I mutter.

"Is it?" Sacha asks. When I glare at him, he raises his hands all innocent-like. "I just ask."

"You've known Ethan for four years, Sacha," I snap. "What do you think?"

His gaze flickers to Jakub, while Isak continues to glare until I roll my eyes and move in front of him. "Just stop," I say warily. "That entire thing is a fucking lie."

"Except one tiny thing," Jakub mutters.

"Which part is that?" Isak asks and I know he's waiting for Jakub to say the cheating part.

I reach behind me and grip Jakub's wrist. "That they're married," I say. The loud inhale that carries through the room once again makes me roll my eyes.

Just as Ethan returns, Caulder comes storming in and reaches my side. "I'm sorry. I tried to warn you. Your stupid phone goes straight to voicemail."

"Wait, you knew?!" Isak asks.

Ethan flinches and turns his face away. I pull him close, hugging him tightly. "It's time," I whisper.

He snorts. "Like we have a choice now."

Ethan flinches again when he looks into the faces of our friends.

"Sorry to make this awkward," he says. "We were planning on telling you today once we spoke to Lucien and B and made sure they were okay to share the spotlight."

Bianca waves a hand. "The stage is yours, darling."

The tension in Ethan makes me hold him tighter. Minutes pass and words don't come. When I look at his face, I find he's truly struggling so I look at Jakub instead. This really needs to start with one of them. The beginning of the story is theirs. I come later.

Jakub gets the hint and moves forward, resting a hand on Ethan's hip in support. As if it were choreographed, the entire room's gazes drop to take in that possessive touch. I turn my face into Ethan's shoulder to hide my smirk.

"We've been married for seven years," Jakub says and comically, there's a very loud gasp that makes me snort. "We met in the AHL. Played together for a season. Got married that summer. Then I was drafted. We made the decision to keep our private life between us. Our parents don't even know we're married. Hell, I don't think mine even know I'm interested in men."

"You kept it secret so you didn't have to come out?" Isak asks, shaking his head.

"No. Not really. But kind of. From the day I met Ethan, I witnessed the prejudice and judgment he faced every day. We started our relationship in secret for both of our sakes because, though he was out, he didn't want to parade around his sexuality when he was already faced with bullshit on every front because of it. It was a mutual decision to benefit us both. My sexuality wasn't a topic of concern and besides the blanket assholery that Ethan faced, he wasn't shoved into the spotlight even more by having an open gay relationship."

"This entire thing is dumb," Sacha says, scowling.

I nod.

"You go through this all days?" he asks.

"Some more than others," I answer. "But yeah. It never ends. Never stops. If it's not some rando walking down the street spewing his opinions, it's keyboard warriors dropping nasty comments on our posts. Even when they have zero to do with being gay."

"We exist," Ethan says. "That's enough offense for a lot of people."

"I hate that for you," Sacha says.

Ethan offers him a smile. "Thanks. We do too."

"So you kept this from us to... wait, I'm confused about this," Isak says, waving his hand to encompass me.

"We've had an open relationship since we met," Jakub says. "In fact, our relationship began... this might be more than you want to know, but we got together at an orgy and... we weren't solo."

I burst out laughing and then quickly cover my mouth. Jakub chuckles at my reaction. Ethan finally offers an actual smile when he looks at me.

"You didn't know that," Ethan says.

Shaking my head, I say, "No. I just assumed it was like you and me."

Ethan shook his head.

"This is the second reason we kept our relationship a secret. We had no intention of a closed marriage. At least not while we were both active in hockey and would likely always be on separate teams," Jakub says. "Being judged for being gay was hard enough on Ethan. Adding to that an open marriage? Can you imagine the shit he'd get?"

"And so you're messing around with Creed?" Asael asks, looking slightly disgusted.

"No," Ethan snaps. "I've been in love with Creed since the day we met, asshole."

Asael holds up his hands, his expression clearing completely.

Ethan sighs. "I'm sorry I kept this from you. It wasn't because I don't trust you. I know it sounds that way, but all it would take is one person accidentally saying something and it would all blow up. One nosy person overhearing something meant for someone else's ears."

"Our parents don't even know," Jakub repeats, emphasizing it.

"Literally the only people who know are the three of us, our agents, and management. Outside of the three of us, they're all legally bound to an NDA," Ethan says. "And I've made it aggressively clear that I would spare no money destroying them if they let even a fucking hint of this slip. This part of my contract—our contracts—are not open to the entire agency. My agent alone knows."

"I wouldn't say anything," Isak says. I frown at the betrayal in his voice, knowing this is what will hurt Ethan the most.

Ethan grips his hand and hauls him close. "I'm sorry. Really. I need you to understand that it had nothing to do with you and everything to do with protecting us. The fewer people who knew, the safer we'd be."

"With my sexuality presumed straight, and us never seen together, there was never anything to tie us together," Jakub says.

"What is the picture from?" Bianca asks.

I shake my head, frowning.

"The airport. Yesterday," Jakub answers with a sigh. "We were so fucking tired that we weren't giving the situation enough attention. So I kissed my husband in public with no thought for those around us."

"So it's clear, I'm not at all upset about seeing it," I say, nodding to Isak as if he still has his phone open. "I'm literally dead on my feet in that picture. I'm not even sure I *actually* saw a thing."

"What that photo fails to show is that I pulled Creed in half a second later and held them both until we were called for boarding," Jakub says.

"Everything else in that 'story' is fabricated bullshit," I say.

"Time for a defamation lawsuit," Astor says, grinning. "My attorney is really good."

"I'm not even going to ask," Ethan says, but then adds, "Text me his name."

"This is all consensual?" Isak asks when the conversation peters off.

"100%," Ethan says. "Jakub has known how I felt about Creed since the day I met him. Creed has known about my marriage for about as long. We entered into this relationship completely honest on all accounts, and I've had Jakub's support from the beginning."

"Him being transferred here really threw a wrench into this, didn't it?" Bianca says.

"Yes and no," Jakub answers, pulling both of us closer once again. I hide my smile in Ethan's shoulder. "The idea was that they'd get settled as a separate couple for the rest of the season and then we'd come together this summer and see how we fell. Obviously, that whole plan was fucked up and this entire thing was... flipped on its head, I guess. It's working out well enough domestically. But we didn't tell you soon enough."

"That would have been nice," Isak says. "We always have your back, but clearly, we didn't know where to point our anger. We didn't know what we were defending."

"I know," Ethan says. "And *this* specifically is what I've been worried about. I didn't want you to think that you weren't important enough to me to know something this personal. I swear to you, Isak, that was never the case."

Isak smiles. "I know. I'm sorry I was a tool, man." He looks at Jakub. "I feel like a really big fool for accusing you of being homophobic."

"And I told you to find dick elsewhere," Three adds, cackling. "You must have been laughing hysterically internally."

Jakub smirks. "I used all your comments as feedback on how I was acting. I had no idea I watched Ethan as much as you all noticed."

"Only because we're always on the lookout for someone ready to give him a hard time," Lucien says. "You were new blood. Watching you was just the natural order of protecting our own."

Jakub smiles. "I really appreciate that. Honestly, the distance between us these last few years has really sucked, but knowing he had a team like you was a constant bolster, knowing that he was okay and looked out for. He's always spoken highly of all of you."

"So," Ethan says, "Any other questions or can we get back to the actual purpose of today? The fact that Lucien doesn't know how to wrap it."

Everyone chuckles.

"One more question," Jakub says, and I look at him with a brow raised. "What did PR say?"

TWENTY-SIX
ETHAN

I FEEL SO MUCH LIGHTER NOW THAT MY TEAM KNOWS. AND while I'm still so fucking pissed about the shit in that article, there's a weight that's lifted from my shoulders because I'm no longer carrying this secret.

My connection with Jakub has always been deep. Special. Our relationship has always been strong and healthy. Keeping it hidden, while there was a level of peace knowing that it's just between us and not under public scrutiny, almost felt dishonest to ourselves. We weren't hiding. Not in the way the world will understand it. But we *were* hiding.

"For now, we're to keep a low profile. The rest of the team will be briefed tomorrow on the situation and how they're to respond to reporters. PR has set up a whole bunch of stupid interviews and a 'domestic' photoshoot." I wave my hand. "Basically, we need to counter this shit with the truth."

"Good. And sue the false news spreader's asses," Astor says.

"I'm concerned that you have a lawyer on standby," Lucas says, eyeing Astor.

"You don't know everything about me," Astor says.

I laugh and it feels good. Jakub's arm wraps around my middle and I lean back into him, closing my eyes. Thank fuck that he's here right now, and this didn't come out when he was still in Vancouver or anywhere else. That would have sucked epically.

"Now back to the festivities," Creed says as he leans into my side. I don't miss the way he also leans into Jakub. Or that Jakub wraps an arm around him, too.

It is too much to want this right here and nothing else? This sliver of happiness. The desire to return to the island resort is so strong that it's almost a longing.

"Yep," Lucien says. "So, who wants to take a guess?"

"You know what I just saw on Viraly?" Three asks, leaning forward. "Not to fuck up today. We can try this with your next pregnancy. But the couple waited until the baby was born and then let everyone see them. They *then* guessed what their gender was."

Bianca looks at Lucien with a grin. "That's fucking awesome. I love that!"

Lucien grins too. "Yep. Noted. But for now, we have some games and shit. Then we'll tell you what we're having."

"As a reminder, we have five boys and two girls," Bianca says.

While our team debates and discusses what this next baby will be born as, I remain wrapped together in the arms of my guys. Caulder and Isak sit close, almost protectively, and I can't help but smile at this too.

By the time we leave, and it's revealed that they're having another girl, I'm feeling good. I've mentally decided that, regardless of how this came about, I'm so ready to drop the secret. Of course, I'm not looking forward to the confrontation with our parents. It's only a matter of time before *that* happens.

I'm second guessing my thoughts that this was a good turn of events when the wall of paparazzi outside of my apartment complex nearly prevents us from getting to our parking spot. Then we just sit inside the car as we're surrounded.

"We should just drive away," Creed says, "though not to my apartment. I'm sure it's no different there right now."

Jakub already has his phone out, calling the cops. When he gets off, he tells us that a squad car will be here shortly. For now, we'll just sit inside my car and glare out the windows at the invading assholes.

"I hate this," I mutter.

Jakub shifts in his seat to face me, gripping my hand and giving

STARTING LINE

the dicks in front of us something to actually photograph. "It's going to be fine."

"I think you should lay on the horn and watch them piss themselves," Creed says, making me burst out laughing.

Without taking his gaze off Creed and me, Jakub sets off the car alarm and the people surrounding us stumble backward in shock. I laugh again and grin at them.

The cops show up a few minutes later and clear a path to the apartment. Since it's not public property, they're being forced to vacate.

"I want all of their names," Jakub tells the cops. "I'll not only be setting up restraining orders for harassment but I'm also charging them with any damage done to my car as they climbed all over it."

"Absolutely, Mr. Bozik," one of the cops says, grinning into the crowd.

"I'm suddenly wishing we lived in a gated community," I mutter.

It's then that one of the reporters breaks free and sprints toward us, camera in hand. He stops in our faces, flashing the camera at us. Time slows down when he shoves Creed out of the way to get a better shot of Jakub and me.

When I say I see red, I really mean it. The next thing I know, I've punched the man in the face and then ripped the camera from his hands before smashing it on the ground. He's lucky I had Jakub and Creed there to pull me back, because I'm pretty sure I would have been beating his ass into the pavement.

He's crying assault charges and property damage by the time Jakub has me near the elevator door. Not thinking clearly, I yell back that I'll be charging him with trespassing and assault on Creed. What I did was in self-defense. The camera? Collateral damage since he's invading my privacy.

Everything is cut off after that when Jakub hauls me inside. I'm still ranting and screaming when he physically drags me into the elevator.

When we're safely in my apartment, Jakub has my face in his hands. "Breathe, Ethan. Look at me and take a deep breath."

It's hard. Really fucking hard. "They put their hands on Creed," I bellow, and try to pull loose. He keeps his grip tight.

"I know. Creed is fine. Creed, tell him you're fine."

Creed moves behind me, wrapping his arms around my chest and pressing his face to the back of my neck. "I'm fine, Ethan," he whispers. "I wasn't hurt. Please calm down."

I'm shaking violently, ready to rip someone in two. More than anything, I really want to hurt that man. It takes Jakub sitting on top of me on the couch to finally pull me from the red haze that clings to my vision.

Taking a deep, shuddering breath, I blink up at him. My tense body goes limp and I close my eyes.

It's then that my phone rings.

Jakub digs it out of my pocket and looks at the screen. Grabbing it from his hands, I smash the answer button and grit into the phone, "You knew what you were doing bringing my husband here. Management did this. This is your fucking fault. You knew it was going to create waves. Well, surprise. You have a motherfucking tsunami to deal with."

Before I get an answer in return, Jakub pulls the phone from me. With a small smile, he gives me a kiss and climbs to his feet. "I'll take this. Keep taking calming breaths." He looks at Creed, and Creed takes his place while Jakub speaks into the phone. He disappears into the other room, closing the door.

Creed gently pets my cheeks, running his fingers through my hair. The hint of a smile plays on his lips. "You were ready to kill someone for me," he murmurs.

My shoulders tense. His hands drop to them and gently rub against me, massaging out the stiffness. "It's been a long time since I've felt that... unhinged."

To my surprise, he nuzzles into my neck. "I love you, Ethan Wilder. You're my fucking hero," he whispers.

Wrapping my arms around him, I grin and close my eyes. "Did he hurt you?"

"No, Ethan. He caught me off guard. That's all."

"If your skin is so much as red..."

My words cut off when his teeth nip playfully at my neck. I shiver, wrenching him closer to me. Before I can contemplate my dick growing hard in my pants, the door to the spare room where Jakub took my phone opens.

Creed sits up and we both watch him walking over to us.

"How much trouble am I in?" I ask.

"Moderate," he answers. "I explained the situation. Having the police there as witnesses will definitely help your case. They were already calling the police department when I was on the phone."

"We're going to have to move," I say.

"No," Jakub answers, kneeling on the couch beside us. He leans his forehead against my temple. "It's going to be fine. We'll go along with PR's plan for now and if it doesn't blow over in a couple weeks, I have my own plan."

"What's that?" I ask.

"Never you mind. However, you're going to need to call your mother."

I flinch and shake my head. "Not today." Then my phone rings.

"Today, miláček. She called no less than half a dozen times while I was talking to PR."

Groaning, I let my head fall back. Sighing dramatically, I motion for him to hand me my phone. "Maybe we should get all our parents on the line so we don't have to have this conversation three more times today."

"Done," Jakub says, pulling out his phone and dialing. Creed glances between us as my phone stops ringing. Eventually he agrees too.

Jakub's parents are waiting patiently. Creed's have just answered when my phone's ringtone pierces the room again. I swear, it's getting louder. I wait for Creed to tell me he's ready, setting his phone on the table next to Jakub's, both on speaker, before I answer the call, putting it right to speaker.

"Ethan Torence Wilder," my mother's voice says shrilly into the room. "You have some fucking explaining to do, son."

Laughter from Creed's phone makes one corner of my mouth quirk up.

"Just so everyone is aware, we have all three sets of parents on our phones. And the three of us are together," I say.

There's a silent pause before Creed's mom says, "Ethan, honey. It's good to hear your voice."

I smile, bowing my head. "Yours too, Mrs. Ayrton."

Somewhat awkward greetings pass between all of us before, for the second time today, we repeat the same story we just laid bare for our team. Our mothers, all three of them, remain eerily silent throughout the entire thing. Several times I touch my screen to wake it up, just to make sure she's still there.

The three of us take turns talking, explaining the situation and our decision. Trying to emphasize that we weren't keeping the secret from them because we didn't trust them or love them, or because we were ashamed of our marriage or whatever. I think we spent more time reassuring them how much we love each other than was necessary.

Just as we're finishing up and our rambling is dying down, Creed's mother says, "Sweetie, did you punch a reporter today?"

I wince. "He shoved Creed," I say defensively.

"He what?!" she snaps, and I relax.

And thus, we explained the second incident that happened today.

"Baby, you need to move out of that apartment and somewhere with tall walls," my mom says. "And maybe a few vicious dogs."

Creed laughs. "It's too cold here for the dogs to stay outside, Mrs. Wilder."

She harrumphs. "Then you three need to be traded to a different team. One further south where it's warm and you can have dogs."

I laugh, letting myself fall back on the couch.

"No team is going to want this PR nightmare right now," Jakub says. "I actually think the PR manager is enjoying this. It's apparently been a long time since Buffalo has made this kind of news. He's got a very detailed plan in place that he was ready to set forward the moment that story hit."

There's a silence that follows before my mom asks, "They were anticipating this situation?" There's a chill in her voice that has my eyes widening. I exchange a look with Creed and Jakub.

"Yes?" I hedge.

"They knew we were married," Jakub says carefully.

I'm startled into jumping when she starts cursing the entire management team, promising them a place in hell for facilitating this mess.

"And everyone knew that Ethan and Creed were pining over each other," my mother says, still in her unsettling voice.

"We weren't pining," I mutter.

"You were pining," Creed's mom says.

Creed covers his mouth and looks at me with wide eyes, as if that will distract me from the fact that he's laughing.

"They literally created this situation," my mom says, distracting me again. "They created this and just threw you into it without a thought or concern for anything but winning."

"That's hockey, mom," I hedge.

She doesn't answer and I have a feeling she's not done with this conversation, though she lets it pass for now. There are some questions about what PR plans to do. Whether we have lawyers and whatever. What our plans are for the future.

When we finally manage to get all three mothers off the phone, mine rings *again*. I'm ready to throw the stupid thing, but Jakub snatches it before I'm able. But he doesn't answer. He looks at me. "I don't think I can take this call."

He hands it over and I see my agent's name. I groan and answer. This day can't possibly get worse. I know I'm challenging the universe with that thought, but fuck. If someone else calls after this, I'm going to lose my ever-loving mind!

TWENTY-SEVEN
CREDENCE

When the phones finally stop ringing, the three of us sit silently on the couch. The anticipation hanging in the air says we're all waiting for the next call. Jakub's agent? My agent? Mine is a literal deadbeat, so I doubt he cares at all. As long as I bring in money.

I really need a new agent. I'll add it to my list of shit to take care of after this storm blows over.

Jakub gets to his feet after a while and disappears down the hall, leaving Ethan and I staring absently at the phones on the table. I can only imagine what's going through Ethan's mind. He's such a kind man, that I know this is weighing on him.

Everyone knows that athletes and everyone under the spotlight have unfair expectations placed on them since they're literally living in the public eye. We're expected to act, speak, dress, and live a certain way. Being gay already challenges those expectations.

Though I know Ethan doesn't hide his sexuality and has always 'dated' in the open, I also know that he's very aware of all the cameras on him. Waiting for him to fuck up. Waiting for a scandal. Just... waiting.

But Ethan's always been a fan favorite. Because he's charming and charismatic. He's genuine, friendly, kind, and generous. That he's fucking gorgeous isn't missed by anyone. I swear, he has one of those smiles that you see in toothpaste commercials.

This was always going to be hard on me, but the pressure on Ethan, both professional and what he's always put on himself, is almost visible now. While he's not obsessed with public image, it's the lies that will weigh him down.

Jakub returns and pulls Ethan to his feet. Ethan looks listless. Drained. Jakub meets my eyes and gives me a small smile before he picks Ethan up and carries him down the hall. I smirk at the image. Jakub is bigger than Ethan, but not by a lot. A couple inches taller, yes, but his bulk is about the same.

For a minute longer, I sit there and contemplate what tomorrow will bring. We have practice. We've already received a text from Coach telling us to be there an hour early. I chew the inside of my lip as I consider this.

I know that he'll be addressing the news that broke today. And while I don't think it's going to be bad, a ball of dread sits heavy on my chest.

To distract myself from those thoughts, I pick up my phone and drop back onto the couch. For the remaining hours we spent at Lucien's, we didn't look at our phones. We haven't been online since —well, I guess since before our trip to the Isle of Kala.

The memories of our trip skip through my mind, and a smile touches my lips. We should have just stayed there. Fuck hockey.

I'm not sure what possesses me, but I click on the ShareIt app in search of the post that Isak showed us. I knew I'd be tagged in a bunch of shit from that, but I'm definitely not prepared for the little red bubble telling me I have over 1000 notifications. In reality, I don't know exactly how many because 999 seems to be the max number it's ever showed. When it moves beyond that, it's just indicated with a little + sign.

Then there are the DMs. I cringe seeing the exorbitant number. Fuck, I don't even want to see what people think they have the audacity to say to me right now.

Biting the inside of my lip, I decide not to look at either my notifications or my inbox. Instead, I scroll, which seems to be just as detrimental. My jaw drops as post after post filling my feed is all about... me, Jakub, and Ethan.

GAY DOESN'T END HAPPY

PROFESSIONAL ATHLETES NOW PUSHING THE GAY AGENDA

BUFFALO ENDORSING THAT IT'S OKAY TO BE GAY TO OUR IMPRESSIONABLE YOUTH

STAR LINEMAN, HOCKEY SWEETHEART, HAVING AN AFFAIR ON LONGTIME LOVE INTEREST

PUBLIC FIGURES FLAUNTING AFFAIRS

I scroll down after reporting a few as false news. But the further I scroll, the more there are. I'm surprised that *not a single one* is in support. Usually there are both sides out there, but no one is even countering the hate on gays playing sports.

Apparently, the lie out there trumps that.

Why hasn't Buffalo answered yet? Why haven't they put up a defense? It's not just our personal lives that are being dragged through the mud, but Buffalo along with them.

I jump and nearly yelp when Jakub's hand lands on my shoulder. His touch is soft, but I was so absorbed in the shit I'm seeing that it feels like he jumped out of nowhere.

His fingers move up and brush through my hair. Then he takes my phone, turns it off, and tosses it onto the chair. "Come on," he says, gently urging me to my feet. I let him and a yawn overtakes me. Once we're clear of the furniture, his arm moves around my shoulders. The next thing I know, he's picked me up with his other arm under my knees.

Laughing, I quickly bring mine around his neck. "What are you doing? You're going to drop me. I'm too heavy for this."

"No heavier than Ethan," he says, kissing my temple. Jakub doesn't wait for me to agree, but heads to the bedroom door.

I try not to stare but end up watching Jakub's face, anyway. I've always acknowledged that he's a good-looking man, but have I ever realized just how gorgeous he truly is? Body aside, his face is just one of those works of perfection. Especially with his unique, almost silvery eyes.

We bypass Ethan asleep on the bed and stop in the bathroom where he sets me on my feet again. I'm distracted when he begins removing my clothes, though he stops at my underwear. With a finger in the elastic, he murmurs, "Take these off. It's not fun bathing in underwear."

It's then that I see he's filled the tub. The steamy air is thick with lavender and sandalwood. Already my shoulders sag a little as the tension tries to fall away.

Glancing down at my underwear, I try to shove away that bit of insecurity that I have. In the locker room, I'm not worried. There's a silent code that you just don't comment on another man's junk. That admits you're looking and then all sorts of uncomfortable moments follow that. Even if someone notes that I'm small, no one says anything. No one even looks at me with that look that says they just *know*.

This is different, though. I'm alone in a bathroom with Jakub, my boyfriend's husband. Arguably, he's already seen me naked. He's seen me hard. He's touched me while I got off. This should be fine.

His hand cups the side of my face and I look up. "I love everything about your body, Credence." My cheeks heat as a shiver races down my spine. "Please don't be self-conscious with me."

Taking a breath, I nod and shove my underwear down. Jakub's soft smile looks back at me. His eyes don't leave mine. His calloused thumb brushes my cheek.

"Get in," he says quietly as he drops his hand to my lower back and guides me to the tub. I do as he says and step into the hot water. Before I even sink down, I'm groaning. Fuck, it feels so good.

When I'm laying back with my eyes closed, Jakub says, "Try not to think for a bit. Just relax. Okay?"

I nod and try to do just that. With all the shit that's happened today, it's proving rather difficult to keep my mind on nothing at all. When I find it's impossible to keep it blank, I decidedly think about the amazing two days we had at the Isle of Kala. The hike to the ruins. Ethan nearly getting stuck in a cave. Swimming with the enormous sea turtles. Floating over the ruins of a pirate ship that we could see clearly on the ocean floor as if it were ten feet under our feet when it was closer to thirty.

Then there was the day in our hotel room with the pampering massage and then the erotic touches that ended in an orgasm that had me nearly coming out of my skin. Who knew that a hot glass dildo shoved up my ass and an unlubed leather glove placing pressure on my cock was enough to have me going wild.

I mean, it was probably the whole experience that led to that point feeding into my explosive orgasm, but still. It was pretty great.

This time I hear Jakub approach and crack my eyes open as he crouches at the edge of the tub. His fingers go back into my hair and I shift so I can lean into him. His other hand drops below the water and wraps around my stomach.

"You okay?"

I shrug. "I made the mistake of going online," I say.

He chuckles. "Don't do that for a while."

"Yeah. I've also made that exact decision in response to going online."

"It's bad, huh?"

"I started to report them as false news, but honestly, we're not going to get them taken down. Everyone is entitled to their opinions as they sit behind their keyboards and spew their bullshit while remaining untouchable. It would be like the three of us trying to herd a thousand children running loose on a farm. Impossible to make it all go away."

"That's an interesting analogy."

I snort. "What's irritating to me is that Buffalo hasn't had a response yet. No one has. They're just letting the nastiness percolate and grow."

Jakub kisses the side of my head and I shift to look at him. His hand draws up my body until his thumb catches on my lower lip. "There's a plan, Creed. Beginning tomorrow, everyone will strike back."

"Why not today?"

He shrugs. "I'm not that concerned with it. Yes, it sucks. Yes, it's all lies. Why do you think that reporter tried to push you out of the picture?"

I shook my head.

"Because seeing the three of us together disproves the entire 'affair' story, doesn't it? And we've been seen leaving the apartment together, getting into the same car, returning to the apartment together. The three of us. But if *those* pictures get posted, someone will eventually question."

"I feel like the airport photo should already make people question," I say, hearing the pout in my voice.

"Your tired expression is being perceived as something else entirely."

I huff. His amused smile makes my lips twitch up too. Then he brushes them against my skin before gently pressing them to mine. My heart stutters loudly. I can feel my blood pressure increase. My stomach flips. It's just like every single time I kiss Ethan.

Thinking of Ethan is enough to make me pull away. "Do you think he's going to be okay with... us kissing?"

The way he smiles makes me think that he's remembering him getting me off on the balcony two days ago. Ethan was definitely okay with it then.

"Yes," he says. "But if it makes you feel better to wait until we ask him outright, then we can do that."

"I feel like maybe it's silly to, but for my own peace of mind, I... I think I need to."

He kisses my forehead and I freaking melt. "If anyone knew you for real, they'd know that every single nasty thing the internet warriors are spewing is a load of shit. You'd not be with a man if you knew they were having an affair. And if they knew how kind-hearted Ethan truly is—it's not just a persona but his actual being—they'd know that he'd never do that, either. I'm pretty sure he hurts a lot more at the idea of hurting someone else."

"What about you?"

He shrugs. "I think if I found my husband cheating, there'd be much more fanfare than me kissing him in front of the other man, don't you think?"

People really are stupid. The dicks who posted the picture painted the story they wanted and now people are actually seeing it that way.

"Time for bed," Jakub says and stands. He offers me his hand and I accept it. After he helps me out of the tub, he hands me a warm towel he'd had in his hands. I grin when I wrap it around myself. There's no towel warmer in here, so that means he'd had it in the dryer. I try to hide my smile at how fucking sweet that is.

When I'm relatively dry, I drape the towel over the bar. Jakub pulls me into the dark bedroom and, for a minute, we watch Ethan sleep. "You want underwear or are you good naked?" he asks.

I glance down, noting that I'm already walking around naked. "This is fine."

"Good. Get in bed."

He gently pushes me to the side and pulls back the blankets so I can climb in. When he's tucking me in, I say, "Aren't you coming to bed?"

"In a minute," he whispers back. "Just going to turn off the lights."

I nod, another yawn overtaking me. Rolling onto my side, I scoot closer to Ethan. As he always does, Ethan feels my presence and moves in his sleep to wrap around me. I smile as my eyes close.

It's definitely more than a minute later when Jakub finally crawls into bed behind Ethan. I feel when he presses to Ethan's back, his chest trapping my arms between them. His legs tangle with ours. Jakub snakes one of his arms beneath us, under the pillows we're laying on. The other circles us both, holding us firmly to him.

Aside from the fact that we're naked, this is a picture that should be out in the world. Showing exactly how we really are. Maybe this started out as two separate relationships, but it is firmly moving into something where we're all together.

The way my stomach dances at the prospect nearly has me gasping. Jakub Bozik is one of the sweetest men I've ever met. He didn't need to take care of me like that. But he did. I think he wanted to. I could definitely fall for this man.

Maybe I already have.

TWENTY-EIGHT
JAKUB

Practice is early the next morning because we need to be on a plane to Columbus this evening for tomorrow's game against the Sails. Though it was supposed to be at ten, everyone is piling in before nine for the mandatory pre-practice meeting.

There's a stranger there when we show up. As we follow our teammates in, everyone is quietly eyeing him where he sits in front of an empty cubby. It wasn't empty before the break though. I can't remember who was there, but someone was for sure. And it wasn't this kid.

He looks like he's right out of high school. He gives us wide, though hesitant, smiles as we gather around and fall onto the benches in front of our cubbies. I keep an eye on Ethan. He looks tired and drawn this morning. The tension in his shoulders suggests he's ready to snap if the slightest negative thing is thrown our way.

Coach Melvin, Assistant Coach Elvyra, and the PR manager step into the locker room at exactly nine.

"Good to see you're all here," Coach says, pulling over a chair and sitting. "Welcome back."

There's a quiet greeting in return as everyone glances at the new kid in the now unassigned cubby.

"I'm sure you know why I called everyone in," Coach says.

"Because there are tools on the internet?" Isak asks.

Ethan smirks a little, though his gaze is far away.

"Yes. Is it safe to assume that you've told the team about your... throuple? Triad? What are we calling you?" Coach asks Ethan.

Ethan raises his eyes and shrugs. "Together. I don't know that we've really tried to make it fit into an already established label. But yes."

Coach chuckles. "Very well. I'm going to begin by reminding everyone that a person's personal life is not up for debate, ridicule, or comment. Not within the locker room and certainly not outside it within earshot of the public. If we find that you cannot offer your teammates respect, you will be removed from this team. Am I clear?"

Everyone's eyes glance at the cubby that had once been filled with a different player. Lipsen? Laposwki? Lorengrove? I'm pretty sure it began with a L, anyway. I think I'm just mentally making shit up right now.

"Yes, Coach," the room echoes.

"Good. Next, we're going to talk about the elephant that just sat on the internet." The room snickered at his metaphor. I don't think it even makes sense. "We all know that it's nothing but lies. In a few, Jakub's name isn't even spelled correctly. We know that the gossip tabloids aren't interested in facts; they will literally take a sliver of shit and make it a dumpster fire if it gets them page views. This is nothing new."

"Why hasn't the team addressed it yet?" Phalyn asks. "So many of those posts are making the entire team into... I'd say assholes, but since they're accusing us of harboring gays, I don't think it's quite a lie. But it's all negative bullshit."

"We have a plan," the PR guy says. "Launch begins today."

"You just wanted to let the keyboard warriors fill everyone's head with shit first?" Isak asks.

"Kind of. Right now, Buffalo's name is on everyone's tongue. You know how I feel about attention; good or bad—it's attention, nonetheless. However, we're about to come back with bullying campaigns, outreach about bigotry against the LGBTQ+ community, and smear campaigns. Tomorrow morning, we're going to blast the truth behind our starting line's personal lives and show the world how idiotic these people truly are."

"I object to this," I say, making the entire room look at me. "Our personal lives are not for public consumption."

The PR guy raises his hand in defense. "Not what I meant, exactly. I'm going to apologize now that you're going to be stuck in interviews almost nonstop for a while, including some domestic photo shoots."

"You can ask us to participate in a photoshoot," I tell him, crossing my arms and narrowing my eyes. "While I understand you think this is some great opportunity for the team, this is literally fucking with our lives. Do you know what it took to get out of our apartment this morning? I had to nearly run a bitch over who insisted on flashing his fucking camera in my windshield."

Creed nods, scowling. Ethan remains impassive. I make a pointed look at him, bringing everyone's focus to Ethan. He doesn't seem to notice. After a minute of silence in which Ethan still doesn't look up, I get to my feet and cross the room.

The movement catches Ethan's attention and I pull him to his feet before retaking a seat in his spot on the bench and pulling him into my lap. Ethan rolls his eyes, shakes his head, but he leans heavily into my arms. I give another pointed look to Coach.

"You're right," Coach says. "While we'd like to get some photos to show what your life truly is, that's not mandatory. I'd like you to do a few interviews, though."

"Can I offer a counter suggestion," Creed says. "I don't want someone in our home with a camera. I get that the world has seen Ethan and me together for years, but that's really not the case. This entire thing is really new and I'm not comfortable letting a stranger in to film us. However, we're together all the time. We have games every other day. We go to events, and we do other work-related shit. And we're always together—the three of us, as well as the entire team. Why not just have a photographer follow us around anywhere outside our home?"

"I like that," PR guy says, nodding with a thoughtful expression. "That will not only show the three of you, but also that the rest of your team supports you as well. In a larger picture, we can emphasize that this team is more than teammates; they're friends." He pauses to look around the room. "That's the truth, isn't it?"

I see many eyes roll but there are nods all around.

"What are we supposed to say when someone sticks a recorder in our face?" Lucien asks. "I'm guessing shoving it down their throat isn't an option."

"Physical confrontation of any kind is prohibited," Elvyra says. She's always so quiet that I forget she's around until she speaks. It's doubly startling because her voice is so unlike the men that make up Buffalo.

"I will practice self-defense," Ethan says, turning his face to look directly at her. "If someone thinks they can lay their hands on me or mine without retaliation, they're wrong."

Elvyra frowns but there are several around the room nodding in agreement.

"My lawyer agrees," Ethan says, eyes hooding.

I happen to know that he's speaking out of his ass right now. He hasn't spoken to a lawyer.

"You may say one of two things," Coach says, moving the conversation along. I have a feeling he agrees with self-defense. "'No comment' or you can tell them you support your teammates. That's it. No conversations. No exchange of information. I don't want you to even say anyone's name. You support your teammates."

"We do support our teammates," Isak says as he glances at the new guy. "So I think I should ask what happened to Crawford, and who's the guy sitting in his cubby?"

Huh. Apparently, his name hadn't started with an L. Who was I thinking of?

"Crawford's contract was terminated for personality conflict," he says, and we all know he's not supposed to tell us a reason. I have a feeling that ties in directly with this conversation, though. Ethan stiffens in my arms, and I hug him tightly. "He will not be picked up by another team. Tomorrow he'll be making an announcement that he's retiring. We have asked Michael Sharpe from our farm league to step in for these next couple games."

"What you're saying is he had some shit to say about our boys," Isak says. I don't miss the way the room cools considerably.

Coach doesn't answer but keeps eye contact with Isak. After a heavy silence fills the room for far too long, Coach says, "Again, I will remind you that you are to make no comments on your teammates' personal lives to anyone. Not where you can be accidentally overheard and certainly not intentionally. This includes social media comments. Am I clear?"

He just gave us a lot of information that he shouldn't have, and I know that this Crawford asshole contributed to the online fiasco.

"There will be no retaliation," Elvyra says. "I realize that it's a lot to ask. I've personally had to stop myself from commenting several times yesterday until it got to the point where I signed out of all my social media apps to take away the temptation. This is difficult to see. Infuriating. I know that. It's rough seeing your friends being talked about with such open hostility when you know everything being said is an outright lie. We are going to strike back, guys. But it needs to be done professionally. We will not stoop to their level of assholery."

Again, the room simmered with her words, and I knew I wasn't the only one wanting to find what Crawford had said that got his contract canceled. As far as I knew, he hadn't ever shown any kind of aggression toward Ethan or Credence. Hell, I hadn't even remembered his name, so I clearly hadn't had any confrontations with him.

"I will send to him a bag of dicks," Sacha says.

A wall of startled silence follows his statement before the room bursts into laughter.

"Fucking Sacha," Three says, slapping his back.

To my surprise, no one, not even the PR guys, speaks against it.

PRACTICE WAS A BREATH OF FRESH AIR. I THINK WE ALL ENJOYED letting some frustration out by expending some energy and slapping the puck with our sticks as hard as we could. I almost felt bad for our two goalies. Phalyn managed fine, but poor Asael looked like he was being assaulted. He laughed about it at the time, but it was almost brutal.

Creed, Ethan, and I were called into Coach's office after we showered. Elvyra and the PR guy were still hanging around too. Once we were seated, the PR guy handed us each a paper.

A list. A very long list. That covers multiple pages. I look up at him with a frown.

"I've canceled the photographer," he tells us. "Actually, I rescheduled him to perform Credence's suggestion." He beams.

"Hold hands on the tarmac," Ethan reads. "Kiss as getting onto the bus. Cuddle, all three together as waiting for room assignments." He looks up with a glower. "We're not doing this shit. You wanted natural. That's what you're getting."

"I mean, we do cuddle when we're waiting for our room key," Creed says.

"This is all based on observation," the PR guy says. "It's not a solid, non-negotiable plan. Improv."

"You're trying too hard," Creed says. "We're not going to set up scenes for your guy. He can capture how we actually behave together, or he doesn't get anything. You think I have the time to think about what we're doing for an audience when we're trying to concentrate on the upcoming game?"

"Good answer," Elvyra says through a cough.

PR guy sighs dramatically. "Your first interview is on the plane. Can you manage that?"

"On one condition," I say. When I'm sure I have his full attention, I continue. "While you don't understand how annoying and frustrating it is to have to explain and defend yourself at every turn, it's already getting old. I can't even tell you how many times we've gone over this in the last week. So, we'll give one lengthy, in-depth interview concerning our open marriage relationship, Creed, my sexuality, whatever. And that's it. Every interview thereafter will need to be with something else in mind. A new angle. A new series of questions. I know this is going to be a wild idea, but they could even talk about hockey."

Elvyra coughs again. I also don't miss the way Coach has to hide his smirk.

"But we're *not* going to keep rehashing the same thing. I'm going to emphasize that this is our lives. This is our relationship. And regardless of the fact that we're professional athletes in the spotlight for the world to see, our personal lives are private. This is non-negotiable."

"Furthermore, we're not some PR project for you," Creed says. "Obviously you get off on this shit, but I think you're forgetting that we're the ones living through this. Those words, those headlines, they're about us. We're living, breathing people, Robert. Maybe you only see the wall of meat that performs on the ice, but this shit affects us. Remember that when you're making your lists and planning some epic response in your own timeframe. For the last twenty-four hours, this is the hell we've been living through. While you sit comfortably scheming on how you can finally put one of your fucking plans into action."

PR guy—who finally has a name, but I likely won't use it—stares at Creed. His mouth opens and closes as he attempts to come up with a rebuttal but fails. He looks a little shell-shocked. I have to wonder what his experience with the team has been before this. Is he used to people just doing as he says? Bowing to his expertise?

"Anything else, Robert?" Coach asks.

PR guy shakes his head. "No. I'll make sure there's an interviewer on the plane when you take off."

"The plane ride isn't long," I comment.

"Would you mind continuing what there wasn't time for over dinner?" he asks, and I have to control my gloating smirk that he's finally figured this out. We aren't his puppets.

"As long as they understand that this isn't a social call and that we have a game tomorrow and won't be staying up all night so he can get a good dish on our lives," I say.

"I'd also like to see his article before he posts it," Ethan says. "I'm really tired of all the fake shit out there. They need to be responded to with nothing but the facts."

"Also, we just came back from vacation together. I think we could be persuaded to donate a couple pictures of the three of us that were actually candid and real to this article," Creed says.

Ethan grins at him.

PR guy beams. "Yes! That would be fantastic. You could email them to me?"

"We'll look over the ones we have and forward those that we approve for public consumption," I say. "Now, with all due respect, Coach, if you want us on the plane on time, we really need to go pack. There's only an hour before we need to leave for the airport, and I already anticipate fighting with the paparazzi just to come and go from our apartment."

TWENTY-NINE
CREDENCE

THE REPORTER'S NAME IS ELROD BARLOWE. ROBERT ASSURED US he isn't one of the assholes online nor has he been with the paparazzi. His face isn't familiar, but that doesn't necessarily mean anything.

When Jakub said we'd give a single long, in-depth interview about *us*, he meant it. We covered everything from our sexuality and how we grew up, to meeting, to dating, and we even touched a bit on our sex lives. Nope, I wasn't at all mortified by these topics at all.

We also discussed some of the pictures that have been popular online that are 'proof' of what they're claiming about us.

Now, I know that being a journalist takes a bit of acting. They have to at least pretend to be interested and sometimes do questionable things to get a story. They have to appear personable and friendly to gain trust.

Either Elrod is really good at all of the above, or he was a little surprised about what was actually happening in those pictures.

"You know," Elrod says as we sit across from him in the hotel dining room where we've been for the last hour and a half, "now that you point out what's going on, their claims just look so stupid. I can't *unsee* your exhaustion, Creed."

"I'm still exhausted," I say. "We traveled almost 10,000 miles over four days. The two days we weren't traveling, we were hiking and swimming and just enjoying the resort, making the most of the little time we had there. I really don't understand how anyone can see anything other than how utterly dead on my feet I was."

While we are taking a leap of faith on this guy, we provide him with our plane tickets (electronic copies, of course) and images of our passport stamps, showing that this is exactly where we were and what we were doing. They go with the handful of pictures we emailed him from the resort too.

Elrod is really excited about the whole thing. He has a lot of questions and while they are along the lines of what the accusations going around implied, I think that he is really looking for the truth of it.

I haven't been a part of a lot of interviews. Most of the questions I answer are during press conferences and while those can be inappropriate and lead to something entirely off topic, I rarely had to sit through anything like this. Even the few times I was interviewed right after I was drafted felt different.

This time, I'm feeling exposed. Like we're putting ourselves out there, raw and bare, for the world to see. This is our truth.

What's going to suck the most is that we know that there will still be some very loud haters. It shouldn't bother me. I've been dealing with the ugly side of people since I was a teenager. Someone is always going to hate what I am.

I have a feeling that this is going to hurt more than anything else that came before it, though. Because there are going to be those that insist that our love, our relationship between three people, is wrong. Disgusting. Unethical. All that crap.

The same things they say about me being gay. I'm used to that.

But having people criticize our little family of three? I can anticipate that being a blow that I'll actually feel.

Ethan's hands close around my face, and I blink out of my thoughts. He's in a considerably better mood as we step out of the elevator and return to our room after the interview, but now I can only focus on what's coming. I think I've been lost in thought ever since we came up to our room.

"What's wrong, baby?" he asks, and my heart does a little dance like it does every other time he calls me baby.

I'm going to call it stress for the reason I blurt out my next question. There's really no other explanation. Considering it wasn't even what I was thinking about, I'm not quite sure where it came from. "Can I see your husband too?"

I blink at him, wide-eyed. Startled.

Ethan is clearly startled as well, since he just looks at me. Right before I begin to panic, he smiles. "Yeah, Creed. Fuck, you have no idea how much I'd love that."

My exhalation is so dramatic that I sway slightly. "Really?"

He chuckles and pulls me to him, kissing my cheek before wrapping me in his arms. "Yes. I think in the back of my mind I was always hoping that we'd be a very intertwined... couple. Uh... triad. You know, I hate that there isn't a comfortable name for this. But that's not the point. I always wanted this, but I was never, ever going to suggest it."

I sink into him, relieved.

"Why did you think I'd be upset about it?"

Shaking my head, I say, "I guess I didn't, really. But what if you were? I didn't want to take that chance."

"Fair." We're quiet. The only sound we hear is the shower and the random door closing beyond our hotel room. "I don't think that's what was bothering you, though. Is it?"

Sighing, I shake my head again. "I guess I'm kind of dreading this story coming out."

"Why?"

"Because there's still going to be backlash, but it's going to feel more personal this time. I don't care if they attack me and my sexuality. But I think it's really going to bother me for someone to attack our relationship."

His arms tighten. "I know. It's going to really, truly suck. I think our best strategy is that we're going to have to stay offline for a while. Ignore it. We can't avoid what happens in person, but that's only one front to worry about."

"Maybe sign out like Elvyra says she did," I say.

"Exactly. We have people who watch our accounts." Ethan pauses. "Do you have someone who watches your accounts?"

Smiling, I shake my head. "It's never seemed necessary before."

"Hmm," he answers. "Well, I'm guessing that we're going to be tagged together—the three of us—for quite some time, so in a third-party kind of way, your account will be watched. We really need to do something about your deadbeat agent, Creed."

"That seems like such a small thing right now," I say.

"Yet, it's not. They're supposed to have your back. While Buffalo was sitting on their ass because Robert thought that letting the drama build was a fan-fucking-tastic idea, our agents were working on serving cease and desist orders. Beginning defamation statements. Commenting on some of these posts."

"When have you even had a chance to talk to them again?" I ask. I've literally been with him every second today. I haven't seen him take a call.

"I get email reports daily when something is happening. Otherwise, it's weekly."

I groan. "You're right. I need a new agent."

The bathroom door opens and a minute later, Jakub is standing close to us. He's not pressed to my back, but I can feel his body heat. "Everything okay?"

"We've determined that Creed needs a new agent," Ethan says.

"Yes, I thought so. Mine is already watching your accounts, though."

I smile, hiding it in Ethan's shoulder.

"Such a papa bear," Ethan croons.

Jakub leans forward and now I can feel more than just his body heat as he wraps us in his embrace. "Absolutely. There's nothing I love more than making it so you don't have to worry about something." His lips press to the spot right under my ear before he murmurs, "That goes for you too, Creed."

I drop one of my hands and grip his thigh to keep him close. If someone had asked if I wanted to be taken care of in a relationship, I'd have said no. I know that the world thinks that's the dynamic between Ethan and me, but it's certainly not the reality. To some extent, we take care of each other.

Like just a few minutes ago when he asked me what was wrong. He's always checking in. Always making sure I'm happy and comfortable.

But really, I'm the one that makes sure he's as carefree as possible. I want to eliminate the pressure he's always carrying by being the starting center. By striving to live up to the expectations of greatness he's achieved and now is expected to maintain. He's always doing charity events and giving to communities that need it. He's a very loud and well-known advocate for the LGBTQ+ people in the world, especially the youth.

When we're off the ice, when we're out of the spotlight, I don't want him to think about anything at all but his happiness and peace of mind.

I've always loved being the one to remove his burdens and take his mind off everything. I fucking love holding him and feeling him sink into me.

But hell, having Jakub do for me what I've always tried to do for Ethan? It should be awkward. Or uncomfortable. I should feel... oppressed? But goddamn, does it feel so good to be cared for. To know that someone is looking out for me, and I didn't even know he was doing it. Because he wants to. Because he cares. Because I'm important to him.

I'm not an overly emotional man, but the way tears sting my eyes has me trying to catch my breath.

And this is why it's going to hurt so bad when people hate on our relationship. This is the best thing that's ever happened to me. More than hockey. Or financial security. Over success. The love and support I have from men who *want me* just as I am? This is everything beautiful and I'm going to hate seeing others comment on it negatively.

I STAY OFF THE INTERNET THE NEXT DAY. ELROD'S ARTICLE WAS emailed to us overnight and, not going to lie, I fucking loved it. Even with as exposed as I felt after reading it, it was perfect. Jakub noted some things that needed to be edited, but when he approved the next draft half an hour later, we knew that the world was about ready to have another field day.

Within the hour, his article and so many fucking posts on all platforms were going to hit the world by storm. And I was trying like hell to stay off my phone. I didn't want to know.

Jakub monitored things periodically, but he somehow kept a frustratingly neutral expression. By noon, I was so antsy that he pulled us from the room and took us to the hotel gym so we could work off our stress.

There were cameras going off there, too. But what were they going to see? Three men working out. There's only so much interaction we can have while working on conditioning. I kept my earbuds in and tried to tune out everything around me.

We won against Columbus 5-4 and were off the next morning to Dallas for a game that night. I hated these turnarounds where we were barely able to sleep between games.

The only notable thing that happened during the Columbus game was that one of their defensemen made a derogatory comment to me about being a gay slut. In the very next play, Ethan ran him over like a steamroller while flicking the puck to Jakub for our winning goal. Then stood over the guy and said, "Courtesy of a gay slut."

I didn't laugh hysterically or anything. The hit was completely legal, which only pissed off the other player more. When he tried to retaliate, he was sent to the penalty box, and we still won the game. I'm pretty sure he'll be slapped with some fines and a very strict warning about his comments as well.

For the last decade, there's been a movement in professional sports to enforce non-discrimination against the federally protected groups—race, creed, sexuality, etc. Once more and more players are entering pro sports open about their sexuality, there have been some ugly moments but always, the LGBTQ+ player has been protected.

Players like the defenseman dickhead won't be tolerated, so he's going to have to come to terms with gay players or take a hike. I really kind of hope he takes a hike. Those are the people that shouldn't be role models for young athletes.

But the Dallas game, that was a disaster. I'd never taken Dallas to be a particularly antagonistic team but by the time the game ended, and we lost 0-1, there had been so many fights on the ice because they couldn't keep their nasty comments to themselves, I was feeling bruises in places I haven't ached in for a very long time.

Now our starting line is standing in front of the press as they spew comments at us. I'm honestly barely paying attention at this point because I'm so damn tired. Between the travel and back-to-back games, on top of the shitshow on the ice tonight, I'm ready to just crash. I'm thankful that our flight isn't until the afternoon and we have no game tomorrow.

That's when it happens. A reporter yells out a question that has the rest of the room falling quiet. "Do you really believe you should be representing the NHL as a trio of homosexuals who can't maintain a sacred relationship?"

Ethan is immediately fuming. He takes a step forward and words begin to tumble out of his mouth before Jakub hauls him back and says sharply into his ear that the microphones don't miss, "Stop." Ethan falls silent, but the fury in his eyes can be felt throughout the entire room. It makes me fidget, and I was just insulted along with him.

Our Coach comes out to bring us off, but Jakub doesn't move. "I suppose it's no different than you, a convicted stalker under two different names, trying to make money off of the hatred you spew when it doens't align with your opinion." Murmurs break out but I'm just stunned by the calm and cool voice Jakub addresses the journalist with. "Yes, I believe three great athletes who have earned their spots in the NHL through their hard work and talent alone *should* represent the league. Our sexuality and personal lives have zero standing in our careers."

Coach Melvin yanks me out from behind the microphones in that moment of stunned silence. As soon as I stumble through the door, more aggravated questions are being shouted. Jakub and Ethan are by my side as I get my feet under me again and Coach is talking to the press.

"Is that true?" I ask.

"Yes. I've had run-ins with him before. The good pious newsie has a criminal record for stalking celebrities and other athletes and has been convicted twice, under two different names. When he acquires a record with one, he legally changes his name and begins again. He likes to give offhand jabs at shit that has no place in sports, so I asked my agent to find out what he could about him. I've kept it in my back pocket for five years."

I laugh, but Ethan is not smiling at all. He's still irate.

THIRTY

ETHAN

I ALMOST CANCEL BECAUSE I'M STILL SEEING FUCKING RED WHEN we get back to the hotel. The audacity of that idiot! I'm so angry, I really just want to hit someone.

I've already texted Elixon to tell him that I'm going to be late. Coach held Jakub back once we arrived at the hotel. No doubt to speak to him about his comment. But fuck that. Assholes like that journalist need to feel some backlash too. They think they have free rein to print whatever the fuck they feel like, true or not, with no consequences.

Well, surprise, fucker. We have your number. Hopefully, you'll feel some actual consequences now.

I'm supposed to be in the lobby to meet Elixon Kipler, another queer player in the NHL. His team plays Dallas tomorrow. I really hope they kick some ass. I'll never have rooted for a team that was not my own so hard as I will tomorrow.

"You going to be okay to go downstairs?" Creed asks me.

I look at him and take a deep breath. It's a legitimate question right now. "Depends," I answer. "If that asshole is here, then no. I'm going to bloody him up if I see him again."

The door opens before he has a chance to respond and Jakub, cool and collected as ever—and also fine as fuck in his suit—strolls in. He smiles at me. A soft, fond smile that somehow forces me to take a calming breath.

"What happened?" I ask.

"Nothing I wasn't expecting. That wasn't a good look. It wasn't how we respond to ignorant people." He waves his hand in an etc. motion. "However, I don't think he disapproved at all. I think that's what he was required to tell me. I have a feeling that you won't be in front of the press for a while, though. You, my love, have no fucking regulation."

I snort and cross my arms.

Jakub grins. With his hand on the back of my neck, he pulls me to him and covers my mouth with his. "Lásko, let me handle the questions, okay? Just let me take care of it."

Glowering at him, I nod.

"If that man is in the restaurant downstairs," Creed begins.

"You and I will be there too," Jakub says. Without breaking eye contact, he says, "Change into something comfortable, Creed. We need to make sure our boy doesn't get himself into trouble and suspended from the team."

"Would serve them right," I mutter. "This is their fault."

He kisses me again. "I know," Jakub says quietly. "And yet, I would gladly live through this a thousand times if it means I finally get to spend every single day with you."

When he puts it like that...

I deflate and frown at him. His smile does nothing to soothe the anger inside me, but it does somehow coax one out of me.

"I know, Ethan," he murmurs. "I truly understand how frustrated and angry you are. We are too. But it's our jobs, it's who we are as people, that we don't sink to their level."

"I really liked your brand of 'fuck you,' though," Creed says. "I can't wait to see the repercussions of that."

"Which we won't see for a while because we're taking a social media break. Aren't we?" Jakub says, turning his light gaze to Creed.

Creed flushes and nods. "Yep."

I laugh and close my eyes. "Fuck, I love you both."

Jakub hugs me and I sigh into him. This is what I needed right now. Just to feel his warmth. His solid, protective presence. "We love you," he answers. "Now, let me get changed and we can head down."

He steps away and I ask, "Do you guys want to eat with us?"

"Nope," Creed says.

Jakub shakes his head. "Enjoy some time with your friend. We'll run interference if necessary."

I'm not really sure Elixon is my friend. He's another queer hockey player, so we've been thrown together for events often over the years. We make it a point to catch up when we're in the same place, just as the rest of us do when our paths cross throughout the season.

I don't hate it. And maybe I could use some time not thinking about all this outside bullshit.

There are, of course, reporters all over the lobby and we're photographed no less than a hundred times as we make our way into the restaurant. I'm led to a table in the back, and I know that Elixon and I will be pictured together all night. There will be no less than a dozen different fabricated stories about this sordid affair.

Right in front of my husband and boyfriend because they're seated a couple tables away.

Elixon looks amused as I drop into the chair across from him. "This is more fanfare than I'm used to," he says.

"Welcome to hell," I mutter.

He chuckles. "I take it things are going well."

"I don't know. Was the post-game press conference broadcasted yet?"

His smile widens wickedly. "Yes. It was."

"Then yeah; everything is peachy."

He laughs as the waiter comes over. I don't even look up as I order. I'm not in the mood to face anyone that *might* be judging me right now. Despite how much my guys calmed me, I'm still furious from the game and then the journalist.

"What happened on the ice?" Elixon asks.

"Which time?" I deadpan.

He takes a sip. "When you basically downed Dixon like you were wrestling and not playing hockey."

"Some assholes can't keep their comments to themselves. I'm really fucking pleased that all five scores were made by the gays." I emphasize 'the gays' to make my point.

He sighs, shaking his head. "This is why I've written off a relationship until after I retire. I don't have the patience for it."

"Do I look like I'm doing well on that front?"

Elixon laughs. "No."

Our appetizers arrive, and our conversation stops while the waiter is here. That's nothing new, of course. I learned a long time ago that we don't speak about anything when a stranger is close. That's why we always ask for a table as far from other patrons as possible when we meet up.

"Otherwise, things are well? Your husband and boyfriend are well?"

I level a look at him as I suck on a crab leg. His gaze drops and he gives me an amused look. "Yes," I answer. "Shitstorm aside, we're... really great." A smile pulls at my lips, and I glance over at them.

"They couldn't stand to be away, huh?"

"No, that's my safety detail. I apparently have no chill and will most likely attack someone who makes a nasty comment," I say, shrugging.

"Good," he says. "I get that America is based on the fundamentals of all these freedoms, but this isn't what the forefathers meant."

"The forefathers also had slaves who they didn't consider people and believed that women were second-class citizens. Queer people weren't even a publicly acknowledged thing, or I think we'd be on the level of slaves."

Elixon snorts. "Fair enough. And probably accurate. I'd be curious to know where the disconnect came from," he says.

After I've sucked the life out of one crab leg, I look up. "What do you mean?"

"Every ancient society and culture reflected homosexuality as a regular part of their lives. Even their deities were almost always bisexual if not pan. The stories, the art... it's all plainly there. And now look at us."

"The answer is obvious, isn't it? Christianity. They basically came in and told every civilization that they were heathens and wrong. They rewrote entire cultures to match their own opinions and beliefs."

"Ouch," he says, chuckling. "Though I don't think you're wrong."

"It's not like I'm a Christian hater. I believe in a god to some extent. But I'm not sure I believe in their God since he seems rather hateful than what they try to claim to be true about him. I mean, if he were real, I can't believe he'd create me as a gay man and then condemn me for being so. Right? But I believe in a divine presence somewhere."

Elixon nods. "I suppose so."

"You don't believe," I observe.

He shrugs. "I've seen more evidence of no god than I have that there is one. Any god. Under any denomination."

"Probably a good thing if one doesn't exist. The entire world would go to hell if he did. There's no one leading a truly sin-free life. Yet, everyone is a judge."

"Any other day, I'd tell you that you're being cynical. But given the current climate hovering around you, I have to agree," Elixon says.

Our meals come and once again, we let our conversation die down. I'm feeling marginally better now that I can breathe in peace again. After we've eaten a few bites, I ask, "What about you? How's Edmonton? How's the love life going?"

He rolls his eyes. "Lack of love life. I honestly have no idea how people find real relationships when they're a celebrity. Everyone wants you for something and it's never for *you*."

I nod. That's been my experience too.

"Otherwise, all good. We're having a mediocre season. Probably going to end somewhere in the middle of the pack." He shrugs.

"Happens," I say. "We likely will too. We started out strong with a ten-game winning streak and then just collapsed. Even with as strong as our starting line is now, I don't think we're going to make up for the lost ground."

"We haven't even seen a streak that long in either wins or losses. Just the way the puck drops, I guess."

I'm feeling better by the time Elixon and I call it a night. Most of that light feeling is erased when we leave the restaurant to a handful of people shoving cameras and recorders in my face and yelling questions. I'd really like to know where security is on these nights. Why are they even allowed in the hotel? Can we enact a law that forbids journalists from staying in the same hotel as hockey players?

We don't allow them in our elevator. By the time the next one returns to the main floor, and they know which floor we're on, we're already in our room.

This room is technically assigned to Creed and me, while Jakub is paired with another player. Three, I think. But now that the world knows, there's no need to pretend. No need to sneak around. I appreciate that aspect of this situation.

Everything else is just making me angry.

I brush my teeth and strip out of my clothes but as soon as I get back into the room, both my guys are on me. I'm laughing as they kiss over my body. Before I can accuse them of planning an ambush, Creed has dropped to his knees and has my cock in his mouth.

Letting my head fall back, I groan loudly.

"How about we relieve some of your stress tonight?" Jakub murmurs as he trails loving but wet kisses along my neck.

"Both of you?" I ask, rocking my hips forward. "Together?"

"Mmm," he answers, dragging his tongue up my neck. "That okay with you?"

A zing of pleasure races through me, and I shiver in anticipation. "Yes, please."

"Both of you get on the bed. Hands and knees. Ass towards me."

Creed looks up, his mouth still wrapped around my dick, but he's still. Jakub runs his fingers through Creed's hair, smiling down at him.

"You too. I'd like to point out I only have a single cock, so you won't take mine tonight, Credence. We're going to sandwich Ethan. But I want you to let me prep you. Is that okay?"

He swallows around my cock as he nods. The momentary tight squeeze has my dick leaking.

"Now. On the bed."

I scramble away to do as I'm told. Creed is slower to follow, glancing at Jakub a couple times before he mimics me. Shoulder to shoulder and hip to hip, he aligns himself with my body. Giving Jakub our asses.

"I gotta say," Creed says. "I've never been more on display for someone since your husband came home."

Chuckling, I lean over and kiss him. "You okay? You can say no, you know."

He nods. "Yeah. I am. This might be the only time I don't feel... judged. Or embarrassed."

"Creed—"

He shakes his head. "I still have moments and I probably will for a while, but I believe you both that you like all of me just how I am."

"I do," I say emphatically. "So much."

The shy smile he gives me is replaced with a sudden look of pleasure as he groans. Looking over my shoulder, I find Jakub's face in his ass. Yep, my cock drips again. That's so fucking hot. His hand works its way up my leg and I feel a slick finger play at my hole. Letting my head fall, I relax so he can push inside me.

Between listening to his slurping sounds, Creed's moans, and Jakub's finger in my ass, I'm falling down a rabbit hole I have no interest in coming out of. I let the day's frustrations fall away. Listening to Creed, I encourage his sounds until they overshadow the words of the reporter and the asshole on the Dallas team. Jakub working on my ass, rubbing against my prostate, I let the feeling of pleasure fill me and replace the tension.

I'm so caught up in replacing all the negatives in my life, I don't realize that Jakub's pulled away until I feel him wrapping a condom around my cock. Blinking, I find Creed on his back, his legs already up with his ass ready for me. I groan, pushing into Jakub's hand while he lathers me with lube.

"Get inside Creed," Jakub says in my ear, then bites my lobe. I shiver. "As soon as you're balls deep, don't move. Understand?"

I nod.

"Then go."

He releases me, and I stumble over to Creed. Lining up, I slowly push inside him. "It's... really hot... that you listen... to him," he says between gasping breaths.

"It is," I agree.

I stop as soon as I'm where Jakub wants me. He shifts my arms so they're over Creed's shoulders and then he's easing his thick dick into my body. I groan, trying not to tense. But I kind of like tensing and making him work for it. It feels good to have him really *push* to get inside me.

As soon as he's seated, he adjusts his position and then takes Creed's legs, pushing his knees further to his chest. "Good?" he asks. I nod, though I'm sure that question wasn't for me.

Creed must have agreed too, because the next thing I know, I'm being fucked with purpose. Jakub's thrusts drive my movement inside Creed's body, which I think he likes since his moans are fucking pornographic.

Or maybe those are mine.

It's been a very long time since I've had a threesome. Not since we were still in the AHL, when we first got together. It was intense then, but it has nothing on this. Not when I can feel my husband's breath on my neck, his dick piercing me. Creed's hands dig at me, trying to pull me closer as he whines and repeats my name like he's praying.

Someday, maybe I'll have the mental presence to be able to drive between them. Control the movement on both ends. But right now, it's all Jakub. When he shoves in deep, my cock pushes into Creed until I'm almost choking. I'm filled to the brink just as my dick is stuffed so deep that I can't catch my breath.

My vision blurs. Pleasure spins around inside me quickly, and it's a different kind of storm than the one I've been stuck in for a few days.

When I come, I'm pretty sure I'm screaming. It's an orgasm so thorough that I feel it throughout my entire body. Every limb. Behind my eyes. Even my scalp tingles and my toes curl. My fingers dig into the bed as I try to ground myself, but I'm just constantly free-falling as it surges through me for what feels like days.

I'm only slightly aware when Jakub begins to clean me. His words are quiet. It's just the tenor of his voice that I hear as he washes me and tucks me into bed with Creed.

When he's finally behind me, I release a breath that I feel to my knees. "I love this," I whisper. "I want this every single day until I die."

"I'll make sure you always feel this," Jakub promises. He pulls the three of us tighter together. "The outside world is just noise. This is the only thing that matters."

I think I say 'I love you' but then again, I might have just said it internally. I'm asleep in the next few seconds.

THIRTY-ONE
JAKUB

A WEEK PASSES AND EVERY DAY THERE'S STILL SOME NEW SHIT being posted online. I'm pretty certain at least half of the images of us are photoshopped. For the life of me, I can't place where they are or when they were taken. The claims get more outlandish such as Ethan and I marrying so I can become a US citizen.

There's even a comment on that one that I was a mail order husband. I snorted at that because, yeah... one who just happens to play hockey? Right.

I keep Ethan and Creed off social media because I can see how much it bothers them. Ethan hates that everyone now thinks he's a villain. He's spent so long giving back to the world now that he has the means to do so and this is how he's thanked.

Creed on the other hand gets incredibly overwhelmed by all the negativity. I think it gives him flashbacks of when he first came out and all the assholes that surrounded him, making his life miserable.

The franchise supports us, and I do show them those posts. There's also a healthy dose of 'reality' being posted daily too, from all the interviews we've done, and pictures taken of us. Since we all liked Elrod and he wrote some great articles about us, we send him random images we take of each other together and at home on occasion.

A second week is quickly approaching and I'm relieved to finally see random supporters again. The comments aren't all 'you're burning in hell' vibes but there are people finally telling everyone else to mind their shit and move on. There are those that support us too. It warms me to see that finally, our support is coming back.

But we're getting stir crazy. We've been at hockey or in our home. Creed hasn't been to his apartment in weeks—not since this shit started. While there are still paparazzi everywhere, they've kept their distance at our apartment since we did in fact slap every one of them with restraining orders. And since we're on private property and have the support of the property manager, there's nothing they can do about it.

Damn vultures.

I lean against the doorframe and stare at both men still asleep, curled up together. They look so peaceful. Like the weight of the world isn't still on their shoulders. I love to look at them together. To just watch them interact. There's nothing sweeter than witnessing the love in their eyes when they look at each other.

Nodding, I step out of the room and quietly close the door. We've done nothing wrong. I'm done letting my guys feel like we're being punished.

Pulling out my phone, I dial the PR guy. He answers and I immediately scowl. I've come to hate his voice.

"Where's this new scandal?" I ask.

"Jakub?" he counters.

"I'm done, Robert. We're not remaining locked in our home for the rest of the season. I don't give a fuck what your plan is, but it's not working."

"It is working. It's just going to take time."

"I've given it enough time. We're not living as shut-ins because the world is filled with a bunch of assholes."

"Mr. Bozik—"

"This isn't a call for your permission, Robert. It's a courtesy. We're done being hermits. I'm taking them to dinner and then we'll see what we feel like doing afterwards. That's it." I listen to him sputter for a minute before telling him 'goodbye' and hanging up.

Then I call Shepey as I make my way to the kitchen. I wince when he answers in the middle of a yawn.

"Sorry. I forget the rest of the world doesn't wake up as early as I do," I say.

He chuckles. "What's up, Bozik?"

"I'd like to take them out tonight," I say. "I just told PR guy to fuck himself—nicely, I think—but I'm done living as if we did something wrong."

"Good for you. This is a bunch of bullshit."

"Yeah. So, I'm hoping you'd assist me tonight."

"Sure. What you need?"

"I'm thinking after the game I want to take them to dinner. And then see what happens from there."

"And you need someone to watch you? Well, I've never been much into voyeuring gay sex, but I guess I can get on board," he says.

I laugh. "No. Actually, I'm asking for something a little more mundane. We're followed constantly, so I'm hoping that you'll chauffeur us to the restaurant. We'll get a rideshare back, but I don't want the press to see the car we get into, and they'll definitely see a rideshare sitting at the arena."

"Less fun, but I'm totally down."

The pan I'm making sausage in gives a loud greasy pop and sizzles before it quiets again. I shake it around and then turn back to the phone.

"Can I make a counter suggestion?" Shepey asks.

"Sure."

"Sceptre. They love that place, and we always head there after a home game."

"That's a little public. Don't you think? A bar is going to be crawling with assholes," I say. "A restaurant isn't going to let those dicks in. But a bar isn't going to have an issue doing so."

"I'll take care of it."

I think about it for a minute as I take out the loaf of bread and start dunking slices into the egg mixture before laying them in a second pan. Shepey isn't wrong. Ethan has mentioned Sceptre to me no less than a hundred times since he's been with Buffalo. I'm sure he'd appreciate being there again.

"Fine," I agree.

"Awesome. I'll take it from here. You cooking, man?"

"Yep."

"You any good?"

I laugh. "I guess. So far, I've had no complaints."

He groans. "I burn water. I miss real food."

Smirking, I say, "We'll have you over for dinner sometime."

At his enthusiastic "Thank you," I know that's what he was hoping for. We get off the phone just as I'm stacking three plates. I set them on the table and turn to head for the bedroom, but both men are already meandering their way to me.

They look ruffled with sleepy eyes and bed hair. Holding out my arms, they walk into me, and I just hold them for a minute. Both of them, Creed included, give me their weight, and warmth just spreads through me. These men are mine. I'll do whatever it takes to put a smile on their handsome faces.

"Morning," I murmur, kissing the tops of both of their heads.

Their chorus back is groggy, and I chuckle.

"Take a seat. Eat before it gets cold."

I receive twin kisses on my neck, as if they've suddenly synced up, before they pull away to do as I instructed. Ethan digs in a little more enthusiastically. He's always been food motivated. It doesn't look like Creed is awake yet. He watches Ethan with tired amusement as he takes bites and chews slowly.

The three of us clean up together and then head into the living room. We turn on Sports Spot but end up spending the rest of the morning talking about nothing and anything. Since we've had nothing to do and were 'encouraged' to keep a low profile for almost two weeks (AKA, stay home and pretend we don't exist), I was prepared for us to start squabbling. To find quirks that are annoying. Run out of things to talk about. Or just get on each other's nerves because there's not a lot of space to get away from each other.

That we haven't only further solidifies that this is exactly how we were always meant to be. This little family we've created right here. It feels so good to look at them whenever I want. To reach out and touch when I feel the urge to do so.

Our parents check in almost daily, knowing that we're getting irritated that we have to stay home. Mine and Ethan's agents check in regularly. We still haven't heard a peep from Creed's. Asshat. Our teammates are constantly ride-sharing weird shit to us for delivery. Their favorite thing is that they've found a local dick shop.

Chocolate dicks. Dick cakes. Fruit dicks. You name it and they make it edible.

I know they're doing it to keep us entertained. We send back pictures of us eating the dicks that they laugh over.

Otherwise, this has been our routine. I honestly don't hate it except for the fact that we're the ones being treated as if this is our fault. We created some huge drama and now we need to hide until the attention passes. I agree with Ethan. Buffalo management did this. I'm not sure how that blame can fix anything, but if we'd had some warning or fucking anything that this was happening, maybe we could have handled it differently.

An hour before we need to head to the arena, I make a point to pack their gym bags along with mine so I can be sure that they have something to wear other than their suits. We're playing the New York Lights this afternoon.

Our game hasn't been affected too much, at least. We're basically in a win-lose pattern, so while it's not ideal, it's not the worst.

Setting the bags by the door, I quickly shower and change before ushering them into the bathroom, too. While they shower, I make protein shakes. We usually eat at home but take our shakes with us. I plan to get us to the arena early so we can spend some time conditioning. The gym in the apartment isn't bad, but our team gym is definitely bigger and nicer. And we know everyone that steps inside.

THE GAME WITH NEW YORK IS A WIN. 3-1 AND THANKFULLY, NY is a decent team to play. No assholes and I overhear several offering Ethan their support and sympathy. We head into the locker room, shower, and get ready to go. Shepey tells me he's going to get the car and bring it closer while I wait for the other two.

After a few more minutes they come over to me, hands linked with their heads bent together while they talk about something quietly. The smiles on their faces and the way they laugh... I want this forever. If I need to completely remove them from this climate so the outside world isn't so loud with their disapproval, then I will. Hockey be damned.

When we step outside, I turn and offer them each a hand. Grinning, they take them. Somewhere in my peripheral vision, I see a flash go off, but then our team is surrounding us. Blocking the view. There are half a dozen team cars right in front of the player exit, so unless someone has a drone overhead, there's no way to tell which we get into.

I push them both into the back of Shepey's gargantuan SUV and since there is room in the back for thirty, I climb in with them.

"Are we being escorted home?" Ethan asks, amused.

"Nope. Shepey is going to be our chauffeur tonight, though. We're not going home. We're going out," I answer.

"Are we allowed to?" Creed asks.

"You're fucking allowed to do whatever the fuck you want," Shepey says, frowning as he looks at us in the rearview mirror. "Fuck everyone else."

Ethan grins.

"Okay, but really," Creed says.

"I already told the PR guy that he can shove his plan up his ass. We're not going to live like this anymore. It's bullshit that the general public can't control themselves and our lives have to be modified to appease them. I'm done. We're going out," I say.

Ethan leans into me and kisses my cheek. "You're so hot when you tell people off."

Laughing, I wrap my arm around him, pulling him into my side. "This isn't anything fancy, but Shepey says you'll be happy about this trip and that's my goal tonight."

"You know we're happy wherever we are, right?" Creed says.

I reach beyond Ethan and touch his cheek. He smiles and I fucking love that there's still a hint of red in his cheeks when he does. "I know. I'm actually really relieved we're not in the least bit annoyed with each other since we haven't gotten away from each other in over two weeks since this stupid cheating story broke. But I mean it. I'm tired of us being hidden away like we're the pariah. The world has a problem with us. That's not our problem; it's theirs."

He leans into Ethan's side, setting his hand over mine, and says nothing else. When I look up, I catch Shepey's eyes in the mirror and his smile.

Sceptre isn't overly crowded. There are other patrons inside but when we pull up, there's a relieving lack of press. The bouncer lets us in and it's a bar, so I can't say it's a breath of fresh air, but it's definitely a breath of something. Something other than home.

Ethan and Creed make a direct path to the pool tables with Isak and Caulder on their heels. Both of them have shown up to our apartment on days off in an attempt to entertain us since we've been on lockdown. I know they miss hanging out.

I sit at the bar and it's almost déjà vu when Shepey sits on one side and then Sacha and Astor on my other. We're sipping on our drinks and watching the rest of our team do their thing.

"Remember that time I told you if you were interested in dick you needed to look elsewhere?" Shepey asks.

"You mean last month?" I counter.

He laughs. "Yeah. Then. Funny, now."

I grin. My smile widens when I catch Ethan with his head thrown back laughing at something.

"How did you manage so long away from your husband?" Astor asks. "That feels like... a lifetime."

"It wasn't so bad at first. The NHL was still novel and new. We were traded a few times in those first few years, so there were always new cities to get used to. But I admit, this season had really sucked being so far apart. I was seriously ready to retire so I could be with Ethan the week before I got the trade call."

"So you were happy about the trade?" Shepey asks.

"We were never *not* happy about the trade. We've been pissed about how it came about, even knowing that this is what we signed up for. But fuck, management knew we were married. They knew Ethan was with Creed. Fuck's sake, they've been hockey's sweethearts for like two years now. I think a warning on either end would have been a nice courtesy because someone had to have known something like this was going to happen."

"Maybe they wanted it to happen," Sacha says. "All attention is good attention."

I frown. "Sometimes, I'd really like to hit that man."

There are still cameras that go off on occasion as we hang out and do our thing. Mostly they're phone cameras of the random patron. We overheard a scuffle at the door when a member of the press tried to get inside.

Shepey grinned as he turned back once they were sent away. "It helps that this is our hang out often," he says. "The manager is a big fan of the Skidmosses, so when I called and explained the situation, he was all about accommodating us."

"They're getting big tips tonight," I say.

"Already has," Sacha says, grinning. He claps my back. "This our family. We take care of family."

Definitely the best trade I've ever had was coming home to my husband and his team. My team. A family like I've never experienced before.

THIRTY-TWO
JAKUB

WE HAVE A TWO-DAY BREAK AND I HAVE PLANS FOR BOTH DAYS. Today, I'm taking my men out again. I have the entire day planned and don't care who sees. However, since I'm planning to head out of Buffalo, hopefully the press won't be around en masse. Tomorrow is all about staying in and spoiling my men for Valentine's Day. I've arranged some help to set that up in our absence.

But today is about going out and enjoying life. Breathing in the frigid fucking air. Thankfully, we have subzero temperature gear, or this Czech would be staying inside during the winters and never coming out.

The sun hasn't even started to peek over the horizon when I get out of bed. I take a shower to help wake me up and then dress in comfortable sweats. Taking our overnight bag out of the closet, I creep out of the room and quietly close the door behind me.

In the kitchen, I prepare a big pot of hot chocolate. While the milk and chocolate are heating on the stove, I pack a soft pack cooler filled with fruits, muffins, bagels, and cream cheese. When the hot chocolate is done, I fill one of the enormous thermoses to the brink and cap it before adding that, three travel mugs, and the cooler to another bag.

I make three trips to the car. One with our overnight bag, the food bag, and their boots. The second trip is for blankets. Lots of blankets. I pile them in the backseat, creating a nest of blankets and pillows. The last is because I've loaded my arms with all our outdoor gear. Everything I could get my hands on. Maybe some extras. You can never have enough layers in this weather. Then I head back to the apartment and gently untangle my guys.

Because Ethan's eyes blink open first, I gently coax him to the side of the bed and silently help him dress. He doesn't ask questions, even as he yawns profusely. He's so adorable, with his ruffled hair and pillow lines on his face.

Then I pick him up, wrapping his legs around my waist. He doesn't argue, even as he sleepily laughs under his breath when I do. He asks no questions when I take him out of the apartment and get him into the running car, tucking him into the back amongst the blankets. I kiss his head and begin to back out when he grabs my wrist.

I expect him to ask what I'm doing, but he doesn't. His expression, though tired, is serious. "I love you, Jakub."

My heart stutters and I lean in to press my lips to his. "Love you, Ethan."

"I'm really, really glad we get to be together every day now."

I nod. For just a moment, I'm choked up and can't get words out. "Me too, zlato. More than happy I'm here."

He blinks slowly, and I know he's ready to pass out again. "Sleep, Ethan. I'm going to get Creed, and I'll be right back."

Locking him inside, I hit the remote start again, so the car stays running and warm for him. Creed is still asleep, so I gently roll him onto his back and slide him closer to the edge. He mumbles something in his sleep.

Brushing my fingers over his face, I murmur for him to open his eyes. Eventually he does. Without a word, I help him get dressed. Like Ethan, he doesn't speak. I'm not sure he's entirely awake and conscious of the fact that I'm dressing him.

And as with Ethan, I pick him up into my arms. He laughs, burying his face in my neck. "What are you doing?" he asks, voice slurred.

"I've already packed your boots and don't want you to walk in the snow," I tell him. Out of context, I'm sure that makes no sense and doesn't really answer his question.

I can almost feel him consider this. His arms tighten around me when I step outside and he shivers. Opening the back door, I slide him inside with Ethan and get him tucked in too. He looks around blearily, but when Ethan pulls him in close, he relaxes and closes his eyes. Once they're both secure, I lock them in once more and head back inside.

Making sure I have their phones and everything else is shut off, I leave the apartment and send a text that we're out and the apartment will be vacant until tomorrow afternoon.

Then we begin our drive with my guys fast asleep in the backseat.

"Would you rather... eat toe jam or belly button lint?" Creed asks.

I glance at them in the rearview mirror as Ethan makes a face. They're sipping on hot chocolate, and each has a bagel. Creed is currently spreading cream cheese onto a second, though his first isn't gone yet.

"That's gross," Ethan says. "Your ass. I choose your ass."

Creed chokes on his tongue, his face turning bright red. Ethan grins at him, and I can't stop my chuckle.

"That wasn't an option," Creed says.

"Isn't it?" Ethan asks, his voice low and seductive.

"Jesus," Creed murmurs, shifting in his seat. He leans forward and offers me the second bagel with a smile.

"Thank you," I tell him. He flushes a little and sits back, turning a stern stare back on Ethan. "Toes or navel. Choose one."

"Navel," he says. "Feet can be absolutely rank. Besides, I've totally licked every inch of your stomach."

Creed rolls his eyes, trying to hide his amusement.

"You going to tell us where we're going yet, manžel?" Ethan asks.

"Nope," I tell him. We're in Canada. We crossed the border when they were still asleep, so they didn't see that. Thankfully, the checkpoint didn't ask me to wake them when I explained I'm taking them on a surprise holiday. Besides the road signs, there hasn't been anything indicating where we are, and they don't seem to be all that interested in signs.

"Would you rather sext all day or spend the day touching each other all over?" Ethan asks.

"Doesn't that seem like an obvious question?" Creed asks as he takes a bite.

"Nope. Because if we sext all day, I bet I could have you frustrated and eager by the time you get home and fuck you into the night. Or, we could touch all day and draw it out that way."

Creed scowls at him. "I still think I'm going to choose touch all day." He looks into the mirror. "Jakub?"

"Sext all day."

Ethan grins. "I knew his answer. That's something we've done; although admittedly, it's when we've been far away and the end result can be pretty frustrating."

I chuckle.

"Jakub, you ask one," Creed says.

"Would you rather role-play as a steamy couple in a hotel room or live out your fantasy in a photo shoot?" I ask.

"We've moved onto sexy, I see," Creed says. "I think the photo shoot."

"Really?" Ethan asks.

"Yep. I've always kind of wanted a boudoir shoot. I think it would be really hot."

"We're totally doing that," Ethan says. "So I choose that, too."

"Would you rather have a threesome with a mutual friend or a stranger?" Creed asks.

"We've done both," Ethan and I say together. He meets my eyes in the mirror and grins.

"Which was your preference?" Creed asks.

"You," I say.

"You're neither, for the record," Ethan says. "You're definitely more than a friend."

Creed's smile is soft and while we didn't technically answer his question, he lets us move on.

Ethan asks, "Would you rather send each other provocative pictures all day or write each other steamy letters?"

"Pictures," Creed says.

"Letters," I answer.

"He's killer with letters," Ethan says, grinning. "I think I've been hard for an entire week because of him."

Creed laughs.

"Would you rather be tied up and teased or do the teasing?" I ask and make sure I'm watching both their faces as best I can while not driving off the road.

"Be teased," Ethan says. "All day long."

Creed contemplates the question. He looks between us, and I try to keep my smile low. I think he'd like both, but it depends on who it's with. I fucking love that he wants to give up control with me. Ethan never wants control. He never has. But I don't think Creed has ever given it up before.

"I don't have a solid answer," Creed says eventually. "I think it depends on the person I'm with and the situation."

That's all the time we have as I pull onto a road and under a covered bridge. The change in scenery catches both men's attention and they shift their focus to outside the window. Creed spots the ice castle in the distance first.

"Wow," he says. "Look at this, Ethan."

Ethan slides across the back seat, crowding in around Creed, and they stare out the window as we approach. "That's incredible," Ethan says.

I wish I could capture the wonder on their faces as I drive. It's so innocent and youthful. The early hour and drive out here is totally worth seeing the awe as we approach.

The ice resort is a few stories tall, but the estate is sprawling and covered with different activities. It's still early morning, before we'd even be out of the house for practice, so we have the entire day to enjoy everything there is to offer.

After we check in, we're heading out to be towed up the snowy mountain on a large four-person tube and then slide down the side of the mountain. We'll be taking a gondola ride back up, where we can enjoy the view of the resort and the snow-covered countryside.

Once parked, I have them stuff all the blankets into the front passenger seat as I go around back and retrieve their outdoor clothes. They dress in many layers before stepping out into the snow where I was dressing.

They're equally impressed with the inside but surprised when I don't bring them to our room. That's a treat I want to save for this evening. When we can stay and just enjoy it. For now, we need to freeze our nuts off.

We end up riding the snow tubes several times because I can't get enough of their laughter. Their grips on each other and me as we're thrown around on the tube, bumping up against the snowy wall and bounced all around have me hugging them tightly. I can't look away from them, even though I feel like that's a dangerous decision. The joy on their faces is something I'll never forget.

They take about a hundred pictures of our surroundings, us together, and separately as we make our way back up the mountain in the gondola. We hike along the trail in the still but freezing air. There's no wind. I didn't know the sides of mountains could be so peaceful and still. Besides a few people around us, there is no sound but the occasional crunch of snow or snap of a twig within the trees.

I hold them to me, and we stare at the world below us. For many long minutes, we remain like this. No pictures. No words. The outside world doesn't exist. It feels like we've finally escaped the burden we've been stuck under for the past several weeks. For this single moment, there is nothing else but the three of us.

"Thanks for taking us here," Creed says quietly. He shifts to look at Ethan and then me. "You know that you can do things with just the two of you, right? You don't always have to take me with you."

"Don't be ridiculous," Ethan says, yanking him closer. Creed laughs when he's almost pulled off balance. But their faces are inches apart now and the laughter dies on Creed's lips. "There will never be a day that we don't want you with us."

"But... you're still married. It's okay to have something that just the two of you share," Creed says quietly.

"We have plenty that just the two of us share. There's eight years of memories and experiences between Jakub and me. Now we're making new memories. Just like this," Ethan says.

Creed releases a breath and looks up at me, his brows slightly knitted together under his hat. I kiss his nose and he laughs a little. "I told you, miláček. You were always meant to be here. There will be some days that we break off into couples or individually. That's healthy. But there will never be a moment when I don't want you both to experience something with me. I want you here, Creed. I want you to be a part of our relationship. Our marriage."

He swallows. "That word, miláček. What does that mean?" I'm impressed that he gets the pronunciation as close as he does.

"Darling," Ethan says. "Or little lover. It depends on his intent behind it."

"So... does this mean that... are you still going to have an open marriage? Will you still be, uh..."

"I already deleted my Drip account," Ethan says. "The day we got together. Actually, the night we jerked off in the hotel room together." He winks, making Creed blush while he laughs. "Yeah," Ethan says when the laughter dies down. He hugs Creed close, pressing them both tighter into my chest. "I think we've been looking for you for the past eight years, Creed. Now that you're here in my arms, I don't feel like there's anything else out there worth looking for."

"What if... later. What if..." Creed doesn't finish when his words trail off.

I kiss his forehead and he sighs, leaning his head on my shoulder as he looks at Ethan.

"If, for whatever reason, one of us meets someone or... something, we'll talk about it. One of the things I've always told you is that Jakub and I discuss everything ad nauseam. But that's always why we get on as well as we do. We don't fight. There's no jealousy. There are never any hurt feelings. Because it's never mattered where we're physically located, we're always a team. We're always first priority. That doesn't change now that you're here. We will still talk until there are no questions left unanswered. We're still each other's biggest priority. The only difference is that where there were two of us, there's three and the three of us are on equal ground. Just because we're married doesn't mean that our relationship comes first or... any of that other hierarchy bullshit. We're completely equal, the three of us."

Creed's mouth covers Ethan's in a kiss that I can almost feel. There's so much emotion behind it. I can feel his relief, his love, his anxiety. His commitment. And his uncertainty and fear. I press my face into his hat, keeping him close.

In all the things we've talked about, I don't think we've ever spoken of his past. Maybe he has with Ethan, but given his response, I would wager a guess that he's been hurt. I know he's been bullied. While I don't know the details, I know enough. But he's never mentioned a previous relationship of any kind.

It doesn't matter right now. I'll never let anyone hurt him again.

My thoughts pause when his mouth lands on mine a moment later. I smile into his kiss and when he melts into me, letting me move our kiss along, I realize how very much I love him. It snuck up on me, even as I knew he was always supposed to be here. I wasn't expecting to love him yet.

But fuck, I do.

I kiss him deeply, hoping he can feel my love for him. I pour it all into our kiss, clinging to him with all the strength I have in my cold body.

THIRTY-THREE
ETHAN

THE COLD ALMOST DOESN'T TOUCH ME. IT'S NOT UNTIL WE'VE slid down the mountain on an old-fashioned sled—the three of us together—and I climb to my feet again do I realize I'm shivering.

Jakub leads us back to the car and grabs a small bag from the trunk before we head into the resort. I'm almost positive he's never been here before, but the way he leads us around, it's like he knows where we're going.

Creed and I follow along, our hands linked together and our teeth chattering, as we marvel at this remarkable place. The tall walls that seem to cut through the grounds must be designed to stifle the wind in strategic places, because I almost never feel it against my skin.

We wait patiently as Jakub speaks to a man and then we're led through ice tunnels that have me grinning. I get the strange sensation that I'm a kid inside an ice maze. As if there was a huge storm and we're buried under the snow. The only way out is to dig and so we dig lots of tunnels and end up playing in them.

The man leads us into a chamber with a sunken hot tub. I nearly groan when I see the steam.

"Yes," Creed hisses.

Of course, that means we need to change right here in the freezing air. When the man leaves, we make quick work of it. We have our sandals and then our swim trunks, all of which came out of the bag that Jakub took from the car. There's a stack of towels inside a case and I really hope that they're super warm.

The water feels extra hot when I step in, and I'm not even sad about it. Almost as soon as we're settled, the man is back with beverages, hot and cold. Then we're alone again, the only sound is the soothing bubbles from the tub.

"This is romantic," Creed says as he stares at the ceiling. There are blue lights set into the thick ice above us, illuminating the room. He, like Jakub and I, has sunk under the water to his neck. "Where did you even come up with this idea?"

"In a ShareIt ad," Jakub says, chuckling. "I found it three days ago and when I inquired, they had an opening for tonight, but not tomorrow."

"What's tomorrow?" Creed asks.

Jakub smirks. "Valentine's Day."

Creed looks at him and then me. He presses his lips together. "Sorry. I've never had a reason to celebrate before, so... I forgot."

Jakub reaches for him, pulling him across the tub with his hand until Creed is in his lap. Creed's gaze darts to mine, his skin flush—which I suppose could be from the cold air or the hot water—before looking at Jakub.

"I don't need you to remember. I enjoy spoiling you and I plan to at every chance I get. Tomorrow being Valentine's Day is happenstance. We have two days off, so I wanted to do something together."

Creed nods. I think it'll take him some time to realize that he has no expectations to fill a role in our lives. All we want is for him to be happy. He doesn't have to remember his own fucking name for all I care. As long as there's a smile on his gorgeous face and he's happy with us, that's all we need from him.

He's used to someone needing him to fill a role, though. To some extent, all of us are. Especially those who have the world watching. As professional athletes, every move we make is under scrutiny, as these last couple weeks have proven. So much is expected of us, not just in behavior set forth by the league itself, but society in general.

We are the role models of today's youth and so we have an agenda that we're supposed to be pushing. Most of the world wants

STARTING LINE

that to be—work hard and it'll pay off. Be a good person. Give back if you're fortunate enough to be able to.

But unspoken, they also want you to be well dressed, behave and speak a certain way, straight, religious, and monogamous. *That's* the message they want the youth of America to receive. And if you deviate from any one of those, everything about your life is questioned. If you don't fit into any of them, you're a fucking nightmare and shouldn't be in front of the camera, corrupting children into thinking anything outside of the status quo is okay.

Creed's lived under that umbrella for a long time. He's felt that pressure both as a child trying to become a professional athlete and as a professional athlete. He comes from a world where being different is certainly not accepted. It's not okay.

He's working on rewriting that in his head and we're going to be here to make every step a little easier.

"The only thing I will ever need from you is your voice," Jakub says quietly. "I need you to never stop talking to me. Everything you feel, you think, you want. And conversely, what you don't want or are uncomfortable with. Alright?"

Creed nods. He shifts further into Jakub's lap and looks at me from where his head is tucked under my husband's chin. I smile, making sure he knows that I'm completely okay with this. Which I am; I want them to be close. In fact, I love that they're close. I'd give anything if we could be together completely, the three of us.

"I want this for the rest of my life," Creed whispers. "I want a family and I want a home. To be loved and never wake up wondering if it's real or not. I mean, I don't want to question whether I believe that I'm loved." He blinks like he's trying to prevent himself from shedding tears. My heart clenches. "And I want that with you."

I cross the tub and crowd in on him, squishing him between mine and Jakub's chest. "I'm glad we're all on the same page," I say. Only because I'm so close, do I hear the way he catches his breath. "And since you brought it up, you want a family? Kids?"

His smile is shy. "Yeah. One, at least."

"Want to get married?" I ask.

Creed licks his lips. "I don't think it's legal to get married to more than one person."

"Somewhere in the world it is," Jakub says. "We'll find that place. Whether the US acknowledges it or not doesn't matter. We'll know it's real."

"And... are we going to share a name?"

"I was going to change my name when we retire," I say. "Ethan Bozik has a nice ring to it, but I'd already begun my career as Wilder and didn't want to change it. But we can discuss that too. It's not a deal breaker."

Creed shakes his head. "No. I like that. If that's okay that I—"

"Yes," I say, pressing a finger to his lips. "Always, yes. If you need us to remind you every day that you're equally ours, then we will."

"I love you," he whispers, his voice shaking.

I look at my husband for a minute before leaning down to kiss him. We don't need words to know what each other thinks sometimes. We've spent so long staring at each other through tablet and phone screens that some things we've learned to read on the other's face. Like this.

"We love you too, baby," I murmur and press kisses all along his face. "Every single day for the rest of my life."

THE ICE BEDROOM IS EPIC. THERE ARE THESE SHARDS THAT HAVE A soft glow behind the bed, rising over the head of the bed at different heights. The bed is on a glowing ice platform, sunken within so that we're surrounded by a short ice wall. It's covered in fur and other blankets.

"As breathtaking as this is, I anticipate being freezing tonight," I say.

"I don't think we're going to want to sleep naked, but it's my understanding that we'll be plenty warm," Jakub says, shrugging. "I've read a lot of reviews and spoken to reception about it when I called to make the reservation."

He brings the overnight bag to the bed and unzips it, pulling out clothing I haven't seen before. Three identical sets. He hands one to me and one to Creed before grinning. "I also bought us matching, corny long underwear for Valentine's Day."

Creed laughs and hugs them to his chest.

STARTING LINE

I'm surprised about how well I sleep. Besides my face exposed in the cool air, which I tuck into Jakub's neck, I'm cozy under the pile of blankets. Jakub sleeps between us tonight, while Creed and I sprawl over his long, hard body together.

We wake to breakfast in bed and the pillars of ice behind the bed blink in a random rhythm, entertaining us with a light show while we eat. After breakfast, we wander the resort for a while longer before climbing back into the car and heading home.

We don't play 'would you rather' this time but ask each other 'get to know you questions' that I found as I was scrolling through ShareIt. Yes, I signed back in, but I've been marking a lot of shit I'm tagged in as spam. Hopefully, if it's done enough, the algorithm will take down the posts on its own.

Not that it'll stop the assholes from making another post, but meh.

We arrive home in the late afternoon and stop for an early dinner since we skipped lunch. The sun is already down by the time we pull into the parking lot of my apartment. Surprise, surprise, there are reporters just off the property line.

I'm in too good a mood to pay them any attention as we each take an arm full of stuff from the car and head inside. Once again, I'm taken completely off guard when we step through the door, and the entire apartment is glowing with little lights.

Not candles, but star lights are everywhere. All over the furniture, outlining the windows, creating hearts on the ceiling. Jakub has us drop our hauls by the door and kick off our shoes as he ushers us inside.

I'm so mesmerized, trying to catch every single detail, that I barely notice when he leads me and Creed down the hall to the bedroom. The furniture is outlined in soft white lights. On the walls are red and pink hearts. Hanging from the ceiling are strands of different length, looking like falling snow or maybe shooting stars.

"This is..." Creed murmurs as he makes a slow circle. His eyes are shiny when he looks at me and then Jakub.

Jakub gently presses his fingers to Creed's jaw. "Happy Valentine's Day, Credence."

Creed blinks, and a tear trails down his cheek. "Happy Valentine's Day," he whispers back.

"Will you let me worship you tonight?"

Creed releases a breath, his lips parted. His eyes shoot to me and I smile. Looking at Jakub again, he nods. "Yes."

"Mmm," Jakub says before turning his gaze to me. "Undress, lásko."

I quickly strip until I'm naked and my cock is waving a white flag. Both of their gazes travel hungrily down my body.

"Good. Now go sit in that chair." He points to the far end of the room. I do without question and plop my naked ass in the chair eagerly. "Place your hands on the armrests." Less eagerly, I do as I'm told and know that this is going to be a torturous beginning of the evening. "No touching yourself. No moving from the chair. No taking your eyes off us. Understand?"

I whine and nod. "Yes."

With a smile that says 'good boy,' he turns back to Creed. "You okay with this?"

They've never been alone before. Jakub preps him most nights we have sex but I'm always in the middle. This'll be the first time it's just them. And fuck, am I excited to watch it. I get to watch!! My dick throbs in anticipation.

"Yes," Creed answers, his voice breathy.

Jakub kisses him. It's slow and drawn out, licking into his mouth in a mess of tongues. His hands move over Creed's body, slowly divesting him of clothes before taking his off as well. When he lays Creed on the bed, he pulls his mouth free.

Jakub's hand trails over Creed's skin, tracing his lines. Creed shivers and looks at me for a second. I smile and nod. His smile in return is nervous.

"You're so beautiful," Jakub murmurs. I nod enthusiastically.

Creed's lips part. His breathing is audible.

Jakub drops his mouth to Creed's chest, feathering kisses over his skin as he spreads Creed's legs to settle between them. I'm not sure he does it intentionally, but knowing my husband, he intentionally doesn't lie on top of Creed, so I have a clear view of what's happening as his hand runs down Creed's naked torso and down to his cock.

His thumb traces the short, thick length, and Creed sucks in a breath. I watch his face closely to make sure he's comfortable.

STARTING LINE

Once more, his eyes scan to mine and I can see he's self-conscious. For a moment, I forget how hard I am. How hot and needy.

"You're perfect," I say. "Every inch of your body is flawless, Creed. Divine."

He gives me a nervous smile and nods. I'm not naïve enough to think he believes me, but it still breaks my heart that he thinks otherwise. And infuriates me that someone's made him feel otherwise.

There's a lot of attention on the pressure that women are under based on the media and fashion magazines. But there's not as much talk to how much pressure men are under. It's not just body shape and tone, but also the size of their dicks. It's ugly and unfair and often results in hurting people like Creed.

Jakub moves down his body, spreading his legs wider so I have a clear view of when he takes Creed in his mouth. I moan with Creed. Creed's hands immediately go into Jakub's hair as he strains to look down to watch. His mouth is still open, the lust and pleasure that paints his face is a work of art.

Jakub somehow magics a tube of lubricant and coats his fingers, easing them into Creed's tight body. I swear, I can feel that echo across mine. I'm not sure if I feel them in my ass, as I have so many times, or feel Creed's tight hole around my fingers. Either way, I'm nearly trembling with need, wiggling in my seat.

Creed makes a choked whimpering sound, his hips rocking up with a sudden jolt, and then Jakub moves off him. "You're like a salty lollipop," Jakub hums, licking his lips. Creed and I watch, hypnotized, as he covers his long, thick dick with a condom and strokes lube onto it. "Should we face Ethan? Make sure he can see it all?"

With a grin, Creed nods. "Yeah. Fuck yeah."

I groan, shifting in my chair. My fingers dig into the arms.

Jakub rolls Creed onto his side before positioning at his back, both of them are facing me now. "Look at him," Jakub murmurs in Creed's ear as he brings his leg up. "Look how hard he is for us. He's making a mess on the chair."

Creed lets out a breath, his mouth opening as Jakub starts to push inside him.

"Think we should make him lick up everything he leaks onto the chair when we're done?" Jakub asks.

The sound that Creed releases has my balls drawing up. He nods, his hands gripping the bed tightly, but his eyes are locked on me. I watch, transfixed, as my husband's massive dick disappears inside my boyfriend's small, taut hole.

"You feel how perfectly I fit inside you, Creed?" Jakub breathes in that voice that can make me come all on its own.

Creed's breaths are stuttered when he says, "Yes."

Jakub slowly pulls out before sliding back in. Deep. As far as he can go. Creed's eyes flutter closed on a long, low groan, even as he tries to maintain eye contact.

"Tell us how much you love this, Ethan," Jakub says. "Tell us how you feel watching us."

"I'm so fucking hard," I say, my hips leaving the chair, looking for any friction at all to touch my naked dick. "My balls are so tight. Every inch of me is tingling with need. I could never imagine how incredible this is. To see you together. The two men I love more than anything."

Creed's breaths punch out of him, his mouth open as he stares at me while Jakub moves in and out of his body at an ever-increasing pace. His hands clutch the bed while Jakub's hand that's not holding Creed's leg up so I can see and give him proper access serves as a restraint to hold Creed in place.

"It's so hot," I whine. "I've never seen anything so hot. I desperately want to be over there."

"What would you be doing if you joined us?" Jakub asks.

"Oh god," I whine, my dick pulses and a fresh stream of pre-cum leaks down my dick. "I don't know. Can I be inside you too, Creed? Can you take both of our cocks?"

Creed moans, nodding. "I've never done that."

"We can work up to it," Jakub says.

"Yes. Oh, fuck yes. I'm going to come right now," I say in an awful, desperate voice. "My balls fucking hurt."

"What do you want?" Jakub asks.

"To see you get Creed off. I want to watch you please him until he covers our bed in his seed," I say. "Please. Fuck, please."

That's the vision I see before me. Jakub shifts his hold so the arm under Creed holding him in place grasps his leg and Jakub's now free hand moves to stroke his dick. Creed becomes increasingly vocal. The whines and whimpers coming out of his mouth have me shaking, begging along with him.

Jakub isn't quick about it, though. He never is. He won't be rushed. Instead, he's so fucking thorough that I swear I can feel his touch as if I were in Creed's place. When Creed finally comes, I'm practically crying for release.

My husband makes me lick my chair first, cleaning the mess I made there. Then he's giving me much the same treatment, except Creed doesn't have to watch. He gets my dick in his mouth as they draw out my orgasm until it's almost painful.

But I'll never complain. They can torture me by bringing me right to the edge, only to deny my release for as long as they want. Because this right here is one of the best nights of my entire life.

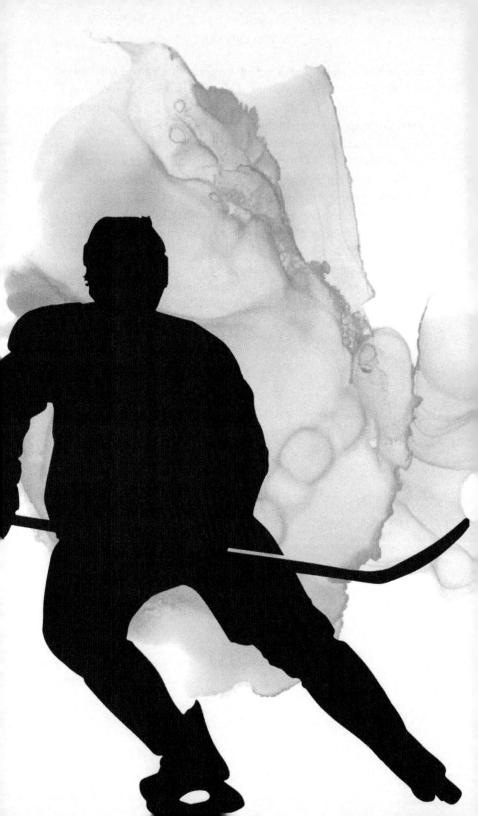

THIRTY-FOUR
JAKUB

Four Months Later—Stanley Cup Viewing Party

The St. Louis Arches and Boston Freedom have been passing their wins back and forth for six games. It's a true showdown right now. Whoever wins this game, wins the Cup. The score is still 2-0 at the end of the second period, with St. Louis in the lead. No one scored in the second period, though there's still a minute left.

Ethan, Creed, and I lean forward slightly when Stark Meierklein of Boston makes a shot at goal, but it's blocked by St. Louis' goalie.

"Ah, hell," Ethan says at the same time Creed says, "Fuck, yeah." There's a moment where they look at each other before laughing.

"Who are we cheering for again?" Creed asks.

Ethan grins and leans over me, smacking a kiss on Creed's lips. "No one in particular."

Creed's phone rings and he reaches for it. The screen says that it's a notification from ShareIt, so I pull it from his hand and open it first. Yeah, I know. Controlling, right? Maybe, but I don't do it to monitor him. I do it because the world has split between Camp Pro Hockey's Sweethearts and Camp WTF Are We Showing Our Kids —This Is NOT Okay.

Both camps tag us in posts. They don't bother me, but they bother Ethan and Creed. Ethan rarely signs into his account anymore and when he does, it's usually while he's sitting in my lap so I can clear out the shit he doesn't want to see first. That doesn't mean all the shit stays out of his feed; because it doesn't. But with me marking everything in his DMs and tags as spam, the algorithm is learning.

Creed remains signed into his app, but he does it so he can be an advocate for our relationship. He's constantly posting pictures of us doing everyday things. He also supports his cousin vocally—while making sure the world knows that's his cousin and not an affair.

As much as he tries to ignore shit and not let it bother him, I can feel him flinch every time a new post calling us heathens and sluts and whatever else they can come up with pops up on his screen. Tagging us, of course.

However, the post that pops that tags him is both amusing and supportive. I hand him back his phone.

Buffalo had a rough February and March. It was the epitome of the world weighing us down and how this shit was affecting us. Our game suffered. We were still a perfect, dynamic team, but more fights broke out than usual because too many members of the opposite teams had shit to say. If it wasn't one of the three of us in the sin bin, it was one of our teammates.

On the ice should have been our escape from the reminder of the storm sitting overhead, but it wasn't. There wasn't any place we could turn that it wasn't slapped in our faces. The entire thing came to a head at the game against, ironically, St. Louis. Someone in the stands by the chute bent over and hollered something obscene to Creed.

Our sweet Creed. Something that I didn't hear because I wasn't close enough, but by the way Creed tensed and his face heated, I knew it was crude. I'm not going to lie, my husband grew wings that day. He practically scaled the wall and punched the guy in the face. Hard. Three times. I'm pretty sure the guy had to have surgery.

Ethan was suspended for the next eight games. Pretty much through the rest of March. That was a losing streak for us.

Two things happened at the beginning of April. Ethan came back, helping us win the last two games of the season. And another scandal broke out.

There's a movie where a superstar football player is suddenly thrown into parenthood when a one-night stand dies, and their child ends up on his doorstep. This is basically the drama that unfolded and was responsible for taking the spotlight off us.

The bio mother doesn't die, but she shows up looking for child support. Of course, DNA tests have been done to prove the child is his. Though this is rough enough, the kicker is that this child is the result of an affair, so now there's a very public and ugly divorce underway too.

And it wasn't a football player. It's a top baseball player.

While I don't envy him and I send him all the best, it's honestly a breath of fresh air when we pull into the parking lot of our apartment and there's not a single member of the press around. No mother's basement journalist. No trashy tabloid wannabe reporter. There's no one there except those who live there.

The first time I realized this, I remained in the car for a few minutes, letting my men sleep after coming back from a weekend trip, and took a breath. Finally, shit could calm the fuck down and we'll be able to begin our lives together for real. I was never under any impression that everything would be perfect from there on out. There will always be shit going down. People will always have an opinion about our sexuality, about gay men in sports, about our non-traditional lifestyle.

That stuff is never going to go away.

But at least for now, we're at peace. In two weeks, we're heading back to the Isle of Kala for a much-deserved three-week vacation where there won't be any cameras at all, except for those owned by the resort. It'll just be us, adventure, and sex.

What more could I possibly ask for?

Isak walks into the room and falls onto the chair. "Why you always have to be so lovey and touching all the time?"

I raise a brow at his scowl. He's not usually like this. I don't know Isak that well, but he's around enough that I know something is clearly upsetting him.

"Today it's bothering you, huh?" Ethan asks, sitting back.

Isak sighs and crosses his arms, staring determinedly at the television.

"We said you could invite your college girl," Ethan says. "We told all of you that, and none of you chose to bring anyone."

Isak continues to glower.

"You don't like her anymore?" Ethan tries.

"I do," Isak says and then sighs. "It's just... She's..."

I think this might be better if it's between the two of them. So I get to my feet and pull Creed with me. "We're going to water... the kitchen," I say.

Ethan laughs and slides across the couch to get closer to Isak. While Isak rolls his eyes at me, I don't miss his smile, either.

Once we're out of the room, Creed turns to me with amusement. "Water the kitchen? That's the best you could come up with?"

I shrug. "I'm not always good on my feet."

Creed laughs. We bypass the kitchen and step onto the balcony overlooking the beach. Because we wanted to watch the Stanley Cup, we decided to stay somewhere that allowed technology for the beginning of June. We invited our closest friends and a guest of their choice. None of them brought guests.

Shepey, Caulder, and Sacha are on the beach, passing a football back and forth. For a minute, we watch them.

"When will your parents be here?" Creed asks.

"Their flight lands within a couple hours of your parents," I say. "Ethan's come tomorrow."

He's quiet for a minute before saying, "It's not that these last few months have felt fake but, in some ways, having our parents here and seeing us together... it kind of makes this feel more real. We always went out of our way to keep our relationship to ourselves as much as possible. Letting our families in makes it feel like we're actually making an announcement."

We've spent the last two months here on a private beach in North Carolina. The entire area is owned privately, only available for rental. We shop every few days and sometimes wander the town but usually, we stay here. The three of us.

So yeah, I get what he means. Creed posts family pictures of us every few days, but in reality, we have very little contact with people. We chose to take this time for ourselves. In a new environment without anyone looking down on us. Judging us. As we continue to build our relationship.

Our friends arrived at the end of May so we could watch the final round of the Stanley Cup together. However, we've not been watching it as often as we thought we might. We completely missed the third game, having forgotten that it was on. Yes, we forgot!

This season had been difficult for all of us. Our entire team felt the backlash of our relationship coming out the way it did. I'm not surprised we compartmentalized the playoffs and focused on just being men. Not hockey players. Not public figures. Not professional athletes. We're just guys hanging out right now.

I wrap my arms around Creed, and he leans against my chest as we watch our friends on the beach. Minutes tick by. Ethan joins us after a while. He stands behind me, his hands on my hips and his lips pressed against the back of my shoulder.

Creed sighs and turns in my arms. I keep him trapped between my body and the railing. He buries his face in my neck, and Ethan tangles his fingers into Creed's hair.

"So... do you have wedding bands?" Creed asks.

Ethan chuckles. "Yeah. We always have them with us but rarely wear them. For reasons you already know, but also hockey. No jewelry."

He nods. "A while ago, we talked about marriage. Kind of."

"We did," I say.

"I've been looking around and... I found somewhere that we can get married. Legally. As gay men and polyamorous," he says quietly. "Not that you have to marry me. I'm just saying that I found somewhere."

"Creed," I say as Ethan gently forces him to look up at us. His cheeks are pink. "Are you asking us to marry you?"

Now his cheeks turn red. "Yes?"

Ethan chuckles. "Then ask, baby."

Creed licks his lips, his eyes moving between us. "Will you marry me?" he asks, voice quiet and quavering slightly.

Ethan climbs my back, hooking his legs on my hips so he can lean over my shoulder and kiss Creed hotly as he says, "Fuck yes, I will." Creed groans, his body sinking into me. Ethan pulls back, letting Creed breathe, and rests his head against mine. I don't have to be able to see him to know that he's looking at Creed like he's the fucking sun.

Creed looks at me, flushed and breathless. I'm more civilized than my husband when I brush his cheek and cup his face. "Yes. Every day, yes."

Likewise, my kiss is softer, though no less filled with how much I love this man.

Creed sighs, a smile on his face, when he rests his head on my shoulder again. "Is it okay if I change my name too?"

Ethan sighs, wrapping his arm around Creed. "You really don't need to ask permission for these things, baby. Yes, change your name too. We will be the Bozik tribe."

He chuckles and snuggles in a little deeper. "Can we tell our parents?"

"Yes," I say.

"Do you want to get married this summer?" His voice is quieter now.

"Yes," Ethan and I say together.

"What country did you find?" I ask.

He laughs a little. "I searched for countries where gay marriage is legal. Then countries where polyamory is recognized and legal. You're not going to be surprised by this, but they're basically opposite countries." He laughs again. "Except Brazil. Both are legal in Brazil."

"Brazil, huh?" I say.

"I may have already downloaded the paperwork," Creed says quietly. "And I might have begun filling it out."

Ethan grins and somehow, his hold on both of us gets tighter.

"I was thinking maybe in August, on our way home from Kala, we can head to Brazil for a week and get married. If you want to," Creed continues.

I press my lips to the side of his head and murmur, "Every. Single. Day... Yes."

"And maybe we can invite our parents and friends?" Creed asks. "Maybe the team?"

Ethan sighs. "Look at me, Creed." Hesitantly, Creed lifts his face. His cheeks are still flush. "We will give you whatever you want. If you want a $100,000 wedding, it's yours. If you want to get married in a sewer, I'm going to silently question your fantasies, but we'll still make it happen. Whatever wedding you want, anything you can dream up, we're going to give it to you, baby."

Creed softens, his eyes glistening. "Thanks," he chokes and then takes a deep breath. "I guess I don't really know what I want. Just the people I want there."

"We'll head into town later and get some wedding magazines. We'll bring an entire carry-on of wedding magazines to Kala," I tell him. "And you can begin planning."

"It's going to be difficult to plan things when we're somewhere without technology," he says.

"Oh!" Ethan says and slides down my back. I don't miss his half hard cock and try to hide my grin. "You know who would organize a fucking epic wedding?"

"Oh, no," I say.

"Our friends!"

That's not what I thought he was going to say. I shift to bring him close again, pressing both my men to my chest.

"Those friends?" Creed asks, gesturing over his shoulder.

Ethan's wide grin as he nods makes me laugh. "This is either going to be epically awesome or a fucking disaster," I say.

"I trust them." Ethan glances at the four of them on the beach. "Mostly. But I definitely trust that they'll organize something that we'll never forget. Caulder will keep them serious and on track and rein in their wild and crazy."

The three of us turn to find that their game of pass has turned into a man pile of them fighting over the ball. Caulder rolls away, laughing as Sacha gets to his knees and spits a mouthful of sand.

"Really?" Creed asks, eyes narrowed.

Ethan rests his head on my shoulder. "Yep."

Honestly, I can't think of anything better than that. We have the next couple weeks to talk to them about it. Our likes and dislikes. Things we'd be willing to have and what is an outright fucking no. But yes, this will definitely be a wedding the hockey world will never forget.

And it'll be the best day of our lives.

WANT MORE JAKUB, ETHAN, AND CREED?

Thank you for reading about Creed, Ethan, and Jakub. I hope you enjoyed their story as much as I loved writing it. If you're not ready to be done with them, you can sign up for my newsletter where you'll have access to another scene in *All Bared*. Access to this story will be granted once my newsletter goes out every third week so please be patient. There will also be an extra scene in my patreon, where you'll find a whole lot of other goodies, including N/SFW art from this story soon!

Are there other characters that piqued your interest as you read this book? You can read more about them in my other books or those to come!

You can find Caulder's friend Egon's bi-awakening story in **Shiver**.

You can get better acquainted with Declan and Zarek in **For Your Mind** (though I strongly suggest beginning with the first book, **For Your Time**) and taking a peek into the gay capital college

WANT MORE JAKUB, ETHAN, AND CREED?

campus of Rainbow Dorset University in the fictional town of Glensdale.

You'll see many more characters that have passed through these pages in more books to come! Including one of the main characters in my next For Puck's Sake story having been introduced in this one. Any guesses as to who that is?!

Make sure you take a peek in the pages that follow for a glimpse into what you can expect within the books I've mentioned (and the next one to come in the For Puck's Sake series)!

AUTHOR'S NOTE AND ACKNOWLEDGMENTS

I've been loving the MM hockey scene for a long time. I've had the books in this series planned for just as long! When I become obsessed with a trope in writing, I can't stop myself from diving in. This was what led me to diving into MM from my comfy seat within the RH world of poly romance (always with MM).

I'm going to begin by saying that while I kept the locations of professional hockey teams reflective of what's current today (as of 2023) in the 'real world', the teams themselves as well as all the players on them (management and every single name within these pages) are completely fictional. Everything about them. Including but not limited to looks, personality, skill, etc. By no means am I writing any 'real' players into my books. Do not attack or become obsessed with an athlete or their family because you perceive a likeness to a living person.

I've also kept the schedule with my fictional Buffalo Skidmoss team loosely based on the Buffalo schedule of 2018-2019 season. This doesn't reflect which games are away/home but does keep the scores and which teams they play in what order. (Yes, I made up the word skidmoss.) The scores are reflective though nothing else about the game itself made it into my book. I've even gone so far as to check the weather for certain dates in history because I'm a little extra like that! The Stanley Cup finals and scores are also reflective of what really went down in 2019.

Why did I do this? Because I find it easier to have a guideline and something legitimate to follow as I bring hockey to life (hopefully with a little more understanding with each book). I like being able to bring back past years in a new light. I'll also note that the suspension of Ethan mentioned at the end of the book is obviously fabricated and I have no idea what the true consequences of his actions might be. Most of those parts are definitely idealistic on my part. I'd like to say that Ethan would be protected in his few moments of lashing out because people think that they can do what they want with no consequences. He may be a public figure but he still has his rights.

As you might have caught on by now, I write poly so you can't really expect me to just walk away from lots of love!! While there's something sweet and holistic about writing monogamy within MM for me after writing 40+ poly books (I haven't examined this so don't ask), there are some characters that just *aren't* monogamous. Just as within life there are people who aren't monogamous. It's not a choice; it's just who they are. While my characters are rarely ever based on living people, I always add in real situations, emotions, and angst. While I don't think authors should have to say this, I feel I now need to point out that just because how the characters in my stories deal with any given situation isn't how *you* might or how *you believe* it should be dealt with, doesn't make it unnatural, unrealistic, or inappropriate. Please keep in mind that everyone is different, as are their responses, emotions, and decisions. Just because my characters are fictional, doesn't mean their situations are completely made up, nor are their emotions.

I *am* new to contemporary writing. While my poly books are almost entirely paranormal thus far, I haven't had a single story idea that's paranormal MM. I don't know why. It's really freaking weird, though. Having said that, you'll sometimes find a few glimpses of the paranormal within my contemporary settings. Like twin bonds and hauntings and stuff. Because, in life, there are those who believe those elements are real. There's an entire television network dedicated to the paranormal (which I may or may not be obsessed with). However, I'm keeping this as real as possible because that's who these characters are! Even though the settings and storylines might have been paranormal in my poly books, and the characters themselves inhuman or magical, that doesn't mean that their emotions aren't relatable and their personal situations and reactions aren't reflective of human nature.

Now that I've explained my writing and why I do what I do, I want to say that I really love my characters and their stories. Oftentimes, I've thought their story through so many times that I can recite it in my sleep. This is why you might come across something that doesn't always make sense because, in my head, I know what's going on. I know a back story or an anecdote that would make a particular scene completely understandable. My team has been with me a very long time so they too know how I work. Thus, if you ever find something that you're like 'wtf is she talking about', please feel free to reach out.

The last chapter where Creed is talking about searching for a place where the three of them can get married legally isn't at all a lie. The countries that recognize polyamory as 'legal' and legitimate are opposite those who allow gay marriage. Brazil appeared to be one of the few (if not the only) outliers, allowing both. Apparently, it's the only country that truly believes that Love is Love.

Thank you so much for reading and I hope you check out my next book! There's a fun gaming twist that I'm psyched to dive into!

BOOKS BY CREA REITAN

MM NOVELS/SERIES

For Puck's Sake
Shiver
Starting Line
Lucky Shot (2023)

For Your Love
For Your Time
For Your Heart
For Your Mind
For Your Forever (2024)

POLY TITLES

THE IMMORTAL CODEX

Immortal Stream: Children of the Gods

Mortal Souls
The God of Perfect Radiance
The Hidden God
The God Who Controls Death
Gods of the Dead
Gods of Blood
Gods of Idols
Gods of Fire

Gods of Enoch

Gods of Stone (2024)

INFECTED FAIRY TALES

Wonderland: Chronicles of Blood

Toxic Wonderland

Magical Wonderland

Dying Wonderland

Bloody Wonderland

Wonderland: Chronicles of Madness

The Search for Nonsense

The Queen Trials

Veins of Shade

Finding Time

Neverland: Chronicles of Red

Neverwith

Nevershade

Neverblood

Nevermore

OTHER/STANDALONES

Hellish Ones Novels

Blood of the Devil

House of the Devil

Harem Project Novels

House of Daemon

House of Aves

House of Wyn

House of Igarashi, 1

House of Igarashi, 2

House of Agni

House of Kallan (2024)

Brothers of Eschat

Unsolicited

Equipoise

Paranormal Holiday Novel

12 Days

Satan's Touch Academy

A Lick of Magic

A Touch of Seduction

Fae Lords

Karou

Sweet Omegaverse

Alpha Hunted

Knot Interested

Omegas of Chaingate

Get Pucking Knotty (2023)

The Princess and Her Alphaholes Anthology (excerpt of *Wrecked*)

Wrecked

Hell View Manor

Stroking Pride (A Sons of Satan Novel)

A Tale of Steam & Cinders

Terror

Haidee (A Ladies of MC Novel)

ABOUT THE AUTHOR

Crea lives in upstate New York with her dog and husband. She has been writing since grade school, when her second grade teacher had her class keep writing journals. She has a habit of creating secondary, and often time tertiary, characters that take over her stories. When she can't fall asleep at night, she thinks up new scenes for her characters to act out. This, of course, is how most of her meant-to-be-thrown-away characters tend to end up front and center - and utterly swoon-worthy! Don't ask her how many book boyfriends she has...

When not writing, Crea is an avid reader. Her TBR pile is several hundred books high (don't even look at her kindle wish list or the unread books on her tablet). Sometimes, she enjoys crafting; sometimes, exploring nature; sometimes, traveling. Mostly, she enjoys putting her characters on paper and breathing life into them. Oh, and sleeping. Crea *loves* to sleep!

Note - Crea is an Amazon exclusive author. If you're reading this ebook anywhere other than through Amazon, it is a pirated copy and has been stolen! Please don't add to that.

THANK YOU

I hope you enjoyed Creed, Ethan, and Jakub's story. They were such heartwarming characters and I simply love the way the three of them just clicked! Sometimes you meet someone and *know* that they're your person. I think that happened in the case of all three characters. Stay tuned for book three - **Lucky Shot.**

Would you be so kind as to take a moment and leave a review? Reviews play a big role in a book's success and you can help with just a few sentences.

Review on Amazon, Goodreads, and Bookbub

Thank you!!

Crea Reitan

PS - If you find any errors, spelling or the like, please do not use your kindle/Amazon to mark them. Amazon's algorithms pull the book! Instead, please reach out to me on Facebook at https://www.facebook.com/Crea.Reitan or via email at LadyCreaAuthor@gmail.com. Thank you!!

Printed in Great Britain
by Amazon